FALLEN

THE CONDUIT CHRONICLES

ASHLEY HOHENSTEIN

Copyrights

This is a work of fiction. All names, characters, places and incidents are either from the author's imagination or are used fictionally; any resemblance to people living or dead, as well as places or incidents, are unintentional and coincidental.

Copyright 2019 Ashley Hohenstein

All rights reserved.

No parts of this book may be reproduced in whole or in part, scanned, photocopied or stored in a retrieval system, nor transmitted electronically, digitally or by means of any other electronic, audio or mechanical distribution without the permission of the author.

ISBN 978-1-7339257-7-8

This book is dedicated to all the aspiring writers out there. May you chase your dreams with ferocious fervor!

A NOTE TO READERS

I have included resources in the back of the book: a Glossary and an
image of the Faction Diagram that you may find useful.
I hope these items make it that much easier to leap back into the
Conduit world and its fantastical characters.

I also want to note that everything in the book is fiction, including the
stories and legends inspired by the various cultures I include in the
story.
All cultural references I make are strictly from my wild imagination.

PART I

ESTHER

*A*kiva had tracked them to this point. He was certain they were staying in this disgusting inn. I looked around the parking lot of the establishment. A few cars were sporadically parked in front of random doors along the bottom floor of the dated building.

"They are in that room, Mistress, room seventy-two." He pointed at the blue door. There were no cars parked along this segment of the building. I wondered if that meant no one else was residing in this part of the inn. It was no matter to me. Let the pitiable humans hear the fracas. They could make up stories about monsters that stalk patrons of destitute hotels such as this one along the highway.

This story could become an urban legend. I laughed to myself at the thought of it.

"Mistress?" Akiva looked at me inquisitively.

"It's no matter of yours," I dismissed his curiosity. My mood shifted from humored to impatient. "Where is Astrid?"

"She should be here in a minute." Akiva felt the shift in my mood and it made him perceptibly nervous.

"Did you express the urgency of the situation, my dear Akiva?" I used my soft voice as I spoke to him. Not because it would settle his nerves—indeed, it did the opposite, and I knew it.

"I did, my mistress."

Before I could continue my inquiry I heard Astrid's voice behind me.

"I am here, Mistress." The pretty blonde cherub of a face was staring back as me. She was small and mighty—electricity coursed through her entire being. Astrid could manifest a voltage that would render you senseless for hours if she wished. It was a magnificent offensive gift.

"Aw, my pet, I was worried about you," I lied, and we both knew it.

"Sorry to keep you waiting. I had a lead on Winston and Lucia, but I lost them a hundred miles east of here." She looked disappointed but that was the least of her worries, because I would make her sorry for that mishap—later. At present we needed to be dedicated to dispatching this lovely pair.

"We are all here now." I smiled and saw both Akiva and Astrid shiver slightly. I was pleased I generated such fear in them. "Do either of you know of Valerian and Nara? We must know our enemies to properly execute them."

"I have met Nara once, before the open battle," Akiva admitted.

"She is a beauty, is she not?" I noted, but Akiva said nothing. "She was once considered the leader of her elected pantheon—the goddess Danu. A mother goddess to the Celts—what a filthy people. Nara was beloved in her time." I thought about her deep red hair and her fair skin. She was striking, always had been. "Do not let her beauty distract you; she is lethal." I turned to Akiva. "Your gift will best match hers, my dear. Nara manipulates wind, the air one breathes, the invisible force that fills the space between. Do not underestimate how effective this can be as a weapon."

I looked at Astrid. "That leaves you and me to disarm Valerian." I remembered the last time I had seen the pretty couple—before the siege of Hafiza. I had approached Valerian, asked him to choose our side. He was a fool and he chose wrong. Now he would die—but not before I killed his precious Nara before his very eyes. "Valerian absorbs energy. He can render you comatose if he is given enough time. His flaw is that he must be touching his opponent. That is where your gift will challenge him. It will be a battle of wills—can he hold onto your scorching skin long enough to drain you as I simultaneously attack?"

"What happens if he drains me?" Astrid asked, worry creased across her forehead.

"Do not worry about that, my pet. If he has succeeded in doing this feat, then you have failed me—which is far more troublesome." I smiled at her and brushed her blonde hair from her face. She flinched, sure I was going to assume control of her body—but that was not my intent. "Have I assuaged your fears?" I asked.

"Yes, Mistress." She looked past me as she answered.

"We must be swift. Akiva, you will do the honors of removing the door when we are in position."

He nodded.

OPHELIA

$\mathcal{W}$e had arrived at The Cathedral the evening before. It was a terrifying experience. The gatekeeper had turned out to be a bigger challenge than Rajahish had led Elias to believe. We both narrowly escaped with our lives. But now here I was, being escorted by the very same monster that only hours ago had tried to kill us.

I was only now getting to my room because I had spent the remainder of last night learning about how the poltergeist named Su became what he is today—a half-gidim, half-man Swali that guarded the entrance of The Cathedral. On one side of the gate he manifested as a black, demonic monster, while on this side, The Cathedral side, he appeared as a handsome young man. I welcomed hearing his story. It was a healthy distraction. Now he was taking me to my room. I was scared. Not of Su, not of The Cathedral, but of being alone. We stopped at a door.

"It's simple. Put your hand on the threshold." Su took my hand and placed it on the doorframe. "Now think of home."

I closed my eyes and my mind zipped from one location to another—all places I called home. Before I opened them, I knew what the door would look like. I swallowed hard, preparing myself for the familiar entryway.

"Excellent." Su clapped excitedly. "The Cathedral has registered your request." I still didn't open my eyes as he continued. "She is some exceptional magic. She reads your desires and creates according to your feedback, both emotionally and visually. She is an empath." Su grabbed my shoulder. "Are you okay? Miss Olly?" I heard the concern in his voice and finally opened my eyes.

I let out the breath I'd been holding. "Yes. Sorry, Su," I said as I looked at the doorway, then held my breath again. "I was just mentally preparing myself for what's behind that door."

"Miss Olly, we can change it." He looked at me anxiously. "It can be any place."

I put my hand on his shoulder. "No, this is my home." I placed my other hand on the doorknob and turned it. The door swung open. I took my first step into the familiar space. The wood underfoot made the memorable creak it had always made when someone walked in. I felt Su watching and it occurred to me, *I wanted to do this alone.* I faced him.

"Su . . ." I began, but before I could finish he responded.

"Never mind. This is a moment you wish to experience alone." I was grateful for his insight. I nodded and then he disappeared.

I took two more steps into the apartment and shut the door. I let my eyes wash over the home I'd shared with Lucas. Our apartment in San Francisco. It was exactly how I'd remembered it. The kitchen that was separated from the living room by a small island where two wooden stools sat tucked under the lip of the countertop. The very place where we'd eat breakfast together every morning. I remembered how the couch felt when the two of us were snuggled up on it together, watching a movie. I looked down the hall. On one side was the door to my room, and then a second door that led to the bathroom. Adjacent to that door was Lucas' room.

I found my feet mindlessly taking me down the hall, to his room. My head was screaming, "Stop!" but my body wouldn't listen; my feet just moved. My hand didn't hesitate. It opened the door, and a

7

familiar scent flooded my nostrils. It was his scent, exactly the way I knew it to be. Fresh and intoxicating.

The room suddenly felt huge and yet too small all at once. I looked at his blue comforter, messily thrown over the mattress I'd always said was too lumpy. On his dresser was a single, framed photo of the two of us on our bikes in Golden Gate Park. My throat got tight.

I walked to his closet and exposed several shirts, neatly suspended on hangers. I grabbed a deep forest green button-up shirt I'd seen him wear several times, pulled it close to my chest, and took in his scent once more. Hand shaking, I reached for the photo and pulled it to my heart, then fell onto the bed.

My eyes swelled with tears; they burned as hot as any flame. Sobs were building in my stomach and making their way up to my vocal chords. My throat trembled, and a piercing scream escaped my lips. It was the sound of my heart being torn in two. It rang in my ears and it still was not enough, so I screamed again and the tears streamed down my face. I let the pain take me—I let it consume me. Lucas was gone. Paralyzed by that reality, I couldn't breathe, I couldn't move. I was broken, floundering and angry. I pulled my knees up to cradle them in my arms. My insides felt like they were leaching out of me, spilling onto the bed. I was trying to physically pull myself back together because reality had torn me apart. I'd never see Lucas again. He was gone.

ELIAS

"*I*s she settled?" I asked Su when I saw him enter the study.

His face was somber. "If that is what you want to call it. She has a room, but she didn't look settled at all."

"I see." I was worried about that when I realized how The Cathedral accommodated her residents. I put my hand on Su's shoulder. He still looked very concerned. "She is strong. She will be okay." I said it for him as much as for myself.

Su nodded assuredly. "How did you find your chamber? Well met?"

"Yes, I am very comfortable." At first, I had conjured Hafiza as my home. But when I entered the familiar space, the events of our final night there flooded back to me and I found it all too overwhelming. So I decided to dream up the bachelor flat that I had always wanted to live in as a young man. It was simple and held no memories or distractions in its walls, only youthful hope.

"That is good to hear." Su smiled. "What are you working on? Is there something I can assist you with?" He peered over my shoulder.

"Possibly," I conceded. I had everything my father had left me upon his passing. He had hidden several documents in the globe he kept in his study. Thankfully, Rand had been astute enough to collect some of my father's belongings the night my parents died. The documents in there directed most of my actions when accumulating information for the summit. My father had been so close to realizing his vision of uniting our people. "I have to find a way to invite the existing Pai Ona to the summit while not divulging our whereabouts to the Nebas."

My father had outlined some ideas he felt may do the trick, but I was not certain I could acquire access to the old channels he believed could orchestrate the broadcast, and I had never sent a mass transmission before. Honestly, I had only seen an old-channels network three times in my life. They were rare, if not considered obsolete. As I understood it, when they were created there were clearly no cell phones, but more importantly, there were fewer Conduits. This meant there were fewer gifts among our people. As it stands now, there are those who possess the power to convey massive messages, but I could not trust this task to a Conduit I did not know well.

I examined the sketch on the paper. It was a basic drawing of what the old channels looked like. The device appeared simple enough. To the unassuming eye, it was a framed metal screen peppered with holes barely larger than the head of a needle. The frame was oak, with small carvings etched into the wood. I had no idea what the symbols meant, only that they were integral for the old channels to work. The device stood vertically on two supporting legs. Next to that drawing was a simpler one—Pierses paper, the only medium that worked with the channel. I pointed at the paper I was holding.

"Here it says something about a broadcast through the old channels. I am not very familiar with them, having only used them three times in my life."

Su picked the sheet up from the desk and examined it thoroughly.

"I have seen this mechanism before, or at least something similar. Before Ruit created the Runes for his family, he used an old network channel on the grounds." I looked at Su in disbelief.

Could we be that fortunate? My father had an old network channel in two of our Haven homes, Hafiza and Chaucer, our home in Vietnam. I had only been in the room once as a young boy, then twice as a man, in order to communicate with Rand after my parents died. I wondered if they would be the same, operate with the same Pierses paper as my father's had. I was eager to find out.

"Will you take me there? May I see it?"

"Of course. Follow me." Su casually walked to the door. I set my things down as I shuffled after him.

He turned to speak to me as he put his hand on the door frame. "You may want those documents for reference, Mr. Kraus."

"Please call me Elias," I insisted again. "You are right." I collected what I had on the communications. By the time I met Su at the door, the hall had transmuted into a dark tunnel in front of us.

"The Network Room is three levels below the ground," he explained. "Hidden within hidden walls."

"Very effective for preventing detection."

"Yes. Ruit was very careful." That was the third time Su had said that, which had me wondering, *could a man who was that efficient and secretive really get ambushed as easily as he had?*

"Step back, Mr. Kraus. Pardon me, I mean Mr. Elias. This room has been closed for many years and I'm not sure of its condition." Su motioned for me to give him more space. "Sometimes things shift in The Cathedral."

"I see." I took a second step back as Su put his hand on the door. It shuddered slightly under his touch then shot open. A plume of dust swirled in the air. I coughed hard after inhaling a lungful.

Su peered into the dimly lit room. "Not to fret, just dust bunnies in here. Everything else looks just as Ruit has left it."

I stepped in behind Su. "Astonishing," I whispered.

"Is it? I have only seen this example of an old-channel network," Su admitted.

"I have seen two before it, and I assure you, this is very impressive." My eyes took inventory of my surroundings. There were over fifteen channels to use, and an entire wall of the rare Pierses paper required to transmit the message. Each channel hung from the ceiling, fastened by two delicate chains. My eyes followed the row of hanging frames to the far-right corner of the room. Below the last channel stood a press of some sort. I walked over to it. I traced my hand along the cover and lifted the top to see there was a powder residue along the side.

"What is this, Su?"

"I believe that will be how you broadcast to the specific Conduits you wish to reach." He stepped beside me. "You see this powder? You can enchant it to allow the message to only be seen by certain individuals. It can be very restricted. You can demand all sorts of stipulations for the receiver to be able to see the message. This is the only way to ensure your communications make it to the proper people."

"Where did Ruit acquire this?"

"That, I do not know."

My mind began splintering into a million possibilities. This was it! This was how we could securely invite thousands of Conduits to the summit. My heart swelled with pure excitement. The biggest obstacle I had identified could be easily tackled. Relief zipped through my body.

I turned to Su. "Sometimes I feel like Ruit was orchestrating this summit before my father ever had the inclination." It was more of a thought than a statement, but I realized I felt it was true.

"Ruit knew many things. Nothing would surprise me. And if you had him on your side, your cause will be blessed." Su beamed at me.

I noticed how he spoke of him in past tense. I knew after speaking to Ophelia that Ruit's family was not certain of how he had died—some even believed he was held captive somewhere. *But did Su believe that?*

"Do you think Ruit is dead? You speak about him as though you do."

"I believe he would not abandon his family." Su looked down. "Or me. Unless something happened to him."

I put my hand on his shoulder. "I believe you are right."

OPHELIA

I hadn't looked at Talia's journal since the night Yanni found us in China. It was a reminder of Lucas' betrayal, his death and the loss of Talia. I pulled it out from my bag now. I was sure it was all in my head, but I thought I smelled the distinct scent of smoke coming from its pages.

I found myself wanting to hear Talia's voice come alive from the journals' pages. Reading her words made me feel like she was still here somehow, or at least it had before everything fell apart—again.

I untied the leather strip that bound it, and the book flopped open to a random page. I caught my breath, not because of what the journal said but because there, on the page, lay the medallion Lucas had used to summon Fetzle.

I replayed the first time I saw him using it, while we were in Chile, fleeing from Vivienne and Nandi—who we believed was trying to abduct me.

He'd put the medallion on the exposed tree roots and recited a few words I didn't understand. All at once, Fetzle had appeared.

How did he slip it into the journal?

I dissected the night in the yurts when I confronted him on his treachery. I'd stuffed the journal in the back of my pants as I laid out his betrayal, so that he couldn't deny it and I could read him with my gift.

Then everything changed so quickly it all became a blur. I retraced my steps. I'd packed my bag while Elias ran into his room to do the same. Lucas stayed with me. He had pulled the journal out of the back of my pants to put it in my bag for safekeeping. I remembered thinking at the time that maybe he was going to take it, but then he'd just handed it over to me.

He must have put the medallion in then. *Had he known he would die? Did he mean to sacrifice himself all along?*

I held the coin tightly to my chest. Tears began to stream down my cheeks. Lucas had left me this precious gift. I let that sink in before I also acknowledged that I had no idea how to use it.

ESTHER

*W*e approached the door quickly. The number on the front read seventy-two. The two was crooked. I felt it was foreboding and extremely appropriate for the circumstances. Yanni always said I had a sardonic sense of humor. He was absolutely right. Thinking of him made my blood boil, which was going to make this kill that much more satisfying.

Akiva ripped the door off the hinges. We entered the room to find it vacant. The bed had been tossed, but everything else was unmoved.

I looked at Astrid and motioned for her to secure the restroom. She quickly obeyed and returned seconds later with confirmation that they were not in there.

My furry turned on Akiva. "Where are they? You said they would be here." I approached him slowly, deliberately.

"They were here, Mistress. I saw them enter this very room." Akiva stepped back as I approached.

"I am very disappointed." Just as the words left my mouth a noise came from behind me. I turned to the entrance to see Nara's body flying toward me, riding a gust of wind. The room that just seconds ago was seemingly untouched now erupted into chaos.

The force of the wind hit me first. It must have been moving at over sixty miles an hour. My body hit the wall hard. Beside me was Akiva's flattened form. She had him pinned to the wall, rendering him useless.

That was inconvenient.

Astrid was approaching Nara from behind, while Nara hovered slightly above the nasty green shag carpet. Her arms stretched forward, directing the wind to continue its onslaught. I could not reach Akiva, to touch him and assume control of his body—I didn't know if that would even serve us as we were.

Astrid was calculating how to get behind Nara without getting swept into the gust herself when Valerian's silhouette appeared in the doorway. He was bare-chested. *Perhaps we had disturbed an intimate moment.* I sniggered to myself.

The wall of wind made it impossible to speak. Astrid had no idea Valerian was behind her until he touched her shoulder. The look on Valerian's face revealed that he had no idea what Astrid was capable of.

He whimpered in pain. It was the perfect distraction. Nara turned to see Valerian fall to his knees from the electrical current pulsing through his body. The wind let up minutely. I reached over and touched Akiva's left palm. His eyes glazed over as I assumed control of his body and its gifts. He could only be released from my command if I willed it or if he was touched by another Conduit. I wanted to ensure I completed this assassination my way. Akiva couldn't be trusted to get it done the way I needed it to be executed.

I flicked Akiva's finger. Nara's head jerked as though she'd just been hit by a semi. Her attention returned to me, fire raging in her eyes. She took a step forward, summoning more wind, but it was a second too late for her stand. I flicked Akiva's finger again. This time my effort was on Valerian. His neck snapped from my gesture, and his body crumpled to the floor in a pathetic heap. Nara tried to divide her focus but Astrid quickly took advantage of the moment, diving under the wind current and grasping Nara's ankle. She screamed in agony. Astrid was holding nothing back. Nara's knees buckled, dropping her onto the floor. The wind around our bodies weakened. We stepped away from the wall.

Nara flung her hand in our direction. The wind picked back up but it was erratic. Again, we stepped forward. Astrid was still gripping Nara's ankle. Nara couldn't fight her off and defend herself from me. Every time she touched Astrid's hand, it just sent a wave of electricity up her arm, causing more pain and depleting her ability to concentrate. I took a third step. Then, with Akiva's gift, I closed my fist and watched as every bone in Valerian's limp body broke.

Nara's face went ghostly white as she listened to the carnage ravaging his body. But that wouldn't be enough. He would recover from that wreckage.

"Astrid, my dear, will you do the honors?" I purred.

Astrid let go of Nara, who was still on her knees in shock, trying to command her gift but failing to do it efficiently enough to hold us back. The weakness of emotions never seemed to fail me. The art of killing was often times less of an effort if you could just expose the feelings beneath. Expose the vulnerability, the fear.

Astrid's hand took hold of Valerian's limp arm. She exuded so much electricity that you could smell the flesh burning on the inside before it was obvious what was happening from the outside. She was searing his flesh from the inside out. By the time the singed skin and flames appeared on the surface he was already entirely incinerated.

Nara's face went blank before it contorted into unadulterated rage. I considered, in that moment, that perhaps I should have approached this a little differently—*maybe I was underestimating Nara's abilities.*

The wind picked up cold and hard. Flecks of ash from Valerian's corpse danced in the air, fueling her wrath. Astrid scrambled out of the room, realizing what was happening. Nara was going to create a hurricane. Akiva and I were both elevated off the ground, our bodies flinging and contorting with the wind. The gusts were getting stronger by the second. Nara's wild red hair whipped around her face like flames. She looked crazed. I enjoyed the image.

I thought for a moment that this could be it. She could dismantle us or at least render me and Akiva unconscious with this frenzy, then she could burn our bodies without a fight. I definitely should have approached this differently, I concluded.

Nara elevated from the hotel room floor. She was wearing a long maroon dress, flowy and now whipping in the wind violently. She began to spin, first slowly then picking up the pace as her hands rose above her head. It reminded me of a figure skater.

I thought how odd it was to have such ordinary thoughts in the face of death. *Was this how everyone's brush with death began, with mundane inner monologue?*

The room began to zip past us. We were in a wind funnel. The wallpaper tore off the walls in random strips. The furniture was slowly ripping apart as it collided with other pieces or the walls. Nara stopped spinning. She hovered over the remains of her fallen partner. She was now the eye of the storm.

I smiled at her. She would be no better than me in a matter of moments. She would be a killer. Nara met my stare and realized I was gloating. It fueled her further. She raised her left arm above her head and directed it toward the large window beside the demolished door frame. What a spectacle. The insignificant humans of these parts would have a wild time trying to explain this disaster. No sooner did the thought cross my mind that my body crashed through the double-paned window, hitting hard on the pavement.

Before Akiva or I could get to our feet the wind gusted again, flinging us back into the air then propelling us back onto the pavement. It happened four times before Nara casually walked out of the wrecked room.

Her voice was hard when she spoke. "You will answer for your trespasses."

I laughed out loud; I couldn't contain myself. "And who will be the judge and executioner? You, my dear Nara? Will you be my reaper?"

She rose both of our bodies higher than she had before, looking up at us with pity. I tried to utilize Akiva's body, but it was useless. He was unconscious.

"I am no killer. I will bring you to be tried. To answer to everyone you have broken." She drew a fist up toward the sky and I began to choke on the air. She was drowning me with the force of the wind. I smiled wildly at her. I had won, no matter what came next.

My eyes shifted to a blur of movement behind her. The sharp smell of gasoline singed my nose.

Astrid was going to set the hotel room ablaze. Nara turned, realizing what was about to happen. She still held out hope that Valerian could be saved. That fool.

Astrid snapped her fingers. A tiny spark ignited and raced down the river of accelerant to the hotel. Nara violently casted our bodies into the air as she ran to the blaze.

The last thing I remembered was seeing the brilliance of stars. Then I woke up in a different hotel, daylight peeking through wooden slats. I sat up to see Astrid in a chair in the corner and Akiva huddled on the ground.

They both stirred when they felt me move.

"Where are we?" I asked calmly.

"In a hotel near the French Quarter," Astrid quickly answered. "I carried you and Akiva through the night after you both were rendered unconscious."

"Did you kill her?"

"No, Mistress. I felt it was more important to save you." Astrid's tone wasn't as confident now.

"Then you are just as much of a fool as she is," I spat.

OPHELIA

I hadn't slept well. I tossed and turned all night. I didn't even dream, which was a rarity for me. So, when someone knocked on the door in what appeared to be the early morning hours, I welcomed the intrusion.

"Come in." I sat up on the couch, the third place I had migrated to as I tried to find a comfortable position in my old apartment. None of the usual spots worked because it wasn't my body that was uncomfortable—it was my soul. I was in some limbo between familiarity and mourning. That terrible place where all you want is familiar things, places and people but they all remind you of your loss—of my Lucas.

Elias peered around the door. "I did not wake you, did I?"

"No. I was wide awake."

He was holding two mugs of coffee in his hands. "Then perhaps you will enjoy a cup of coffee." He smiled genuinely.

I returned the gesture, but my smile didn't feel as warm as his. He was so patient with me. I was distant and moody these days. Torn between emotions and regret. But Elias didn't skip a beat. He just continued to let me be where I was—as he persisted, slowly waiting out the storm within me. I wasn't that patient. I could never put up with someone like me.

"Thank you. Have a seat." But as soon as I said it, I regretted it. My heart was squirming. This place belonged to me and my Lucas. It was our place. I didn't want memories of Elias to taint that.

"You know, she changes on cue. Should you desire a different location or change of scenery."

He read me so well.

"How do I do that?" I managed to choke out. Elias still hadn't sat.

"Stand up. As things shift, you may not find yourself in the same position or on the same furniture." I stood as he continued. "Place your hand on the lamp in front of you. It could be any object, really."

Again, I did as instructed.

"Bring a place you desire to be in your mind's eye. Explore every detail, make it vivid. Now close your eyes and ask her to assist you."

I looked at him speculatively.

"She will always bring you back here, to this place—to your home. But you can get away if you wish. Su explained all of this to me in great detail last night. I will also show you how to teleport to just about anywhere on the grounds." He smiled as he spoke. It had an air of childish enthusiasm I hadn't seen in him before.

I closed my eyes and felt the air move around me. When I opened them we were exactly where I'd imagined.

"Take a seat," I insisted as I threw myself on the bed. It was my dorm room from my first year of college in Chicago. "I've always wanted to have a hot guy in this room, serving me coffee," I joked. "I couldn't have fathomed it would happen this way."

Elias smiled again as he sat at the end of the bed. "This was your dormitory at university?"

"Yeah. How did you guess?" I laughed. I needed something ridiculous like this to help pull me out of my torment.

"Call it a hunch."

"Anyone could've deduced that from the mess, two beds, kitchenette and the Katy Perry and Lady Gaga fanfare on the walls." Life was simpler yet so much more complicated during this season of my life. I considered how we always seem to be trading one set of complications for the next—they don't go away, and every situation seems like it's the worst when you're in it. There was some grace in remembering that because it meant my current season would also pass.

Elias handed me the coffee he'd been patiently holding. "What is on your agenda for the day? Would you like to assist me with some summit preparation?" His eyes lit up with anticipation.

Elias was so honorable. He had continued to invite me to help him with everything he did regarding the summit since we had arrived here at The Cathedral. All for the sake of the transparency he'd promised in Jammu.

"What's the task?" I asked as I took my first sip of perfectly tailored coffee—he knew just how I liked it.

"Su showed me the old network-channel chamber Ruit kept in the lower levels. It is like nothing I have ever seen before. My father had a room for the old networks, but it had only a single channel and the required Pierses paper was in short supply. Therefore he did not use the channels often. This room has seventeen channels and stacks of Pierses paper. But the most unique and exciting contraption is this enchanted exacting press." Elias shifted in his seat excitedly as he spoke. "This press allows you to put very detailed specifications on the broadcast, so only those you wish can see it. It is miraculous—it will allow us to weed out anyone with Nebas affiliations from even hearing of the summit. Can you imagine?"

"What is Pierses paper? Like the sister books?" I asked.

"Exactly. The Pierses were composed with the enchanted paper. It is part of their magic. Where it originated, I cannot say. But it is finite, so to have so much of it at our disposal is incredible."

His excitement was infectious. I found myself smiling and buzzing in my seat. "It sounds remarkable. How will you determine the specifications for the recipients?"

"I researched all night and made a list of what I believe will effectively divide our friend from foe." He leaned in as he spoke. "There are so many layers, so much we can do to keep those we wish to attend safe. I want to show you. Do you want to help me?"

"Well, how can I resist now?" I said. Elias was so pumped up, it would feel like I was kicking a puppy if I refused his invitation. "Let me finish my coffee and shower. Come get me in thirty minutes."

ELIAS

*W*e finished working on the broadcast for the day. Susuda offered to show Ophelia the gardens while I determined what our next plan of action was.

My father had left me four large files of information he had accumulated concerning the summit. The first file was inside the globe Rand had salvaged from the fire the night they died. Within that folder were clues to where I could find a second compilation of information in Hafiza. From there I was able to determine the whereabouts of two other hidden compartments containing important research about his plans.

For the majority of the last two years I had only concerned myself with sifting through the information about finding a location. Once we secured the location that could safely accommodate thousands of Conduits, I was immediately concerned with how we would discreetly invite those Conduits. My father's research indicated the old channels were the best route. I wondered if he knew the venue he was researching would contain an extremely efficient network room.

I had to trust that he also had accounted for what he felt needed to occur at the summit. Before Hafiza fell I had taken the opportunity to read about his intended agenda, something momentous enough to draw the Pai Ona out of hiding. When I first saw the term Katuan Trials, I did not fully understand what they meant. I was too young to have ever heard of them. Fortunately for me, my father had given me enough material to track down further intelligence on what these entailed.

Hafiza's library contained a volume on the Trials, and The Cathedral's library housed two huge books on the details of the Trials. One thing became abundantly clear, in order to perform the Trials, we needed something called the Katuan Stones.

I knew nothing of them, except that they were enormous in size and ancient. Their inception occurred during a convening of gargantuan proportion. They were said to govern the Trials with clear precision and tradition.

I rubbed my brow. *Where on earth would I find these magical stones? Exactly how big were they, and how in the world would I transport them?*

There was a tap at the door.

"Come in." Su made his way to the table I sat at, papers and books littering its surface. "That was quick. Ophelia got tired of walking so soon?"

"No, Miss Olly asked to be alone." His face said it all. His eyebrows furrowed and the smile that usually adorned his face was transformed into a thin line.

"It is not you, my friend, let me assure you. She is going through a great deal at present." He looked at me skeptically but did not protest. "Perhaps you can help me?" I was aware that Su had been alone for so long that all he really desired was company and purpose. I could understand that.

"How can I serve you?" he asked, and his demeanor changed instantly.

"Let us call it help. Not serve. That makes me feel like some sort of master, when you ask to serve me."

"I see. In that case, how can I help you?" His smile had returned and I was glad to see it.

"I understand that you have read every book in the library, many times."

"That is true."

"What can you tell me about these two volumes? What do you know about the Katuan Stones?"

"I can tell you whatever is in the text." I looked at him, afraid that was the extent of it. I could read the text myself. "Or I could show you the Stones."

I stared at him blankly for a long moment. "You have them here?" I managed to stutter out.

"They have been here since I first arrived. I think they have always been here, for safekeeping. The Stones hold an exorbitant amount of power," Su said matter-of-factly.

"Please, by all means, take me to them." I could not believe how fortunate we were turning out to be. This was the second stroke of incredible luck since we had found our way to The Cathedral. Third, really, if you counted the place itself. On one hand, it made me feel as though this entire mission was ordained, and on the other, I found myself distrustful of the ease of it. It felt to me that someone else must have their hand in this event, someone who wanted to remain unseen. Anyone who chose the shadows left me trepidatious.

Su walked to the door and stepped just inside the hall. As soon as I was in arm's reach, he took my hand in his and we teleported to a cold, dark chamber.

"Give me a moment to light the fire."

Within seconds the hearth was full of warm, red flames that plainly illuminated hundreds of enormous stones stacked upon one another. I moved closer. There was nothing exceptional about them. They just looked like large blocks.

"How can we be certain that these are the Katuan Stones?" I was careful not to touch them as I made a closer examination. I had read enough to know that an exchange happened when you touched the Stones. I did not yet know what that exchange meant so I intended to keep a safe distance until I understood the consequences of such actions. Su had apparently become familiar with them some time ago. He walked up and put his hand on the closest one.

"Katualapa." He almost whispered the word, but the stone responded nonetheless, shaking under his touch.

"Incredible," was all I could think to say. After a long moment in silence, I was better able to formulate my thoughts. "Why did the Stone respond in that way?"

"It was the original incantation word. It doesn't have the same effect as it once did, but it stills incites them."

"Brilliant, simply brilliant." I took Susuda in for a hug. "Do you know what this means?"

Su shook his head no—he was such an honest soul.

"It means that as soon as we finish the broadcast we can begin preparations for the Trials. It means the summit my father dreamt of will be actualized."

OPHELIA

*E*ver since I had found Lucas' coin in my bag, I'd been trying to decide what to do about it. I didn't know the words to call Fetzle, but something in me knew I had to try. I needed to tell her what had happened to her friend, to our Lucas.

I sat in The Cathedral's vast gardens, flipping the coin in the air, mustering up the courage to try and call upon her. *What would I say? How would she react?*

Su had been kind enough to leave me alone, but I didn't know how long it would be before either he or Elias came looking for me, so I needed to make a decision. I didn't even know if The Cathedral would allow a troll on her grounds. *Did magical Haven gardens have different rules?*

I stood up and started pacing. There was no one around. The best time to make contact, if that was possible, was now. My feet led me to the base of a beautiful maple tree. I knelt down, swallowed my fear and said the first thing that came to mind as I placed the coin on the exposed tree roots. I repeated the phrase three times aloud, "Please come see me, Fetzle. Please come see me, Fetzle. Please come see me, Fetzle."

Nothing happened. I internally scoffed at myself. Of course

nothing would happen. Lucas had some special phrase when he called her. I stood up to leave when the tree began to shake, and there, in the canopy of the tree manifested the familiar face of Fetzle the troll.

She looked surprised to see me, as I expected she would. Her head tilted curiously at me. "FetzlecomestohersnamebutswheresbeLucas?"

I took a couple of steps back, mindlessly chewing the inside of my cheek as I collected my thoughts, and decided what I would say. "Hi, Fetzle. Do you remember me? My name is Ophelia Banner, and I'm friends with Lucas and Elias."

Fetzle waved her hand in the air, while taking a couple steps toward me. I had to take ten steps back for her two. "OfscoursesFetzleremembersstinkyOphelia."

I frowned but let it go before Fetzle noticed, or at least that's what I hoped. "Right. Well, I called you."

Fetzle's eye got bigger, as though to say, "Duh, I get that." So I continued. "I have some bad news. Terrible news, actually. Lucas was, well, Lucas was killed by Yanni."

I looked nervously at Fetzle, not sure how she would react. She stared blankly back at me for a long, excruciating moment.

"Fetzlethinksno," she said as she shook her head.

"I'm sorry, Fetzle, but it's true. We were ambushed in China by Yanni. There was a fire and a fight, and Lucas saved my life." I played with the hairsy charm on my wrist. It caught Fetzle's eye, and it was then that she realized I must be telling the truth.

She began to shake her head more violently. "Fetzlenotbelieve. NotsFetzlesLucas." Fetzle began to pace, then abruptly crumpled to her knees.

"Fetzlesonesfriend." Then the tears came in thick sobs, like I'd never seen before. "LucasFetzleslastfriends."

I moved slowly to sit by her side. "Elias and I are your friends, Fetzle," I assured her. She said nothing in reply.

Sitting closer to her, I realized it wasn't really a watery liquid that fell from her eye, but more a snotty, clear ooze. It was still so odd to consider I was sitting by a real-life she-troll, breaking the same terrible news to her that had been tormenting me for days—the loss of our Lucas.

Suddenly, Fetzle's demeanor changed completely. "TellsFetzlealls-sheknows."

I looked up at her wiping her face. I hated talking about it. I hadn't talked about it. But she deserved to know what happened to Lucas. So I told her everything, from our travels to the journal that I found that had led us to China. I decided to leave out Lucas' betrayal. It would only hurt Fetzle to think Lucas was less of a man than she believed him to be, and that was if she believed me. When I was done, we sat in silence for a very long time.

"Fetzlethinksits-stopsignoringthatswar." She inhaled sharply as she continued. "Fetzlethinksits-timetocollectshershe-trollsandhelpsthis-goodConduits."

I digested what she was saying.

"TheseNebasisverybadsFetzlethinks," she declared.

"I agree, Fetzle. Something must be done. But what will the trolls do? What will you do?"

"Fetzleknowsnotyet, butstodaysFetzletakingsbacksherskingdom!" Fetzle was ready for action. She stood up, perhaps a little taller than before, and began to walk to the tree she'd manifested from.

"Fetzle! Wait!" I jogged up beside her. "How do I reach you if I need you?" I opened my palm to show her the coin Lucas had left for me. "I don't know how it works."

Fetzle took her big finger and gently closed my hand around the coin. "YouputstheHilliotorootsstinkyOphelia, threetimesshes-sayssomethings, onlyFetzleknows." She leaned down close so I could whisper in her ear, or at least where an ear should have been.

"Fetzle, my friend." I said it confidently, so she knew I meant it.

"Fetzlelikes." She smiled her frightening smile at me. "Nowsthe-Hillioknowsourwords, nootherswordsworks. Opheliaused-heronescallFetzle-withnowordsalreadys."

I realized that must have been how I got Fetzle here today, with my single free-calling card. She called the medallion a Hillio. I looked at it again in the palm of my hand. I would treasure this gift, for so many reasons. Fetzle met my gaze when I looked up.

"Goodbye, Fetzle. Be safe." I whispered the words but I knew she heard me. Then she was gone and I was alone, once again consumed by the loss of Lucas.

ESTHER

I watched the way Claudia moved. She was fierce, but could not always be trusted. I had no choice but to bring her into our small hunting party. We needed more fire power at our disposal. Something was amiss; I could feel it in my bones. Too many Pai Ona were mobilizing, seeping out of the security of the shadows. I decided we needed to form larger bands to offset the occurrence.

Whatever was provoking their peculiar behavior needed to be discovered and squashed. Yanni and I had worked for too long and too hard to see it all collapse now. I decreed that no one be left alive. Every Pai Ona was to be killed on sight no matter the spectacle.

I chose Claudia for her talents. She was easily underestimated, and good with humans. She had shoulder-length blonde hair—the soccer mom cut, she called it. She wore pastel blues and pinks most days. Today she had on a lavender camisole atop a pale pink sundress. She didn't have remarkable features. In fact, it was just the opposite—she had a face that made you think you had seen her before because it looked like so many others. Brown eyes, simple nose, round features and the perfect straight-white-teeth smile.

I never understood why she chose this side—our side. I supposed that was part of my unease with her. I liked to understand people's motives. Yanni would tell me all the time that that was not necessary when you played on the darker side of the world. He believed some Conduits were just drawn to malevolence.

It could be true, but it did not bring me comfort. Claudia was a talented Illusionist. She could create massive distraction with her gift. All she needed to do was make eye contact to reflect a person's greatest fear. As long as she held that eye contact, all they could see would be the thing that terrorized them most in this world.

If we'd had her with us during our combat with Nara and Valerian, Nara would not have gotten away.

The past was the past, but the defeat plagued me. Something about Nara's righteousness made me sick. It was that interaction that brought to my attention the fact that I was missing something. She was too confident. *Why had they returned to combat with us?* It was uncharacteristic of the Pai Ona to stop and fight and not turn and run. *They had already eluded us, so what made Nara and Valerian risk their lives and come back to the hotel room?*

I issued an order to kill on sight to everyone else, but we were on a different mission. I needed to uncover what was happening in order to keep the upper hand we had fought for. I preferred my enemy weak and skittish.

"Esther." Claudia refused to call me mistress. It wasn't a requirement, of course, but I liked her less for it.

"Claudia," I responded sarcastically. She ignored my tone.

"Astrid reported a Pai Ona pair moving just south of us in Rio. We could cut them off as they move to cross the border." Claudia's voice was deeper than you would expect it to be. Not manly, just huskier than most ladies'.

"Why would you assume they are coming north, my dear?"

"Astrid implied she has already seen this Soahcoit once before. Winston and Lucia."

My eyes got large. There was no need to restrain my excitement. I was eager to capture any of the Conduits who had spent extended periods of time with Viraclay, the miracle golden child, defender of the weak and knight in shining armor... *blah blah blah.*

I needed him and his pet, Ophelia. Their capture would end any resistance, squash any hope. But we'd lost them. I clenched my jaw. Lost them the night that my Yanni, my Atoa, my other half was taken from me. The back of my neck got sweaty as I thought about how he must have felt, alone, without me. Eagerness swelled in my chest, in the chamber where I contained my thirst for vengeance. I'd had to compartmentalize after his death, or it would consume me—drive me mad. I had no right to go mad until I completed our mission and avenged his death.

"We will not wait idly by the border. Get exact coordinates from Astrid. We are already two steps behind." I turned to Akiva. He had not been the same since the encounter with Nara. It made no difference to me. I could use him, literally, when I needed to. "Akiva, do not disappoint me."

"Yes, Mistress." He took his place behind me while Claudia got on the phone with Astrid as she, too, followed.

OPHELIA

I made my way down to the galley. It was my fourth full day in The Cathedral and I felt like my body had finally acclimated to teleportation. I wasn't sure that was exactly what The Cathedral did to move us seamlessly from one room in the castle to the next, but it was what we decided to call it. All you had to do was step into a passage and put your hand on the wall. Once you made contact, you visualized where you wanted to end up on the grounds and—*bam!*—after some odd physical sensations, you were there. It was convenient, because the place was massive, but I felt sick the first couple of days during the transportation. The nausea subsided today.

Susuda had said we could explore every inch of The Cathedral in this way, from her vast gardens down to the third subterranean level. Anything further than that, not even he could teleport to.

So I had The Cathedral zip me down to the stairs above the galley. I still needed to get some exercise, so if it appeared to be a straight shot and I couldn't get lost, I started having her drop me off a short way from my ultimate destination. Su was waiting for me when I arrived.

"Hey, Su! How come you're always down here?" I asked playfully. "You don't even eat."

"I am the gatekeeper; I can sense where you're moving to in The Cathedral. Every person within these walls registers in my senses. I can see who they are with and where. I also feel the presence of those loitering outside the gate. It's, after all, my job," he said proudly, and continued. "You are correct, I cannot partake in the joyous act of eating. I can, however, live vicariously through your taste buds." He grabbed a stool and dragged it to the countertop where I usually prepared my meals. "Food is different than it was in my day. Such a variety. I wish nothing more than to taste a single delicious bite."

"So why can't you eat?"

He suddenly looked so sad. "I've tried. This form doesn't allow me the decadence of food."

"I'm sorry." I really was. I liked Su, a lot. He was a great guy who had been dealt a crappy hand. I admired his human form. Anything was better than that gidim monster he became as the gatekeeper. But this state he was easy on the eyes. He had dark hair, straight and cropped at his shoulders. He once told me he was grateful he'd gotten a haircut only days before his transformation. His skin was caramel tan, which made his green-gray eyes stand out even more. If Su were to describe himself, he would say he was an exotic Sumerian man. I thought he was just plain exotic, damn the Sumerian. He'd been in his early twenties when he became whatever he was five thousand years ago.

"What is on the menu today?" he asked eagerly.

"I thought I would make Elias and I some poached eggs atop of those fresh croissants you hunted down yesterday—where on earth did you find those anyway?" I looked at him curiously as I pulled the eggs onto the counter.

"France," he said simply. "But do not worry, I always implement wards to keep the gate secure while I am away."

"I know you are very cautious Su." I assured him. "But seriously, when did you have time to go to France?"

"As a gidim, I can move through gates and across borders no one knows about. My gidim form is ethereal unless I will it to be different. It makes international travel very swift."

It didn't feel very ethereal when he was trying to prevent us from entering The Cathedral, I thought. "You'll have to explain this to me in more detail one of these days."

"It would be my pleasure." He leaned in close to smell the croissants as I cut them. "Will you describe the taste?"

I laughed. "If you insist. But I feel like I'm torturing you."

"Not in the slightest," he assured me.

I prepared the rest of breakfast as Su described his favorite meal that his mother made in ancient Mesopotamia, an onion soup. I always thought he would be sad when he spoke of her, but he wasn't— he looked back on his human years with fondness, despite the fact that they had been ripped away from him, all because a few Conduits couldn't sort out their own problems amongst themselves. It made me angry, but Su seemed resigned to his fate as a half-gidim poltergeist, half-human keeper of The Cathedral. He adored Ruit for giving him some purpose in his eternal life.

When I was done, Su summoned Elias. He met us in the dining room. I couldn't tell you what the dining room was next to, because that isn't how The Cathedral was built. She moved, shifted constantly and manifested upon necessity. I don't think Elias or I had the slightest idea of what she was really capable of. It was all too magnificent to comprehend. For a Haven, The Cathedral was like the Winchester Mystery House, while Hafiza was like the Eiffel Tower. You know, the tower is nice and all, pretty incredible really, but it doesn't keep growing, expanding and changing. Albeit I hoped the Winchester Mystery House had stopped growing since Lady Winchester's passing.

The analogy made sense to me, anyway.

I set Elias' plate down across from mine.

"Thank you, Ophelia. It smells delicious." He smiled at me. I'd noticed that since our discussion in the hotel in China he no longer called me Olly. I wondered why that was. Maybe it was his way of keeping his boundaries clear since we could in no way, shape or form be together without causing massive destruction—*or so the prophecy foretold.*

"Ophelia is a fine cook, is she not?" Su suggested.

"Indeed, she is," Elias agreed with a mouth full of food.

"Stop it. You two are going to make me blush," I said as I took my first bite, careful to dissect every flavor so I could describe it to Su as best I could. He was definitely teaching me how to appreciate my food, something I neglected before our meeting.

I described the buttery texture of the pastry, combined with the richness of the slow-cooked egg.

Elias laughed when I finished my description.

"Can you do better?" I challenged.

"I will not know unless I try."

We all laughed as Elias' attempt nearly mimicked mine.

"I think it sounds delicious," Su decided.

We wrapped up breakfast and Su insisted on taking the dishes back down to the galley.

"Can I speak to you?" Elias asked.

I looked around as I formulated my sarcastic quip. Sometimes his formality brought out the smart-ass in me. "Looks like it's just you and me."

He smiled at my humor. "Of course. I apologize. I am so used to company and enforcing impeccable manners."

We walked over to a sitting area a few feet from the formal dining room table. "Don't worry, spend some more time with me and I'll rid you of all those manners," I joked.

"One can only hope."

We sat in two overstuffed chairs opposite one another. "So what's on your mind?"

"How are you holding up here?" The question was far more complex than either of us wanted to dive into, so I kept it light, hoping he would do the same.

"What's not to like? The Cathedral is amazing. I think I could dream up a McDonald's and she would manifest it. The travel nausea stopped today, so that's a good thing." I paused. "And I'm coping with all the other stuff as best I can."

No need to tell him I'd had a heartbreaking conversation with

Fetzle yesterday, or that I found myself sobbing most nights before I went to bed and afraid of the boredom when I woke up. My grief didn't need to be his burden. It was complicated enough, Elias planning an event for thousands of Conduits, but if we just focused on the relationship Lucas and Elias had, it was enough to make anyone's head spin. Lucas had betrayed Elias' parents, he was involved in their murder, in the murder of countless others, and he'd put my life in danger trying to have Elias killed by our enemy. They had never liked each other, but now I knew it hurt Elias to think of Lucas. Yet, he only ever expressed concern for me and my loss. The loss of a friend I trusted and loved and looked to for strength up until only moments before he died, when I found out about his fierce betrayal. But I wasn't mourning that man, I was mourning my best friend. I knew enough about psychology to allow myself the grace to be angry with the betrayal and still love the betrayer.

Elias let me lose myself in my thoughts for a moment before continuing. "We are very close to perfecting the enchantments on the broadcast. Would you concur?"

"I would."

He smiled. "Yesterday, Susuda shared with me the whereabouts of the Katuan Stones."

Bewilderment flashed across my face.

"They are integral for the success of the summit. I will explain in further detail at dinner."

I waved him on. "Yeah, that's fine. I'll get the 411 at dinner."

"The truth was, I had no idea how long it would take to procure the Stones. This development rapidly moves up our timeline." He sat up on the edge of his seat. "There is still so much to do, but I believe we will be able to send the broadcast within two days and expect the first arrivals within a week."

I let that sink in. This place would be buzzing with thousands of unknown Conduits in a matter of days. I realized that was why Elias was having this conversation with me. He was worried I wasn't ready for this type of excitement after having just lost Lucas. He was asking if he could move forward with the summit he had been planning for years before he met me. The very summit his father had planned for years until his death. Elias was willing to put things on hold if I needed more time. I didn't deserve that kind of selflessness, yet he continued to give it to me. Tears welled up in my eyes. Worry stretched across Elias' face. This was what he was afraid of. My mental state.

I put my hand up. "I'm fine." I swallowed hard to steady my voice. "You never cease to amaze me. I would never want you to put the brakes on the summit and all that you have worked toward for me." I leaned in and put my hand on his leg. "Elias, we are a team. We're going to make this summit great, together. The sooner the better."

I said the words and I meant them. It would be a welcomed distraction. I wasn't going to be the weakest link. And I would still mourn, in silence, in solitude, and maybe even among friends.

He squeezed my hand but didn't say anything. We were a team, and that was all either of us needed to know.

ESTHER

"*A*strid has indicated that Winston and Lucia were seen entering that establishment." I pointed to the bar across the street. It was a quiet night in Santa Elena de Uairen, a town just over Brazil's border into Venezuela. "I want to be clear. It is in my best interest, therefore your best interest, that we capture Winston. Feel free to dispatch Lucia; she is of no interest to me." I smiled my wicked smile and met each of their gazes one by one. "If you should fail me…" I spent extra time glaring at both Astrid and Akiva on that point. "… Again… I will dispatch of both of you. Because you will no longer be of use to me. Am I understood?" I clasped my hands together gently, waiting for each of them to concede. One by one, they nodded in assurance. "Very well. Let us be victors this evening."

I turned and began to traipse into the bar. My scarlet gown moved over my skin in a sensational way. It had been one of Yanni's favorites, so it seemed appropriate for the occasion. I had braided my long black hair, and the very tip of the braid tickled my calves through the dress. Beside me walked the soccer mom, Claudia, to my right, and the platinum blonde gothic cheerleader, Astrid, to my left. Akiva continued with his despondence. He stepped behind, guarding my back—or avoiding the fight; I had not decided which yet.

41

I opened the wooden door that led down into the dark tavern. *Why on earth did people frequent these places? Disgusting humans.*

It creaked, as did the steps as we made our way down into the dark narrow cavern of the basement.

It smelled awful, like stale beer and mold. I heard Claudia actually scoff at the odor behind me.

My black leather heels scratched at the dilapidated wood stairs as we descended. The floor was concrete at the bottom. The place was a long tube with rounded ceilings and tiny chandeliers intermittently hanging the length of the room. Along the right side of the tunnel were private booths, and on the left was a bar that stretched the entirety of the wall. Heavy curtains divided the booths so you couldn't see the occupants. It reminded me of a speakeasy I used to frequent during prohibition. I thought of Yanni in suspenders and smiled.

With one finger, I motioned for the three of them to investigate the booths while I would peruse the patrons at the bar.

I was half-way down the room before a bartender approached.

"Señorita, que puedo conseguirte?" He was a young man with messy golden hair and bronze skin. He had a wrinkled buttoned-down shirt on. I could not see his pants but I assumed they were just as disheveled.

I gave him an icy stare before responding. "Do you speak English?"

He nodded.

"I am looking for a friend. You probably IDed him and his attractive companion. They look far too young to be in this sort of establishment."

Recognition lit up his eyes. So eager to help, I thought. *What a pawn.*

"Oh yes, they slipped into the back. We have a small game room back there."

"Wonderful. I appreciate your help. I am sure I will be back in a moment to order that drink." I smiled at him a sultry smile. He cleared his throat uncomfortably.

"Yes, of course."

I winked at him, then turned to see my entourage had heard the bartender and were already slinking in that direction.

I kept my pace slow and casual. I didn't need to be the first to set eyes on the youthful-looking couple.

A thick velvet curtain was partitioning the room. Claudia took hold of the left panel while motioning for Akiva and Astrid to flank the other side. I stood back a few feet, waiting to make my own entrance.

Claudia mouthed a countdown from three. On one, she drew back the curtain to find a wall of tables and chairs. Just as the last gap was filled by a flying dart board, I caught a glimpse of Lucia's angelic face.

"Tear it down," I ordered through gritted teeth.

I should have known this was not going to be simple. I watched as Astrid, Akiva and Claudia clawed at the barrier of furniture.

"What are you doing?" the bartender shouted behind us.

"Claudia, take care of him and any other patrons foolish enough to still be in this bar." Claudia immediately dropped what she was doing and went to terrorize the bartender into leaving. Sweat began to bead on my forehead. My neck felt scratchy from the heat. Winston knew I was here. That meant he could focus his Calentar gift on me, he would boil me alive.

"Move faster," I shrieked. I was ready to start ripping off my clothes. Lucia had built a wall of furniture, that resourceful little harlot. It wouldn't keep us out for long, but I could boil in my own skin before we made it through.

Claudia made her way back to my side. She was drenched in sweat. I had mistakenly said her name out loud, giving Winston another target. Her eyes were pleading and growing red around the edges.

"What the fuck is this?" she cried.

I shoved her aside and took control of Astrid's body with my touch. "I'm going to burn it, Winston!" I threatened. "You and Lucia can die in there, huddled together in heaps of ash for all I care."

No one responded. My skin started to steam and sizzle from the extreme temperatures inside.

They had to be running out of furniture for Lucia to play with. I directed Astrid's hand onto the closest chair and sent a current hot enough to set it on fire. I had her reach for another and another until there were seven fires ablaze in the pile of broken junk.

I turned around to see Claudia writhing in pain on the floor, completely naked, having torn off her clothes.

Suddenly there was a crash of timbers from the game room. Winston barreled through, making eye contact with me, and the pain I had felt paled in comparison to the excruciating sensation that filled every cell of my being now. My vision was blurry, distorted, but I saw Lucia's petite figure clinging to Winston's arm.

"Akiva, get her!" I roared. She nearly slipped from his grasp but he seized her hand. She yelped in pain.

"Winston!" she cried as Akiva's grip tore them apart.

Winston froze.

"Call off the assault," I mumbled, nearly inaudibly. "Now, or Akiva will tear her apart and toss her into the fire." I meant to have Astrid give Lucia a warning shock as well but I was too weak to maneuver her body. Claudia still lay on the floor, tearing at her own skin.

The intense fever subsided slowly as Akiva held tight to Lucia's tiny body. She was a child when they consummated. Her seraph face was framed with kinky black curls. She chose to wear attire that indicated she was older than the fourteen years she had lived as an Unconsu. Winston glared at me, waiting to make his next move.

I still couldn't think, so I released Astrid's body with my mind. I needed her to be able to act quickly.

"Take me instead," Winston asserted. "You don't really want Lucia."

I was still collecting myself, determining what I would do next. Claudia was composing herself as well, but she had torn her clothes apart during her panic, so she was standing there, shamefaced, covering her intimate parts. I had to laugh. The woman had nothing to be ashamed of—except for her irrational behavior. But how is one to act when they are being boiled alive, *really*?

When I felt I could speak without trembling, I did. "It is you that I wish to speak to. But seeing as how Lucia keeps you from poaching us all where we stand, I believe I will have Akiva hold tight to her." I straightened my drenched clothes. "We need to catch up, Winston. I have been dying to hear how hospitable Elias Kraus has grown to be."

I got within arm's reach and slapped him across the face, dragging my nails through his skin, leaving four lovely gashes across his cheek.

"First things first. Astrid, contain the fire before the local authorities are called. Claudia, find some clothes." I stepped closer to Akiva and Lucia and took a beautiful tendril of Lucia's hair between my fingers. It reminded me of my beloved's. "And you, my dear Lucia. Do me a favor, my precious girl, and don't attempt any more construction."

I chuckled to myself. Who would have thought a Mason would give us such grief? I had never considered the benefit of having a master builder among the Nebas. It was time to reconsider.

ELIAS

I prepared dinner this evening. Su had met me in the galley and asked if he could relay the story of the Katuan Stones to Ophelia. He loved telling stories and he was good at it. It was also likely he knew it much better than I, seeing as how he had read the books here in the library multiple times during his stay in The Cathedral. Therefore it was easy to comply with his request.

Su helped me carry dinner up to the room we had deemed our dining area. We could have decided to eat in a different room every night, but familiarity becomes more important the longer you are in the throngs of change.

I thought about The Cathedral and all her magnificence often. This was no traditional Haven. It changed like a living organism. Over the last week, as we prepared for the summit, I had been in more rooms than I could count. Some rooms I feared I would never see again. The day we arrived we were hurtled into a huge hall that had the most stunning stained-glass window I had ever seen, with golds and greens and rich hues of yellow. I had yet to stumble upon that grandeur again.

She also had a courtyard and a lawn that spread for miles, if she wished. We could spend years here and never see all that she had to offer. Su had explained to me during one of our explorations that he had always thought Ruit had made The Cathedral. But it was not the case. Ruit had only created the key that could open her. She was just as much an anomaly to him as to anyone else.

We arrived in the dining room to find Ophelia had yet to arrive.

"Susuda, do you believe you have seen all that The Cathedral has to share?"

"I have lived here for two thousand years and have yet to have seen everything on the grounds."

I considered that. What a strange thought, not even two thousand years was enough time to see it all. Su interrupted my thoughts.

"I look forward to seeing what she will do with the Stones."

I nodded in agreement, not yet certain what that truly meant. Su and I had spent the afternoon looking over the documents my father had left me in conjunction with the text we had at our disposal. We concluded that the best way to re-create the Katuanak Arena, where the Stones were first created and endorsed as essential to the Trials, was to coordinate with The Cathedral. Lay our plans at her steps and see what she would create in collaboration with the Stones. It was as good a solution as any, since it was obvious we could not build an arena ourselves. My father suggested as much in his own notes. He did not know he was looking for a Haven as grandiose as the legendary Cathedral, but he knew he needed some place with extraordinary transformative powers.

This time my thoughts were interrupted by the appearance of Ophelia in the doorway.

"It smells amazing," she observed as she made her way to her seat. Su pulled it out for her while she sat. I had to catch my breath; she looked so fetching. She wore a long dress that fell above her ankles. I could tell she was spending time in the sun by the way her skin glowed. Her freckles looked a touch darker. When she caught me staring, I had to find busy work with the table settings. After reading the prophecy, it became clear that Ophelia was not going to entertain our connection. On one hand it was a relief, because I knew I did not have to fight the urge to be with her all on my own. On the other hand, I

47

missed her. I missed the friendship we were building. I missed the familiar buzz between us. She had all but snuffed that out with the shield she had acquired from Lucas. Frequently, I wondered how much of her distance was the prophecy and how much of it was guilt from losing Lucas, knowing he wanted her affections.

"I think you have set and re-set the table enough times, Elias," she joked.

I did my best to brush off my embarrassment. "Indeed."

Su began to dish up our dinner.

"Do we have to describe the food before or after you tell Ophelia of the origins of the Katuan Stones?"

The question caught Su off-guard. I had to laugh. He was just as eager to hear about our meal as he was to share an epic story.

"I think you can share your food experience after."

"Oh, Su, you're going to tell the story? That will be lovely." Ophelia beamed at him with enthusiastic delight.

"It is my honor, Miss Olly." Su settled into his own chair and clasped his hands on his lap. "I am only relaying the story I read. I was not there for the first Katuan Trials. But there are many written accounts, from the first Trials to the last, which occurred nearly four thousand years ago. Katuanak was an ancient fortress built by many. It was said that over five hundred Consu participated in the Covening that created the Katuanak construct. The fortress encompassed an enormous arena. After centuries of being on the planet, many Conduits desired to participate in assembly and communion. It was said that the inhabitants of the Katuanak fortress sent invitations far and wide to all the Conduits in the world, to every pantheon and all the continents. The invitations intrigued each recipient, and the over-seeing Conduits were astounded to find that all who were invited had decided to attend."

"Where was this massive assembly?" Ophelia interrupted.

"First you must understand that populations were much smaller than, so the Trials probably only consisted of about a thousand Conduits in all. The Katuanak fortress was built and stood for many years until the final games on the island of Atlantis."

I watched Ophelia's expression closely, curious of how she would react. She was surprisingly stoic. It took a lot to shake her these days.

"The lost city of Atlantis?"

"Exactly," Su said confidently.

"Well, I can't say I'm surprised. It was an island said to have extraordinary power, right? It would make sense that Conduits were behind that. I didn't mean to interrupt. Please continue."

I smiled at her and she winked back while Su continued.

"It certainly did. Atlantis was the ideal spot to build a Haven such as the Fortress of Katuanak because it was a land inhabited solely by Conduits. A place where they could express their abilities unhindered. The large Paksyon that convened the fortress inlaid many enchantments into the Stones, all so their intentions for the Trials could be met without exception. It was agreed that the Trials were created to unite the factions from all corners of the world, to remind the participants that as Conduits we have the gift to create, destroy and transform, just as the original brothers did. Ultimately, the Katuan Trials served the sole purpose of amalgamating the Conduit people. It is unclear when the first Trials began. Not much has been recorded on individual victories or team triumphs."

Ophelia interrupted once more. "Slow down, Su. What are Conduit factions?"

"May I?" I turned to Su to make sure he was okay with me answering that question. He nodded and I proceeded. "Conduits used to be divided into factions according to the characteristics of their gifts. It is an antiquated tradition, but it will be used during the Trials to form teams. If you can withstand your curiosity, you and I can go over what I have found on the subject tomorrow afternoon."

"If it isn't pertinent to the story right now, sure," she agreed.

"It is not," Su assured her. "It is my opinion it is best understood by inspecting the diagram in the library. You two should start there tomorrow."

"That sounds like a perfect plan." Ophelia nodded in approval. "Please continue."

"I won't go into details about teams; you two can discuss that tomorrow. But there are thirteen Champions per team, chosen by the Katuan Stones. It is a great honor to be chosen as Champion. The Trials were not just about the three challenges themselves, but also about fellowship. So for a fortnight before the Trials begin, each day marks the reception of new arrivals, feasts, minor competitions, music and merriment of all sorts. Upon the fourteenth day, the Opening Ceremonybegins, and the Stones announce the Directorate, the Champions and their Katans. The Katan is what you call a team. The teams have three days to acquaint themselves with each other's gifts and learn how to work together before the first Trial. On the third evening, the entire congregation of Conduits attends the Champions' Ball, an evening of grandeur and celebration." Su leaned in, excited. "Everyone dresses up, even me. There is also a Victors' Ball. We will dress lavishly then as well, to pay tribute to the victorious Katan."

Ophelia beamed at him. His enthusiasm was contagious.

When he was through reveling in the delight, Su returned to the story, or as it had become, the tutorial, which, I supposed, made sense, since that was how it was written in the text he had read. "The three challenges set before the teams were that of creation, destruction and transformation. The Katuan Stones defined each challenge a specific rubric the morning of the Trial in front of the audience. The challenge can be different at every Trial. It's hard to say because the Trials took place every hundred years. However certain elements were consistent, such as the Katans geting two days before the second Trial to strategize and a single day before the final Trial to prepare."

"Every hundred years?" Ophelia said skeptically.

"That is a drop in the bucket for a Conduit, especially one of that time, who was yet to have anything to fear. The Nebas was not even a word among the whispers." Su looked off, beyond us both. "But that did not mean there were no wars taking place."

We both knew he was talking about his own transformation into what he was today, all because he was caught up in what he was told was the war of the sisters.

"We all know it was not entirely peaceful, Su, and you and those you love are a terrible testament to that." I leaned over and squeezed his shoulder with my hand.

"It was not all peaceful," he said solemnly, shook his head and began again. "On the morning of the last challenge of the final Katuan Trial to ever take place, devastation befell. As I said before, the Stones were enchanted, built with boundaries to keep the Trials within their purpose—unification, camaraderie. During the final challenge a death occurred. Onlookers believed it was an accident. A Champion got too close to the flames. No one meant to push her. In truth, no one was said to have actually seen the incident that lead to the death, but the Stones had been built with a single severe consequence upon death. The Katuan Trials would end, never to happen again. So it followed that the Katuanak Fortress began falling apart, the Stones vanished into the water, some rolling into themselves, while other stones flung themselves into the other structures on the island. Every Conduit had to flee the island as it slowly and destructively deteriorated into the sea."

"So that's how Atlantis disappeared? Seriously? And now we are bringing these disastrous Stones into The Cathedral?" Ophelia looked between us frantically.

Su spoke first. "The Stones have been here for longer than I have."

That did not appear to assuage her fears. Her eyebrows shot up.

"My father uncovered a written work that suggested the Katuan Stones would let commence one last Trial with the intent of transformation. A loophole of sorts, within the intention enchantments. They require a word, a word we have." I attempted confidence but was not certain I convinced anyone.

"Okay, so we have a word that may work to rouse potentially homicidal rocks to judge us, put us in groups, pit us against one another, and we have to hope no one breaks the rules."

I thought about her argument, both as a whole and in its parts. "I want you to know I understand your apprehension. It is going to take something monumental to pull the Pai Ona who have lost everything and live in hiding into risking exposure by coming out. This is monumental." I spoke with my eyes as well. "The Stones are just, the Trials

51

are harmless, and the Conduits we are inviting are on our side. We are ensuring that with the broadcast we are building. There is a risk... many. But there was always going to be a risk."

Her eyes softened and I knew she understood. But before she could say a thing, Su chimed in. "And there is going to be a ball!" He put up two fingers. "Two of them!"

OPHELIA

*E*lias and I had finished working on the broadcast for the morning. I felt it was ready, but he was still unsure. I couldn't blame him; a lot rode on the success of the invitation. The networks room was dusty from years without use, so I decided to take a shower before we had lunch and met in the library to learn about the Conduit factions.

I looked in the mirror. My strawberry hair was damp but manageable today. My eyes looked tired. I realized it had been days since I'd had a good night's sleep, and it was showing. Black circles gave my exhaustion away. It was days like this I wished I was better with makeup. Upon closer examination, I noticed my freckles had darkened from spending my afternoons on the lawn. I kind of liked the way they looked. They detracted from my sunken eyes.

After one more quick inspection, I decided there wasn't much I could do to fix it and gave up. My stomach was telling me it was lunch time, so I threw on a pink cardigan over my lime green sundress and stepped into the hall. A second later I was in the galley, searching for what I was going to make us for lunch. I landed on grilled cheese sandwiches and tomato soup. I stepped into the pantry, when I suddenly felt the hairs on the back of my neck stand on end. There was a noise, a hum or a hiss, gently bouncing off the walls.

"Hello? Su? Elias?" I said as I turned around to make sure I was alone.

The noise didn't let up, nor did anyone reply. I replaced the can of soup onto the shelf and stood there quietly, trying to determine which direction the noise was originating from. My feet attempted to follow my ears as I walked down the hall, up the steps towards a dark passage. The further I got the less I could see. I lowered my shield slightly and manifested a flame in the palm of my right hand. I smiled at it because it reminded me of Aremis. My left hand stayed on the wall, and I gingerly put one foot in front of the other, feeling for any steps or discrepancy in the floor that I couldn't see by my tiny light. After a few minutes I found myself at a dead end. The passage just ended. The stones were cold and damp down here. The deep hiss, which was what I concluded it to be, was definitely coming from the other side of the wall. I pressed my ear against the cold stones. Vibrations permeated my head, slow and rhythmic. I closed my eyes and expanded my senses, daring to drop my shield further.

"Miss Olly?"

I screamed—a bloodcurdling scream. He screamed back, and then we both stood there laughing, the flame skipping above my head.

"Su," I grabbed at my chest, "you scared the daylights out of me."

"What are you doing down here?" he said through his own panting.

"I heard something." I stopped to see if I could hear it once more but it was gone. "A hiss. Have you ever heard a hiss down here?"

Su grabbed my hand to escort me into the light. "No, I have not."

Maybe I was going crazy, a thought that I had considered more than once.

"You say you heard a hiss?"

"I guess that's what you would call it. Never mind." I waved my free hand. "It was probably nothing."

"Well, I'm glad I found you. I was looking for Mr. Elias." Su turned and took both of my hands into his. "I transported the Stones into the great hall. Would you like to see them?"

"Would I!" The light from the galley illuminated where we stood, so I extinguished the flame.

That was all he needed to teleport us to the hall. At first I thought the Stones were very unassuming. We walked the thirty feet or so to fill the gap between us and where they stood stacked in the middle of the great hall. As we got closer, I realized they were far larger than I'd thought at first glance.

"Su, how on earth did you move these things?"

"One at a time," he said proudly.

Now that we were only a couple of feet away, the stack of Stones loomed overhead like a skyscraper. The symbols etched into the huge slabs of rock looked vaguely familiar. I got even closer and traced a large circular shape with my index finger. The engraving shimmered under my touch, and I felt a strange pulsating move up my spine.

"Did you see that?"

Su was behind me now. "See what?"

"The shimmer under my touch, there, on the symbol."

Su leaned in closer as I removed my hand.

"I hope you have not touched the Stones," Elias' voice echoed from across the room.

Before turning around my eyes met Su's, and we silently agreed we wouldn't say anything. I faced Elias with my nervous grin. I thought he suspected something, but he said nothing.

"They are huge!" I observed.

Elias agreed. "Magnificently so. I am surprised Su was able to move them so quickly."

"One at a time," Su repeated.

Elias put his hand on Su's shoulder. "Thank you."

"What are you going to do with them?" I asked.

"Good question. I believe they will do what needs to be done once we encourage the collaboration with The Cathedral." Elias looked up at the huge wall of Stones. There had to be hundreds of them. They were so large it was difficult to tell. "But first I must conclude some additional research and we must have lunch and talk about Conduit factions."

The mention of lunch made my stomach growl.

"Lunch sounds like a good next step," I agreed.

Su started walking toward the hall entrance, where we would teleport. "Oh, what is on the menu?"

Food was the easiest distraction for him. "Grilled cheese sandwich and tomato soup," I said as I fell in step beside him and Elias.

I turned to look over my shoulder one last time before we exited the great hall. I could still see the vague shimmer where my hand had traced the symbol. My cheeks warmed, and I considered telling Elias that I did in fact touch the Stones, but decided one little fib couldn't hurt. Besides, I hadn't *denied* touching them. I just wouldn't say anything.

ELIAS

*W*e stood in front of the large diagram Su had spoken of the day before. It was impressive in size. I had seen a smaller example in the back of one of my father's books.

"What are we looking at here?" There was a smile in her voice. I was happy to hear it. The closer the summit got, the lighter her spirit seemed to grow.

"Well, from what I have gathered from a variety of texts that my father had in addition to what Ruit collected and stored in the library here, there are six teams. Each Katan, or team, starts with thirteen Champions. Twelve of the Champions represent a faction of Conduits."

She interrupted. "Only twelve?"

"The thirteenth Champion on the team can be from any faction. A wild card of sorts. I was not able to find anything that explained why the Champions are chosen in this way, or the significance of thirteen."

"Why were we factioned to begin with?"

"That is a good question, one I do not know the answer to either. Knowing which faction they belong to certainly makes it easier to identify an individual Conduit's gift." I walked over to the bookshelf adjacent to the diagram. The binding of the book was not titled, but I knew which one contained the faction list and descriptions. I had read it many times already. "Let me show you what I discovered." I pulled the heavy book from the middle shelf and hoisted it onto a table that stood in the center of the room. A plume of dust spewed from the cover as I opened it. I had moved the book several times over the week, but still dust seemed to collect instantaneously on its pages. Ophelia sat in one of the four chairs surrounding the table. I sifted through the pages until I found what I was looking for. I pointed at the diagram again, then paused when I saw Ophelia get up.

She walked over to the diagram on the wall and ran her finger over the shape several times.

"Circles," she whispered. "These look so familiar to me."

I looked at her curiously, wondering if she would say more on the familiarity. But she did not so I continued. "This faction is the Elementals." I pointed to the symbol in the book that represented their designation. It was a four-point star. "They represent any Conduit who can manipulate earth, wind, fire or water. Within each element are further divisions. Remember how Vosega said he was a Vulcan?"

She nodded. The smaller divisions were not depicted on the large diagram she was still examining.

"That is one of three divisions within the Earth Elementals' designation. There are also Minerals and Quakers. Minerals command control of metals, stones, salts, anything that is found in the earth in its most basic form. Quakers shake the earth, move the plates within the earth's surface. Vulcans specifically work within mountains, creating volcanic activity."

Ophelia resumed her seat beside me and scooted in closer to look at the book I was referencing. It listed all the factions, subfactions and the symbols and gifts associated with each. "But the Katuan Stones don't divide the factions up into these subfactions when they create the Katans?"

"Not that I am aware of," I admitted. There really was so little that I truly knew about this process and the rituals we were going to be participating in only days from now. It made me uneasy, but I had

trusted the process thus far and it had served us on this journey. I saw
no reason to stop now.

She pointed to the symbol society had deemed the Vitruvian man.
"Was da Vinci a Conduit?"

"Yes," I replied, and she did not flinch with surprise. "This faction
is the Corpori. It includes any Conduit who can affect or compel the
human body. There are many subcategories in this faction, with a
wide variety. Ranging from Healers, like my mother, and Body
Snatchers, like Esther."

Mentioning Esther did create a visible response, and I felt bad that
she was still so shaken by her. I moved on quickly. "These are
Ramalans. They see the future and are very rare." I pointed to their
symbol of the eye. "Bustanys influence plants." Their symbol was a
tree with deep roots.

"What's this one?" She pointed at the Taqa symbol, a cup.

"Taqas manipulate energy into things like shields or camouflage." I
waited to see how she would respond with the mention of something
she associated with Lucas. Ophelia looked down at her hands.

Whatever she was thinking, she decided to keep it to herself.
"Please tell me about the rest of the factions," she said with a vacant
smile. My heart ached for her pain.

I took a deep breath and continued. "We have the Incantors, who
create spells, manipulate language. Mapping, and even truthsaying
falls under a subcategory in the Incantors faction." Ophelia leaned
down to look at their symbol more closely.

"Is this a hand over a mouth?"

"Yes."

"Who decided on these symbols?"

"I cannot tell you." I shrugged. More of the unknown. "I only know
what is in these pages. Animos influence dreams, visions or inspire
creativity, like a muse. The Tahwils are Shapeshifters or Giants.
Circuitu are a very diverse group. They manipulate weather. Some are
Calentars and Latterns. Varons have power over animals or can speak
to animals. There are the Ancients, who are only distinguished by

their age and eclectic abilities. And there are Adfectors, Conduits who deal with emotions, like you." I smiled.

She ran her finger over the Adfectors' symbol, a knot between two hearts.

I watched as she examined each faction. "I have met or heard of many Conduits who express gifts from most of the factions. But I don't think I've met a Bustany or Varon. Are they rare?"

"Not necessarily. In fact Taqas and Ramalans seem to be the rarest, from what I understand."

She nodded. "Maybe I'll meet a Bustany or a Varon at the summit," she chirped.

"You most definitely will. It will be hard to avoid getting to meet every kind of Conduit." I paused. "But no one can know what you are." Or what we suspected she was, a Sulu.

"I understand, Elias," she said seriously.

I put my hand on hers. "I know you do. I am just worried."

"I'll be discreet. I have my shield up, remember?" She pulled her hand out from under mine and stood up again to further examine the diagram. "What's this?" It was a blank section in the center.

"I wish I could tell you." I made my way to her side. "Perhaps it is the space between the gifts. Some Conduits express gifts that do not quite fit in a single faction. Nara, for example. She manipulates wind."

Ophelia looked at me thoughtfully. "I didn't know that." She pointed to the Elemental. "So she fits here."

I pointed to the Circuitu. "She can create hurricanes, so she is also a manipulator of weather. Therefore, she can also fall here."

She nodded in understanding. "Everything is always so complicated. How will the Katuan Stones pick their Champions?"

I lit up, mostly because I had the answer to this question. "I will show you." I grabbed a rolled-up sketch Su and I had been working on and gently sprawled it out on the table. "Su and I have been re-creating the Katuanak Arena and the placement of the Katuan Arch." We both leaned over the table. I pointed at the plans. "See this arch here? This is where every Conduit will enter into The Cathedral. As they pass under the Katuan Arch, they will be measured by the Stones.

This is how they will determine the Champions, Directorate and the Master of Ceremonies of the Trials. They become familiar with their abilities through proximity."

"Cool."

"Indeed," I agreed. "The Arena will be a collaboration between the Stones and The Cathedral. We are very fortunate that The Cathedral is a master transitional Haven. Susuda is certain that the Katuan Stones and The Cathedral will be able to build something of this grandeur and sophistication."

"Will we be able to see the Trials?" She pointed at the arena seating. "Do we sit here?"

"Yes, and there will be projections and other ways to view the more intricate goings-on of the Trials. As I said, there will be a large variety of Conduits in attendance, with gifts we cannot even imagine."

"Do the Unconsu participate? Can the Stones choose one of us to be a Champion?"

"No. The Trials are dangerous. Feats that may only harm a Consu, but could kill me or you. As it were, we will be the only Unconsu in attendance and we will be spectators for this event."

"Sounds like fun! Oh, can we make popcorn?"

I laughed aloud. "That can be arranged."

ESTHER

"How much longer can you endure? What are you fighting for?" I circled Winston's broken form. Akiva had been especially ruthless today. "I know you have means to contact Viraclay. Share your method and I will make your death swift and spare Lucia's life." I looked at her mangled body in the corner. She was barely holding on, and Winston knew it. "Still you stay silent as Lucia suffers. What kind of Atoa are you?"

Lucia's dry voice croaked quietly, "Winston, they cannot break us."

I laughed until my face hurt. "Is that what you truly believe, dear Lucia? There are ways, tortures greater than physical pain. I was hoping to be kind and spare you the agony, but you two are proving to be more stubborn than I had anticipated." I played with a tendril of my long black hair as I considered which avenue I would use next, what tool would make the biggest impact. "Astrid!"

She quickly stepped into the room. "Collect the vice."

"As you wish, Mistress."

"Have you heard of the vice?" I leaned down to make eye contact with Winston's battered face. "It was manufactured by my father. He commissioned it from a great builder, whom he later murdered. Fear not, it is not to torture your physical form—that has proven useless.

The vice latches onto your thoughts." I grabbed Winston's black hair and pulled his head up to look at Lucia. "Each one of her thoughts will be excruciating as the vice twists and contorts them into fragments and splinters, until there is nothing left but mania. Can you imagine?" I threw his head to the floor. "Will she be as pretty when she has gone mad?"

OPHELIA

*T*his was it, the last step before we sent the broadcast and the summit was officially put in motion. I was ecstatic. I could only imagine what Elias was feeling, watching all of his hard work, all of his father's hard work come to fruition.

I'd been shying away from intimate moments with him, but this was all too monumental to let that prophecy get in the way. I took his hand in mine. "How are you feeling? You must be dancing in your skin with anticipation." My eyes met his. There was something else there. I let my shield drop to feel what it was. It was fear, intense fear. I squeezed his hand harder. "What? What's wrong, Elias?"

He cleared his throat uncomfortably. "I cannot get anything by you." He knew I'd used my gift to peek into his emotional state. If it bothered him, he didn't let on about it. "There is so much riding on this moment. So much riding on the success of the summit. Now that it is so close, I find I am more afraid. What is wrong with me?"

"Nothing. Nothing is wrong with you. We can do this," I assured him. "We are a team."

He smiled, but it was half-hearted. I couldn't possibly understand what this fully meant to him. He had lost so much to get here. But I wanted him to know I was with him. Before I could say more, Susuda returned. He wasn't frightened at all. In fact, he looked elated.

"It is ready." The three of us stood on the threshold of the great hall. The Katuan Stones were still piled in the center. "Would you like to do the honors, Elias?"

I let go of his hand as he solemnly placed it on the wall. He took a deep breath. "Hold on." With that, he put his other hand on the arena plans he and Susuda had prepared and said what we hoped was the magic word, "Brilfalti."

Instantly, the room began to spin and shift, all at once. *It worked!* I cheered silently in my head. The floor vibrated beneath our feet. It reminded me of the transitions in Hafiza. I struggled to stay standing. Su took my arm to keep me steady. I stared at the Stones in the center of the room. One by one they began to move, slowly at first, then each one began flying in the air above our heads. A wind picked up with the momentum of it all. My hair whipped around my face erratically. Su laughed wildly beside me. I found his joy comforting in such a chaotic moment. He wasn't afraid so I guessed I shouldn't be either.

Suddenly the Stones stopped moving, hovering in midair before flying to opposite corners of the transforming room. I blinked, and when I tried to refocus on my surroundings, I could see things were no longer as they had been only minutes ago. Where the wide-open floor of the hall had been, divots appeared. No, not divots—steps. Below the steps, in the center, where the Stones once lay, was a huge oval platform. Above us hung an enormous metal chandelier. The hall had transformed into a grand coliseum with archways on every level. There had to be enough seating for over five thousand people. It was magnificent, and not unlike the Roman coliseum in its design. The smile on my face was so wide it hurt my cheeks.

I turned to Elias. He was awestruck. They'd done it. The summit was happening.

ELIAS

Ophelia and I had spent all morning double-checking the broadcast. She looked over my checklist, and with her assistance I felt we covered all our bases. Now that the collaboration between the Katuan Stones and The Cathedral was complete, everything was in order. It was time to invite the guests. Still, I hesitated. Re-reading our work.

When I sent the broadcast, only those without known affiliation with the Nebas would receive the letter. Once they physically touched the envelope, the second enchantment would determine if they held any malefic intent toward other Conduits or an affinity for the Nebas. If they passed this tactile enchantment, they were granted a warning that would appear on the outside of the envelope, which read:

'This broadcast is meant for those purest of intent. Should you falsely claim allegiances of truth for either side you will bear the mark. Open with the knowledge that all trespasses will be revealed in the contents of this message.'

I smiled to myself as I considered Ophelia's brilliance in this additional step of the enchantment. If they did not proceed with opening the letter, they would be marked. If they did open the letter and they were in fact aligned with the Nebas, the contents would be blank and they would be marked. The mark itself was subtle, only visible to those who knew to look for it. A faint shadow of an impression in the shape of a square would be visible on their right palm. Su had the ingenious idea of informing The Cathedral. This meant she would take an inventory of anyone with the mark who approached her gates.

The last precaution was the most crucial. Once the letter was opened, an honorable recipient would be prompted to share their blood. They would be given a final warning, which read:

. 'If you share your blood on this paper you swear your allegiance to the Pai Ona. A blood promise that binds you to never kill or harm another of our people. If your promise is broken, not only you, but your family will pay the price, forever marked by your treachery.'

This final and severe binding would certainly discourage anyone with questionable motives. The blood bonds in a contract such as this are nearly impossible to break. It would require expansive amounts of energy. After participating in the binding, the instructions on how to reach The Cathedral, date and time of the impending summit would be revealed.

I felt good about our work. But I hesitated. I had yet to place the broadcast in the channels. The truth was—I was afraid. Not only would we know who was our friend and who was our enemy—lines that could never be redrawn once they were exposed. But some of these people may be people I thought were my allies—who my parents thought were friends. It would also make clear our true position in this war. Were our numbers few or many? This broadcast would immediately change everything. I was so lost in thought that I jumped when I heard Ophelia's voice behind me.

She stood there with Su, a bottle of champagne in hand. "What are you waiting for? It's time to celebrate!"

"I was just double-checking our enchantments, confirming that they are thorough enough."

"That broadcast is tighter than Fort Knox." She came closer when she saw the worry line cross my brow. "This is what you've been working for. What your father desired more than anything else. You've done him proud. Stop second-guessing how amazing you are."

She kissed me on the cheek. The feel of her skin on mine was enough to erase any doubts.

Together, we could execute this summit. She fortified my resolve. I turned back around and, one at a time, sent the broadcast through each channel. One by one, they disappeared into the ether, on a mission to expose the state of this war.

My heart was racing out of my chest when I put the last one in. The champagne popped behind me, Ophelia squealed with enthusiasm and I dissolved my fear.

OPHELIA

The last two weeks passed by in a blur. Once The Cathedral and the Katuan Stones did their thing and Elias sent the broadcast, there wasn't much left to do in preparation. At least nothing I could assist with. Su ran around and collected a vast array of foods. Although Conduits don't require food for sustenance, they enjoy it. So Elias said we needed plenty available for the variety of celebrations and festivities that would take place leading up to the Trials. I, for one, was looking forward to seeing what other Conduits would cook up.

Then there was the arguments stage. Apparently, at the end of the Trials, the Oracle Aurora would be overseeing any dispute hearings that needed to be resolved. Elias said this formality was to alleviate any bad blood among the Pai Ona, to create harmony. The way I understood it, it was pretty simple. If a Conduit suspected another Conduit to have hurt either them or their family, they could be heard in front of Aurora. I envisioned something like Judge Judy, but Elias said these disputes were far more serious, with accusations such as collusion with the Nebas or even murder. Aurora was the most powerful Ramalan in existence today, so that was why she would be hearing the arguments. It would be up to her and her gift of foresight to determine the truth of it all. That wasn't a job I'd want.

In addition to preparing the plans for the stage, Elias was running around planting arsenals and back-up plans, should The Cathedral be breached and a battle begin. Most of this planning took place between him and The Cathedral. I wasn't sure how the preparation made me feel. On one hand I felt safe in The Cathedral, and on the other hand all this offensive planning made me uneasy. Uneasy or not, I knew that this time we wouldn't be caught off-guard if Esther and her minions found us.

I didn't want to get in the way, but I'd been chewing on a couple of questions I had for Elias, and since we were now at the eve of the summit, it felt like it was now or never. He was only going to get busier as people arrived. We agreed to have dinner together for the first time in two weeks.

Elias insisted on cooking, so I sat waiting in the dining room, nervously playing with my hairsy charm, a habit I'd grown to find comforting in a weird way.

"I hope you are hungry. I may have gotten a little carried away with our menu," he said as he entered the room, Su in tow, carrying several dishes.

"It smells amazing," I said as they laid the spread out on the table. I smelled sweet and savory spices wafting in the air.

"Three different Indian curries." Elias smiled proudly as Su removed the lids from the serving dishes. "This one is spicy, just like you like it." He pointed to the one closest to me and then took a seat.

Su turned to leave. "You aren't joining us?" I asked.

"Not this evening. I need to be on watch." Su's smile was faint. Disappointment shadowed the gesture. "But you can tell me all about it tomorrow."

"I will," I assured him, and he perked up slightly, then he was gone.

The mood in the room shifted. I realized this was the first time in a very long time that Elias and I had been alone together.

"Well, please dish up," Elias said as he poured both of us a large glass of wine.

We didn't talk much as we ate. The meal was delicious, and I definitely ate more than I meant to. When we were both too stuffed to eat another bite, we migrated to the fireplace on the opposite end of the room. There was a small love seat directly in front of the hearth. It comfortably sat us both, without feeling too cozy.

I took another long sip of my wine before diving into my questions.

"Are you excited?" I asked.

"Terribly anxious, I am afraid, but with that comes some level of excitement." He looked past me for a moment, his strong features hypnotic in the firelight. I followed his jaw line and noticed the stubble on his chin. The green-gold eyes that captivated me so intently were lost in thought. I leaned in; I had a sudden urge to comfort him. Maybe it was the wine, maybe I was the one who needed the comfort.

I nestled under his shoulder. "I'm sorry you're so stressed. But I think you've done an amazing job of putting this event together. How many Conduits are we expecting, anyways?"

"I hope we will see at least six thousand attendees."

"Wow," was all I could muster. This place was going to be very different by tomorrow evening. There wouldn't be any moments like this available to either of us.

As if on cue, he wrapped his arm around me and I let my shield drop. I'd been wearing it like armor ever since the night Lucas died but tonight would be the last time I could come out from behind it until the summit was over. Something about that limitation made me want to let loose a little. The buzz between us materialized on my skin. I let Elias' emotions wash over me. It was a flurry, a rarity for a man that's usually so calm and collected. I felt his anxiety, his fear, his love for me, his concern for my well-being, sexual frustration and, somewhere deep inside, a pinch of pride.

"You should indulge that feeling a little more," I said.

He pulled back so he could see my face. He knew I'd let down my shield but he didn't know what I was talking about. I expanded the

71

sense I inherited from Rand, dove a little deeper into Elias' feelings. I could sense the ounce of gratification.

"That feeling, the pride and gratification you're stuffing down, deep down inside you. Give it a little more space to breathe. You deserve it. Your father would be proud of you. *I* am proud of you."

We sat in silence for a long moment but I felt him fan those lost little feelings, and it made me smile.

When I noticed his mood shift back to anxious, I decided I might as well ask my questions.

"So where will these six thousand Conduits sleep?"

"Here, same as you and I. Su will carry them through the gate, walk them through the Katuan Arch and show them to their rooms."

"All by himself? That's a lot of greetings."

"He is quite capable. I do not think we know all that he is capable of. He feels confident that he can tackle this chore."

I just nodded. Elias was right. I was sure I didn't understand all that Su could do.

"There is enough space?"

"Absolutely. The Cathedral is truly miraculous."

"What can I expect for tomorrow?"

"Arrivals. We have two weeks of arrivals, and during that time there will be an assortment of festivities that you are welcome to participate in. Things like dancing, fencing, eating." He squeezed my arm playfully. The electricity between us amplified at the tighter touch and sent tingles into my abdomen. "There will be music, games, all kinds of entertainment."

"Are you putting this on?"

"No, I am leaving that up to the Pai Ona themselves. Each of their rooms will have a welcome letter that encourages them to participate in or organize whatever they wish during arrivals."

"You seem confident they'll decide to orchestrate these things."

"I am. Many of our people have been stifled for too long. Afraid to use their gifts freely, fearful of detection by Yanni or Esther and the Nebas. I believe they will be elated to have the freedom to just be and share in fellowship."

"You're probably right," I agreed. "Will you be busy the whole time?"

"No busier than I am now."

So busy, I thought.

"Will I see anyone from Hafiza?" This was the question I'd been ruminating over most.

"If they survived, they will be here."

If they survived. I considered that. I could only hope some of my friends had survived. Suddenly, I felt vulnerable. I replaced my shield, cutting off my connection to Elias. He didn't say anything, but I wondered for a moment how that made him feel.

He whispered, "Keep your shield closely around you." With that, he gave me a tight squeeze and pulled away to stand up. "I am going to bring the dishes down."

"I can help."

We made our way to the galley in silence. I was mentally preparing myself for the onslaught of strangers that I'd surely meet tomorrow while Elias washed up and I dried the dishes. *Maybe some Conduits would arrive before I even woke up.*

I was so lost in thought that it took me a moment before I realized I could hear the hissing noise again. I stopped drying the dish I had in my hand. Elias looked at me with concern.

"What is it?" he asked.

I was straining to hear if there was anything else distinct about the noise. "Can you hear that?"

Elias strained his own hearing, hearing that was probably better than mine.

"I hear nothing." More concern in his voice.

"I hear a hiss or a hum—I can't quite discern what it is."

Again, we both stood there in silence, listening. Then the sound was gone.

"It's gone," I said. "Sorry, I didn't mean to worry you. It's probably just me."

Elias didn't say anything. We finished the dishes in silence, but before we left the galley he grabbed my arm and turned me toward him.

"If you keep hearing it, let me know, okay?"

"Of course."

He pulled me in for a hug. "We are doing this. We are going to unite the Pai Ona and end this war."

"We are," I assured him.

PART II

ELIAS

J was so bloody nervous. Everything I have been working toward, everything my father had been working toward hinged on the next few weeks. It felt heavy, suffocating—*how could it not?* The Pai Ona would begin to arrive tomorrow morning. One by one, in pairs and small groups, and if all went well, all of them would be ready to decide when the summit was over. *Would they stand and fight or would they continue to lose this war in the shadows?*

I hoped I could show them that hiding was not fighting, nor was it serving the purpose that many had expected. We were not waiting out the Nebas, holding fast while they imploded on each other in a fury of distrust and violence. We were, in truth, sitting ducks being plucked off one by one in silence and solitude so that the carnage was obscured and imperceptible.

I could do this. I could establish this horrific truth—make it known and undeniable, so that they would need to act to survive.

My father had laid it all out. He had devised the precise agenda that would create the biggest impact. Fellowship and reunion, the trials followed by the arguments and then the call to action—the bidding. I was shaking as I replayed the exact order of things.

Deep in thought, I barely heard the tap on my door. I opened it to see Su pacing nervously.

"What is it? Is everything okay?" I asked, shaken by his anxiety.

"Everything is fine." He paused. "There is someone at the gate. I know it is a day early, and I have not completed all of the wards. I refused to let him in, but he insists you come out to speak with him."

My eyes narrowed. I considered who it could be and decided that whoever it was, he had been clever enough to get this far—to find the gate a day early. I would speak to him.

"Take me to the caller."

"As you wish." Su bowed slightly, and I followed him into the corridor where he promptly put his hand on the wall, and we were instantly on the roof of Fort Bhangarh, where Ophelia and I had first entered The Cathedral.

It was dark. My eyes adjusted slowly to see a figure at the far end of the structure. He turned, and I knew who it was, without question.

"Rand," I whispered, although I meant to call to him. He immediately appeared at my side. I held him, as he did me, in a warm embrace. I was so afraid he had fallen with Hafiza.

"You look good, my boy." He had not called me that in years, since my parents had died.

"So do you."

"I needn't come inside." He looked to Su. "But I do require a private audience."

"Of course." I addressed Su. "Let no one in but me. Keep Ophelia safe and well-tended, please. I will be back shortly. If she asks where I have gone, tell her I had an errand to run in town."

"I will hold the gate." Then Su was gone.

I brought my full attention back to Rand. "Where would you like to conference? Off the grounds, I presume?"

"If we may, let us run. I have fallen in love with the inhabitants of Bairat. It's a forty-five-minute run with your skill. Would you entertain an old man and join me? I won't keep you long."

He patiently waited for my response. I considered his proposal. This wasn't a whimsical request; I knew him better than to assume that. But that was a substantial distance, and it worried me to be that far from The Cathedral and Ophelia. I weighed my options and decided I wanted to trust Rand. Somewhere deep down inside, I knew I had to.

"Let us make post haste. It makes me uneasy to be that far away from Ophelia."

"I completely understand. I would not ask such a thing of you if it weren't pertinent." I nodded at him. "Shall we?" He turned to the north then paused. He put his finger to his lips, suggesting he was considering something of importance. "Let me leave you with this ponderance: who killed Alistair?"

Then Rand took off at a pace slightly faster than he knew I could keep. I quickly chased after him, my mind swarming with questions. But he knew it would—that was his intention. He wanted me to consider his question the entire run so he could swim around in my thoughts and feelings until we got there.

He was cunning—but to what end?

ESTHER

*L*ucia lay writhing in pain. I had hoped her misery would bring me even an ounce of satisfaction, but it did not.

"Why do you stay silent? You can end this for her. End her anguish," I whispered in Winston's ear. Resolve resonated from him. "Alright. Apparently we must try a new tactic." I touched his shoulder and assumed control of his body.

Winston stiffened. He was trying to shut me out. But it was futile. No one had ever succeeded in evicting me from my host once I took control. In fact, I think the struggle made it more painful for the victim. Nonetheless, Winston was trying his hardest to resume control of his body.

"Please don't fight it. It only makes it worse," I purred as I brushed his filthy hair from his face. I looked at Akiva. "Remove the vice from Lucia. We are going to implement a new type of torture."

Winston continued to wiggle under his skin, and it occurred to me —he wasn't fighting my control, he was attempting to hide something. Something that was imprinted in him. He was afraid I would get access to it. I commanded his body to stand and face me. It responded immediately.

"Curious. What is it you are trying to hide, my dear Winston?"

He, of course, did not respond, as he could not with me maintaining my will over him.

Lucia was now free of the vice. I walked over to her shaking form. "Do you have the same secret?" I cocked my head at her. She said nothing. I touched her forehead, releasing Winston and possessing Lucia. Her thoughts were weaker, since she had just withstood several hours of mental shredding. I felt the same resistance seizing her body. It wasn't her strength, it was the thing itself fighting my influence. There was some sort of defensive action surrounding the imprinted information.

"I am so intrigued," I cooed. "I have seen nothing like this until now." I was distracted, lost in considerations. Akiva left the room to replace the vice in its chest for safekeeping. I paced the small chamber, Winston's limp body on one side and Lucia's on the other. What were they protecting, I wondered. The next course of action occurred to me. I would tear the secret out of them. I heard the door latch, and turned to see Winston holding hands with Lucia, breaking my domination over her. My skin began to burn and itch. From the sound of the screams coming from the hall, I was not the only one.

The room we were in was narrow and tall, spanning three stories until it reached a small circular skylight, the only manner of illumination for the chamber. Clay bricks lined the walls. They began to move and shift and shake. I made eye contact with Winston. All I needed to do was touch him, just graze him, really, to command his willful body. They could not get away, not after what I witnessed inside them. It was essential that I discover the content of what they were hiding.

Sweat pooled under my arms and on my forehead. My head felt foggy from the escalating temperatures. I could not make my legs move. My body was trying to shut down, to preserve itself from the heat.

"I will find you," I muttered, hating the sound of my voice—the weakness. The stones from the walls began to fall and stack around me. One by one, Lucia systematically encased me in a boiling tomb, while strategically not compromising the building itself, which could then topple on us all.

81

I heard Winston's voice, frail and shaky. "Hurry, my Lucia. I haven't much strength left to contain them."

Then the light was snuffed out by the final stone being placed over my head. The fire in my blood heightened, and somewhere between consciousness and death I realized that there was something bigger going on here. The Pai Ona moving, the defended messages—there was something huge happening.

ELIAS

*I*t was a decaying restaurant. The family that ran it grew very excited when Rand and I walked in the door. Rand spoke fluent Punjabi with the patriarch. They quickly served us hot tea as we took our seats opposite one another in a small booth.

"Have you considered my question?" Rand asked after he took a long drink of his tea.

"Considered it, yes—long before you proposed the question. I concluded that it was Salzar or Yanni. They were both in Chicago. I barely got out of there with my life."

"Why would they kill him?"

"Because he was helping me," I said, irritated with the direction of our conversation. I could tell Rand knew more than he was letting on. He wanted me to reach his conclusion before he confessed it. It was an effective persuasion tactic, but I needed him to be plain with me. "You know it was not either of them?"

"I do." He raised an eyebrow. "Drink your tea, my boy." He pushed my glass toward me.

"You would have me believe a Pai Ona killed him just before he was going to give me answers—save me all the trouble of decoding his journals?"

"I would," Rand said matter-of-factly, then changed the subject completely. "How is our darling Ophelia? I heard about Lucas."

Of course he had. I sighed. I knew Rand well enough to know that whatever answers he intended to give me would be on his terms, so I might as well play the game. I took another sip of my tea. "Ophelia is coping. Some days are easier than others, as is to be expected. Susuda, the gatekeeper, is good company for her. She really enjoys his companionship."

"How are you holding up? Are you bowing under the weight of the world?" Rand's question was sincere, but it dug at something in my gut. I did not like what it implied—*that I could break.*

"I am fine," I said curtly, knowing that Rand would taste the truth.

He leaned back, evaluating my mood. "We have never spoken about the evening your parents died. Why have you not asked me about what I saw?"

Another diversion tactic, I thought. "I was there, the same as you. Was there more to your story?"

"More, perhaps not. Different, I believe so." Rand sat up again, all implications of casualness having escaped his body. "There were two intruders."

I slumped back into my chair and let the magnitude of that sink in. "Two? How can you be so certain?"

"I met one while I was on the first floor, then watched the second tackle you down the stairs."

My leg shook anxiously under the table. The back of my jaw was tingling. "Why are you just telling me this now?"

"You never asked. I waited for you to ask, my boy." Rand reached for my hand as he spoke.

I thought about pulling away, but I desired the comfort—the assurance. He continued, "We know one of the traitors is dead."

I waited patiently for him to continue. His eyes rolled back into his head. Rand could be easily distracted, which always made sense to me—tasting emotions in the air would be intrusive at times. But now was not the time. We needed to discuss Rand's timing and appearance. *What did all of this mean?* "It would seem that Lucas is gone. There has been no sign of his resurfacing since Yanni found us in China. How can we flush out the second assassin?"

Rand squeezed my hand tightly. "There isn't time. I cannot stay. Know that I will be watching and waiting for the right time to strike—should the spineless snake emerge from the shadows. No one must know I'm here." He pulled me into him from across the table to whisper in my ear. "No one can know I'm watching."

Then he was gone. Vanished from view so quickly that not even the air around him stirred. I sat there silently, motionless, for a long time. I considered what Rand meant by this strange meeting. *What had he intended to share besides a vague warning?*

I paid for the tea and mindlessly walked out of the cafe. My feet felt heavy as I made my way to the border of the city, where I would begin to run.

It seemed logical that there were two intruders. I always knew my parents had to have known their assassin—or better yet, assassins—because they got into the Haven. Two-on-two combat made far more sense than a single attacker.

But what did Alistair's murder have to do with my parents? Unless they were killed by the same people.

If I found out who killed Alistair, I would know who the second traitor was. Rand wanted me to be prepared, in case the traitor somehow slipped into the summit. I had to double the wards immediately. I would also find time to complete my translation of Alistair's final journal. Perhaps there was a clue, an insight into who had betrayed him.

My body began to buzz with that familiar call to action. I had to get back to The Cathedral, to coordinate with Su. If a traitor entered the walls of The Cathedral, we would be ready.

OPHELIA

J lay there with my eyes wide open in bed. The time was ticking by at a snail's pace. I expected to be anxious and have a hard time getting to sleep the night before the arrivals began, but this was ridiculous. I rolled onto my right side again.

Maybe I should just get up, have coffee and go to bed early tonight. This was so inconvenient. I wanted to be at my best today. Exhaustion wouldn't help me with that. I sat up, threw off my blankets and decided it was time to succumb to consciousness. As I trudged into the kitchen I wondered if anyone had arrived yet. *Could I sense them if I took down my shield? A little peek couldn't hurt, right?*

I clicked on the coffee pot and slumped on the couch. Slowly, I pulled away the second skin, the shield I'd inherited from Lucas. It was a legacy that I'd never be able to truly thank him for. Once the guarded layer was gone, my senses felt alive. Ignited with the other gifts I'd accumulated from other Conduits I'd encountered in my new world. I hadn't had much time to engage it, but the last time I took my shield down and really explored my extra gifts I thought I detected some of Talia's power accessible to me.

Aside from the really obvious enhancements I'd found, like manip-ulating fire and metal or Lucas' shield, I hadn't tried to see what else

I'd picked up along the way. Could I boil blood with a look, like Winston? Could I blur the mind like Talia? The problem was I needed an eager guinea pig to find out. Once Lucas was gone I didn't have a Consu to train with, and I wouldn't risk hurting Elias to find out what I could do. Not that he'd had any time to entertain my experiments since China anyway. Susuda wasn't human or Conduit. He didn't really know what he was. So I couldn't be sure that his response would be that of a Conduit or human.

The coffee pot stopped percolating and I stood to grab myself a cup of coffee. I could try to boil water, I thought. Winston could boil all kinds of things. After my coffee was dressed up just the way I liked it, I sat back down and put a glass of water on the coffee table. Winston never told me how he made things heat up, so I just started by staring. Really focusing on the liquid. Nothing happened. I narrowed my focus further, every ounce of energy pointed directly at the water in the cup. Still nothing.

Maybe I needed to expand my energy, I thought. I cast a net of intention as wide as I could. And I caught a sensation under the net. No, not a sensation—a vibration. A hiss or a hum, the very noise I'd heard the evening before with Elias. Except this time it was louder, so loud it made my body vibrate the same way a strong base does in a car. I forced my net downward, toward the dark passage off the galley. I pushed and pushed until the noise was so deafening in my ears I thought my eardrums may explode. *What was it? And how come only I seemed to hear it?* I pushed past the discomfort. It got quiet for a second and everything stopped—the vibration, the hissing. Straining my senses, I waited in silence.

Then, erupting through my body, it roared back to life, but his time I heard it. "Sulu." I screamed, then reinstated every ounce of my shield I could find, desperately clawing at it to protect me. I sat there shaking for a long moment while my thoughts and fears came into focus. *Someone or something already knew what I was.*

ELIAS

I was walking down the passage that The Cathedral had been providing me to the broadcast room when I heard a rustling behind me.

"Sorry to interrupt, Mr. Elias, but I have someone who is eager to see you, and I didn't think it was appropriate to bring her down here."

Her? *Maybe it is Aurora*. My heart skipped a few beats at the prospect of her arrival. I knew she was going to come. I looked at my watch. It was early. I had not been able to sleep after my brief encounter with Rand. "Is she our first guest?"

He nodded.

"Yes, of course. Take me to her, Su."

"This way." He took my hand, and within seconds we were in a small room. It was dark, bare.

"Aurora?" I asked into the dark.

"No, Viraclay, it is I, Nara." Just then her sleek form manifested out of the shadows. Her hair was hanging limply onto her shoulders, knotted and dirty. Her clothes were in tatters. My eyes fell upon her face and I knew the worst had happened. I stepped toward her, ignoring all customs or courtesies of her time, and took her in my arms.

Nara leaned in, and although her sobs were silent, I felt the vibrations in her chest against mine. We stood there for a long time before she pulled away and sat at a small table in the corner. I realized Su had silently excused himself.

"We were ambushed. Valerian was…" The words choked off in her throat. "I watched them kill him. There was nothing I could do."

I took a seat beside her. "I am certain there was nothing you could do."

"She is a monster. A fiend, and she must be stopped." Rage lit up Nara's face, where sorrow had just been.

"We will stop them all. I promise. We will avenge Valerian."

Her lime-green eyes met mine. Even in the dark I could see their vibrancy. "I wish to kill Akiva. When the time comes, his flesh is mine."

I nodded, certain I could not dissuade her, and not entirely clear I wanted to.

Several minutes went by before she spoke again. "I am proud of what you are doing here. I stand beside you through it all. If ever you should need me, whatever the task, do not hesitate to call."

"You bless me with an exceptional honor."

"The honor is mine." She stood and bowed slightly, and I reciprocated. "Now leave me to collect my thoughts and gather my wits."

"As you wish." I turned to leave and said a silent prayer. I asked Malarin to ease her pain.

OPHELIA

*A*fter I heard the mysterious voice this morning, amplified without my shield filtering it, I spent the rest of my waking hours before I saw Elias rationalizing what I'd heard. I reasoned that maybe I was going crazy, or perhaps I'd imagined it, since no one else seemed to have any idea what I was talking about. Either way, I decided not to tell Elias about it just yet. I didn't know what to tell him anyway—*that I was hearing voices?* He had so much on his plate, I couldn't bother him with this. Whatever was happening to me, whoever knew what I was hadn't threatened me, so I'd just keep my shield up. I'd keep an eye out and if things got weirder or if I sensed a threat I'd let him know. In my flurry of thoughts, I promised myself that if the right opportunity presented itself to tell him, I would.

When I made my way down to the arena I noticed both of them looked exhausted. Elias was busy greeting everyone after Su escorted them to their rooms. I decided it was best if I was out of the way for now. So I found a vantage point to watch for familiar faces.

The Katuanak Arena was swarming with moving bodies. I stood above the commotion on a small balcony. I'd never been a fan of large crowds, but there was something different about this menagerie of people. Unlike the years of my mortal curse, where crowds meant inexplicable swells of emotion and outbursts from strangers' secret lives, now I could control my gift. I could turn it off or on. It helped that Conduits were in far more control of their emotional climates, as well. The combination of these two factors meant that crowds didn't have the same dreadful effect on me. I could just hate crowds for the pure and simple reason that most people did—they were chaotic and clumsy.

Elias snuck up behind me, and I jumped when I heard his voice in my ear.

"Astounding. Thousands of Conduits ready and willing to hear our cause—to change our world."

I let my shield fall slightly. I felt his excitement. I let it warm me— wash over me. It was good to feel and see him more excited than anxious. I even let the electricity between us ignite, and the familiar buzz pulsated up my shoulder where he held my arm. I turned to see his face light up, both from his enthusiasm at the event taking place before us and the realization that my guard was down.

He leaned in closer. "I love this feeling, but I worry about who may discover your abilities when you are exposed."

I immediately shut him out, replaced my shield and decided that I wouldn't allow myself that moment of weakness again. I returned my gaze to the crowd. *Was now the right time to tell him about the hiss?* The last thing I wanted to do right now was feel rejected and crazy. Besides, he was right. I needed to keep my shield up. That would prevent any voices from speaking to me, *right?*

"You understand my fear, don't you? I would love nothing more than to embrace you, completely unfiltered—open."

I stopped him. "I get it, Elias." I did get it, but my pride was hurt as well. I felt rejected, like every time I tried to let him in, it was the wrong time. I either needed to get better at picking the moment or maybe it would never be the right time. I knew it was silly to drop my shield, and to feel rejected. He was right. We'd agreed to this for my safety but my heart still felt the pang. I'd let the excitement get the best of me.

I did what any normal self-respecting woman would do, I ignored the hurt and changed the subject. "How many Conduits have arrived so far?"

"Nearly two thousand."

"Wow." I considered what four more thousand would look like in here. I watched the strangers busily moving. Among their movements was the occasional hug—a reunion between friends or lovers, for all I knew. According to every Conduit I'd every spoken to, a peaceful congregation of this size hadn't occurred in over three thousand years.

"I believe the majority of them will arrive in the next day or two." Elias' arm moved to the pillar behind us. "As far as The Cathedral's ability to accommodate, Su assures me that she has been busy but nowhere near exasperation. She is prepared for an assortment of guests."

"That's good, because there certainly is an assortment." I moved my gaze from one face to another. There were brown faces, blond heads, dark eyes, braids, capes, gowns and fashion I didn't have a name for. "How will I see anyone I know in this bunch?" I mumbled the question as much to myself as to Elias.

"Trust me, you stand out. They will find you." He squeezed me tightly with both of his hands on my shoulders. "I must be going. I have a few tasks to attend to. Will you be okay here?"

I waved my hand in the air at him. "Go be the host. I'm fine. I'm going to stand here for a bit longer—take it all in—before I escape back into my room for some me time."

"I will check on you later," he whispered in my ear before moving swiftly out of sight, so fast I didn't know which direction he went in.

I leaned against the pillar and watched the sea of faces, searching for a familiar one. I didn't know how long I stood there before I decided to call it quits. We had two more weeks of arrivals and festivities—that should be plenty of time to run into anyone I might know in this crowd. I turned to leave, to scale the steps, when a flash of an impossible face caught my eye.

I whipped back around, searching for the eyes I recognized. My heart raced and fluttered in my chest—it couldn't be him.

He was gone.

My eyes narrowed onto the back of a bouncing head of brown hair. I leapt off the balcony like a ninja, a feat I'd never tried before and wouldn't try again if I wasn't in such a hurry to see that face.

I pushed through the crowd and ignored the mutterings I left in my wake. The head of brown hair rose above the others. When I was sure I was in his earshot, I couldn't contain my excitement.

"Aremis!" As soon as I said the name aloud I felt foolish. He was gone. I knew he was gone.

But the head of brown hair stopped, and he turned to meet my gaze. He was tall, thin, thinner than the Aremis I knew. He wore a familiar slack-and-vest ensemble. His hair was long and wavy but shorter than last time I'd seen Aremis. It felt like he turned in slow motion to meet my stare.

The air expelled from my lungs when I took in the full sight of him. He could be Aremis' son. *Did Aremis have a son?* If so, he had never mentioned him.

A grin spread across his face. It was Aremis' smile. I looked into his chocolate eyes. They were Aremis' eyes. I knew those eyes. My mind had to be playing tricks on me.

The man spread his arms wide. "Miss Ophelia."

It was Aremis, it had to be. If this was a dream, I'd revel in it. I ran to him. I leapt into his arms and squeezed him tight and hard.

"Aremis? How?" I was crying now. It was so familiar, so safe. If this was a dream, it was the realest dream I'd ever had. I pulled back and saw that we were creating quite the spectacle. My cheeks got red with embarrassment.

"Come, let us find a quiet nook to reacquaint ourselves." Aremis put his arm out and I latched on. It had to be him. I stared at his face as he navigated us out of the grand arena. It was Aremis, I decided. Every cell in my being confirmed it. He was just twenty years younger than the Aremis I knew from my time in Hafiza.

We moved out of the crowd into a narrow passage. It was then that he spoke up.

"I am unfamiliar with this Haven. What way should we go?" I marveled at his voice and the joy it brought to my heart.

I didn't say anything. Instead, I put my hand on the nearest wall. I thought about a beautiful meadow with a soft babbling brook running through it. I visualized a quaint table for us to convene at as the warm sun shrouded our skin.

"This way." I held on tight and felt the familiar sensation of teleportation as I escorted Aremis into my vision.

"Miss Ophelia, that is impressive," Aremis conceded as he patted me on the forearm.

"It's not my parlor trick. It's The Cathedral." I walked us over to the table and chairs.

"I'm afraid I've just arrived." He took his seat across from me.

I couldn't wait any longer. "How is it that you're here? Elias and Lucas saw you die. I cried over your loss."

He reached over and took my hand. Squeezed it gently. "I am so sorry to have hurt your heart. If I had known what this was, what I was, I would have told you. I assure you of that."

"What are you?"

"I am a Phoenix." The word sounded funny in his slight Irish accent.

I let that sink in. *A Phoenix? What did that mean?*

"I know a flurry of questions follows that statement. And I am afraid I don't have most of the answers. I did not know what I was. I've never heard of a Phoenix before my rebirth—I cannot say that is the true name for my form. But it felt fitting enough for me."

He looked down at our clasped hands and squeezed mine once more. "I remember my life, my Natasha, and my death. I woke up in a daze under piles of rubble, all that was left of Hafiza after Yanni and Esther sieged the castle. I had all of my memories, but they were being filtered through a veil of innocence—of newness."

"You woke up in Hafiza?" My brain was trying to catch up with his story.

"In what was left of her, yes. I lay there for a long time, unsure of what was happening, realizing something was very different. It turned out I was in infant form. I couldn't really move, not much. I grew until I was a toddler, then child size—large enough to walk and move the debris. I cannot say how long I stayed down there in the dark. I can say that I seemed to age a couple of years physically approximately every week. I crawled out of the rubble naked as a babe and the size of a ten-year-old. I saw my face for the first time in the reflection of the river that ran the valley below Hafiza's perch. I had my gift. I commanded fire just as easily as the day I was consummated. It was so strange—imposing all the familiar gifts I had become accustomed to but through the filter of a child's innocence. I had to keep from sight and continue to move, since an adolescent growing at an unnatural rate would surely be noticed. I travelled all the way to Oslo, Norway, before I had the appearance of a respectably aged man."

I was counting backwards in my head. *How old was he, physically?*

"So you're about twenty years old?"

"In my approximation. I feel like a youth of twenty." He smiled the smile I loved so much.

"When will you stop aging at this rate?" I asked, realizing he would be over a hundred in a year. *Would I lose him again?*

"I am afraid I don't know the answer to that, Miss Ophelia. I don't know what I am or how this new gift works. I was in Oslo when I got the call for the summit. I was so relieved. I would be reunited with you and maybe, just maybe, some of the Ancients would have answers for my condition."

I squeezed his hand this time. "We'll get answers. I know it," I assured him.

"I hope so. Enough about me. I see momentous changes in you, my courageous friend. Tell me, how did this come to be?" He gestured around him. "How are we here? Please tell me everyone survived the siege. What is this change I see in you? How is the company of Elias and Lucas?"

I let my head fall. I knew I'd have to explain what happened during this summit. I didn't expect it to be to Aremis. I was instantly relieved that the first Conduit I had to tell about Lucas would be him. I could fall apart with Aremis, I could cry and be angry and explain the betrayal in my heart.

When I looked up at him, my eyes were brimming with tears. He looked at me with that warm, comforting stare, and the floodgates opened. Tears streamed down my cheeks, sobs shook from my chest, and I explained everything. I told him about our travels, Fetzle and the hairsy charm, the blessing I received, the way my gifts emerged. I told him about Talia and how Elias and I grew closer. Lastly, I told him about Yanni and Lucas. I told him everything about that night, every detail and regret, and my friend, my Aremis, cried with me.

ELIAS

*I*t had been a successful day of arrivals. Seamless, really. I could not have asked for a better response. By Su's count, we were at four thousand, six hundred and two Conduits. He reported that all of them had been gracious and excited to be participating in the summit. Many expressed pure astonishment at the sight of The Cathedral and the arena, and true peace of mind. I had hoped that the others would trust that I had secured a site that would not put their lives or the lives of those they loved in jeopardy. It made me happy to hear that they had come to that conclusion. This meant they would be more inclined to trust me when I made the bidding of war.

The bidding was a formal declaration of war. It meant all those who aligned with our side would be nearly compelled to act. I needed the bidding to be received. It could not just be a call to action—it had to be extreme, almost a deployment, but by choice.

The day was rounded out by the discovery of Aremis' miraculous resurrection. There were concerns to be had, since no one knew what to expect with his rapid aging, but the look on Ophelia's face was wondrous. Her eyes truly lit up, in a way I had not seen since Lucas' death. She looked more whole. It gave me a sense of peace I had not been able to put my finger on since China. Her loss would affect me, that was to be expected, but her recovery somehow healed my wounds as well. Also, I knew she was in good hands while I was busy tending to matters of the summit.

Aurora had not yet arrived today. This was troublesome to me, especially after hearing of Nara's narrow escape and Valerian's demise. *Had Aurora been ambushed en route? Was she going to attend at all?* She knew what this meant to me, what it meant to my parents. She would not disappoint. Still, something was not right, and it gnawed at my gut.

OPHELIA

I'd been so surprised to see Aremis yesterday that I'd stopped my search for anyone else. I spent the rest of the day with him. It was surreal and healing. I felt a little more whole today. More whole than I'd been since Lucas died.

Aremis agreed to meet me at the base of the grand staircase. Together, we would scan the crowd for familiar faces. Su said he would let me know who of our Hafiza companions was in attendance. But I couldn't wait. I was eager to see my friends, to fill the voids in my heart.

I pinned my damp hair into a messy bun on top of my head and stuck a cute yellow flower accent on the right side. I examined my work in the mirror. It was still so strange to be back in my San Francisco apartment—exactly the way I remembered it. The mirror was old and had a silver hue to it. My building had been built in the forties, which gave it character and flaws.

The Cathedral had meticulously recreated everything I loved about the place, including my wardrobe. I patted at the yellow skirt I'd rummaged out of the far reaches of my closet. It had white polka dots on a smooth and flowy material. The hem fell below my knees, but the waist was high and tight just under my ribcage. The skirt coordinated perfectly with a classic silk blouse that tucked neatly into the waist band. As I admired the outfit I realized it looked like it came from the era of the apartment's construction, the 40's. I slipped my dangly pearl earrings into my ears and fastened my mother's pearl necklace around my neck. As I twirled slightly the skirt flared out around me. I had loved this outfit when I found it in the thrift stores on Haight and Ashbury, and wore it regularly for months, but then something changed. Something new caught my attention. Peering into my closet, I tried to remember what outfit had replaced this one as my top choice. When the memory failed to appear, I let it go. It didn't matter, not really.

I knew why I had chosen this one today. I'd been wearing it in my dream last night—more a flashback to the first night Lucas and I went out on the town after we had become roommates.

I was wearing this ensemble when we met after work. I saw the way he looked at me. There was a distinct twinkle of desire in his eyes.

It worried me, for two very important reasons. Firstly, I was enjoying our living situation and I didn't want anything to get in the way of this burgeoning friendship. I already felt so much more peace around him. I was terrified to lose that. Secondly, I felt a wave of desire touch my own belly. I had not felt a surge like that—ever. That was scary, which meant the clothes clearly needed to be stuffed away somewhere in the back of my closet. Apparently I blamed the outfit, so that's where it went, in the receding corners of a musty rack.

I felt the hairsy charm on my wrist, but that was no longer a concern to be had. Lucas and I would never exchange flirtatious friendly moments ever again. My eyes began to burn as tears swelled up.

I sternly looked at my reflection in the mirror. "Not today, Olly! You just did your eyeliner!" Then I promptly turned around and headed toward the door to meet Aremis.

He was standing there, patiently waiting for me. I had a quick flash of Jack in the Titanic waiting for Rose, and I giggled.

"What?" Aremis looked around where he stood. "What is it that I am missing?"

"Nothing. Did you ever watch the movie *Titanic?*" I realized this was entirely possible, since he enjoyed reading romance novels.

"I absolutely did, along with everyone else—about a dozen times." His smile got larger. He appreciated the reference and realized my association. "I would love to be Jack."

I just beamed back at him. As he stood before me, no older than twenty-one in physical age, he could have easily been a Jack Dawson.

"You would make a fine Jack," I agreed. "I, on the other hand..."

"Nonsense. You would be a splendid Rose. Rose with a little flare." He winked.

"That's what you call it." We both laughed.

After a moment Aremis' face got very serious. He hooked his arm in mine and we retreated up the stairs a ways. His grim stare locked on mine and he spoke in hushed tones. "I have been considering your developments. I agree wholeheartedly with Viraclay. You mustn't express any gifts during the duration of the summit. I will not say more on the matter, but understand that I believe, as he does, that we cannot risk your exposure."

I waited to respond, weighing his words. Honestly, I saw no reason to use any of my gifts during the summit. That being said, I had no idea what to expect from this gathering. I'd hoped that we could get some answers about the Sulu—find out if that was what I was. Elias had assured me that he would conduct a very cautious investigation, and I trusted he would.

Aremis' eyes grew worried at my silence. I put my hand on his shoulder.

"I understand. I'll stay nice and shielded—mum's the word." I pretended to lock my lips and throw away the key.

His shoulders relaxed and he kissed me on the forehead. We turned to resume our position at the bottom of the stairs, a perfect vantage point when hunting for familiar faces. As we moved back to our assumed position, I saw two eyes glaring at me, but it wasn't a pair I knew. They belonged to a man with light brown hair cropped up neatly into what I would describe as a bowl cut. His pale skin was milky in its shade. His nose was sharp and thin. It perched above a narrow mouth with pursed full lips. He was tall, slim, and wore red robes. I almost missed his companion, a petite woman. She was a foot shorter than him. Her robes were orange and gold. Her hair was white, braided over one of her shoulders, long and thick. Her hair was the same exact color as her skin, so her only distinct feature was her pale blue eyes. They just stared at me.

I squeezed Aremis' arm, ready to lean in and ask who these two ghostly gawkers were, when they approached us.

We met on the third stair. The man bowed ever so slightly. "Aremis, you have changed." He had a very minor Hungarian accent. There was no question in the statement, just an observation. The man's chocolate-brown eyes turned back to me. "Ophelia Banner, it is nice to make your acquaintance." He bowed once more and his silent companion did the same.

My mouth grew dry. I was finding it difficult to form words.

Aremis didn't skip a beat. "Almus, Inca." Aremis bowed, and because I couldn't communicate any other way, I complied and bowed as well. "It has been at least four hundred years since our paths have crossed."

My brain started retracing scenarios where I had heard those names. It hit me like a lightning bolt. Talia's journal. Almus was Huan's brother—Alistair's father. Ruit's son.

Almus' eyes hadn't left mine. I could tell he saw my revelation.

"Nandi expressed great admiration for you before she passed to The River Tins." The small woman squeezed her husband's arm.

"She was our sister." Inca's voice was raspier than I imagined it would be, considering her tiny frame.

I licked my lips vigorously, trying to create enough moisture to use my mouth for speech. I must've looked ridiculous, but it worked.

"She spoke of you two as well." This caught them off-guard. They looked at each other inquisitively. "She saved my life."

This provoked everyone in my company to nod empathetically, as though they'd just begun to understand our friendship.

"She was one of the most honorable of our kind," Almus stated confidently.

Aremis stood silently during the exchange. I wondered what he was thinking.

"I'd completely agree," I conceded.

"We would like to convene over a drink during the summit. Would you consider such happenings?" Almus asked.

I looked up at Aremis, not really sure what to say. I didn't know these two. *Did he trust them? Talia seemed to.* Almus saw my silent exchange with Aremis and quickly added. "Aremis may join us. We have much to learn about his transformation, as well."

That seemed to satisfy Aremis, and he answered on behalf of both of us. "Let us convene on the fourth day. I'll send word."

Everyone bowed once more, and the couple faded into the crowd silently.

"Do you know them well?" I quickly asked.

"Well? Certainly not. Do I trust them? I do. And I feel better that I will be accompanying you on your date." He patted my arm. I took that as a sign the conversation was basically over for the time being. I was okay with that, because I hadn't exactly shared everything with Aremis. I didn't explain that I still had Talia's journal, or that it was where I'd learned about Almus and Inca. I trusted Aremis with my life, but I felt like I'd be betraying Talia if I let anyone else into the pages she shared with me. I was weighing all of this when a familiar face came into focus.

I flew off the stairs, shoved myself through the horde until I was facing him. My fencing master, Ying.

"You're alive!" I wrapped my arms around his neck. He didn't immediately reciprocate the gesture. I ignored the awkwardness and kept on. After a long moment he wrapped his arms around me as well, and my feet lifted a few inches off the ground.

A bell of a voice interrupted us. "Pardon me, but I would love to meet you. I'm Aruna, Ying's Atoa." She had a voice that sounded like birds chirping. I felt drawn to her instantaneously. Ying put me down in front of the vision he called a wife.

Aruna was a little taller than me. She had long thick black hair that peeked out from behind a brilliant fuchsia sari. Her eyes were blue with green flecks. I was mesmerized by them. Her skin was caramel and flawless. Her smile was bright and big, a little too big for her face, but it did nothing to detract from her beauty. She took my hands in hers and squeezed them gently.

"My Ying tells me much of your courage and strength. I'm eager to make fast friends with you."

I reluctantly took my eyes away from the vision of a woman in front of me to wink at Ying.

"You said nice things about me? I'm a little surprised," I mocked astonishment.

Ying's face stayed stern. "I could have used more time to teach you," was all he could muster.

Then his expression morphed completely. I don't think words could describe it. Sadness, relief, bewilderment blended together on a face I'd never seen show more than minute shifts in expression. I turned to see what he was looking at—to see what rattled him. My eyes fell onto Aremis, who was slowly approaching us.

When he was a foot away from Ying, both men grasped each other's shoulders. The Conduits around us had made room for the exchange to happen. The men simply stood there, holding each other's shoulders, not saying a word—staring into one another's eyes. Unexpectedly tears began to stream down both their faces, and long thick sobs left their mouths.

I started crying silently, as did Aruna. She pulled me in to hold me, and I let her. I wasn't sure what I'd just witnessed, but I knew it was something beautiful.

ESTHER

*J*called back all the hunting parties. We had a new agenda. I
needed to know what was being imprinted onto the Pai
Ona, and that required living, conscious captives.

Akiva arrived in my chamber, with Lucifer by his side.

"Everyone has arrived, Mistress. Everyone who is still alive."

I snapped my head in his direction. "We have casualties?" We had
not suffered any casualties, aside from those at Hafiza, since the last
open battle.

"Yes, Mistress," Lucifer answered.

"Who? Who did we lose?" I demanded.

"Owney, Adolf and Dagmar."

"Three? How do you explain losing three of our most seasoned
killers?" I kept my voice as calm as I could. Owney was an incredible
marksman. His skills were invaluable. Adolf incited hatred and fear—
perfect for creating chaos in the masses. And my dear Dagmar, she
had been a merciless child killer in her heyday—an unruly pastime,
but her siren's song created blinding pain in all those who heard it.
Each gift would be missed in this upcoming collection. Thinking
about their abilities, now lost to me made me fume with anger. I
walked toward Lucifer and Akiva. Both of them backed away upon

my approach. "I did not hear your explanation. How did they meet their demise?"

Lucifer's voice shook when he answered. "We were ambushed outside of Marseille, France. We'd been tracking a Soahcoit when, out of nowhere, seven Pai Ona came up on our flanks. There was no time to fend all of them off."

"But you survived?" I hissed.

"Barely," Lucifer insisted.

I turned my back to the two men, thinking aloud. "When was the last time we were ambushed?"

"Until recently?"

I scoffed at Akiva, knowing he was referring to Nara and Valerian. He continued. "More than three hundred years ago."

"What was happening during that time?" I asked, knowing the answer.

"The Pai Ona were mobilizing for the last open battle."

My long hair whipped around before I was facing them once more. "When was the last time you encountered seven Pai Ona working together?"

Neither of them said a word, following my train of thought. The Nebas had been terrorizing the Pai Ona for years with nearly no resistance, picking them off one by one. Now here they were mobilizing, ambushing and killing our people. They'd killed my Yanni. My anger peaked. I could no longer contain it. I reached for Lucifer, seizing his body. In turn, his burly hand took Akiva's neck into its grasp. Akiva clenched his fist by his side, crushing the hand I was controlling. The scene was enough to let me take a deep breath and regain control of my fury.

Akiva rubbed at his neck, and as soon as I released Lucifer's body, he began massaging his own crumpled hand.

"I am upset, gentlemen." The statement was an understatement. "I know something is happening, and yet here you both stand before me, without any idea of what this something is. Therefore I stand here ignorant." Neither of them met my gaze. "Gather every Nebas you can find. We need to determine what is happening and how soon it will be taking place. I don't appreciate being blind to our enemies' intent. We must collect intel, and that will require a living, conscious captive to interrogate. Specifically, one with limited offensive or defensive gifts. Am I understood?"

"Yes, Mistress," they agreed in unison.

"Good," I purred. "Now find me more Nebas, and quickly. I want at least thirty more hunting parties mobilized by tonight."

ELIAS

Susuda looked at me in his curious way. I knew he wished to say something but was not sure how he intended to say it.

"Out with it, Susuda. What ails you?" I sat across from him at the bar.

"Mr. Elias, I met with Jezebel today."

"Was that a pleasant reunion?"

"Yes, it truly was. But she brought something to my attention, something I am confident you have considered but we have not discussed."

He had my attention. I sensed there was something of great consequence coming next. "Please do not hesitate."

"The Loktpi—you have one."

I looked down at the ring Rajahish had fashioned for me. He had not allowed me to be present during its creation, but he had requested that I decide what form I desired the Loktpi to be forged into. I chose a ring. It seemed like the easiest and most inconspicuous object to tote around.

Su continued. "Jezebel has one, as do Almus and Inca. Theia's was brought here for safekeeping after she was murdered. Yours was Nandi's, but we do not know what happened to Alistair's, Huan's or

Ruit's. If someone were to come possessing any of the missing keys, what would you have me do?"

Before the summit began, I had considered the possibility that the other three keys were in the hands of our enemies. *But if that were the case, and they understood their value, would they not have used them already?* Furthermore, they would still need to find The Cathedral in order to enter, and that would require access to the broadcast or cooperation from Rajahish. Both scenarios were unlikely. Then, of course, there was Susuda himself. We possessed the Loktpi, yet still he guarded his gate. The key did not mean he granted easy entrance.

"I have considered this possibility. First, the would-be intruder would need to find The Cathedral, which is not impossible, just not likely without assistance from someone within our confidences. I feel that we have taken all the precautions we could to eliminate this from happening with the bindings in our broadcast. Would you agree?"

"Yes, I agree. But what if they got to Rajahish?"

"It took me years and many lucky strokes to find him. But let us imagine they did. What would you do if someone approached with a Loktpi?"

"Am I safe to assume they are Nebas?"

"It would seem so, for if they have the Loktpi, they took it from Alistair, Huan or Ruit's bodies."

"It is my job to keep The Cathedral safe, to keep her hidden. I have wards that I put in place to assist with the amount of guests we are entertaining, but if it were one person or even many approaching, I would kill as many as I could. There would be no questions, I would not wait for an explanation, there would be no mercy."

We stared into one another's eyes for a long, serious moment.

"That is exactly what I would expect from you, Susuda the gatekeeper."

OPHELIA

*D*ay three of arrivals was very different from day two. As Elias had said, there would be festivities, and the first on the agenda was a fencing competition. I watched the arena as the bustle went on all around me. Aremis had run into Natasha's brother. It only seemed right to give them their space to grieve and connect. I knew that this was an unprecedented gathering, but in the last seventy-two hours I'd seen and felt so much genuine emotion, witnessing reunion after reunion. It was enough to melt your heart and break it at the same time. I was still eager to find out if Rand, Winston or Di had survived the siege. So I was delighted when Di appeared in the arena below me. The arena itself was magnificent, surrounded by huge, circular stadium seating that overlooked the main stage. But there was more to it. There wasn't a bad seat. No matter where you sat, you could see everything—every player, every movement—as if you were in the front row. I knew it had something to do with the collaboration of gifts between the Katuan Stones and The Cathedral. I was grateful for it, because unlike everyone else around me, I didn't have the superhuman vision they were blessed with.

I watched as Di gracefully moved around the arena. She wore thin metal armor that I was pretty sure was more for show than protection. Her perfect blonde hair was pulled back and up into an assortment of elaborate braids. Di wasn't using her charms on her opponent, a burly man named Thiago.

If I understood the rules correctly, these two could only use their combat abilities in the ring—no Conduit gifts allowed. I held my breath every time the bare-chested Thiago swung his giant ax in Di's direction. Neither of them would intentionally cause serious damage, but they weren't holding back either. She was so nimble, moving more like an angel than a warrior. Di struck Thiago hard in the chest with her long sword. There was blood, but surprisingly less that you would have thought, and the wound started to heal almost immediately. I stood and cheered. A strange sensation crept up the back of my neck, the kind where you know someone is watching you.

I turned around to see a tall man with olive skin staring at me. There was no malice in his chocolate eyes, but he was definitely focused on me. His long black hair was swept into a braid with colorful ribbons weaved into it. He smiled at me when I met his gaze. I gave my nervous smile back and returned to my seat, feeling exposed and vulnerable from the stare I could still feel on the back of my head. Di delivered another crushing blow, this time creating a gash in Thiago's chest so large he knelt down to compose himself, which apparently was the end of the match. I cheered for my friend, relieved to see she was alive and well.

I still felt the strange man's gaze upon me, so I turned, only to see he wasn't in his seat. Relief washed over me, until I turned back around to see him a few feet from my face.

"Hello, little darlin'. I'm Realto." He put his hand out for me to shake it.

"I'm Ophelia." My voice came out as more of a whisper. I took his hand, shook it quickly then moved aside. "I have to go congratulate my friend on her victory," I mumbled, pushing past the person next to me and scuttling down the stairs.

I looked back once to see him watching me, but he didn't follow, and I was relieved for that. I barreled out the door at the bottom of the arena. There were hardly any other people down here. It was the area where the participants got ready for whatever competition they were participating in. I turned a corner and saw Di standing there, so I ran toward the little goddess.

"Di!"

A childlike smile spread across her face, and she giggled.

"Ophelia!" she chimed back. When I was close enough to throw my arms around her, she took me by the shoulders and just stared into my eyes. It was not the hug I'd anticipated, but it was intimate none-theless.

"I'm so glad to see you," I said as I let my arms fall to my sides, giving up on the hug.

"It is I who is happy to see that you are alive and well." She giggled again before letting her hands fall to her sides, no longer gripping my shoulders.

"Have you seen Ying and Aremis?" I asked.

Her eyebrow raised slightly at the mention of Aremis' name. "Aremis is alive? That is a pleasant surprise."

"He is a Phoenix. I'm sure he'll tell you all about it."

She just nodded. Nothing could surprise this old soul; she'd been on this planet for too long. "I must be going. I will be challenging the victor of the next sequence."

"Okay." I hadn't really expected hugs and tears when I saw Di again. This seemed very appropriate for the stoic goddess of love. "I'm so happy to see you," I repeated as I began to move in the direction I'd come from.

I was almost past her when she clutched my wrist. I yelped. Not because it hurt but because it surprised me.

"Where did you get this?" She inquisitively looked at the hairsy charm as she spoke. "Who gave you this magic?" Her voice was sterner with the second question.

I pulled my arm away and plucked at the charm nervously. "It's a hairsy charm. A friend gave it to me." I don't know why but I felt nervous, like I was being scolded.

"Hairsy charm?" Di spat the words. Even in her bell-like voice the words sounded insulting. "What fool identified this magic as a hairsy charm, a troll?"

My cheeks got hot. "Well, actually, yes, it was a troll. Her name is Fetzle and she's very nice. I think it was kind of her to share her magic, even if she gave it a silly name."

"This is not troll magic. This is ancient magic from The Pierses themselves. This magic never should have been in the hands of a mindless troll," Di sneered, and her features were distorted into those of a snotty teenager.

"Fetzle isn't mindless. You aren't being very nice, Di," I asserted. "You don't even know her."

"Never mind your affinity for trolls. You must hide this." Di leaned in closer so she could quiet her voice. "The Pierses are hidden for a good reason. If someone were to see you with a token of their magic, it would not end well."

She took my wrist forcefully into her hand. I had this sudden fear that she was going to just cut the charm off. That would feel like she was cutting off my final connection to Lucas. I wouldn't have that. I couldn't have that. I pulled my wrist away once more. Di looked up at me. Curiosity spread across her brow.

She reached for me again, and without thinking, I took control of the metal she wore on her forearm, physically binding it to her breast plate. Curiosity morphed into bewilderment, with a hue of anger.

"I won't cut it off," I asserted.

Di's voice got soft and alluring when she spoke next. She was seducing me. If I hadn't had my shield up, it would've worked. I remembered how her gift had mesmerized me during our time in Hafiza. "Ophelia, release my arm. I will not be removing your token. If you will let me, I will disguise it." A playful smile danced at the corners of her mouth. It was all part of her allure.

I immediately withdrew my influence over the metal. I knew the type of tone Di was using well. She meant 'now,' otherwise there'd be consequences. I also knew that I never should've exposed my gift to begin with. I chastised myself internally. I'd let my emotions get in the way, and as a consequence I'd let someone witness my strange developments.

"I'm sorry, Di, I don't know what came over me."

She ignored my apology. "May I?" This time she asked for my wrist, and I gingerly placed it in her petite hands. "I will perform a small enchantment. It will render the charm invisible to all but your eyes."

She gripped the bracelet with both hands, mumbled several words in Asagi, and when she released me, I could see the hairsy charm but I could tell something was different.

"You can't see it anymore?" I looked at her, waiting for her to answer.

"I cannot."

"Well, thank you," I said. "I don't want to upset anyone by wearing it."

Di just stood there, staring at me. My face got warm with embarrassment for my behavior and the awkwardness of standing there in silence for an extended period of time.

"I should be going, so that you don't miss the next match."

"Ophelia." Di's gaze met mine. Her eyes were gravely still. "You must guard that gift you have with relentless restraint. Should you expose your abilities to the wrong eyes, you will kill us all."

I started shaking at the solemnity of her voice. The prophecy came flooding back to me. The jovialness of these games, of this summit— my veil of security that I'd shrouded myself in—was shredded in an instant.

"I—" I wanted to say I understood, that I'd be more careful, that I wouldn't let her down. But instead I turned and walked away.

ELIAS

I was just settling in for the evening. Three days into arrivals and I was feeling much more confident in the success of the summit. The only thing missing was the Oracle. Her tardiness was troublesome. So when I heard the knock on my door at this hour I was hoping it would be news of her arrival. I opened the door to see Di and Aremis. It was the first time I had been close enough to either of them to give them a hug. I leaned in and took Di in my arms. She let her body relax, but did not hug me back. Aremis on the other hand took me in his youthful arms, now younger than mine, and squeezed me hard.

"Come in," I said as I moved out of the doorway and into the small flat I presently called home. It was not ideal for entertaining so I quickly manifested another more inviting space with a touch of my hand on the door frame. Now we were in the common room of the West Wing in Hafiza. "Can I get you a refreshment?"

Di did not sit, while Aremis found a comfortable chair. "I would like a glass of wine."

"Indeed. Di?"

She shook her head. Her demeanor was now making me uneasy. It was clear she was agitated.

"Red will suffice?" I asked Aremis.

"Of course."

I poured both of us a glass, handed one off to Aremis and took a seat opposite him while Di still stood like a statue in the center of the room.

"I am happy to see you both, but what brings you to see me? I can sense it is not a leisure visit."

Aremis met my stare, also painfully aware of the frustration rolling off Di. "It is not, I'm afraid. We are concerned for Miss Ophelia."

My heartbeat quickened, and I felt sweat instantaneously pooling on the back of my neck.

"She is Sulu!" Di asserted. "You know she is." It came out as an accusation, and I was certain that was Di's intention.

"Do I?" I stood now. "I know she has uncharacteristically advanced gifts for an Unconsu."

Di interrupted me. "I witnessed her manipulate metal today. Ophelia has somehow acquired Ying's gifts?"

I let out a deep breath. I turned to Aremis. "And you, have you seen her talents?"

"No. She told me."

I put my wine glass down forcefully. I thought Ophelia understood the necessity of discretion, but here we were, only three days into the gathering, and she had already exposed herself to people. "To speak plainly, Di, I do not know what she is. Can you definitively say she is a Sulu, based on the legends you have heard? She is special, and special can be scary," I admitted. "I thought we had an accord about her keeping her gifts secret. Did anyone else see?"

"No, thank the strokes," Di hissed. "She could not contain herself when she thought I was going to cut off the Pierses token she is wearing around her wrist."

"The hairsy charm. You attempted to cut off the hairsy charm?" I rubbed my brow.

"It is not ridiculous troll magic. That token has a variety of powers. A troll had no business sharing it."

"Perhaps not, but it was a gift that was given to both Ophelia and

Lucas, and now that he is gone, it has become a representation of him in her life. I can see why she overreacted."

"She cannot overreact or expose what she is. It will incite panic," Di argued.

"How do you know that's what it will incite? What if it inspires?" Aremis suggested.

Di turned her icy stare on him. "Don't be a fool, Aremis. The Pai Ona are skittish. New is not assuring right now. They want security, some semblance of certainty. Introducing Ophelia will ignite terror. No one has forgotten the prophecy. Have you?"

"I hear you, Di, but something new could bring hope. The prophecy says she may save us all."

"Or she may destroy us!" Di was now in Aremis' face. "We all know what Ophelia is, because she is destined to be with him." She pointed at me. "But knowing what she is and seeing what she's becoming, inexplicably—you would be sorely misled to believe that will inspire hope and not fear."

Aremis stood and towered over Di. "You are afraid."

I had seen enough. This was not getting us anywhere, and I could not argue with either of them. That being said, I was not willing to risk Ophelia's life to discover if she would inspire hope or fear. I stepped between the two of them. Di turned around, facing the wall, and Aremis returned to his seat.

"You are both here because you worry for Ophelia and for our people?" Di's face softened when she turned back around to face me. "Because we do not know what she is or how her exposure may affect the Pai Ona, I see no other way except secrecy."

I put my hand on Aremis' shoulder. "Ophelia is still new to this world. It has not even been a year since we swept her away to Hafiza in the middle of the night. She shows amazing restraint and courage in almost all circumstances. But she is fallible, just like you and just like me. I am assuming both of you impressed upon her the importance of her discretion." They both nodded. "I will talk to her again. In the meantime, what can you find out about Sulus? Inquire, but be inconspicuous about it. Di, what do you know about this token?"

"I dare say, not much. I only recognized it from its likeness to Walthrup's. The very thing he was killed for."

That was the first time I had ever heard Di say her Atoa's name. I had no idea he had been killed for a Pierses token. No wonder Di was so on edge.

Aremis interjected. "I did not know, Aphrodite." Whatever discord was between them had dissolved completely. They were back to sharing the same sad fate of the Poginuli, and that trumped any animosity.

"I disguised the token, but she must maintain control and not let anyone see what she is becoming." Desperation slipped into Di's voice this time, her hard exterior crumbling at the mere mention of her lost companion.

I sighed. "We are in agreement there. I will speak with her in the morning."

OPHELIA

I woke up to Elias at my door. I had a feeling I'd get in trouble for losing my temper with Di the day before. Elias impressed upon me again how important it was that I keep myself shielded. I knew he was right. I just listened and did my best to reassure him that I wouldn't make that mistake again. When he left, I gave myself a serious talking to and resolved to not let my shield down again during the remainder of the summit. It was clear what was at stake. If I ruined this opportunity for Elias and the rest of my people because I couldn't maintain self-control, I'd never forgive myself. Once I was dressed, fed and sure I could keep my cool, no matter what came next, I made my way to Aremis' room. We were scheduled to meet with Almus and Inca today.

Aremis and I walked in our familiar arm-in-arm down the hall to their quarters.

"Does it seem odd that they are inviting us to their room for a drink?" I asked.

"Not in The Cathedral. It's private, and they can make their chamber into whatever they would like."

I wondered what we would find behind their door. Another thought occurred to me.

"Could it be a trap? I mean, if they could make it into anything they want, it could be a trap, right?"

Aremis patted my arm in that comforting way he did. "Miss Ophelia, I may be wrong but Viraclay has given you an exorbitant amount of freedom in The Cathedral. I know him well. I believe he must feel very confident about the precautions he took when creating the broadcast and inviting so many Conduits. Wouldn't you say?"

I stopped walking. I thought about what Aremis had said. We did all we could to ensure that no Nebas traitors were able to even learn about the summit. I felt confident in our work, *so why was I second-guessing it?*

"Okay, I'll buy that," I agreed.

We turned down one more corridor and there, at the end of the hall, was a large red door.

"Looks like that's our spot." I pointed to the door.

"So it would seem."

We walked faster with our destination in sight. When we were feet away, the door opened and Almus stood tall and welcoming in the threshold.

"Come in," he said as he stepped aside, exposing an elaborate courtyard. Ivy draped the brick walls that framed the space. Above us hung an ornate crystal chandelier. It was dusk wherever we were, and the sunset colors of deep purple and baby blues with a flash of magenta painted the sky. A huge gold fountain nestled into the furthest corner. It depicted a merman on the backs of two large fish. Below the chandelier stood a mahogany wood table with four chairs. Fruit, cheeses and meats littered the table, along with a large decanter of red wine.

Inca appeared in the courtyard to our left. "Please take a seat."

"Thank you for hosting us," Aremis said as we sat.

I admired Inca's beauty again today. She had braided her hair on top of her head in a way that hinted at her real age—ancient.

"Where are you from, Inca?" I asked.

"Originally, I inhabited the cold wetlands of Finland." She poured us wine as she spoke. "As you know, Almus and I have migrated across the globe in more recent years."

I wondered how much she thought I knew about her family and how she thought I knew it.

I just nodded. I still hadn't decided how I was going to navigate around Talia's journal without exposing its existence.

"Where are you from?" Almus interjected.

"I'm from the United States. All over the US, really, but I'd call San Francisco home."

"A beautiful and busy city," Almus observed.

"I always loved it."

Almus turned his attention to Aremis. "I must know your secret, friend. It would appear time has erased your years by plenty."

I was grateful for the shift in gears.

"Well, it was an unexpected surprise that I could only learn upon my death." Aremis lifted his glass. "I will tell you all about it, but first let us toast. To new and renewed friendships! May the strokes be in our favor!"

"May the strokes be in our favor!" we repeated in unison.

With that, Aremis started into his story about his resurrection. When he finished, he pondered what he didn't understand about the occurrence.

"I have so many questions. Such as, can I only resurrect if I am killed by fire that I am manipulating? Can it only happen once in my lifetime? Will I stop aging at the rate I am aging when I reach my consummation year? Some of these questions I may never have the answer to," he admitted. "I must believe that Chitchakor was not finished with my stroke."

We all sat in silence. I suppose we were all considering Aremis' questions. I looked at my young Aremis. He was handsome in his youth. My thoughts were interrupted by Inca's raspy voice.

"We have many questions for you, Ophelia Banner, but my good sense tells me that first we should share our intentions with you."

"Intentions would be great, but I would also like to know more about Talia—I mean Nandi's family." I purposefully dropped Talia's name to see how they responded. They were both surprised by the name I used. They knew nothing about her affiliation to me as Talia. I noted that for later consideration.

"Certainly," Almus quickly took my cue. He reached for his Atoa's hand as he continued. "Inca and I met on the shores of the Amazon in Colombia. My family visited the country often while I was a youth. Inca found herself there, starved for heat and fertile soil after growing up in Finland. She stuck out like a sore thumb among the natives. Naturally, between her gifts and her appearance, they considered her divine."

I intersected. "What are your gifts?"

Without speaking, Inca stood and walked to the wall of ivy. She put her hand on a single leaf. Within seconds, the wall that had gaps of brick peeking through dense vines was completely covered. Additionally, tendrils of ivy traced the veins of the cobblestone on the floor until it grew to climb the legs of my chair. "I encourage the growth of plants and the like."

"I see that." I smiled genuinely. "What a beautiful gift." As Inca took her seat again, I put all the moving parts together. "That would be very helpful for the indigenous people you and your family visited regularly."

"It was invaluable to our people," she agreed.

I thought about how she referred to them as 'our' people. *Were they really? Or was she, like many other Conduits, manipulating people with her gifts in order to create followers?* If I considered that to be the motive, then that lumped my dear friend Talia in their deception. *Was that what I thought of her, as well?*

I turned to Almus, almost unable to stop myself from speaking. "And you, you could help them conceptualize how to create their own agriculture or any other invention you thought would benefit them."

"You have put much thought into this?" he asked.

"No. Actually, these are thoughts coming to me as we sit here and as I consider what I know about the tribes Elias and I visited earlier this year." I thought I should add, "I don't usually just speak what I'm thinking. I'm sorry for my abruptness." I wondered if Almus had implanted something into my psyche to encourage this frankness. "Did you implant a thought into my mind that would create this candidness?"

"I did. I admittedly planted the inception upon our first meeting. But I assure you, it will not make you disclose anything you do not wish to share. I only wanted to increase your likelihood of investing your trust in me and my wife."

Aremis looked at me, worried about my findings or perhaps my response. I nodded at him.

"I will let this go, on one condition." Almus and Inca looked at each other, had their own silent exchange, and nodded in agreement. "Be honest. Was it difficult to implant on my unconscious?" I wanted to know how effective my shield was against this sort of thing.

I could see by Almus' expression that he wasn't expecting that to be my question. I desperately wanted to lower my shield and get some insight into what he was feeling with my gifts. But I chewed the inside of my cheek instead because I'd promised Elias only this morning that I wouldn't expose myself, no matter what.

"I found your head very difficult to penetrate, especially for an Unconsu. I left shades of my imprint but I was not certain if any of it had anchored."

"This is very important." My tone got serious. "Does this forthrightness only pertain to you and Inca?"

"Yes. I swear it." My psychology senses told me he was being truthful, and that would have to be enough.

Aremis spoke up. "Why? What is it you are looking for?"

"My father is missing, presumed dead. My brother Huan was murdered after infiltrating the coterie of the Nebas. My son was assassinated after convening with Viraclay. Now, Nandi is gone after befriending you." There was no accusation in his voice, mostly pain. "My mother and my wife are all that I have left. I must keep them safe. I must understand who our enemies are and why."

Tears welled up in my eyes as I spoke. "I'm no enemy to you or your family. I loved your sister Nandi. She saved my life. I wished I could've done the same for her. She was killed by Vivienne. I couldn't save Nandi but I did avenge her. Vivienne is dead."

Disbelief saturated Almus, Inca and even Aremis' face. *Had I left that part out when I told him my story?* I realized that by sharing that, I may have also exposed more about myself—I was alluding to how powerful I was.

"How did you—Vivienne has killed many powerful Conduits." Almus was almost speechless. *Subtext was, she has killed beings with huge powers—how could you have done the job?*

"How doesn't matter. I was lucky," I fibbed. "What matters is how you knew I had befriended Nandi."

"From our Runes, bestowed upon us by my father to all of his children." He pulled up his sleeve to expose his on his forearm, while Inca exposed hers on her neck. "Nandi sent us a farewell moments before her death. In her message she asked that we help protect her dear friend—Ophelia Banner."

My heart swelled up and my throat got tight. I was going to cry again.

"So why, then, would you suspect Ophelia as an enemy?" Aremis asked.

"She would not be the first being to betray our family," Inca said briskly. I understood who she meant. She meant my Lucas, and she was right.

I cleared my throat and pushed past the tears. "I understand your precautions. I can promise you that I'm truly sad to have lost Nandi, and that I'd never do anything to hurt her or anyone she loved. Not now, not ever."

Inca and Almus exchanged another silent conversation before nodding at me and agreeing that they felt they could trust me. It occurred to me that they were not sharing a silent exchange the way Aremis and I did, they were using their Runes. I touched the back of my ear, simultaneously imagining Almus in my mind's eye.

"There is one more thing." Almus' eyes got huge when he heard my voice in his head. "Nandi gave me her Rune."

Inca was massaging her husband's arm with concern. I saw the moment she realized what had him alarmed by the look on her face. I turned to see all kinds of bewilderment on Aremis' face. I reassured him with my eyes—I hoped my expression said, I'm alright and I'll fill you in later. His shoulders relaxed slightly, so it must've been enough.

I returned to my internal exchange with Almus.

"I'd love to learn more about this gift Nandi gave me. Can we talk about this later?"

Almus' voice rang loud and clear in my head. "To be sure. Another time."

We all settled back into our seats.

"Can we dig into this great spread you have here, Inca, and talk about something a little more lighthearted for the time being? Maybe we can talk about how you and Aremis met?" I suggested as I reached for a piece of cheese.

"Now that's a waggish story," Aremis said.

ELIAS

Ophelia had confided in me that she had noticed a particular Conduit by the name of Realto watching her closely over the past few days. Naturally, when I noticed him moving toward her in the crowd, I decided to make my way to her side. To see what his gawking was truly about. I made it to her only thirty seconds before he did.

"Realto is approaching," I whispered in her ear, and felt her body stiffen. "I will not let anyone harm you," I assured her.

Realto presented himself a moment later. He bowed slightly upon his advance, a white flag of sorts. He was not here to cause a problem.

"Viraclay, I have yet to make your acquaintance and show my gratitude for your obliging my attendance to this rather extravagant shindig." He gestured around flamboyantly with his hands. It occurred to me that he may be gay as I took in the entire sight of him. He had long black hair he wore braided over one shoulder—laced in the braid were shiny colorful ribbons. He wore a pink vest over a teal button-down shirt, and if I was not mistaken he was wearing purple leather chaps.

"I am thrilled that you could attend," I politely replied. "How have you found your accommodations? I hope they suit you."

"Most assuredly one of the most purtee'est places I've ever seen," he said before turning his attention to Ophelia. "I'm actually here to speak to this beautiful little darlin'."

I could not place his accent. *Was he from Texas?* One moment he sounded Victorian, the next he had a southern drawl. Odd.

Ophelia did not say anything.

"What is your business with Miss Banner?" I reached for her hand and took it in mine, to let her know I was not going anywhere and to let him know she was important to me.

"Nuttin' unscrupulous." Realto put his hand to his chest in an exaggerated gesture implying he would never dream of such a thing.

"Certainly. Nevertheless, Ophelia and I are very close. You may share with me whatever it was you intended to share with her. What say you, Ophelia?"

She must have been satisfied with her own read on him because she drew her eyes away to speak to me. "I don't see why not. I'll share whatever you tell me with Elias at some point."

"Have it your way, darlin'. I was only tryin' to be sensitive to the lady. Can we excuse ourselves from this bunch? Just over there should do just fine." Realto pointed to a small alcove, just outside the arena. "You may not want other ears to hear what I'm 'bout to share."

Ophelia nodded, and we led the way to the small space. I squeezed her hand, silently comforting her—or at least I hoped that was what I was doing.

When we were all situated out of the crowd, Realto cleared his throat uncomfortably.

"I know your folks." It was a simple statement that had a significant impact. I felt Ophelia's hand shake ever so slightly.

"You do?"

I wondered if she was worried he may be threatening Eleanor, or was she more excited to learn who her father was?

"I do, darlin', and I swear I'm sorry to be the bearer of bad news."

Ophelia let go of my hand completely and crossed her arms.

"Continue."

"I'm old, much older than this country. But I've spent the majority of the last one hundred and fifty years in Texas, near the Mexico border."

Ophelia mindlessly interrupted him. "In a small town called Loredo."

"Yes, that is exactly it, darlin'. My town is sweet, remote and hardly touched by evil. 'Hardly' being the important word in this narrative."

That explained the strange accent. I knew from Ophelia that she believed she had been conceived in Texas. *But how could Realto know anything about her conception?*

"It was July 1989. Mount Redoubt was showing signs of a pending eruption. I know because my dear friend Oya came up from the south, stopping at my place in Loredo before continuing her journey to meet her lover Vosega in Alaska. He is an Elemental, the one responsible for the eruption. It was an accident."

Before he went much further down this rabbit hole, I interjected. "We know Vosega. Ophelia spent several days with him this summer."

"Wonderful. Then I won't have to explain how he likes to drink." Realto waved on. "Darlin', you sure do get around." He shook a playful finger at her. She ignored the comment completely.

"You were saying?" she prompted.

"Well, I had a favorite café I frequented. They had the best pancakes this side of the Mississippi. They were more like flapjacks— small and almost crispy on the outside. My mouth is watering just thinkin' about 'em. The café has changed hands since, and let me tell you, they're not the same. But I digress. Oya and I were enjoying our meal when a familiar unsavory Conduit sat in a booth across from us —Nestor Marini."

Realto paused. He was waiting to see if we knew of Nestor. I looked at Ophelia; she was stoic.

"We know who Nestor is, and of his reputation," I conceded.

"I was not gonna allow him to stay in my town. I realized from his interactions with the wait staff that he had already been there several times without my knowin'. I marched right over to him and, in not so many eloquent words, demanded he leave Loredo at once. Oya bolstered my threat with a brief light show. She is an impressive combatant. The monster agreed he'd leave immediately. I reckoned that was the end of it. I was dreadfully wrong. It would be the last time I saw him in the café, but it would not be the last I saw of him."

"Oya saw him." Ophelia said it more as a statement than a question. I wished I could read her better.

Realto continued, not certain what to make of the interruption. "Six months went by. Oya was returning south after Vosega created too much of a ruckus up north. Once again, she stopped in. After only three days she decided to continue her journey, but not long after we waved goodbye I found her back on my doorstep. She was in tears. She said she heard screams, terrible screams, coming from a ranch she passed about fifteen miles out of town. The ranch was just over the border." Realto reached for Ophelia's shoulders. I hesitantly let him. "It wasn't a safe time to be a hero, but Oya would have it no other way. That girl is as stubborn as a mule. She knew we needed to stop whatever was going on out there. So later that night we crept to the house she identified the screams had been coming from. I ask that you forgive me for this next chapter in the story. I cannot repeat what we saw. My heart won't let me. But I can show you. I'm a Projector."

Realto's hands lit up. He projected the images onto the wall of the alcove. It was just large enough for the three of us to see.

It was dark. I identified the back of Oya's head leading Realto into the house. Just as they slipped into a window, the screams began again. They were bloodcurdling. My skin crawled from the terror they portrayed. The home was a single level but the screams sounded muffled by depth. In my mind, it indicated a basement on the property. Oya figured the same. She found her way to a thin wooden door that opened to a staircase. There was a flickering glow at the bottom of the stairs. As we watched, Ophelia reached behind and took my hand. She was trembling again.

We followed Oya as she took the stairs quietly two at a time. The screams grew louder and more agonizing. I thought if this is a Conduit inflicting this pain, the screams must be the only way they did not hear their approach. There was nothing to be heard but those terrible screams.

Oya pounced onto the dirt floor of the basement. She caught the assailant off guard and struck him with a pointed flurry of lightning. The screaming turned into pleading, cries for help. Realto got to the basement floor just behind Oya.

"Get her out of here. I will deal with this fiend," Oya growled as she shot another lightning bolt from her fingers, striking the attacker in the chest. Realto looked on as a man, nearly naked, tried to get back on his feet. He had strawberry-red hair flailing around his face from the electricity. His skin was fair and he had deep blue eyes—his eyes were hot with terror. He knew he was outmatched by Oya's skill. Realto made his way into a metal cage that had been opened while the man accosted the hysterical young woman, strung up three feet off the ground with chains. She was completely nude. Every inch of her body was purple or bleeding, her thick dark brown hair matted around her face. She was sobbing uncontrollably. Realto's gaze scanned her body and stopped at her belly. She was pregnant. Realto looked away and we saw from his projection that he was vomiting. When he looked back at the young woman, she was staring back at him. Ophelia fell to her knees as she dry-heaved herself. I looked up at Realto. He understood my message and immediately stopped the projection.

I had only seen pictures of Eleanor, but I knew it was her.

Ophelia was not crying, but she stayed on the ground for several minutes. I held her, and Realto waited patiently for her to compose herself.

Slowly she rose to her feet. When she was ready to speak, it came out in a faint whisper. "What happened to her attacker?"

"Oya tried to kill him, but he took hold of a charm from a table in the basement and transported out of the house. He did not go unscathed, I assure you. She would've finished him off if he hadn't ran like a yellow-belly coward." Realto's voice was more resolved as he spoke. "Oya and I took the young lady—Eleanor—back to my home, where we nursed her back to health. She was seven months pregnant at the time. When I came home one afternoon, she was gone. I assumed she was afraid he would return. I couldn't blame her, and I wasn't sure I could save her if he did. So I didn't look for her."

Ophelia was wringing her hands, growing angrier with every minute. I could feel it reverberating off her, even through her shield. "Who was he?"

Realto looked at her with disbelief, as though she had missed the punchline somehow. "Darlin', it was Nestor."

Ophelia stopped moving her hands, stopped breathing—then she touched the wall behind her, melted into it and was gone.

I looked up at Realto. He shook his head. "I'm sorry, I truly am. But the girl deserves to know her origins, to know what her mother went through to have her."

"Whether right or wrong, she knows now," was all I could say and then I, too, dissolved into Ophelia's room.

OPHELIA

I couldn't breathe. I couldn't breathe. I was tugging at the buttons on my shirt, trying to undo them but my fingers were clumsily useless. I leaned over and put my hands on my knees. My vision was starting to get hazy. I needed to calm myself.

I just kept seeing Eleanor's mangled body hanging there, her eyes pleading for rescue—her swollen belly. I dry-heaved again. My head was spinning and tumbling and turning, trying to make sense of what I'd just heard. Eleanor was brutally tortured and raped by her father, by my grandfather. I dry-heaved again.

I heard a chirping voice behind me. I'd had The Cathedral transplant me to the gardens, where I'd hoped I could be alone—or at least avoid Elias. I didn't want to talk right now.

"Are you okay?" the voice chirped again. "Can I help?"

I looked between my legs, upside down, to see a woman dressed in a sparkly spotted bodysuit of spandex. It was mostly golden brown with random specs of white and black. To top it off, she had on ankle boots covered in wild brown feathers. She was tiny—you'd have to be to pull that look off—and had a sharp nose. Besides her eyes, it was the only really distinct feature on her face. Her eyes were intriguing, gray, almost foggy.

"I think I can help," she repeated, and she stretched her neck up in an inquisitive way. Her short auburn hair was spiked out all over her head. *She was something else.*

"I'm okay," I managed to mutter.

"You don't look okay." Her neck extended again and she cocked her head slightly. It reminded me of a bird. I stood upright and turned to properly face her. She was now feet away from me, her hand outstretched.

"My name is Sparkle Bantee. You can call me Sparkle." She smiled and her entire face lit up like a Christmas tree.

I moved to shake her hand despite desperately wanting my solitude.

"My name is Ophelia Banner. You can call me Olly."

"Olly. I like that. Olly, Olly, Olly. It's catchy."

I smiled at her. *What was this woman doing to me?* I'd just heard devastating news—I was the product of incest. I saw the mangled body of my mother. *How could I be smiling?* She must have seen the bewilderment in my eyes.

"Oh, don't worry. I know it's weird to be feeling one thing, but also another. Especially when one of the feelings is bad. I can tell yours are bad." She said it with empathy, through a contagious smile. "It's my gift. I sprinkle happiness. I induce joy. I bring sparkle." She laughed.

"I see," I said. "I think maybe I should be alone to feel what I need to feel."

"I don't think so," Sparkle insisted. "We can talk about it. You can feel it—it will just be filtered through a lens of happiness. I promise it won't change how you feel in the long run, it will just make this part— the hardest part, the rawest part—not so bad."

"But shouldn't we experience it all to be able to move on?" I asked.

"Why? Why should we filter misfortune and heartache through a foggy lens of pain? There is no additional closure in this. There is only additional pain. Often we feel like we don't do a thing justice unless we allow ourselves to be terrorized by it. I see everything about my life through joy. I choose happy, and trust me when I say life has not been all laughing monkeys and lovely roses." She giggled.

I laughed at her metaphor. "Is it really a choice? Your gift is joy, right?"

Sparkle's face got a little serious. I say a little because she was still smiling. "My gift is to give happiness, not to embody it. I choose to live what I can give."

We sat there silently for a while. I thought about what she said. *Why did holding onto joy despite the circumstances feel like a betrayal to what happened and the person who was hurt?* What a terrible thing to perpetuate.

"Okay, Sparkle, I'm going to tell you a pretty bad story. About a bad man doing a terrible thing to two beautiful women who never deserved it. I'm going to try and process this your way."

I smiled half-heartedly.

"I will listen with all of my heart." Her eyes were soft, warm and comforting. I found myself telling her every last detail. And when we were done, I did feel better.

ELIAS

$\mathcal{I}$ had already called on Aremis, Di and Ying to see if she had visited their quarters. I was pacing in her chamber when she appeared. I was so relieved I nearly tackled her with my hug.

"I have been so worried about you. Are you okay?" I pulled her back to examine her person. She appeared unscathed.

"I'm sorry I worried you. I am. I needed time alone." She threw herself on the couch as she continued. I waited to see if she was going to change our setting. It was apparent that she did not like sharing the space she had with Lucas in San Francisco with me. I was not offended by this realization. I could respect her feelings about keeping this part of her life separate, sacred. But when she did not change it immediately, I decided to sit down. "I ended up not being alone—not exactly what I'd intended but I guess the painter knows better than me. I met a woman named Sparkle. She spreads joy. Which was the last thing I wanted, but apparently, I needed it. I feel like a weight has been lifted. I know who my father is. As disgusting as the truth is, it's just that—the truth."

I just stared at her in amazement. She was handling this better than I could have imagined. Better than most. Any single aspect of the story we had just heard would be difficult to swallow, but she was embracing it all—head-on.

"You look like you are doing okay," I admitted.

"I think I am. I mean, I'm not going to go screaming from the rooftops that I'm some product of an incestuous psychopath. I know who I am, and some sociopathic sperm donor doesn't get to define me." She looked down at her hands. "I wish I could hug Eleanor. Tell her I'm sorry and that I understand why it must've been so difficult for her to parent me, to take care of a daily reminder of torment and abuse. She never told me. I don't think she ever told anyone. What a burden that was for her to bear."

"You cannot blame yourself for that. She chose the best way she knew how to deal with a terrible situation." I reached for her leg. I half expected her to pull away, but she did not.

"I know, I just wish I could hug her now."

I had nothing to say to that. No comforting words, nothing. So we sat there in silence. Comfortable silence.

A rap at the door interrupted the tranquil moment.

Ophelia stood to answer it. Su stood patiently on the other side.

"Sorry to bother you, Miss Olly. Is Mr. Elias with you?"

"You're never a bother, Su. He is. Come in." Ophelia stepped aside and Su walked over to me.

"Mr. Elias. You have been summoned to join the faction of Ancients in the ballroom."

I could not hide my alarm. Su saw my reaction and immediately followed up with his own concerns. "We can take extra measures to ensure your safety. I didn't sense a trap. I will be there with you, if you wish."

I stood to face Su. "No, I will be alright. I am just taken aback. The Ancients are reclusive, distant. I worry about what has them moved to action. I need to change into something more appropriate for their audience, first. Please let them know I am on my way and will be arriving shortly."

Su disappeared and in his place stood a worried Ophelia.

"Can I go with you? I can see you're worried about this." Lines creased her forehead.

She had had a hard enough day without worrying about me and my responsibilities.

"I do not believe I am in any danger. So you should not worry about that either." I rubbed her shoulder gently. "Relax. I will come and tell you all about this meeting when it is through. I should mention that I would have you attend, but I do not wish to offend the Ancients. They have different customs, several I know nothing about. Therefore it is best if I abide by their terms—learn the ropes before I change the rules."

She nodded. "I understand. Please find me as soon as you're finished. I'll have some food ready for us odd 'eaters'." She said the last part drawing quotation marks in the air and smiled.

"That sounds perfect." I pulled her in for a hug and then quickly escaped to my room.

I put on a robe that my father had left me written instructions to have made in the event that I entertained the Ancients during the summit. His instruction also cautioned me. He said they had strange customs but they were not violent, and although they may be peculiar, they should be harmless. I tried to comfort myself with his words.

As soon as I was dressed, I transported myself to the ballroom. I was relieved when Di approached me—she, too, was in a similar robe.

"Viraclay." She nodded. "I am here as the official ambassador to the Ancients." She knew how to command respect even with that cherub face.

I looked beyond her to see twenty-one hooded figures on the opposite side of the ballroom floor. They were not ordinary sizes; I could see that from this distance. They had to be twice my height, at least.

"Should I be concerned?" I asked in a hushed tone, not certain where Aphrodite-my-friend started and the ambassador to the Ancients left off.

"Nothing to be concerned about, Viraclay. They are very diplomatic."

"Very well. Let us proceed." We both slowly approached the hooded figures. When we were a few feet away, Di stopped, as did I. As though on cue, all of the figures turned to face us and removed their hoods in sync.

I controlled my expression. I knew what I would see, but knowing and actually seeing are two very different things. Before us stood the Ancient gods.

I bowed as my eyes went down the line. First to the falcon-headed Horus, then to the canine face of Anubis, followed by Bastet. Atop Bastet's shoulders perched her feral cat head. Inkenga's face was that of a man with long protruding horns growing from his crown. They had to be six feet long. After him stood Ganesha, one of the most distinctly recognizable Ancients with his elephant head and four arms. Hanuman smiled a mischievous grin. His entire body was blue. I could see most of it since besides the cloak he only wore a small cloth between his legs, his most unique feature was his monkey face. Shiva's face was stoic as his three eyes stared back at me. Water flowed down his face but somehow never pooled at his feet. Khnum's wide ram eyes watched me take in the sight of each of them one by one. Taweret had the most intriguing look to her. She was a hippo with breasts, a crocodile tail and, somehow, the majesty of a cat. Thoth and Sekhmet stood closest to one another. I wondered if they were a couple. Thoth's head shifted in and out of two forms, a baboon and an ibis bird. It was disorientating to watch. Sekhmet on the other hand peered at me through enormous lioness eyes.

The Indian and Egyptian pantheons were certainly the most famous, but not the only Ancients in attendance. Anansi, in his gigantic spider form, had perched on the wall behind the rest after his robe fell to the floor. His mound of eyes watched me closely. Adjinakou also took the form of an elephant, but he was double the size of his companions. In close second was Nanook, the polar bear god. No less impressive was Pamola, with his massive moose head, eagle wings and talons. One of the friendliest faces was that of Urchuchillay. His expression almost made me laugh aloud. He was a llama man-god, furry all over, with a long neck and smiling llama face. The only

Ancient who looked entirely normal, by human standards, was Ixchel. She could be anyone's grandmother, but I knew she turned into a fierce jaguar.

The final four stood slightly away from the rest. Itzamna had a man's body and an iguana head. Gukumatz lay beside him, coiled as a feathered serpent. Tlaloc and Tezcatlipoca were both stout and block-ish-looking men. Tlaloc had uncharacteristically large googly eyes and long white fangs, too large to be held in his mouth. Tezcatlipoca on the other hand was primarily in human form, with the exception of a snake for a right foot and two thick lines running down the length of his body, one yellow, one black.

Twenty-one Ancient gods stood before me, all in their supernatural forms. Altogether, they were an incredible sight to take in, in both stature and anomalous qualities.

Anubis stepped forward. Di took her place by his side. He looked mountainous next to her delicate frame. Three times her height, and shoulders that spanned at least seven feet.

Anubis placed one large finger on Di's shoulder. Di's mouth began to move, but it was not her voice that came out. It was a deep baritone, a haunting spectacle. Anubis was speaking through Di. No wonder they needed an ambassador, I thought. I would be hard pressed to allow him to do that to me in our first meeting.

"Thank you for your welcome into the summit. We are old, and many have forgotten we ever existed. It was an honor to be considered."

I bowed ever so slightly again. "The honor is mine. It is me who feels privileged to have you accept my invitation to oversee the summit." That was exactly how I had invited them, as spectators. They did not enter through the Katuan Arch as the others had. My father had left instructions for me to do so. He understood that they could be powerful allies, but they appreciated their privacy—demanded it. They would not likely heed a request to participate but they might agree to come watch.

"Not all of our people could be here to witness. They send their gratitude as well."

These were clear formalities that we needed to parade through.

"Please extend my appreciation to them as well."

Di nodded, *or was that Anubis?* Either way. "We are impressed by what we have seen thus far. We have convened and decided we wish to participate in the Katuan Trials."

My mouth slacked. I had to quickly compose myself. "It would be a colossal tribute to the Trials for you to take part," I agreed enthusiastically. I felt like to the attending Conduits seeing the support of the Ancients would be remarkably impactful. It could sway them all to take up the cause.

"We are glad you see the value in our involvement. It has been many centuries since we have let foreign eyes gaze upon our forms. We see that this is our time to choose, to stand with those we believe are just. We stand with you, Viraclay." Then Anubis asked, "When will the Champions be chosen?"

"The Opening Ceremonyis in one week's time. I can arrange for the gatekeeper to escort you through the arch for admittance into the Trials."

"We look forward to it." With that, Anubis removed his hold from Di's body and returned to his companions. Di looked dazed for a moment—not a common look for her. When she was fully cognizant, she resumed her place by my side. We both bowed. The Ancients reciprocated the gesture then replaced their cloaks to cover their exotic forms.

I was in awe as we left the ballroom. This was a crucial piece, in so many ways. I waited to say anything to Di until we had shut the door.

Before I could speak, Di interjected. "I asked the Ancients about the Sulu."

My face got tingly as the color fled my cheeks. "What did they say?" It came out as a whisper.

"Ganesha shared what he knew with me, before you entered the room."

"Can we convene in my chamber? I wish to discuss what Ganesha shared with you. I also would like to hear what you know about the

Ancients—how you became their ambassador. I must collect Ophelia first. She will want to be a part of this conversation."

Di nodded and turned to leave and then decided she had more to add. "Viraclay, you must know, Ganesha's experience with the last Sulu is… complicated."

I nodded in understanding. "It makes no difference. I am of the mind to share any findings with Ophelia, as I promised her I would."

"I will see you in your chamber in an hour's time."

"That will be more than enough time," I agreed.

"One last thing. I will be bringing the gatekeeper, Susuda. He can help explain the formation of the Ancients—although he most likely does not know their similarities to his own makeup."

Interesting, I thought. "You know better than I."

Di was gone before I could say another word.

OPHELIA

$\mathcal{A}$fter Elias described his meeting with the Ancients, he explained why we were going to sit down with Di and Susuda for a conversation in his room. I was excited, nervous and intrigued all at once.

There was information about a Sulu—about me. What a day of revelations. I was exhausted and exhilarated simultaneously. After finding out what I had about my mother and father today and not dying, I was sure I could handle anything else anyone threw at me. I hoped I wasn't wrong.

I looked around. I didn't know this place, the place he manifested as home.

"When did you live here?" I asked as I walked around the oversized sofa. It was a quaint apartment. I was sure he'd lived in far more glamorous places than this. The floor was a light wood. It accented the deep chocolate brown walls nicely. All of the furniture was white or tan. It lightened up the space significantly. There were high ceilings, and tall windows on every wall, draped with shear white curtains. No art, nothing else adorned the walls. The kitchen was open, with white cabinetry and white tile.

"I never actually lived here, until now. It is a flat I imagined when I was eighteen. When I wanted freedom. I thought this place would be an ideal bachelor studio." He took a seat at the small dining room table and gestured for me to sit.

I smiled at him. "It's a pretty sweet apartment. I could see how the ladies would like it," I joked.

"I was eighteen. A boy could dream," he teased back.

Su and Di appeared in the seats across from us at the table. I jumped at their manifestation.

"Sorry, Miss Olly, we should have knocked." Su blushed.

"Do not fret. We were expecting you," Elias assured him.

Di looked at me inquisitively. We hadn't seen each other since that day after her match, the day she'd disguised my hairsy charm. I played with it instinctively, to make sure it was still there. She watched my hand tug at my wrist. "Hello, Ophelia," she said plainly.

"Hi," I said. I felt exposed. I wanted to say I was sorry, again, but decided to keep my mouth shut.

"Let us begin. Su is here to share his input about the Ancients, then he has agreed to leave before we discuss other matters." Su nodded in agreement with Di. "The Ancients are older than anyone knows. It is suspected that they belong to a civilization that thrived on what is now Antarctica. Before it was sheathed in ice, the Ancients drew the maps we know exist today. But they were not always as they are now. They were not always beastly. Their strokes were the same as yours and mine, same form, similar powers. Conduits driven to take on a new power, a new image among the humans, to distinguish themselves as supreme and undeniably different. Thus they founded a large Paksyon. There were fewer Conduits then—a hundred, perhaps less. Every Conduit on earth allied with the Paksyon, and together they performed huge Covenings. Hurricanes of magic, creating cataclysmic transformations. They imposed their gifts onto each other and transmuted their forms into creatures they admired. This is, in many ways, how our friend Susuda was created."

Su jumped in. "I have explained this to Miss Olly, but not to you, Mr. Elias. Di recognized the similarities in me from her time spent with the Ancients. My inception is of magic similar to Covening, not so different from the shaping of a Haven. My father was Consu, my mother was Swali. I held a cursed dagger upon my transformation to this form—all of this magic was fused together when the Conduit Ureshkigal tried to kill me. You see, my father tried to save me, as did my grandmother Inanna. Each of their efforts resulted in their gifts imprinting on my soul, creating this: a Swali with magic who can move between portals and take two different forms—that of the gidim beast from Ureshkigal's curse, the thing you call a poltergeist, and this form, my birth form."

Elias interjected to clarify, "Your gifts are imposed magic, the same as a Haven's. The Ancients transformed themselves into what we see now by similar means. Only yours was accidental and theirs intentional?"

"If it is to be believed that our gifts were created similarly, then yes," Su concurred. "My current form, the Ancients' current forms are a culmination of powers. So much energy went into the transformation that we are no longer mortal, no longer Conduit, we are something more. The manifestation of a powerful magical cocktail."

"Thank you, Su. You have played your part. Please dismiss yourself," Di instructed. Su dissolved from his seat without question. "So now you know how they came to be as they are. For centuries, they played an integral role in several civilizations. I met many of them when they were still overseeing Egypt. They had grown bored, indifferent about human society by then. Populations were so large that it no longer benefitted them to be so conspicuous. Instead, they found it a hindrance—the burden of fame. Too much was being asked of them, so when things began to change and the worship of pagan gods dwindled, they welcomed the turn of the strokes and went into hiding. Holed themselves up in the tunnels of Antarctica. I am the only company they keep beside themselves."

I was trying to keep up. "They live in the ice?"

"Below it. The tunnels were built by their first civilization. They know them well."

It made sense. Conduits were not affected by temperature.

Di continued and I observed that the Di I was seeing now was more like a general, very matter of fact. *It made me wonder how many hats she really wore.* "They have not left the safety of the tunnels for thousands of years. It says much that they have come and now wish to participate in the Trials. Which brings us to you." Di pointed her gaze at me in an almost accusatory fashion. I wanted to explain that I had no idea what a Sulu was, nor did I ever intend to become one, but it seemed like a moot point. I said nothing and she continued. "Ganesha left me with this." She put her hand on top of her head and a green glow appeared. "It is all he knows of the last Sulu on earth. It was nearly 5,000 years ago, in Caral, present Peru. Sulus are vortexes of power. Consider it a typhoon of energy. Ganesha says they can manifest in a handful of ways, but it is the Sulu that attracts then reflects the powers of others. How or why this happens to only a few Conduits is unknown. Ganesha explained that when the last Sulu disappeared, there was a massive worldwide vanishing of Conduits."

"What do you mean, disappeared?" Elias asked exactly what I was thinking.

"Ganesha and many of the others were participating in a retreat during the time it happened so he is unclear about the details. Only that they were in seclusion for a hundred years, performing an extensive Covening. When they returned to their homes, in various places around the world, all of the known Conduits of their domains were gone. Other younger Conduits were now in their stead. Ganesha sought out the Sulu and discovered that they, too, were gone."

"So what you're saying is that Ganesha believes the two phenomena are related?" I asked.

"He does. Not only because of this experience."

Elias leaned in. "Did he know another Sulu?"

"He did not know another Sulu. As the strokes would have it, when Ganesha and many of the other Ancients were conceived, there were stories of a Sulu before their time. Just before their time. The accounts described a similar sequence of events. A Sulu was born, disappeared, and along with him an entire planet of Conduits."

I leaned back in my chair, as did Elias.

"I told you this was complicated," Di concluded.

We all sat in a heavy silence for a long time. *What did this mean about me? Was I going to kill everyone? Was I some sort of monster?*

"Di, did he say whether or not the Sulus were consummated? Was their consummation the inciting incident?" I took a deep breath, afraid of the answer.

"No. The Sulu Ganesha knew was consummated for many years before anything happened."

I internally sighed with relief.

Elias stood up from the table. "You will tell no one what you know. Not a single soul can know what Ophelia is, or what a Sulu is suspected of doing. Am I clear?" His tone was authoritative. I wondered what Di thought about taking orders from him.

"I agree. It will only create hysteria." She looked at me. "They would kill her."

I swallowed hard. Elias knelt beside me, staring deeply into my eyes before he spoke.

"This is one story. One interpretation, with many mysteries. We will learn more. In the meantime we will keep you safe and these secrets hidden."

I felt the sincerity in his voice. He was sure he could keep this hidden, keep me safe.

I put my hand on his cheek to reassure him. "I believe we will do our best."

ELIAS

*I*t had been a long three days with very little sleep. It was not that I was being torn away from my chamber to deal with various complications concerning the summit—on the contrary, things were going very smoothly. Seamlessly, rather. The arriving Conduits were few now, as the Trials grew closer. Those who had surfaced in the first few days were happy to organize daily festivities and competitions. I was surprised at the fluidity of it all. It really took on a rhythm of its own, as though it was in our makeup to congregate and participate in the Katuan Trials.

The sleeplessness stemmed from Aurora's extended absence. *Was she safe? Had she been ambushed?* Then there was the alarming revelation that Ganesha had graciously shared about the last known Sulu he had come across during his vast time on this planet. I lay in bed, restlessly tossing about, considering the implications of his observations. Ganesha's experience of the vanishing of an entire generation of Conduits appeared to align with the looming prophecy about our destruction, should Ophelia consummate. But the prophecy gave an alternative fate, a prosperous one—right? I grappled with question after question, all of which would fall on deaf ears, since little was known about Sulus. Rumors, speculation, myths, really—all saturated with mystery and fear. If I continued to investigate, I also ran the risk of drawing attention to Ophelia, something I was unwilling to do.

I looked at the clock beside my bed—4:03 a.m., and I had not closed my eyes for more than thirty minutes all night. I needed to do something soon, not later, not after the summit. I needed answers now. Methodically, I traced back every instance when the term Sulu was interjected into a conversation. Slowly, my groggy thoughts made their way back to the conversation with Nara in the kitchen at Hafiza, after Ophelia's first lesson with Ying. Nara had said that we knew of only one other Sulu and that the similarities were striking. I had dismissed the conversation at the time. Everything was still so new, and it was unclear what was truly happening with Ophelia and her gifts. But now Nara's words were all I could think about. I needed to speak to her immediately.

OPHELIA

*D*eja vu. I know I've been here, in this place, in this cave, dozens of times. I have Lucas' ashes at my feet. Tears stream down my face. I feel the wretched sensation of my heart being torn from my chest as I watch a fireball dive toward my friends—toward Elias, Aremis and everyone else I love.

Yanni whispers in my ear. "I always knew you were a killer."

Then a new voice, a vaguely familiar voice fills my other ear. "Of course she is a killer. She is my spawn, my warped seed. The progeny of terror. Conceived in terror only to bestow terror."

I want to scream back at him, deny his callous words. But as I watch everyone I care about burn in front of me, I know he must be right. I must have been born with the sole purpose of creating destruction.

I sat up in bed. I was drenched in sweat. My heart was racing and my mouth was dry. The dream changed. It had only changed two times since it began. The first was after Aremis died—or I thought he did, and he did, but now he was back. That whole concept made my head spin. The second time was when Lucas died. After Lucas died, his ashes replaced the pile at my feet that were once Aremis'. Now,

Nestor had entered the dream. The monster I now knew was my incestuous father.

"I need to shower." I said it aloud to myself, then threw the sheets off the bed and stumbled into the bathroom. I looked around and thought, *I guess I could have dreamt up a better bathroom.* The one in Hafiza was nice—spacious. Unlike my tiny bathroom in my San Francisco apartment.

Maybe another day, when I want to take a nice bath. I'd consider a change of scenery then. But for tonight, to wash off the stench of that nightmare, my familiar shower would work just fine.

I let my nightgown slip off my shoulders and stepped into the basin. The water warmed me instantly. It felt amazing as it trickled down my back. When I considered myself thoroughly cleansed and toweled off, I grabbed a clean nightgown and picked up my journal to note the change in the dream. It sickened me to replay the new development, but something in my gut said it was important—that following the progress of this dream would have purpose someday.

I replaced the journal on the shelf I'd been keeping it, beside Talia's journal. I pulled hers out and browsed the odd language in the first half, before she began her entries to me.

It was like nothing I'd ever seen before, yet somehow vaguely familiar. Elias hadn't recognized it either. After mindlessly flipping the pages, I closed the book and traced the inlay and the stone on the front.

I wondered what kind of gem it was. It was brownish, rich in facets, and had a subtle but rapturous shimmer to it. I replaced it back on the shelf and decided I was wound down enough to try and go back to sleep.

My bed had gotten cold. I wiggled under the blankets, trying to create a warming friction. As I wiggled my eyes got heavier and heavier. I found myself falling into a deep, dreamless slumber.

ELIAS

"*N*ara, may I speak to you in private?" I asked her as she removed her shield. It looked like something from her Celtic heritage. Something she wore when she was known as Danu, a goddess of the Tuatha De Danann. Although Ophelia and I slept or attempted to sleep at nightfall, most of the other guests continued with the competitions throughout the night. They had no need for sleep. I was happy to find that Nara had just completed a combat round. This particular competition required the combatants to use only their gifts for weapons. Nara beat the illustrious Dracula. Her wind was well-matched with his speed and transformative powers. It was nearly a draw, but Nara caught him off-guard in the final moments of the last round as he transformed from a bat back into a man. She reverently bowed in the direction of her opponent before addressing me.

"Of course, Viraclay. May I change? You can meet me in my quarters in ten minutes' time."

"I will be there in twenty. Please take your time. Can I bring up some wine?" It was early for me, but late for her.

"That would be agreeable," she replied before disappearing.

I vanished into my own room and collected a vintage I thought

Nara would appreciate. I took the scenic route as I made my way to Nara's chamber, being sure to wave and connect with as many new faces as possible along the way. It was my part, I was here to build trust and relationships so that when the time came and I asked for their bidding, the Pai Ona would rise to the call. In the midst of the games, laughter and camaraderie, I had to remind myself of my purpose.

Her door was shut when I arrived. I knocked and she quickly answered.

She did not smile anymore. Come to think of it, I am not certain she ever smiled much to begin with. But since Valerian had died I never saw her smile. Not once.

"Come in." She moved aside. I noticed that her room had evolved since the night she had first arrived at the summit. There was a window now, framed by crimson drapes. It was still a small space but it had life in it. The little table we sat at the first night was now under the window. It had a bouquet of colorful gerber daisies on it. A large chaise lounge chair was positioned by the wall opposite the window. The chaise was upholstered in a rich brown velvet. Two throw pillows lay strewn across its back. They were white and embroidered with intricate green vines.

Nara caught my stare.

"This was our apartment in Paris. Nothing spectacular, but our home for many years." She sighed as she took a seat at the table.

I pulled out the wine, but realized she did not appear to have a kitchen. "I can go retrieve some glasses."

"I have two." She pointed to the corner china hutch behind me. I had not noticed it. "We did not require a kitchen, but we did require glasses. It was Paris, of course." Still she did not smile with her mouth, but there was a smile in her eyes as she remembered this season in her life.

I quickly grabbed the glasses and sat down. I had already opened the bottle, so I poured us both a healthy glass.

Nara seemed to inhale her first taste. "This is good," she assured me.

"I am pleased that you like it."

"I know you did not come to speak to me about wine. What can I assist you with, Viraclay?"

"When we were in Hafiza, you came to me with your concerns for Ophelia's safety." I paused to see if mentioning our time there would upset her, but she appeared unmoved so I continued. "You said to me that we have only seen one other of our kind with the type of ability Ophelia was presenting, and she suffered a fate worse than death. You also said the resemblance was hard to ignore. You believed even then that Ophelia was Sulu."

Nara nodded. "I remember the conversation well."

"Can you tell me more? At the time I doubted that Ophelia was a Sulu. But..." I considered what I was about to do. I was going to let someone else know what Lucas and I had concluded—that Ophelia *was* Sulu. "I have reason to believe she is indeed Sulu."

"I understand. I understand why you did not want to believe it then and why you hesitate to tell me now. You should be fearful of who knows, but not of me. I will never harm you, your cause or your Atoa." Nara met my eyes and held my stare for a long time. She wanted me to believe her, to trust her, and I did.

"I need to know all that I can about Sulus. You were referring to Aurora when you said we have only seen one other of our kind display gifts like Ophelia's?"

"I was." She leaned back in her chair and took another sip of wine. "What is it that you know about Aurora's captivity? About the Oracle herself?"

"She is a Ramalan, a prophet. Apollo abducted her from her home in Poland, where she was revered as one of the three Zoyas. He killed her Atoa and kept her prisoner in Delphi for hundreds of years."

"Yes, that is the story that we all know," Nara said matter-of-factly. "But there is more to every story. Why do you think we keep the details secret? Is it for the Oracle's dignity, her safety? Or to protect others, ourselves?"

"It would depend on the details."

Nara nodded and pointed at me with her free hand. "Exactly. I will tell you what I know, but you must keep it to yourself. There are those who wish to go untethered to the atrocities I will share. I cannot say that I am innocent in all of this, because if I were, I would not know what I do. I can say that I have atoned for my sins and I will continue to do so by protecting your Ophelia."

My shoulders eased slightly with her last statement, but I felt a knot tugging in the depths of my stomach. I had this feeling of betrayal, one I felt often when I found out secrets of the world I grew up in. *Why had my parents chosen to keep me in the dark?*

"Aurora had been held captive for nearly three hundred years when I met her atop the mountain where the Oracle of Delphi presided. She was beautiful, as she is now. Even in chains, she looked majestic. You see, it was not just humans who sought her visions, it was also our kind." Nara's eyes narrowed in disgust. I saw the inner turmoil boil up inside her. "The history books will tell you that the Oracle was actually three women, not one. There is truth in this, but not the way you would expect. Aurora had the gift of sight. The person to her right was an Amplifier."

I interrupted. "You mean to tell me Apollo had multiple captives? One was Aurora, another an Amplifier with the ability to strengthen the gifts of those Conduits around them?"

"Yes. The Amplifier strengthened the gifts in their presence, advanced Aurora's sight, but they were not captives. The other two Conduits, male or female, who lay beside Aurora in her chains, were willing participants."

I clenched my jaw, considering what this meant. "How do you know this?" I just could not bring myself to believe it. This whole war started because of the cruelty of Apollo. If others participated willingly, they were no better than he.

"I participated."

The air fled my lungs. I could not catch my breath, the gravity of her words suffocating me.

"Hundreds of years on the planet, and life became stale for many Conduits. It is hard to understand, but I think that is why we condoned it—participated in it. Valerian and I decided to travel to

Delphi. In order for Conduits to be seen, they had to agree to trade their gift. This was how a Sulu formed. Aurora sat between an Amplifier and another Conduit. When I sat on her other side, she would share with me my future. But the beauty was in the vortex the three Conduits created. Aurora could temporarily manifest my gifts when she was touching my skin. Not the way Esther does, by taking over another body. This was different, this was Sulu. Aurora could manipulate her own wind."

I put my hand up, gesturing for Nara to pause. She did so. I took a long swig of my wine before speaking. "So Aurora could absorb?"

"Only in the Sulu vortex, and only her. I did not acquire any further gifts, and when I left the circle, my gifts left with me."

"How do you know that for certain?"

"Because she was captive for hundreds of years. If she accumulated powers and maintained them, I believe she would have escaped on her own. Or someone would have seen her manifesting other powers than her sight. It was the Sulu created by her power and the others. And although she did not keep the gifts, I have yet to hear of another Paksyon being able to achieve what she did. So there was something special about Aurora."

I rubbed my forehead nervously. "What you are saying is that our people held Aurora captive, not just Apollo, and that she, with the assistance of an Amplifier and another Conduit, can transform into a Sulu?"

"Yes, and before I go on I must say once more that I know my actions were deplorable." Nara reached for my hand, something she had never done before. "Will you forgive me?"

I took a deep breath. It was not my place to judge Nara; she clearly judged herself. This did bring to light why so many secret Nebas rallied to Apollo's side. They were all convicted when he was—if he was to be held accountable, then someday they could be. It also explained why Aurora did not trust anyone. She could not. Nara waited patiently, pleading with her eyes as I considered the actualizations of what came from Aurora's captivity. "I forgive you. It is not my place to judge your strokes."

"Thank you," she whispered.

I began to think aloud, connecting the dots. "Thank you for your honesty. With this information, it becomes clear why you were so fearful about who knows about Ophelia. She is Sulu, possibly a more powerful Sulu than Aurora could ever be. The similarities are striking and cannot be ignored. Many of our kind participated in the Oracle's captivity, which makes them possible traitors. We have no way of knowing who those individuals might be." My throat was tightening after every realization. "There is nothing we can do to stop her gifts from growing. Unlike Aurora, she accumulates every gift she comes into contact with." I poured myself another glass of wine and finished it in one swallow. "How do I keep her safe, Nara? How do I keep her hidden from sight? And where is Aurora?"

OPHELIA

"I wish to show you something." Almus led me down a small garden path. "I have to ask your discretion, because Inca forbade me to share this knowledge with you."

"I don't want to cause any problems for the two of you." I felt compelled to say that, even though I had no idea what he was talking about.

"I know that. She knows that. This is between us. Fret not that she will blame you, should she find out that I took it upon myself to elucidate without her consent." He patted me on the shoulder. It was meant to be a comforting gesture, but Almus was not exactly congenial—instead, he was awkward. I smiled nonetheless. "Let us take this conversation to a more private setting."

This had become our code for 'use your Runes'. I brushed the skin behind my ear and heard Almus' familiar voice, now in my head. "Let us walk, Ophelia."

I kept with his pace. I could tell he was really grappling with confiding in me.

"I'm sure, whatever it is, it can wait," I insisted. The hardest part about having an inner dialogue was controlling your expressions so that you didn't look like a crazy person if someone saw you.

"Nandi... I mean your Talia."

I interrupted him. "I've told you, she will always be my Talia, but call her what is natural for you."

He nodded. "Nandi told you about my son Alistair, no doubt."

I stiffened slightly. I knew Alistair had been murdered. "Yes. She said he and his grandfather were very close."

"So you know he was assassinated?" His voice was low, hushed—even between our minds.

"Yes, I knew that."

"He believed as I still do that my father, his grandfather, is still alive. He was on a mission to find him. We all have been. My wife believes that his Runes betrayed him somehow. That he shared his with the wrong person after his Theia was killed. This is why she does not support me showing you how to share your Rune."

I thought about what he was saying long and hard. I'd suspected I could share it, just as Talia had with me, but I never thought I'd discover how, not after I lost her. *What risk was I taking by sharing it? Could someone tap in?*

"What do you mean by the Runes betrayed him?"

"Therein lies the problem—we are not certain. Did he just share his Rune with a Nebas in hiding, someone he assumed was a friend? Or is someone able to listen to our conversations? How they could, I do not know."

"So Inca's fear is that there is a transmission glitch that may have occurred when he shared it last?"

"That is correct. If we are to believe that, that is where the betrayal happened."

"Why are you so sure there was a betrayal? That he wasn't just hunted down like so many before him?"

"It is possible, but he contacted me and Inca that night. He was terrified. He said he had shared his Rune with someone and that he had no idea what he had done at the time. He said he felt he was being watched. He apologized through tears, told us he loved us, and then was abruptly cut off." Almus rubbed his temples. "That was the last time I heard from my son, and I had no words of comfort, no solutions—I did not even understand his problem until it was too late."

I put my hand on his shoulder sympathetically. "You couldn't have known. How could you?"

"I knew he was frightened."

I didn't know what to say to that. So I said nothing. We walked in silence for several yards down the garden path.

Almus picked back up the conversation in our heads. "Inca does not want to put you in danger. Nor do I. But Nandi shared a sacred family gift, and you are only using half of its potential." He stopped and looked at me earnestly. "We can share our Runes with one other individual. I want to show you how to share yours. Who you choose to give this gift to is up to you. But I caution you, choose wisely and do not give them the secret I am giving you now—not immediately. See that they are responsible with this power, that they keep it secret and safe. Because once a Rune is given, it cannot be rescinded. They will be forever capable of communicating with not only you, but anyone else who shares the Rune. You open us all up to trespassers."

I digested what he was saying. It was a heavy responsibility, a huge consideration—if I chose to share the Rune with someone else. I was honored that Almus felt I deserved this insight. After all, it was his family's legacy, bestowed upon them by their patriarch.

"I'm honored. I promise to be responsible and only share my Rune when I can be certain it will be left in capable and trustworthy hands."

Almus pulled me in for a very awkward hug. "I believe you will." When he was satisfied with our exchange, he pulled away and continued walking.

An image filled my mind's eye. It was Almus. He was brushing his Rune while reciting three words. I didn't know the words but they sounded like, "Plitos, Milti, Damilton." I repeated them with him and he nodded enthusiastically. After we repeated the phrase several times and I felt like I had it, I asked him what they meant.

"They mean, 'mine is yours, ours is theirs.' Do you feel like you can remember it?" I recited it several more times, perfecting my enunciation.

"I think I got it, yes."

"Excellent. The second piece to the transfer is in the touching of first your Rune, then the place in which you would like to implant the Rune on your chosen companion. To initiate the transfer you must recite the phrase while first touching your Rune then complete the transaction by reciting it as you touch them," Almus explained.

It all made sense to me, because that was exactly how I remembered Talia giving me mine.

"I understand." I met Almus' gaze. "I'll be careful, and I will not betray your trust in me with this information," I assured him once more within our exchange.

"I know." He turned around and we began back the way we came. "Now I just need to convince Inca of this."

He flashed an image of a red-faced Inca across our conversation. We both laughed out loud.

ELIAS

I sat decoding Alistair's journals in my chamber. It was the first time I had had the opportunity to pull them out without interruption since the arrivals began. The process was slow, methodical. Even though I had the keys, he rotated between the codes at random and what he wrote was often also cryptic, not written in entire sentences. I still held out hope that there would be more answers within their pages. There was a reason why he took such great measures to keep things secret. I knew there had to be.

The knock on my door was unexpected. I sighed and put the journal I had been working on away inside the safe before opening the door.

I was alarmed to see who was calling on me. It was Almus, Alistair's father.

"Almus, how can I assist you this evening?"

"I hope I didn't interrupt anything."

Nothing I would confide in him about. "Nothing of importance."

"In that case, will you share a stroll with me?"

"Indeed," I agreed and shut the door. We began our walk down the hall. "Almus, I understand you have been meeting with Ophelia, helping her understand her Rune," I said as Almus took step beside me.

"She is a wondrous woman. I can see what my sister Nandi saw in her, and what you see in her."

"She is exceptional."

"I value the time she and I spend together. In many ways, she reminds me of Theia. Kind, smart and empathetic to others."

"I did not know Theia, but if those were her qualities, then it sounds as though they were indeed very much alike." I stopped walking and turned to face Almus. "I doubt that your intention for this meeting was to talk about Ophelia—or Theia, for that matter. How can I assist you?"

"Very pointed, but I can appreciate a man who does not trouble with pleasantries. Has Ophelia told you all she knows about our family? That my mother and I believe my father Ruit is alive and that..."

He paused this time, choking on his words ever so slightly.

"...That I believe Alistair's Rune betrayed him? That he shared it with someone he should not have trusted?"

I had my own questions. "Were you the one orchestrating the expectations of my arrivals to the villages your family frequented?"

The question caught him off-guard. That alone told me he was not the one.

"The villages were expecting you?"

"Every one of them." I continued walking. "I have to admit that it made my welcome far easier than I had anticipated it to be. If it was not you, then I am forced to believe it was your father that had the foresight to pave the way for Ophelia and I." I lifted my hands, gesturing to the grand hallway we were walking through in the greatest Haven the world had ever seen. "Why would your father want that? How could a man with so much foresight, so much skill, be ambushed?"

"He did have great foresight, and if this is where he wanted you to be, this is where you were meant to be. His alchemy was vast—the Loktpi, the Runes, and countless other spells, creations and wards, all stored in his head, for the most part. So how did he get ambushed? I have asked myself over and over. He cannot be dead. He was worth more alive," Almus reasoned.

"But this Rune—it cannot reach him?" I asked.

"No."

"Can it reach Huan, or Nandi, or your son?"

"No, but we know they are dead. Their murders were witnessed."

"How could someone detain your father, as powerful as he is, without him contacting you?"

"These are all valid questions, but you are missing the point. How many Nebas were there, that they had the gifts to ambush and capture my father? That one of them manipulated my son into sharing his Rune? You saw him, his last night?"

"I did."

Almus pulled up his sleeve to expose his own Rune symbol. "Was he touching this?"

I remembered that night well. "Yes."

"He was not speaking to me or his mother, or grandmother, or aunt. He was speaking to someone who led to his murder."

"You mean to tell me that your son was sharing the conversation I was having with him with someone else, and you believe this person was his assassin?"

"I do."

I stopped and faced him again, putting my hand on his Rune. "Then, dear Almus, we could be in greater danger than we know."

ESTHER

"*M*istress, we have collected a Pai Ona we believe you will find worthy of your interrogations." Akiva stepped into my room as he spoke.

"Why must you disturb me?" I growled. "I had a moment's peace for the first time since..." I did not want to say it aloud. My room was dark. I lay on the fainting chair in the center of the vast chamber. It was upholstered in a plush, violet chenille fabric. I was appreciating the feel of it on my skin for the first time in days. What used to be one of my favorite sensations was now a horrific reminder of my loss, my lust for revenge and my rage. But only a moment ago I'd found a whisper of that sensation again, that peace. Ripped away from me by this bumbling idiot.

I got to my feet and walked over to Akiva. I tore my nails across his cheek and watched the blood ooze from the three identical wounds. It did nothing to bring back the peace, but it felt mildly comforting. "Whom did you capture, and in what condition?"

Akiva composed himself before he spoke. A moment longer and I would have torn through his face again. Just before I raised my hand, his voice interrupted the silence. "Filbert Ortega."

"Realto's lover?"

"Yes, Mistress."

"Realto was not with him?"

Akiva shook his head no.

"And his brother Mikkel?"

"No one was with Filbert at the time of his capture."

"Curious. So many moving parts and they leave this sweet lamb to his own devices." It seemed too easy, but why look a gift horse in the mouth? "I will meet you in the cell."

"Mistress." Akiva bowed and backed out of the room.

I paced in my room. *If this was a trap, why would they let us get Filbert into the compound?* Realto and Mikkel would know how difficult that would make retrieving Filbert. No, it had to be a pleasant turn of the strokes. Filbert would be easy to maintain control over. His gift was weak. I made it a point to know my enemies well, much better than the opposition knew of our gifts. Filbert was an Aromatic. He could manipulate humans rather successfully with his gift, but unfortunately for him, we Conduits were far less affected by our sense of smell. His brother Mikkel, on the other hand—now, he would be problematic. Valuable, but problematic. The last known living Epochus. I had been searching for him for centuries, but his ability to distort time made things very difficult. Now I had his beloved brother at my mercy.

"Thank the strokes!" I clasped my hands in delight. This almost made up for losing Lucia and Winston.

ELIAS

*M*y discussion with Almus had me on high alert. *What did this all mean? Would I find the answers in Alistair's journals? Should I share them with his father? Was that the honorable thing to do? Where was Aurora? Did any of this affect her attendance to the summit? How could it not?*

I had so many questions. I had hoped that the summit would bring resolutions, not further inquiries. If what Almus suspected was true, then this traitor may also have the Loktpi. *Rand knew something about Alistair's murder. Should I reach out to him?* I sat staring at the journal. I needed to make deciphering the entries my top priority. It was time to get to work. If they held no answers, then I was no worse off than I was now, but if they held answers and I simply had not prioritized the contents of the writing I had in my hand—well, that would be terrible and I could not live with myself.

I pulled my chair up to the desk and got busy.

ESTHER

"Filbert," I purred in his ear. "Filbert, Filbert, Filbert. Where have you been hiding? More importantly, why are you scurrying about now?" I circled his chair twice before straddling him. "Not just you." I pecked at his chest with my finger. "But many other righteous Pai Ona have been busying about these days. I need to know why, and I am certain you are the man to tell me."

Filbert had not said one word since his capture. Instead, his blue eyes glared back at me with disdain. He must have been in his late forties when he consummated. His hair had flecks of silver around the edges, and his eyes were framed with thin lines. I ran my fingers through his hair. "Do you think Realto was disappointed when he discovered you were his Atoa, so much older than the young stallion?" I pulled at the ends and heard the tearing of hair follicles from his scalp. I gripped tighter and yanked hard. I looked inquisitively at the fistful of hair in my hand. "You still have a full head of hair, mature or not." I stepped off his lap and blew the hair in his face.

ELIAS

I had not slept at all. Aurora still had not arrived. I had sent Susuda out last night to see if he could track down her whereabouts. But she was a master at staying undetected. I did not know where to have him start.

It was Opening Ceremonies today. The arrivals had been a success. I felt that everyone was now buzzing with excitement—eager for the main event to begin. The Katuan Stones had proven to be very accommodating, with the assistance of The Cathedral, molding and shaping to whatever event took place in the grand arena each day.

In all honesty, I did not have any idea what the Opening Ceremonywould entail. None of the texts we had to reference outlined the specific events that would take place. I wondered if every ceremony was different, depending on the audience and Champions chosen to participate. It was this not knowing that kept me up all night. *What if the Stones failed? What if the ceremony was a flop? What if the magic of the Stones was already exhausted?*

I pulled on an undershirt as I contemplated all of the ridiculous outcomes. As I buttoned up my final button on my light blue dress shirt, I felt the anxiety begin to make me lightheaded.

"Get it together, Elias." I said it aloud, willing the calm into my body. I took a seat in the center of my apartment, cross-legged, elongating my back and closing my eyes. A quick meditation would at least slow down my heart rate, quiet the quick-firing thoughts. After a moment or two I felt better. When I opened my eyes I had the aura of calm. Now I just needed to maintain it.

I had agreed to meet Ophelia down in the galley, to have a private breakfast before the events of the day began. It was nearly time. I threw on a casual cardigan and stepped out my door before teleporting into the passage that led to the galley.

OPHELIA

*I*t was Opening Ceremonyday. I woke up giddy with excitement. For so many reasons—for Elias, to see his hard work realized, because we were going to witness something that hadn't happened for thousands of years, and because I got to practice with my Rune. I was walking and talking to Almus as I made my way down to the galley to meet Elias. It was an odd sensation that required I divide my attention. I had to listen to Almus transmit while concentrating on the placement of my feet.

Talia had said that different people communicated differently with their Runes. It turned out Almus used words and images. That meant I was getting flashes of what he was trying to convey while my brain tried to simultaneously translate what my eyes were absorbing in front of me.

I could've sat in my room and waited for the conversation to be over, but the way I saw it, if I was going to use this Rune right, I'd need to perform daily tasks without anyone suspecting the internal dialogue occurring in my head. So I ran into things and walked like I was drunk while I practiced dividing my attention.

I was so distracted that it took a familiar face standing directly in front of me with a plate of food before I realized he was there.

"Miss Ophelia, I prepared your favorite," Winston's voice chirped.

I refocused all my energy to confirm what I was seeing. Excitement swelled inside of me. Winston was one of the last of my closest friends from Hafiza to be accounted for, and here he was!

I screamed. "You're here!" I jumped into Winston's arms, barely missing the plate of food he narrowly managed to set down and out of my way.

Almus' voice came in louder. "Are you okay? Where are you? I can be there at once."

I shook my head and popped back into the conversation with Almus while squeezing Winston as tight as I could around the neck.

"I'm fine. I'm sorry. I just saw an old friend I'd suspected was dead. Can we resume this conversation in a little bit?"

"Of course," Almus agreed and then signed off.

I let go of Winston's neck and only then realized how uncomfortable that outburst of emotion made him. I chuckled.

"Where have you been? We were all sure you must have fallen with Hafiza when you didn't arrive at the summit over these last few days." I stepped back and took in the sight of him. Nothing had changed. He was still the ancient sixteen-year-old boy I remembered.

"We were late. It couldn't be helped."

"We?" I peered around him to see a small young woman I had only seen in a photograph. "Lucia?"

She smiled a sheepish smile. "In the flesh, Miss Ophelia." She had a thick accent—although from where, I had no idea.

"May I?" I spread my arms, implying a hug.

"Please." She filled the gap between us in an instant and wrapped her tiny arms around me. She had to have been fourteen when they consummated. "I love hugs," she said as her head lay on my chest.

What a pair these two made. When she pulled away I felt a lingering sense of attachment to my new friend. I wondered what her gifts were. I suspected from our brief interaction that I could learn whatever I wanted to about Lucia. She would be an open book.

. Lucia made her way to Winston's side where she scooped up his hand. "My Winnie speaks very highly of you."

I internally chuckled at the doting nickname. "I think Winnie is pretty awesome as well!"

Winston rolled his eyes at me using his pet name. "I prepared eggs Benedict for you. Come take a seat."

Winston pulled Lucia to the opposite side of a counter while I took a seat on a stool I'd used from time to time down here. "Did you make enough for Elias? He's meeting me."

"Yes." Winston gestured over his shoulder to another plate of food. I smiled at him, feeling a little more anxiety leave my body, energy I didn't realize I was still holding onto as I waited for all of my friends to be accounted for.

"When did you get in?" I asked between bites.

"Late last night," Lucia answered.

"Does Elias know you're here? He'll be excited to see you."

"The gatekeeper said he would inform Master Elias of our arrival," Winston said matter-of-factly. "How do you like the dish? Did I prepare it as you remembered?"

I nodded as I chewed.

"Winnie told me all about his time in Hafiza. He loved cooking for you. He returned to me with all sorts of new recipes. I am happy to say he learned some amazing new things about the culinary arts while in your service." Lucia's smile was contagious.

I swallowed. "He is one heck of a chef. But better than that, he saved my life—he and Aremis built me a way to get out of the fortress unscathed. If it weren't for Winston, I may not be here today." I felt my throat get tight. "I owe him a lot."

I almost thought I saw Winston blush with flattery. I hoped I did.

"Never matter that. It was under the specific direction of Master Elias. It is he you should thank."

"Thank me for what?" Elias came up from behind me and patted my back gently before quickly making it to Winston's side. "It is you I thank."

Elias took Winston in close and tight for a long silent hug.

"Susuda's just informed me of your arrival as I made my way down here. I would have found you sooner."

"It was late. We are sorry for our tardiness. It could not be avoided." Winston's voice implied there was more to the story.

Lucia took Elias by the shoulders. "Viraclay, you have grown to be such a strapping man."

I wondered how long it had been since they had seen each other. I thought about how young Elias must have been. *Was he ten, fifteen, or in his early twenties like Aremis?*

"Aremis!" I shouted. "Have you seen Aremis?"

Lucia and Winston hung their heads low, as though it was up to them to break the bad news to me. "Surely you know what happened at Hafiza," Lucia said.

Just then, I heard Aremis' familiar voice behind me. I didn't need to turn around to know he was in the doorway. Winston's face read like a billboard—pure disbelief.

"I heard a rumor I died."

ELIAS

I observed Ophelia as she watched Aremis and Winston reunite. Her reaction was almost more precious than the two old friends. She was beaming, watching them hug and share in each other's disbelief. I leaned over, once I sat down beside her with my plate. "So much for a private breakfast." I meant it lightheartedly, and she knew it.

"This is better," she whispered back.

"I agree." I took a bite. Winston had outdone himself.

We listened as Aremis relayed his story. When it became Winston's turn to explain his and Lucia's absence until today, the mood shifted. Winston did not say it, but I saw it in his face. He did not want to disclose what happened in front of Ophelia. I considered explaining that our dynamics had shifted since Hafiza, that I would relay whatever he said to Ophelia at some point, but decided I would wait to enlighten him at a later date.

"Winston and I are so excited to see all of you. We wanted to be sure to reunite before the Trials begin. But, if we may excuse ourselves to collect our wits and prepare for the rest of the summit, it would be greatly appreciated."

Ophelia was the first to speak up. "Naturally. Go, rest. We can hear all about what you've been up to some other time." She stood to give both of them hugs as they made their way to the galley exit.

"I am going to take my leave as well." Aremis smiled at me when he dismissed himself. "I just wanted to see my young friends before the ceremony began. May I walk with you to your quarters?"

The question was directed at Winston but Lucia answered. "Please." The three of them slowly made their way out of the galley, Lucia latched between the two young men.

I turned to Ophelia, who was also watching them go, still beaming. "Are you excited about today?"

She nodded enthusiastically as she took a bite, then paused, her expression instantly changing to forlorn. "Do you think Rand is going to show up late, too?"

I had promised to tell no one of Rand's visit, and for the time being I decided that also meant Ophelia. He was up to something. My gut said trust him and keep his whereabouts secret. "I am certain Rand is safe, wherever he is. One day he will entertain us both with a wild story explaining his truancy." Deep down, I hoped I was right.

We both chewed in silence for a few bites before Ophelia spoke up again. "I'm really excited about today. How about you?"

"Excited, anxious, terrified." It was a vulnerable admission, but I knew Ophelia would understand.

She took my hand. "It's all going to go smoothly, I just know it."

"Your optimism is appreciated," I said as I took my last bite and cleared both of our plates, since Ophelia had already finished. "Let me clean these plates and then we can find our viewing balcony."

She jumped up and ran over to a box in the corner. "First we have to celebrate your amazing achievement! Whatever happens next, you've brought six thousand Conduits together for the first Katuan Trials in over three millennia." When her head popped out of the box, she had a bottle of champagne in one hand and two flutes in the other. "One glass won't hurt."

I left the plates in the wash basin and took one of the flutes in my hand while Ophelia popped the champagne. The cork flew up and bounced off the ceiling. She beamed with delight while she filled both of our glasses to the brim.

We raised our glasses in unison. "To an amazing summit," she hailed.

"To ending the war," I replied.

OPHELIA

*O*ur balcony was far above the rest of the arena seating. There were seven others at the same level, each overlooking the mass of Conduits below eagerly shifting in their seats, waiting for the Opening Ceremonyto begin. The noise of the arena was surprisingly minimal considering how many people were attending. But I supposed that was because Conduits could hear exceptionally well and didn't need to shout at each other. In the center of the coliseum was a large circular stage with a single podium.

"Who's that for?" I asked Elias.

"I am not certain, but I would postulate that is where the Master of Ceremonies will stand as the Champions are announced."

"Who is the Master of Ceremonies?"

"I am afraid I do not know. The Katuan Stones selected them, just as they have the Directorate and the Champions."

"How will we know who they are?" No sooner did I ask the question than the arena itself began to shake beneath our feet. Not violently, like an earthquake—more like a drumroll. My attention went to the podium. A figure began to manifest, fuzzy at first and then unfortunately clearer. I slumped back in my chair, disappointed. "It's Realto."

Elias put his hand on my cheek. "I know seeing him must be a painful reminder, but you are not the sum of your parents or their crimes."

"I know. I just..." But before I could say more, Realto's voice reverberated off the walls and I forced myself to change my attitude. It wasn't his fault, and I wouldn't let my evil incestual father ruin this for me or for Elias, because I knew if I let this bother me, it would bother him. I whispered, "I'm fine."

Then we both focused on the flamboyant Master of Ceremonies. His voice was proud, loud and electrifying. He wore a bright red leather bodysuit. It clung to him like plastic wrap, so tight it could've been translucent. His hair was pulled into a long pony tail that sat on the top of his head, making it flip around everywhere as he spoke.

"Good morning y'all! My friends, my people, I've been chosen to perform the rites of the Master of Ceremonies. It's my honor to bid the will of the Katuan Stones and begin the Opening Ceremonyof Katua."

The arena roared with enthusiasm. It was infectious. Elias and I both stood to cheer in applause as well.

Realto continued. "The Katuan Stones appraised each of you as you entered the grounds of this sacred place, The Cathedral."

Again cheers exalted from the arena. We returned to our seats while still clapping.

"As you have all been measured, many of you have been found worthy of honor, yet few of you will be convoked to participate in the Trials." Realto stiffened, and you could tell something was being conveyed through him. A light circled him and then grew into a massive projection, similar to the one he had showed me of my mother and father. I shivered slightly at the memory, but stuffed it down. I knew now why the Stones had chosen him. The light narrowed into pixelated images. It was a parade of Conduits moving through the Katuan Arch, and I thought I saw a flash of my own face, the day I saw the Stones for the first time. I looked over at Elias to see if he saw it too. I couldn't tell, but I felt guilty having not ever told him I'd touched the Stones.

I leaned over. He leaned into me. "There is something I should tell you, although it's probably silly." He looked at me curiously.

"Nothing you could say would be silly." His eyes returned to the flash of faces, familiar and otherwise.

"That day Su brought the Stones up…"

Realto's voice interrupted me. "The Champions are chosen. Are y'all ready to meet your Champions?"

The mass of Conduits got to their feet, screaming, clapping and jumping. It was like nothing I'd ever seen before, more exciting than any live sporting event I'd ever attended. Elias grinned at me and stood himself. I followed, relishing his excitement just as much as my own.

"Six teams, thirteen Champions per team, each Champion representing a faction. The Ramalans!" Hundreds of shouts grew above the rest and I realized these were the Ramalans of the crowd. Man, did Realto know how to incite the masses. "The Varons!" One by one, he called the name of each faction, and each group tried to be louder than the one before. "The Elementals, the Tahwils, the Circuitis, the Adfecors, the Bustanys, the Incantors, the Corporis, the Taqas, the Animos!" Then he paused for effect. "The Ancients!" The assembly went silent as the gigantic Ancients moved from out of the shadows of the archways that led to the arena. One by one, all twenty-one Ancients emerged and threw off their cloaks. A silent moment that seemed to last forever passed through the crowd, and then it was pandemonium. The arena shook, but this time it was from the stomping feet of its spectators now overwhelmed with excitement. Each Ancient bowed and clapped, which I assumed was their form of celebration. Elias took my hand in his, jumping and cheering, and then, without thinking, he kissed me and I kissed him back, drunk on the moment. We kissed heavily and hard, until we needed to either come up for air or rip each other's clothes off right then and there. I felt tingles everywhere, and had he invited me to, I would've left all of that elation for a few moments of pleasure with him—damn the prophecy. But he pulled away, as he always did.

"I am so sorry," he said through labored breathes. "I got carried away."

"Me too." I wiped at the sweat that had already built on my chest, from just that moment of titillation. "Don't apologize. Let's just get back to the show." I said it playfully and returned my attention to the stage.

"Team Quitsee, rise when you see your face," Realto roared over the noise, and immediately everyone got silent once more.

One by one, faces illuminated the projection in front of us. I didn't recognize most of them, but when a handsome black man's face with a charismatic smile appeared, I asked Elias, "Is that Martin Luther King Jr.?"

"Yes. He is an Adfector." Elias then pointed at the next face that appeared. "And that, that is Stalt."

He waited for the recognition to light up my face. "The Stalt? The Vulcan?" I said through a laugh.

"The one and only." We both muffled our laughs.

"Team Finesol, rise when you see your face."

This time I knew two of the faces, Inca and Winston. I cheered wildly for them.

"Team Klison, rise when you see your face."

Di, Ying and a man I was pretty sure was Al Capone were part of the Klison team.

"Team Panjoin, rise when you see your face."

Aremis was chosen to be on Panjoin, and another familiar face flashed before me. I looked at Elias when we saw it. "Is that Abigail?" I remembered the young woman's face from the photograph I'd seen in Hafiza. I thought she'd been my grandmother Lilith but was sadly mistaken. Her story was one I couldn't forget, and now I knew it was similar to my mother's and grandmother's tragic tales.

"It certainly looks like her," Elias agreed.

"Team Opaly, rise when you see your face."

Vosega's face beamed above us, then Sparkle's and Nara's, and even another familiar face that I vaguely remembered from Hafiza.

Elias said her name was Renata. But it was the last face that startled us both.

It was mine.

PART III

ELIAS

*T*ime slowed down. No, it stopped. I could not comprehend what I was seeing for a long moment. Eyes from below darted to find her, to find us, to see our reactions. Ophelia's expression displayed her shock. I imagine it mirrored my own.

I pulled her down, out of view. Realto went on, "Team MisaKa, rise when you see your face."

"What were you going to say earlier? About the day Susuda retrieved the Stones?" My eyes were searching hers, looking for answers I knew she could not understand.

"I… I touched them. Before you said not to, I had already touched them." Her voice was quiet, absent of emotion.

I sat back onto the floor and leaned against the wall. My thoughts were jumbled, jumping from one scenario to another, berating me for not warning her sooner, for not giving better direction to Su. I knew not to touch the Stones. I did not entirely understand why, but I knew. *Why had I not informed Ophelia sooner? How could I be so stupid?* I threw my head against the wall behind me.

Ophelia sat down in front of me and put her hand to my chest. "Stop. We can fix this. We'll just substitute someone else. Obviously the Pai Ona feel honored to be chosen."

The applause was still erupting all around us as the final faces of the final team were displayed.

I shook my head. "It is not that simple, Ophelia." I took her hand in mine. "When you touched the Stones, you were weighed against everyone else who walked through the Katuan Arch. It's a contract. By choosing to familiarize yourself with the Stones you agree to participate in the Katuan Trials in whatever station you are assigned. It is not negotiable. To negate your participation is to negate the contract. The Trials would end before they ever began. The summit would be over. This would all be for naught."

I looked up at the elaborate domed ceiling above our heads, the manifestation of the grand arena orchestrated by the collaboration of the Katuan Stones and The Cathedral. It would all be for nothing. I would not put her life at risk for these Trials. I could not allow her to be looked upon by inquiring eyes. She would be seen for what she was —different, extraordinary. Sulu.

I did not look at her as I got to my feet. Realto was now announcing the members of the Directorate. "You will not be in harm's way," was all I could say before I stepped out of the confines of the balcony. I would find Susuda. We would convene the Directorate and we would cancel the Trials.

OPHELIA

The Opening Ceremonyhad concluded, but I couldn't say who was on the Directorate or the last team. I was in a daze —shock, really. I stumbled out of the balcony shortly after I heard the final applause. My thoughts were bouncing around my head like a throng of ping-pong balls. I couldn't sort out what I was feeling; my head wouldn't quiet enough for that. As I walked down the stairs and Conduits emerged from the arena, I got pats on the back, words of encouragement and some very strange looks. A small clique at the bottom of the stairs leading into the banquet hall, where the next event took place, was exceptionally pointed with their stares. Three of them, all people I'd never met, bore holes into my body with their eyes. I recognized their faces, though. They had been selected as Champions as well. One of them was a young woman with long, silver-white hair that fell to the middle of her back. Her features were sharp, angular and attractive. Beside her stood a man with no hair. I couldn't tell if he had shaved his head or if it was naturally that bald. Behind them both stood a much taller woman, Amazonian-sized. She towered over the two of them. She had dark features and deep-set eyes. In the shadow of her brow, her eyes sparkled gold with a ring of red.

I looked away when I got closer, but I heard the tall one snarkily assert to the others, "Now the Trials will be over and the entire Kraus cause will die with them. All because she couldn't keep to herself, as an Unconsu should."

My skin got hot. *She didn't even know me.*

I had to get some air or a drink. I put my hand on the threshold as I walked through and evaporated into the galley, and then let out a big sigh of relief when I realized no one was down here. I bee-lined it to the first case of wine I saw and cracked open a bottle of cabernet. I poured a big glass and perched myself up on a barstool beside the island where we ate breakfast.

Two more deep breaths and half a glass of wine later, and my brain started to slow down. I could think. But no sooner did I formulate my first solid thought than the hissing erupted in my ears.

"Goddamit! Who is that?! Who is there?" I shouted to the empty room. I stormed out of the galley, my wine glass in hand, stomping all the way down the dark passage the hiss had led me to before. "Who is there? Come out, you fucking coward!"

I stood there in the dark, the hiss still ringing in my ears. But no one manifested in the dark with me. It was just damp and cold. After several minutes I walked back to the familiarity of the galley. The hiss slowly grew quieter until I was in silence again. Until Susuda appeared.

"Miss Olly!" He ran to my side. "Do not fret, Mr. Elias is taking care of this. The Trials will not go on. You are in no danger." Su put his arms around me.

The Trials would not go on because of me? Because I was an idiot and touched the Stones? No way! This was my bed; I had to lie in it. The summit was our last hope of uniting the Pai Ona. I'd be damned if my curious fingers were going to put a stop to that. It became clear—I'd participate in these Trials. I wouldn't shatter all of Elias' hard work because I was an idiot. I wouldn't jeopardize the future of my people for my own safety. None of us was safe while this war continued. The show must go on. The summit must take place, no matter the cost.

I reached out to Almus with my Rune. "Will you stand with me?"

I waited patiently for his reply and turned to Su.

"Take me to him," I demanded. I put my glass of wine down. "Now, Su."

ELIAS

"I won't allow it!" I thundered as I slammed my fist down on the table.

Di was by my side. "To refute the Katuan Stones' decision is to forfeit the Trials completely."

Winston stood up. "She is mortal, and although the games are not fatal to a Consu, she could die."

"We have healers on hand. We can keep her safe," Confucius argued.

"There is nothing a healer can do if she is mortally wounded, like beheaded, incinerated, and the hundreds of other ways Conduits can damage each other," I said sternly. "I will not risk her life for this."

"Then you forfeit the games and the summit." Di looked past me when she spoke, not wanting to make eye contact.

"So be it." I moved toward the door. "I will make the announcement."

Almus stood. "Ophelia would like to speak."

I looked at him skeptically. I knew what she would say. I did not need to hear it. I would not entertain it. "This is not up for debate."

Almus ignored me and walked to the door, where Ophelia stood, waiting patiently on the other side. I saw it in her shoulders, felt it in her body language—she would argue my ruling. She would sacrifice her safety for this damn summit.

"May I speak?" She asked the question more out of formality than anything. To appear complacent when we both knew she was anything but. She was her own woman, and she would do what she felt was right, what she felt was for the greater good. I took a deep breath and let it out slowly. I followed behind her as she made her way to the head of the conference table.

She looked at me for a brief instant, her eyes trying to convey something I did not understand. Then she addressed the room. "I don't know why the Katuan Stones chose me, but it is done. I honor the traditions of our people, many of which I don't understand or have yet to learn about. I know the importance of traditions and their place in a community. I won't be the one to deface this sacred ritual. I'll participate in the Trials, no matter the consequences." She said the last part through gritted teeth. "This isn't a decision to be made by a committee. It's my choice, and mine alone."

Ophelia made eye contact with everyone in the room, waiting to see who would object to her declaration. No one said a word, not even those who had sided with me only moments ago.

"Very well. Now that that's settled, let the games begin." The last remark was meant to be cheeky but it made my skin explode with goose pimples. I knew better than to contest her publicly. She turned to leave and I followed. The moment we were out of earshot, I put my hand on hers and my other to the wall, transporting us to my chamber.

"You do not know what you are agreeing to." I was going to let her see all of my fear. It would do me no good to hide it. She needed to know. I fell to my knees. "I am begging you to revoke the declaration. No one would blame you."

Ophelia looked at me, her eyes going soft, and she got to her knees beside me. "Don't worry about me, Elias. I can do this. I'm not just some weak little Unconsu girl."

I took her hands in mine. "I know. It is not about your capabilities, it is about your vulnerabilities. Your mortality, a thing we can do nothing to change."

Something flashed in her face. "But we can. You heard what Di said. Consummation had nothing to do with the Sulus' strange disappearances." She leaned in closer and kissed me passionately, her tongue moving intuitively inside my mouth, before pulling away and tracing my earlobe. It took everything I had to pull her away.

"I know what Ganesha said, but that is different from the prophecy. The prophecy is what restrains me," I said breathily.

Ophelia's face changed from anticipation to disappointment. She sat back on her heels. "Well, I've made my choice. The only choice you have is whether or not to consummate with me. If you feel, as you say you do, that it's still too risky, then there is nothing else to say or do."

"It is not that simple."

"Isn't it?" She looked into my eyes. "Destinies can change. I know they can. But you have to decide you're going to design something different for yourself." She took my hands back up into hers. "We can design something different."

I shook my head solemnly. "There is too much at stake to guess."

"There is too much at stake not to try and change it." She got to her feet. "I'm participating in the games. I don't care what you say." Then she put her hand on the threshold of the door and she was gone.

OPHELIA

*Y*esterday was a whirlwind. After the Opening Ceremonyand banquet, I had hoped to discuss more with Elias, to make sure we were okay. But he was busy. I suspected that the errands he had to attend to had something to do with my being in the Trials. It was safe to say it threw a wrench in the works. So I refocused on basic, silly things like sleep, food and survival. I didn't know exactly what I'd signed up for, but having an Unconsu participating in the Trials had to change a few things… or at least I hoped it did. Su came to my room last night with a message from Elias. The note said he would be here in the morning to walk me to the Opaly training course.

So here I was, waiting not so patiently for Elias to arrive. I sat on the couch, my leg nervously shaking. When I heard someone outside the door, before they knocked, I opened it. To my surprise, it wasn't Elias. It was Winston.

He handed me a tray of food. "Have you eaten?"

I took the tray as Winston walked past me into my apartment. "I'm not sure I can."

"Try." He took a seat on the couch, where I'd been sitting.

I lifted the lid from the plate of food and saw he had brought me oatmeal and fresh fruit. I had to smile at Winston. This was thoughtful, not a characteristic I necessarily gave him enough credit for. I took my seat beside him and picked at the fruit.

"Eat the oatmeal," he prompted. I looked at him sideways, because the way he said it made me feel like there was more to the request.

Still uncertain of what was in the oatmeal, but sure whatever it was, it was Winston's way of looking out for me, I took a bite. *It tasted like regular oatmeal.*

"You are brave. You have changed since the fall of Hafiza. Some of it is good, some of it is sad."

Without realizing it, I stopped chewing. I was bewildered by this outburst of compassion. It wasn't like Winston to be so talkative, much less empathetic. I looked at him as he continued.

"Lucia and I almost died on our way here. Esther captured us." He put his hand up before I could say something. "We are here now." Winston positioned himself to face me. "The war is coming. Your choice to face your fear will change the world." He leaned in for his final admission. "Nothing will happen to you during the Trials." He looked at the oatmeal. "You have many allies." He glanced at the oatmeal once more and winked.

With that, he stood and promptly left my apartment.

I stared down at the oatmeal. What could he have put in there to make me invincible, I wondered. *How long did this invincibility last?* My thoughts were interrupted by a knock.

"Come in."

This time is was Elias, and he looked terrible, like he hadn't slept in days.

"Are you ready?" He glanced at me skeptically and I had to check my ego, because I wanted to sound more assured than I really was.

"As ready as I'll ever be. Let me finish the oatmeal Winston was kind enough to bring me."

"Indeed."

"Anything you can tell me about today?" I asked between bites.

"Only what little I know." Elias paced in front of me, perhaps the most distraught I'd seen him yet. "Today you meet with your Opaly team, your Katan. From what I have gathered, the Trials are different every Katua, and we will not learn the specifications for each Trial until immediately before they proceed. However, it is understood that every member of the team must participate in some way during each challenge. So today is an opportunity to learn how each of your gifts works. But Ophelia, I must caution you…"

I put my hand up to stop him. "I know, don't let anyone in on my abnormalities."

His shoulders slackened from around his ears ever so slightly.

"Your Katan will keep you safe, I have been assured of that. And if they do not, many other Conduits who will be in the arena will ensure your safety. That being said, I want to be plain here. This is extremely dangerous. The other Champions are lethal, with a variety of gifts at their disposal." He got to his knees in front of me and took the tray away as I swallowed my last bite. "I know you are doing this for me, for my cause. I have pulled whatever strings I can, called in whatever favors I could, but there are still Conduits among us who cannot be trusted—or worse, hold a grudge against my family and would gladly see this all fail. So I do not wish to give you a sense of false security." He lay his head on my knees. "Trust those you can, and fear those who give you reason. A simple accident could hurt you, but intentional malice will kill you."

I put my hands on his head. "I'm doing this because I believe in what you and your father want to achieve. Because I don't want to lose any more friends, and the success of this summit and the bidding is the only thing that can give us a chance at that. I'm doing this for me."

That last statement drew his eyes up to meet mine.

"I'm part of this world. My fate is intertwined with the annihilation of our kind. I want to prove to myself that I'm good, that I fight for the right side." He started to interrupt but I put my index finger to his mouth. "If I can compete with giants, gods—these people, everyone here can fight for what they know is right."

He nodded thoughtfully, and slowly got to his feet. Then he put his hand out and lifted me to mine. "Shall we, Miss Banner?"

It sounded silly coming from him, but I hooked my arm in his and we gave each other one more serious glance before teleporting into the Opaly training room.

ELIAS

One of the arrangements I had made with the Directorate was that I would be allowed to oversee her practice with her team. It was encouraging to know she already had five known allies within her company. Vosega, who would guard her with his life. Aruna, who had already expressed an affinity for her, knowing what Ophelia meant to Ying. Nara had promised me she would do anything for the cause and to see the Nebas destroyed. Renata had spent time with us in Hafiza, and although Ophelia and she had not actually met, Lars, Renata's husband, had been Di's right-hand man. He had died in the siege of Hafiza, and Renata felt she should carry Lars' torch. Then there was Sparkle, a joyful Conduit Ophelia happened upon here, in The Cathedral. I did not know her well, but Ophelia spoke very highly of her.

That left seven other hearts Ophelia would need to win over. I had no doubt she would do it. I peered down into the training court. Perhaps a football field long and nearly that in width. It was vast, with plenty of space to practice any drills or demonstrate any talents. There were a few statues strewn about the space and I pondered their purpose. The farthest wall held a small arsenal—bows, swords and various axes and spears. The room was lit by a large circular skylight. Otherwise there were no other windows.

Shiva's huge frame towered over the rest of the group. He dwarfed Vosega, which was not an easy thing to do. I wondered who would take the lead. Shiva seemed like the obvious choice—he was far older than any of the other Conduits. His sheer size gave him presence, and he had years of experience being a leader. Twelve of the thirteen bodies were standing around, waiting on the last member to arrive. Borte hurried through the door at last. Of all the Conduits, it had to be Borte. I internally moaned. I wondered if anything was said about her tardiness. If someone did make a comment, it was brief, because it took no time at all for the introductions to begin.

OPHELIA

I was standing next to Sparkle when Borte arrived, and was instantly happy to have a friend by my side, because the look on Borte's face was piercing. She surveyed in my direction, then, when she seemed to realize who I was, her glance turned into a lethal glare. Vosega came up from behind and whispered in my ear. "Don't mind the old witch; she isn't partial towards me either. She was Yessica's stepmother. Abhorred Lucas, and didn't much care for her stepdaughter."

I tried to shake the stare, but it was disturbing. I leaned into Sparkle, hoping her gift could ease my discomfort.

A slight woman who had been casually leaning against the far wall addressed the group. "Hello. My name is Kassandra. I'm the Ramalan of our ragtag team of misfits. I think we should all begin with formal introductions. Let's start with you." She pointed at me. I instinctually stepped back.

"Me?" I put my hand to my chest then cleared my throat. "My name is Ophelia Banner. I'm not sure what else to say except that I'm unfortunately the short straw in this bunch. I'm an Unconsu." I shrugged.

Shiva met my gaze. He was trying to speak to me with his eyes but I wasn't catching his drift. Borte's shrill voice filled the quiet space.

"Shiva says he would not call you the short straw." I was back to being aware of her painful stare. She addressed everyone but never took her eyes from me. "I am Borte, wife of the Great Khan and translator of all languages, including body language." She looked to Shiva, who bowed in approval. "I am representing the Incantors of our team. Usually, I would say that my gift is best suited for diplomacy, but in this case I feel I give us a great advantage." She gestured to Shiva and then to Kassandra. "Considering that the Ancients require a translator, which I can do easily, and our Ramalan can only speak her visions through sign language. Isn't that correct, Kassandra?"

"It is, Borte. I can only depict my visions through sign language, the dear curse of crazy Kassandra." She bowed in Borte's direction. "A pleasure to meet you and have your assistance."

Sparkle chimed in, "My name is Sparkle Bantee. I'm an Adfector. I spread joy. Useful for creating cohesion on a team." My girl Sparkle gave Borte the closest thing to a nasty look that she could conjure.

Renata, the beautiful face I recognized from the projection as having been at Hafiza, stepped forward next. She had shoulder-length brown hair. Nothing remarkable about that, but her face was exotic. I'd seen my share of ethnicities, and knew when I was looking at a beautiful blend of backgrounds. That was Renata. Her heritage wasn't discernible, which made her even more mysterious and attractive. "IIIIIIIII..." she hit a high-pitch stabbing note, "...am Renata." She ended her name with a deep low tone. "I'm a Timbress and I represent your Taqa faction. I manipulate noise. I can create a variety or deafening noises or mute a room." She stepped back and folded her arms across her chest.

Vosega was shirtless, of course. He moved out from behind me. "I am Vosega, Vulcan, Earth Elemental and eager to succeed in the Trials." That got a round of smiles. He turned to Shiva. "What do you do, besides being very large?"

Shiva's smile turned wicked. He looked at a statue that stood across the room. I couldn't see what it was from here. I thought it was a man atop a mountain. I didn't have a very long time to examine it because it exploded into a million tiny pieces in front of my eyes. I was grateful we were far away from the plume of dust that erupted in its place.

Borte sounded bored. "He is Shiva, the destroyer. He breaks bonds —between atoms, people, things."

"Well, that will be useful during the Destruction Trial." Vosega tipped his head in Shiva's direction.

A gust of wind swept past my hair. It swirled and turned where the statue once stood. Now in its place was a playful dance of dust and wind, creating pretty patterns in the air. Nara put her hand on my shoulder as she moved in front of the group. "I am Nara. I am your Circuitu. Some think of me as an Elemental, but the Stones decided that I manipulate weather, not only the wind." The dust began to spiral, a fierce wind picked up in the room, and for the first time in my life I saw a tornado. Then it just disappeared as though nothing had happened.

A white-haired man walked over to the pile of dust. He swept more of the statue's remains into a small mound then dropped something from his pocket into the center of the dirt. As he backed away slowly, a sprout began to shoot up from the pile. First it shot up then began to crawl toward us like fast-moving vines, and when it reached my feet I realized that was exactly what it was. "My name is Friedrick Olmsted. I'm a Bustany, at your service. I create plants from seeds and nurture their swift growth."

There were only four introductions left to make, and I knew who one of them was. Aruna moved into the center of the room. We instinctively moved around her. "My name is Aruna. I'm your Varon. She began to whisper in the air, words too quiet for me to hear. Everyone else could probably make them out with their super-hearing. She raised her arms to the sky. The gesture brought my attention to the skylight I hadn't noticed before. A shadow filled the span of the hole, with several dotted shadows around it. I couldn't make out what they were until they were only a few feet away. They moved so quickly, effortlessly, in the air. Huge wings gently came to a stop as the most enormous bird I'd ever seen stood at attention in front of Aruna.

"I speak with birds." She reached up and stroked the enormous bird's beak. I didn't know my birds well but it looked like an eagle. "This is Nince. He is a thunderbird. Only one of fifteen left in the world. These are his cousins." Instantly, a flurry of swallows landed all over Aruna, on her head, her outstretched arms and shoulders. She giggled as though they were tickling her. Then she threw her arms up once more and Nince and all of the other birds began to take flight. Just as quickly as they had arrived, they were gone. I must've looked as flabbergasted as I felt because Aruna walked over to me and put her hand on my cheek. "I will better acquaint you with Nince another time. He liked you."

"He liked me?" I whispered back, but she was gone, already returned to where she was standing before her introduction.

"Am I supposed to top that? Because it ain't happening," a gruff male voice said to my left. "I'm Tete. Take a wild fucking guess what I am." Then, where Tete had just stood, was a fearsome gargoyle. I wondered if he'd morphed into a statue, but then he blinked and the look of it was alarming. Animated stone was the stuff of anyone's nightmares. His oversized mouth opened to expose monstrous teeth.

"Well, this is just too good to be true," a sassy female voice said as she walked in front of me to face Tete's gargoyle form dead-on. I waited for something to happen, but nothing did. She moved and I saw that Tete was standing there frozen, his terrifying gargoyle face unmoved. With the stillness I noticed every feature, his large teeth, thick single furrow above his eyes. He had wings. They were folded, but even folded they looked enormous.

"Is he made of stone?" I leaned over and asked Sparkle.

"He is, but I didn't turn him into a statue. He did that himself." The female returned to stand in front of me, she was wearing sunglasses. "My name is Medusa." She stuck her hand out to shake mine. I noticed her leather gloves. "He's just frozen. I can undo it at any time by looking back into his eyes." Medusa worked her way down the line, making formal introductions with each of us. "I'm the team Corpori.

Now let's set Tete straight." She put her finger to her lips. "But shhhh, don't tell him. He'll have no idea." Medusa turned back to Tete, and instantly he reanimated.

Medusa took off her gloves to greet Tete and stuck her hand out to him. "Hi, Tete. I'm Medusa."

Even in his gargoyle form, you could see his confusion. Nonetheless, he took her hand and shook it courteously before morphing back to his male form. But when he morphed back, he had no clothes on. My cheeks burned bright red when I found myself face to face with an entirely different view.

"He's cute." Sparkle tittered and Tete winked at her as he walked out of the center of the room. *She was right, he was attractive.* He must have been twenty when he consummated. His thick black hair, muscular build and tattoos suggested he was a Pacific Islander.

Kassandra took another eyeful before turning her attention to our teammate, a tall, skinny man with blond hair and gray-green eyes. He wore long, silky silver robes and black gloves. "And you? Who are you?"

"I'm Klaas Vaak, your Animo." I only realized he had his hand in a small pouch when he removed it and waved it in the air. I thought I saw a shimmer of glitter fly from his palm, then everything went dark.

I was in the cave, the cave that had been haunting my dreams since the night Hafiza fell. My chest got tight. This wasn't a dream, *unless this was all a dream.* Panic choked my throat. Then it was gone. The light was back. Klaas stood in front of us, his demeanor unchanged. I looked to my right. Friedrick's face mirrored my terror, and to my left Sparkle's jovial features were contorted and strained.

"My friends call me Sand Man," Klaas said.

"Keep that creepy parlor trick for the opposition, asshole," naked Tete growled.

Kassandra wiped the sweat from her forehead and regained her composure. "Alright, boys. Klaas, um, Sand Man was just sharing his talents just the same as the rest of us. What are those, exactly?"

"My dust hurtles you into your deepest and darkest nightmare. I put my adversaries to sleep."

"I think we all got a good enough taste of that gift, wouldn't you agree, guys?"

Kassandra looked at everyone and I almost laughed when I saw the uncomfortable look on Shiva's face. He seemed too big to be scared of nightmares. Then it occurred to me. "You didn't really show us yours," I observed aloud.

Kassandra looked at me keenly. "Touché." With that, she placed her hand on my shoulder, closed her eyes and her body began to convulse. When her eyes reopened, there was nothing but white in her orbits. It appeared she was having a seizure. Kassandra fell to the ground. After a while she stopped moving and stood as though nothing had happened, and brushed herself off. Her hands started gesturing wildly.

Borte started rambling off what she was hearing or seeing, however things were translated to her. "You cannot hide who you are. The prophecy foretold your weakness. You will choose, and many will die. When you drew the circle, you drew our fates. Only one can stop you."

Everyone was silent. Everyone was staring at me.

Kassandra reached for me again, and this time I flinched. "Hey, hey, I'm not going to hurt you. They don't call me crazy Kassandra for nothing." She laughed, and the climate in the room lightened. "Let's practice some drills."

Everyone started to move toward the center of the room. I heard Kassandra, just barely. "Beware of the trio."

I turned to see her smiling and shrugging at me.

The trio?

ESTHER

"*L*ucifer, I need you to make yourself useful." Lucifer appeared before me. His cologne was salty. I didn't like it at all. "Besides showering off that disgusting stench you are wearing, I need you to track down H.H. Holmes for me. I need his interrogation tactics. Mine are falling on deaf ears."

"Mistress, I can do that. Do you know his last whereabouts?"

"If I did, I would not ask you to track him down." I leaned into Lucifer's muscular frame, and although he was a foot taller than me, he leaned back. "Follow the blood trail. He will be found somewhere under a pile of mutilated bodies, like he always is."

"Of course, Mistress." He backed up. "I will not disappoint you."

"No, Lucifer, you will not," I agreed as he quickly left me alone in the room with my defiant captive, Filbert. I turned my attention to him. "Certainly you have heard of Holmes' work, Filbert. He is exceptional, really. I would keep him around, on hand, if he didn't have such a thirst for blood. It is hard to keep him from making a mess." I took Filbert by the shoulders from behind. "His preferred mutilation technique involves the pear of anguish and these disgusting beetles. He names them—can you imagine?"

Filbert did not flinch. I had to admire his resolve. "If you were willing to explain that hidden little gem in your psyche, I could call him off—he would never need to come to the compound." I touched his scalp with my fingertips and dug my nails in. His body jerked as I assumed control. There it was, a mysterious box hidden in plain sight. I just didn't have the combination to open it.

I released his body. Waves of rage began to erode my mood. "I'm getting bored, Filbert." I flicked his ear. "I hate being bored. We have been at this for almost a week."

For the first time since we'd chained him up, he initiated eye contact.

"Almost a week? Six days and twenty-two hours, four minutes and six seconds." His French accent was thick, and it made me laugh.

"You've been paying attention, after all?" I laughed again.

His eyes flicked to the door. I listened, realizing he was waiting for something. I heard nothing. My eyes got wide. *I heard nothing.* Filbert was staring at me, taunting me with his gaze. Lucifer was gone, the only Conduit who could thwart Mikkel's powers.

"Akiva!" I screamed. The door flung open. Mikkel stepped in. Everything started to move exhaustively slow. Everything but Mikkel — he moved effortlessly through the time warp he'd created.

"We should kill her," Filbert suggested as Mikkel untied him.

"We should, but we will need help. She has over two hundred mercenaries on the grounds." Mikkel hoisted his brother over his shoulder. "I entered the compound the moment Lucifer left. If he returns, he will disrupt the time warp. I must get you to safety."

"Let us cut off the head of the snake," Filbert insisted.

Mikkel paused, considering his request. "Brother, we haven't the time to watch her burn."

"Very well, then I leave you with this. See if my gift does not make you writhe now, you disgusting cunt." Filbert gently blew in my face and I was surrounded by familiar scents. The scents of my Yanni, mixed with burning flesh and death.

OPHELIA

*B*orte leered at me. I didn't know what I'd done to offend this woman, but boy, did she seem to have it out for me. Maybe it was because I cared for Lucas, while she, on the other hand, loathed him.

The others trickled out of the room in front of me. I ducked behind them, hoping to slip out without having to face Borte in that awkward way, when you get caught in close proximity to someone you'd rather avoid.

No such luck. It was the two of us funneling out side by side. Just when we hit the narrowest part of the exit, she reached over and grabbed my arm.

"I must speak to you in private, Miss Banner," she demanded. "Now." She pulled my arm in such a way that I felt like I was five years old again, getting in trouble with the yard duty during recess.

"Okay. Can you let go of me?" I yanked back my arm. "You've got some grip."

Borte didn't say a word. She just kept walking until she felt we were at a suitable distance from prying ears.

"You have something I must translate." She put her hand out like I was going to give her something right then and there.

207

"I do?" I looked at her, puzzled.

"You do. I must see it," she demanded.

"I'm afraid I don't know what you're talking about, Borte." I patted my clothes to show her I wasn't hiding anything.

"It may not be on your person. But you have it. I can smell it," she accused.

"I have no idea what that means, and I think I'm offended," I responded indignantly. "Besides, if I did have some strange document, why would I need to share it with you? Maybe I want to keep it private."

She scoffed. "It isn't considered private if you are too stupid to translate it."

"You're a very rude woman." It was all that I could think to say. I'd only met her a couple of days ago and she'd managed to insult me twice, not to mention the evil death stares I've been getting all day.

"Your Atoa has my husband locked up, awaiting some formal argument. How am I a rude woman?" she contended. "You prance around here pretending this is all okay."

"First off, I have nothing to do with the arguments or the accused." I really had no idea what she was talking about. "And secondly, if I had some remote language I needed transcribed, you'd be the last person I'd come to." With that, I turned around and hustled my way down the hall, out of sight, then transported myself straight to the wine cellar beside the galley to grab a good wine.

I was leaning up against a barrel, still mulling over that strange interaction with Borte, when Elias appeared in the doorway.

"Were the drills that terrible?" I didn't say anything. "I suppose it is never too early for a good glass of wine. What did you choose?" He walked over to see the bottle in my hand. "Oh, a 2002 Rombauer. What a refined palate you have, Miss Banner," he teased.

"Is it a good one? I was distracted when I grabbed it." I examined the label as I spoke. "I think I should stick on the side of two-buck chuck right now."

Elias laughed. His smile instantly made me feel better. "Well, you may be hard pressed to find a Charles Shaw in The Cathedral's cellars, but let us take a look, shall we?" He took the Rombauer as we entered the cave room lined with bottles of wine from around the world. Elias replaced the bottle I had and began inspecting what else was on the shelves. "What has you drinking at three today? Anything I can help with that drowning in a bottle could not rectify?" he said playfully as he looked over his shoulder at me. I got tingles in my lower abdomen. They raced up my spine and gave me goose bumps on the back of my neck. He was so damn sexy, and there wasn't a single thing I could do about it. It just made me want to drink more.

I sighed. "No, nothing you can do a darn thing about." I said it, but realized that maybe that was wrong. "Are you keeping prisoners here? Awaiting formal arguments?"

That got his attention. "Who told you that?" He looked at me sharply.

"You are, aren't you?" I accused.

"I am not holding anyone captive. The Cathedral is," he admitted. Then he continued to peruse the wine selection.

"What do you mean, The Cathedral is?"

"Exactly that. We sent the invitations to prevent any imposter Nebas from attending the summit. The Cathedral has her own wards that alarm when she suspects nefarious motives. She arrested three Conduits upon their arrival. Thus, we are now faced with the tedious task of determining where they are. I had not intended this, I assure you," Elias said, exasperated. "It creates dissention in the summit and uneasiness about our security. I wish The Cathedral would have approached me first, before taking her own measures. But it is done, and we need to handle it as diplomatically as possible."

"Borte thinks you have Genghis."

"I know she does. I have spoken to her several times about it. I explained the situation as best I could to her. But she is convinced that this is my doing and that I have detained Genghis to be tried during the arguments in front of Aurora."

"Has Aurora arrived?"

"No." Elias stopped at a particular bottle and withdrew it from the shelf. "This bottle should suffice. May I join you? I think I need a drink now."

I nodded, then continued with my inquiry. "Why didn't you tell me this before?"

"When you were chosen as a Champion, things got complicated and I have been a bit preoccupied." I knew it was true. "I did not mean to keep it from you."

"Okay, I believe that." I grabbed two glasses from the hanging rack and a wine opener.

"Allow me." He took the wine opener and began peeling the foil around the top of the bottle as he spoke. "The judge should be Aurora, but she has yet to arrive. I know not what keeps her, and yes, it concerns me, especially after Nara and Winston's ordeals."

I hoisted myself up on a barrel and sat with my legs dangling. Yep, he deserved a drink.

"Is there something I can do?"

Elias poured each of us a heavy pour and handed me a glass. "I am afraid there is nothing any of us can do at present. Wait it out and hope for the best."

"What do you think happened?" I asked.

"Best case scenario, Aurora is being very careful and taking her time getting here. Worst case scenario, she was ambushed and killed when she came out of hiding." He took a seat across from me on another barrel. "The most likely scenario is that she is too afraid to come out of her safe haven at all, and therefore will forgo the summit entirely. Which is the worst case for our cause, because it shows lack of faith from the Oracle, who sees futures."

"I was referring to the Khan. What do you think The Cathedral did with him?"

"Oh, right." Elias expelled a loud sigh. "Su and I have discussed it in great detail. Wherever The Cathedral is keeping her captives, they are below this level. Su's experience with The Cathedral allows him to access some of the deeper chambers with her consent, but he cannot locate anyone or travel freely below this floor. He suspects she is detaining them below us."

"For the arguments?"

"No, likely not. I haven't the faintest idea what she intends to do with them, or her purpose behind the abductions. She shares a language with Su, and she refuses to elucidate her intentions with him. He assures me that she would never harm anyone, but then again, this has never happened."

"Who else did she take?"

"Besides Genghis, George Thracian and Cadmus."

"Do you have reason to believe they aren't upstanding guys?"

"Genghis has been known to turn a blind eye to things. He certainly is not what I would consider upstanding. But the other two, they have impeccable reputations."

I took a sip of my wine. "So you have three crazy wives chasing you, wondering where their husbands are, and a missing Oracle who is key to the success of the summit and the bidding?"

"When you put it that way, it dwarfs some of the successes we have seen thus far."

"Then let's only acknowledge the successes." I raised my glass. "How about the look on everyone's faces when the Ancients appeared, prepared to participate in the Trials? And I didn't die today during drills!"

"Cheers!" Elias smiled at me as he raised his glass. "To our triumphs."

ELIAS

 $\mathcal{I}$ escorted Ophelia back to her room after we polished off the bottle of wine in the wine cellar. I told her I would be back to accompany her to the Champions' Ball later that evening. Tomorrow the first Trial, the Creation Trial, would take place. It all came up so quickly, three days of preparations could not have been enough to prepare Ophelia for what she was about to face.

When I got back to my apartment, I was surprised to see Realto waiting outside my door.

I approached slowly, preparing myself for whatever the Master of Ceremonies might ask of me.

"Viraclay. May I call you that?"

"Of course. How may I assist the Master of Ceremonies?"

"I'm not here as the Master of whatever. I'm here about my Atoa, Filbert."

I softened my demeanor, realizing this was strictly a personal visit. "Please come in."

We entered my apartment and took a seat at the dining room table.

"He hasn't arrived. He should've been here a week ago. We're like many of the other Soahcoit, we've adjusted to spending years apart. But he and his brother were fixin' to meet me here."

Tears began to stream down his face. "I know somethin' real bad has happened. I was going to leave, to go looking for them, but now I'm this Master of all get-out, and I don't know what to do."

I handed Realto a tissue.

"Where do you believe they are? Perhaps I can send someone to do reconnaissance at their last known whereabouts."

Through sniffles, Realto's face lit up. "Would you? Could you do that?"

He reached for my hand across the table.

"They're both good men. Useful allies. And I'd be forever in your debt."

"Well, I cannot promise we will find them, but if you give me locations to investigate I will send someone."

Realto's sniffles returned to sobs. He laid his head on the table and let it all out. I just sat there and listened, offering the occasional tissue and holding his shoulder to let him know I was listening.

When he was ready to leave, I saw him to the door and was disappointed to see Borte standing there when I opened it.

"I will be in touch, Realto," I called after him as I shut the door. Borte had already invited herself in.

"He was crying. Do you also have his partner imprisoned?" She did not sit. Instead, she stood with her arms crossed in the middle of the room.

"No, Borte, I do not, just as I do not have your Khan imprisoned." Exasperated, I sat on the sofa. "I have no fresh news."

"Are you even looking for him?" she demanded.

"The Cathedral is the most powerful Haven in the world. She acts on her own. I cannot say why she abducted your husband when he entered the gates. Perhaps if we knew why... what he did to offend her?"

The little woman growled at me. "Offend?! How could he offend a place he has never seen before?"

"I do not know."

"What if something were to happen to your Atoa? She is fallible, after all."

I got to my feet. "Are you threatening Ophelia?" I did my best to maintain my composure.

"No, I am threatening you!" she asserted then stomped to the door. "My husband is being held against his will. If I find out you are responsible for this, I will kill her." Borte slammed the door behind her.

OPHELIA

*T*here was a gentle tap at my door. I got up groggily from the couch. That bottle of wine I'd shared with Elias had laid me out. I answered the door.

In front of me stood a Conduit I'd never met before. He was large, easily taller than six feet, with dark chocolate skin and bright green eyes. He was sheepishly looking at something he had in his hand.

"Can I help you?"

"I hope I can help you." His voice was deep, soothing. "My name is Cline, and I think what you're doing is really brave, Miss Banner." His striking eyes met mine and shot tingles up into my scalp. "To put yourself in danger so that the Trials may continue is honorable."

"Thank you, Cline. I'm sure many others would've done the same."

He shook his head. "Most people wouldn't risk their own safety for a cause. I assure you."

I was going to argue with him, but I realized it made no difference. He was entitled to his opinion just as I was mine, and I liked to think most people were selfless. Cline continued. "I'm an Armorist. I create a variety of shields in the form of clothing." He lifted the piece he had in his hand. "I made you something. It won't be cheating, I promise you that."

The thought hadn't even occurred to me, but I was glad Cline had considered it. That was the last thing I needed to do, to be kicked out of the Trials and end the summit for cheating. I moved aside. "Come in. Tell me about this gift you've made me." I smiled at him. What a generous man.

Cline stepped into my apartment and looked around thoughtfully. His eyes stopped when they landed on a picture of me and Lucas on the mantel.

"You knew Lucas Healey?" I asked.

"He was a talented Shield. We never met, but we tend to hear about those with talents similar to our own."

I nodded. "He was a dear friend." I consciously made sure not to choke on my words as I spoke about him. I wanted to be able to talk about him without falling apart.

"I'm sorry for your loss." It came out awkward and forced. I wondered why that was. Cline seemed compassionate enough to be sincere. "May I?" Cline gestured to the small dining room table.

"Oh, of course." I moved the bowl of fruit to the countertop in the kitchen as Cline displayed his handiwork. It was an all-black body suit.

"I hope I got your dimensions right. I have a good eye for these things, but sometimes I miss the mark."

My cheeks flushed pink as I considered wearing this in front of six thousand Conduits. Cline noticed.

"I can fix it if it's too big." He clearly misunderstood my embarrassment. "It will tailor itself some, once you put it on."

Tailor itself? What did that mean? Was this thing alive? "Is it alive?" I stuttered.

"No, but it has an intelligence of its own. Think of it as A.I. technology. It's intuitive; it's supposed to be." Cline pointed at the seams. "These aren't just stitches. They have symbols sewn into them. Each symbol offers a different type of protection. This one," he ran his finger over the tiny stitch, "repels fire, and this one will prevent anything from penetrating the suit. I put seventy-three different protective symbols into the seams. You won't be able to be harmed by poisons, heat, impaling... Even certain Corpori and Animos will struggle to latch onto you."

My head started swimming as he listed all the different ways I could die. I knew the Trials were dangerous for an Unconsu, but I guessed I'd naively shut out what I was actually going to be facing. "Remind me, what can Corpori and Animos do?" I muttered.

"Oh, of course, I remember hearing that you were not raised knowing what you were, what we are. Pardon my assumptions. Corpori are Conduits who can manipulate the body, while many Animos can weave things into our minds. The armor will protect you from some of those gifts. I can't guarantee it will keep all of them at bay, because they come in such a wide variety that it's difficult to account for them all."

I took a deep breath, letting tomorrow's events truly sink in for the first time. My knees started to shake, I sat back down to steady them. I'd been so caught up in helping salvage the summit for Elias that I really didn't think about what I'd agreed to participate in.

"Are you okay, Miss Banner? You look like you might be ill."

I thought I might be ill. I had to snap out of this. *Remember, Olly, you aren't some normal Unconsu. You are a Sulu, an anomaly. You have gifts of your own and you can heal yourself. The beauty of this gift is that now you'll be able to use some of your extraordinary capabilities and you can attribute it to the armor. Cline just gave you a massive advantage in more ways than one.* The pep talk worked. I could feel the blood flooding back into my cheeks.

"I'm sorry, Cline. I guess I was a little in shock, if I'm being honest." I smiled at him, trying to assuage the anxiety I saw building in his brow. "I hadn't really listed the ways I could die in the arena tomorrow. I didn't let myself think about it, but I needed to. Thank you."

Cline sat down beside me. "I'm so sorry. It's the night before your battle and I show up to bring worry and fear. This was so thoughtless of me." He was wringing his hands. "Forgive me?"

"There is nothing to forgive. You've given me a tremendous gift. I can't thank you enough." I smiled again. "And you're sure it isn't cheating?"

"I asked the Directorate. It was agreed that this is an unprecedented event and that there are no restrictions on an Unconsu protecting themselves in the arena."

There were those words—unprecedented, Unconsu, arena. I shook off the unease that they gave me and hid the feelings in a box deep in my subconscious. Fear wouldn't serve me—not now, not tomorrow, not ever. I'd decided I would never let fear consume me again when I was crawling out of the tunnel that led me to safety the night Hafiza fell. This was no different from that. The danger had been real then and it is real now, but this situation would help prepare me for the battles to come. The Katuan Stones had chosen me for a reason.

"Should I try it on?"

Cline's face lit up. "Oh, please do. It would be an honor to see the fitting."

"I'm going to change in my room, Cline," I teased.

Blushing, he said, "Oh, of course. I didn't mean to imply that you would…"

I waved my hand to brush him off as I stood and headed down the hall. "I'm kidding. Give me a second to change."

I was in my room before Cline could say anything else. The material felt strange in my hands. It was like nothing I'd touched before. The best way to describe the texture was scaly. I put the bodysuit on the bed while I slipped off my clothes. I sat on the edge of the bed and pulled one pant leg on. The oddest sensation crept up my leg between the fabric and my skin. It was as though a billion little ants were marching up my body. It tickled and kind of burned at the same time.

I pulled the second leg on and the sensation intensified. In my mind, I was praying that the weird feelings stopped or I'd have to insult Cline by refusing to wear his armor. It would be too distracting to wear this in the arena. It was bad enough I was going to look like I was trying to be Cat Woman when I had this thing on. I quickly pulled the rest of the suit up. The moment it slipped over my shoulders, the prickling stopped. Relief washed over me. Then I frowned. There were no clasps or zippers to fasten the armor.

I walked over to my door to examine what I looked like in the mirror and stood there for a moment, admiring the black suit. It fit pretty well, considering Cline didn't have a single measurement of my body. Then, right before my eyes, the suit expanded and then retracted to fit perfectly over my skin. Heat washed over me, then melted away, as did the black fabric. It literally melted into my skin. I could no longer see where I began or the armor ended. Consequently, I was now stark naked and glad I'd taken a moment to look in the mirror before traipsing out there to show him.

Cline had some questions to answer now. I hurriedly put my clothes back on and looked in the mirror one last time. The hairsy charm was gone. I ran my finger over my wrist. I could feel the outline of the bracelet but not seeing it on my wrist made me nervous. It had become a security to me, a reminder of my Lucas. I wanted to pull it back out but couldn't find the seam of the suit that I'd somehow managed to squeeze it under. A strange rippling moved up my arm. The suit was doing something to the bracelet. They were interacting somehow. Panic. I was struck with panic. *Was I going to lose the hairsy charm to this armor?*

The rippling moved into my chest. I felt pressure over my heart. I was having a heart attack, I thought. But then the pressures eased and was replaced by an icy cool. The cold moved into my heart then through my bones. Then it simply disappeared. I rubbed over the hairsy charm on my wrist, but I couldn't feel it. My eyes welled with tears. I'd lost it. Somehow the armor had absorbed it. I wanted to crawl back onto my bed, curl up into a ball and cry.

A knock on my bedroom door reminded me that action was not a possibility right now. "Are you okay, Miss Banner?"

I swallowed the sobs and wiped at my eyes. "Yes. I'll be right out." One last look in the mirror—still dressed—and I opened the door.

Cline's face said it all. He was damn proud of his work. "It fits you beautifully."

"It does seem to fit. I have some questions, Cline." I moved toward the couch and he followed.

"Oh, of course."

"Does it come off?"

"Yes!" He reached toward my chest and I instinctively pulled back. "Pardon my touch, Miss Banner. I only intend to show you how to remove it." He placed his fingers on the top of my sternum. "Trace the seam that begins here, down to your navel. The armor will reappear in its original form, and you can slip it off. But there really is no need to, once it's on. It conforms to your skin. You can use the facilities, wear your clothes over it, even share in relations in the suit."

I frowned slightly. "But there wasn't a hole down there."

"The armor is now one with you. Every part of you, even your head."

"Okay." I understood what he was saying but I still had one major worry. "I had a bracelet on, and it slipped under the armor and now it's gone. Did the armor absorb it?"

"No, it wouldn't do that." Cline reached for where the cuff of the sleeve should be. He felt around but quickly concluded what I had—that it was gone. "That is strange. My armor has never done that before. What kind of bracelet was it?"

"Just a token I got from a friend." I wasn't going to tell Cline, a man I barely knew, about the hairsy charm, especially after Di's harsh reaction.

He nodded knowingly. He was aware I wasn't being entirely honest. "I'm sorry about the bracelet. You know, if it were a special bracelet, say with magical properties, it is likely the armor incorporated the magic into itself. It's built to conform to its host, including amplifying any magical gifts present to begin with."

I sat there, stunned, wondering whether Elias had agreed to let Cline create this armor for me and if he'd known all that it could do. A part of me still wished I had the familiar braid to play with, but the idea that whatever magic the hairsy charm held was now part of the essence of the armor was enough to ease the anxiety of feeling like I'd lost it completely. It was all silly anyway. Lucas was gone, and I'd never see the trail of his whereabouts that the charm left. Maybe this was a good thing, a way of helping me let go.

"Are you okay, Miss Banner? You look like you're far, far away."

"I'm good, Cline. This armor gives me great peace of mind. You are so generous and thoughtful." I patted his hand and smiled the most gracious smile I could muster. "I mean it. You may have saved my life."

"You honor me by wearing it. Now I should go and leave you to rest before I overstay my welcome." Cline stood and walked towards the door. "If you have any more questions, at any time, please contact me, no matter the hour. I will see you tonight at the Champions' Ball."

"I will. See you tonight," I assured him as he closed the door.

ELIAS

*A*s I got ready I tried to quell my nerves by considering that Ophelia was in great hands with Sparkle, Vosega, Nara and Aruna. Then Cline came to me and asked if he could manufacture armor for Ophelia, and I was all too eager to acquiesce to his request. Fortunately for me, the Directorate members felt the same, that it only made sense to equip the Unconsu with some sort of shield. Of course, I knew she was not as helpless as it may seem, but in order to pull off this continued secrecy of her true nature, it was pertinent it still appeared that she was a normal Unconsu.

Cline's armor would allow Ophelia some grace in defending herself without casting suspicions, and quite honestly, every little bit of protection helped.

I charged Su with tracking any leads he could concerning the whereabouts of Realto's partner and brother along with Aurora, who had still not appeared. He would make haste after the evening's festivities were concluded.

The knot in my stomach was from Borte. She was a determined woman. I wished I had more to give her. Sadly, I did not, and now I had to fear for Ophelia's safety around her. I tried to abate my fears by reminding myself there was nothing I could do at present.

Tonight everyone would amass as the Champions' Ball. The Trials would begin first thing in the morning. This was another concession made for Ophelia. Since Consus did not need to sleep, the first Trial would usually play out immediately after the ball. The Directorate unanimously agreed that would not be fair to the Opaly Katan, since all Champions had to participate in order to not get disqualified, and Ophelia could not go day-in and day-out without sleep.

I looked at myself in the mirror before spritzing my tuxedo coat with cologne. I had so many emotions and thoughts regarding the summit, all complicated by Ophelia's admittance into the Trials. On one hand, I wanted to cherish every moment and all that it took to get us here, in this place, with six thousand other Conduits. On the other hand, I was wracked with anxiety about the coming days. *Would we be able to keep Ophelia safe and her gifts concealed? Would the Trials be enough to unite the Poginuli and the Pai Ona? What if they were not? What then? Where was Aurora?*

Su interrupted my train of thought as he entered my chamber.

"The ballroom is ready, Mr. Elias." I admired Su's attire. He had put thought into his appearance—he, too, felt the occasion. He shuffled nervously under my assessment. "Is it too much?"

"On the contrary, I find it very suitable." I smiled at our gracious host turned friend. Su wore a burgundy robe with a gold sash around his waist. His pant robes were a slightly deeper shade of red. The contrast was rich, and he looked very dapper. "You clean up nicely."

Su smiled and looked down at his robes. His long black hair was braided. "I haven't had a reason to dress up in centuries."

I considered how Su had expressed how lonely he had been before meeting Ruit and being tasked the job of the gatekeeper. I was happy to see that he was enjoying the buzz around The Cathedral. Instead of overwhelm or frustration, he took the busyness in stride and stayed present among all happenings.

"Well, you have outdone yourself, my friend. Do you think Ophelia is ready for me to escort her down to the ball?"

"I was just at her chambers before receiving the message that the ballroom was ready. She looked beautiful. But I needn't say more. I dare not spoil the unveiling."

My heart skipped a beat. I had been waiting for weeks to see her in the dress I had bought her. I wondered if she liked it then brushed off the thought. She would have told me if she disapproved.

"I am ready to meet my date." The two of us entered the hallway. "Would you mind attending to any early guests?" I looked at my watch. "We still have thirty minutes until the formal attendance time, but there are always the eager early birds to account for. We will be just behind you."

Su nodded. I saw a flicker of disappointment flash in his eyes and realized he wanted to see my expression when I saw Ophelia. I leaned in. "I promise to describe every ounce of excitement I feel when I see her." I knew this was what Su wanted, just as he enjoyed the description of the taste of food. Our insights reminded him what it was like when he was mortal. My assurance lit him up again, and we went our separate ways.

I cleared my throat as I approached Ophelia's room. She had such a hold on me. I shook off my nerves and removed the pin I had been saving from my pocket. It had been my mother's. I found it in her chamber in Hafiza, before I ever met Ophelia. Something about it called to me, and I knew I had to give it to the woman who stole my heart. The timing had never seemed right until now. First there was Lucas, then there was the mourning of Lucas. I never wanted Ophelia to feel pushed or pulled by me. But tonight felt right.

I had selected her dress with the pin in mind. The brooch was gold, with deep red rubies and clear sparkling diamonds. The stones were set together in the form of a blossoming rose. It fit nicely in my palm. I looked at it one more time, realizing I had broken into a sweaty mess.

"Are you going to knock already?" Ophelia's voice was muffled on the other side of the door. "I know you're out there."

I stifled a laugh. "Patience is a virtue, Miss Banner."

"Not one I possess."

"Very well, then. I will not keep you waiting any longer." I tapped on the door. It swung open slowly. I had to catch my breath at the sight of her. The dress was Gatsby-inspired fashion. Gold sequins hung to the ground. The material underneath was sheer and flawlessly draped her skin, accentuating every curve. The neckline dipped in a classy way to just above her navel. She spun in a gentle circle, and I was reminded that the back was also exposed and trailed into a long train. My eyes made their way to her face, framed by tamed wavy red hair. Her lips were a crimson, perfectly painted the same color as the ruby earrings I had purchased to go with the dress.

"What do you think?" She bit her lip, nervously waiting for my approval.

"I think... I reason... What I am trying to say is that I have never seen anything more stunning in my life. You look ravishing."

Her cheeks flushed. "You don't think it's too much? I guess you're wearing a tux." She gestured to my suit. It was a traditional black tuxedo, but I wore a matching gold dress shirt with red cufflinks. "I mean, you look amazing. I just don't want to be overdressed," she stammered.

"You won't be, trust me."

"This train is cumbersome. I'm afraid I'll step on it." She looked over her shoulder at the trailing material.

"If I may?" I opened my palm to show her the pin. "It was my mother's and I think she would be honored for you to wear it tonight."

"Elias." My name came out breathy from her perfect lips. "Are you sure? I mean, you have so few things left of your parents'."

"I bought the dress with the pin in mind. It has always been meant for you." I knelt down beside her right leg that was generously exposed by a slit. "The woman who sold me the dress showed me how to bustle the train, here, alongside the slit. May I?" I looked up at her. She nodded.

My heart started racing. I slipped my hand just inside the top of the slit and took the excess material in my other hand, trying to mimic the exact fold the dressmaker had demonstrated. My head began to swim from the proximity of Ophelia's skin to mine. I looked up to see she had closed her eyes with anticipation and yearning. She bit again at her lip. This time it looked like an entirely different gesture. I fastened the pin quickly, but lingered just a little too long, taking in the scent of her, the feel of her hot skin against the back of my hand.

I took hold of her thigh, and a gentle moan escaped her mouth. It took all I had to tear myself away from her. I gently kissed her leg before commanding my body to stand. I met her gaze again. We stood there in tense, seductive silence for what felt like forever. She put her hand on my chest.

"Well, at least your heart is pounding as terribly fast as mine is."

"Terribly fast," I concurred. "We should be going before either of us suffers from cardiac arrest."

We both took a deep breath. Ophelia hooked her arm in mine. "Will there be dancing?"

The tension was subsiding. "There will be as much dancing as you would like."

OPHELIA

J was doing my best to exude calm, non-sexual energy. I felt like I was failing, miserably, but somehow Elias was able to contain himself. He was such a pillar of control. We were entering the ballroom arm in arm, ignoring the impulse both of us had had only moments ago.

I didn't think anything in the world could distract me from his aroma and touch, until the curtains parted, exposing the ostentatious ballroom. It was enormous, circular, with tall, domed glass ceilings. The stars twinkled in a clear sky above our heads. The walls were draped with thick purple velvet curtains. Between the curtain panels hung an enormous painting of each chosen Champion. I thought I was going to be sick. I hadn't spotted my face on any of the canvases yet, but the idea that there was a gigantic painting of me looming about made me nauseous. *I didn't even like selfies.*

I squeezed Elias' arm. No one but us two and four other Conduits were in the room, but I whispered nonetheless, "You didn't tell me there would be a giant painting of me in here."

"I did not know it was part of the Champions' Ball tradition until this afternoon, when signor da Vinci brought me his works to be displayed."

"Leonardo da Vinci?" I gasped.

"The one and only."

My feet stopped working. I didn't know what to say. Elias turned to face me. He took both of my arms into his hands.

"There will be many Conduits joining us shortly. I expect you will meet individuals that will astound you. I encourage you to just take it all in. Be amazed, be excited, laugh, smile, dance tonight—we have worked hard to get here and you are now a Champion of the Trials. Trials that have not taken place in over three thousand years." He leaned in and kissed my forehead. "But should it ever become too much, should you need to escape, your wellbeing is always of top priority. I will be close, but do not hesitate to leave without me."

I took in all that Elias said, stared deep into his eyes and decided right then and there that I was going to make this evening all that it could be. "We'll have a wonderful time together tonight."

ELIAS

$\mathcal{O}$phelia flitted around the room gracefully. It was a joy to see her so happy after so many days of sorrow.

"Master Elias." Winston came up from behind.

"I always hated that you called me that. You have never worked under my employ." I turned to hug my dear friend. Just behind him stood Di and Renata. "Ladies," I acknowledged their presence.

As usual, Di looked stunning in a pale pink gown that had a long flowing train. Renata was also dressed for the occasion in a black dress. It was modest compared to Aphrodite's but I had never seen Renata wear a dress. It was flattering on her.

"Viraclay, the ballroom is astonishing. You have outdone yourself," Renata imparted.

"I wish I could take the credit, but this is all The Cathedral's doing. We are just so fortunate she is willing to cooperate with our wishes."

"Your father would be proud, as would your mother," Di stated as she raised her glass.

"To your parents," Winston inserted.

"I will drink to that," I agreed.

We four took a sip of our champagne. I could tell they were

waiting to say something. I glanced back at Ophelia, who was laughing with Aremis and a Conduit named Korbin, a Champion on Aremis' Panjoin team.

"Well, what are you three waiting to discuss?" I was not in the mood for small talk, but rather eager to tackle the real subject.

"We know where they are. We could strike now," Di was the first to get to the point.

"Di, we have always known where they were," I reminded her.

"Yanni is dead. They are weakened," Renata added.

"Possibly, or possibly by killing Yanni we have poked the beast. Enraged the bull."

Winston stopped my train of thought. "They almost killed her. They almost killed us. Esther has not resorted to torture in years, since before the last war, and Viraclay, may I remind you, she saw the broadcast. She was not able to access it, but she knows something was amiss. She will be like a dog with a bone."

"We must attack now!" Di demanded.

I quieted my voice. "I hear what you are saying. Each of you." I made eye contact with them one by one. "We are so close to the bidding. If the Pai Ona bid, we will attack. But we need the numbers to offset the unknown. We know they are in Chernobyl. The Nebas compound has been there for thirty years. Before that, it was Oradour-sur-Glane. Why do you believe the Nebas let their location be known?"

"To taunt us," Renata answered.

"Or to bait us? I will not be baited." The answer hit its mark. I could see it on each of their faces. "We have waited this long. We are close to a true advantage. Stay with me, friends."

Their silence spoke volumes. It was not submission, but it was concession. "We will avenge our fallen. I promise."

Just then da Vinci approached. With a nod, each of them diverged in a different direction. I was satisfied with the outcome of the exchange as much as I could be. Putting out one fire at a time.

"Signor da Vinci, you have outdone yourself." I kissed the elderly

Conduit on the cheek. He was not old in terms of years on this earth, only old for his consummation age.

"Signor Viraclay, has she seen it? Has she seen my masterpiece?" He clasped his hands together in anticipation.

"I believe she has, signor."

OPHELIA

"Jesus Christ," I said as I slapped Korbin on the shoulder. Before I could comment more on his dirty joke, I felt a tap on my shoulder.

"I'm sorry, I know who you are, but have we met?"

The color in my face must've disappeared. The man in front of me had shoulder-length brown hair, tan skin and brown puppy-dog eyes. He wore white robes with a golden sash around the middle. The resemblance was unmistakable, but it was the expression on his face that told me who he was.

"Um, I'm sorry, I…" Korbin was unsuccessfully stifling a laugh. I shot my hand out to shake his. "I'm Ophelia, and you must be Jesus."

"What a pleasure, Ophelia. I think sacrifice is the bravest act anyone can partake in. Bravo to you for putting yourself in harm's way to see the Trials carry on." He ignored my hand and leaned in and kissed my forehead. "Bless you." Then he walked away.

I whirled around to see two shit-eating grins. Aremis and Korbin couldn't hold their laughter anymore.

"That guy just can't get out of character," Korbin teased.

Then all three of us were laughing.

"Pardon me, can I join the flock that appears to be having the most fun?" a man's voice with a distinct German accent asked.

"Come on over, Berty. Keep the girl company while we fill our glasses." Korbin took my flute and winked. I turned to Berty, now on my left.

"Hi, Berty. I'm Ophelia but you can call me Olly. Berty must be your nickname."

"Aw, yes, it is." I looked at the older gentleman with wild white hair and a hefty mustache on his upper lip. He looked modish in his black suit and thin tie. "My full name is Albert. Albert Einstein."

I tried to hide the shock, remembering Elias' wise words in my head. *Be shocked, be amazed, have fun.*

"Of course you're a Conduit. I should've known."

"I'm going to take that as a great compliment."

"You should," I agreed. "It was nice of you to share your knowledge of the universe with the world."

"I gave them some answers but left them with more riddles, I assure you." He looked at me with a look I was getting to know well, speculation. "You're a curious one. You see, I see the strokes, what humans call energy. Energy moves differently around you, especially for an Unconsu."

I didn't skip a beat. "Well, Cline over there was nice enough to make me fancy armor."

"This was before that. I noticed it the moment I saw you."

I started to feel uneasy, exposed. Berty leaned in. "Don't worry, your secret is safe with me."

I appreciated his discretion but I wanted to change the subject, take the light off me. "Tell me about time travel."

"Ahhh." He scoffed and waved his hand in the air as if he could swat it away. "Silly humans. Time is a tapestry, not a linear line. You can cut it, manipulate the strings, but you can never return to it." He paused, as though he wasn't sure how to phrase what he wanted to say next. "Beings are obsessed with time travel because they have a wild desire to change their fates, maybe even a prophetic fate." He paused again to make sure I was following him. "Often our most pivotal points in our lives are unintentional. That's the curious thing about fate, it appears to be the summation of mindless choices or what we would call accidents."

I nodded. Something deep in my soul knew that what he was saying to me would have great consequence for my future.

"So if that's all we are, fated beings who stumble around making careless choices, I find setting an intention, a true purpose, integral in my life. Perhaps by setting an intention we are willing our unconscious choices without realizing it." That was heavy and important. Berty wanted me to understand how I could change my fate. Then he chuckled. "But of course, these are just silly ramblings from a crazy old man."

Berty's turn to change the subject. "Tell me about this Cathedral!" He put his hands up in the air. "She is magnificent, and you have been here for weeks."

Just then Korbin and Aremis returned, and I decided I liked Berty, even if he was onto my abnormalities.

ELIAS

The ball had been carrying on for nearly four hours with no sign of the party dying down. Ophelia was exuberant. I currently watched her line-dancing on the ballroom floor, with Medusa, Ying and Di attempting to learn the steps. It had to be one of the most comical scenes I had ever witnessed. The band led by Elvis and Mozart had been playing a variety of music as the night carried on. This particular number had been requested by Ophelia and Realto, who appeared to be in better spirits once I had assured him I was sending Su out this evening.

After my conversation with Di, Winston and Renata, I added the lands around Chernobyl to Su's destinations. In the event that Aurora, Filbert or Mikkel were being held captive, Su could at least confirm their whereabouts.

The Ancients attended the ball and even partook in food and drink but refrained from dancing. I could tell by Ganesha's glances in my direction that they had been discussing matters that concerned me. So when he approached as the entourage of gigantic Ancients moved toward the exit, I conceded to his touch—or communication, rather.

Ganesha's trunk fell on my shoulder and his voice echoed in my head. "Be careful of those three. They mean to harm Ophelia. Much pain and distrust there. They will incite restlessness among the attendees if they have the opportunity."

I knew exactly who he was talking about. "Thank you," I said aloud.

The enormous elephant head bowed slightly and the Ancients excused themselves from the social.

Ironically, all of the Conduits I worried about were standing against the same wall. Leviathan, Helia and Constance huddled in a corner, while Borte brooded only a few feet away. The truth was, I empathized with Borte, but she would not trust me. Both George and Cadmus' Atoas had been very amicable and were willing to wait until the arguments to see if The Cathedral would lay out her plans for the three captives. Borte was relentless. I would be the same, so somewhere in my heart I understood. As far as Leviathan, Helia and Constance were concerned, I knew not why they held such ill will towards Ophelia. I took a deep breath; I guessed it was time to find out.

I walked over to the clique in the corner. "Good evening."

"Is it?" Helia responded, and I realized she must be the leader—of what, I did not know.

"It would appear that most of us are having a good time."

"Hmmm," was her reply.

"Helia, have we formally met? Aside from the time of your arrival, that is?"

"No," she cut me off, giving me very little to work with.

"It feels as though you hold some ill intent towards me or my friend, Ophelia."

The other two just waited for her to answer all of my questions. "Well, it must not be too malicious, since your watchdog let me in."

"True, Susuda is very protective, of Ophelia especially." I meant it to sound threatening. "I am curious, why would you attend an event that you clearly despise?"

"Simple, really. To insure you don't succeed in uniting the Pai Ona.

Everyone should know what comes out of an alliance with the Kraus family," she hissed, and then the three of them moved around me, leaving me alone, with more questions than answers.

OPHELIA

"Ophelia!" Nara's sweet voice caught my ear.

Sweat pooled on my brow. I'd just got done dancing with Aremis. Turned out he was a very skilled swing dancer. I spun to face her, smiling. But my smile faded when I saw the two people beside her. It was Zavier and Abigail, from the photo I'd found in Hafiza. Abigail looked so much like my grandmother Lilith that I'd been hoping it was her image, evidence that she was still alive, that she had not killed herself in a mental institution after my mother was born. Instead, the image belonged to Abigail, a young woman who Nara and Valerian had met one summer after her parents were brutally tortured and presumably murdered. The story still gave me the chills.

I knew she was here. I'd seen her face on the projection during the Open Ceremony. Seeing her face immediately conjured up gruesome imagery I had to shake off.

"Nara," I greeted her with a slight bow as the three of them approached.

"I have someone I would like to introduce you to," Nara said as they filled the gap between us. They stopped in front of me. "This is Zavier." The young man stepped forward and put out a hand for me to shake.

"Hello, Ophelia. My dear friend Nara tells me much about you. But I believe you will find you're more eager to meet my Atoa." Zavier let go of my hand and moved aside so that his pale-haired beauty of a wife and I were standing face to face.

She bowed slightly and put out both of her hands. I placed my right hand into hers. She took it and gave it a gentle kiss.

"Nice to meet you." She pulled my hand to her chest. "Lilith Abigail Platz." Lilith's eyes met mine, and there was no doubt in my mind that this woman, younger than I was, was my grandmother.

"I need to sit down," was all I could say.

ELIAS

$\mathscr{I}$ saw Nara setting a chair behind Ophelia, at which point she fell back into it. Curious about what was going on, I started in their direction.

"Viraclay, can I speak to you?" Vosega's voice boomed above the music.

This was a conversation I had been avoiding. I respected Vosega and I hated to see him in pain about his son's recent passing but I had so many mixed emotions about the circumstances leading up to Lucas' demise. It was one thing to console Ophelia, and it was an entirely different thing to explain to a father his son's betrayal.

"Vosega," I turned to greet him properly. "Is this conversation pertaining to Lucas?"

"You were with him the night he died?"

"I was."

"I want to know it all. What happened?"

I looked back over my shoulder but Ophelia was gone. I decided now was the time to be honest with the man, to explain what we had discovered and how Lucas had saved our lives.

"Come, let us find a more private venue." We walked toward the door. I grabbed Aremis by the arm on my way out and told him to tell Ophelia I would be back shortly. I did not want her present for this conversation; it would only upset her.

OPHELIA

$\mathcal{N}$ara excused herself once she escorted us up to my room. So now I sat awkwardly in silence between Zavier and my long-lost grandmother, Lilith.

"Do you guys want tea, or something stronger, like wine?" I got up and went toward the kitchen. "I'm going to go with wine." I poured three glasses, although they hadn't said yes or no to the offer.

I handed them their glasses and sat back down at the dining room table. I took a long drink of my cabernet before starting the real conversation.

"So, where have you guys been?" It wasn't the most important question, but it was a relevant one.

Zavier answered. "We don't stay anywhere for any extended length of time. Abigail, I mean Lilith, has had a very troubling past, and therefore she doesn't like to stay anywhere for very long."

I felt this flood of anger when I realized that Lilith had been alive all this time and had never returned to check on her daughter or grandchild. She'd just left us to fend for ourselves. Prey for the same monster who broke her to break my mother next. I turned to Lilith. "Which past? The one where your parents are tortured and you witness it through the panels of the wood floor in the basement, or the past where you're tortured by a depraved Conduit named Nestor? An Incubus that impregnates you multiple times?" The moment I said it, I regretted it. Whichever story was true, they were both devastating. "I'm sorry. I'm just in shock."

Zavier responded again. "That is to be expected. To answer your question, both stories are true. Lilith's parents were mutilated in their home in Poland, not Canada, while she was stuck beneath the floor boards watching the life slowly drain from their faces." Zavier adjusted himself in his seat. You could tell this was hard for him to retell. "Unfortunately, she never got away when her father instructed her to run. Nestor was lying in wait for her to disclose her location. He took her captive and kept her locked up for three years. I found her in an institution in Connecticut. She had escaped Nestor's clutches, but he left her..."

"You met in the institution?" I repeated. I tuned to Lilith. "Why aren't you speaking?"

"He left her cursed. She cannot speak in congruent sentences. She can only put together pieces. It comes out as gibberish."

I looked in my grandmother's eyes. There was so much pain there. I recognized that pain; I used to see it in my mother's eyes.

Zavier continued. "We met in the institution. I was a resident psychiatrist. When we realized what we were to each other, we fled."

But there was a piece missing—Eleanor. "Why didn't you take Eleanor with you? Why did you fake your death? She was just an innocent baby." I was flustered, for my mother and all that she'd lost by not knowing her mother or who she was, what she was.

My eyes were on Lilith, but her eyes were pleading with Zavier to explain.

"We couldn't risk Nestor following us to claim his child. Lilith had seen him do it before, chase after his progeny. The baby was safer not knowing her parents," Zavier said confidently.

My eyes never left Lilith's face, and I saw something there—regret, shame... deception. "But she wasn't safer."

Lilith's eyes locked onto mine, desperate to hear what I would say next. "Nestor found her. He found my mother and he raped her. He broke her. Together they created me, an incestuous daughter that my mother struggled to look at. Eleanor was defiled by her own father and she never knew to be fearful of him until it was too late. Now I have to live with the knowledge that I'm an abomination, the product of an evil man and his abandoned daughter."

Tears streamed from Lilith's eyes. I was torn between wanting to reach out and comfort the grandmother I thought I'd lost and letting her see what her decisions did to her family.

Zavier spoke up again, and I had to give the man credit for standing by his partner. "Lilith was broken when she made her decision to leave. It wasn't an easy one. But she would never be able to tell her daughter what had happened, who her father was. That was no way to raise a baby."

"How do you know about her past?" I asked plainly. "You know so much."

"Writing is true," Lilith answered.

"It isn't always easy to understand, but it allows her some level of communication through the curse," Zavier explained.

Lilith moved closer. She reached for my hand. "Sorry." Tears, once again, stained her cheeks. She lay her forehead on our stacked-together hands and just repeated over and over and over again, "Sorry."

Zavier put his hand on her shoulder. My heart softened. The anger that I'd felt completely melted away. I could feel Lilith's true feelings, not through my gift but simply from her presence, and she was undeniably devastated.

ELIAS

*N*ara came to me after I had finished my conversation with Vosega. She told me about Lilith and that she and Ophelia were up in Ophelia's room, talking. I had the urge to go up there and see if she needed me, but decided I was better off waiting for her to come to me. So I continued to play host. By five a.m. I had to get some sleep. Susuda had implemented stricter wards while he ran around to the locations Realto and I had suggested.

I was surprised to see him manifest at my door as I approached.

"Mr. Elias, I am just checking in before I proceed to my next location. It would appear that the wards held up as expected."

"So it would seem." The mention of the wards triggered my curiosity about Helia's admission into The Cathedral. "Su, do you remember admitting Helia, Leviathan and Constance into the gate?"

"I do, but I promise you they didn't arrive with ill intent. I would have seen it. I've watched it grow, aware that they desire your failure in uniting the Pai Ona. That being said, both The Cathedral and I have not felt the intent was lethal, mostly bitter rage."

"I see." My thoughts were slow in the early morning hours. "So you can sense if they get dangerous? You will tell me?"

"You will be the first to know," he assured me before flitting away.

I crawled into bed. My thoughts were disconnected but continuous. At least I had Su's assurance that he would know if things got worse with the trio. It was not enough to assuage my fears, but I was glad to know I would have warning. I was not certain I ever really fell asleep, but when light peeked through my shades, I remembered what today entailed, and there was no sleeping after that.

·

OPHELIA

I slept. I actually slept the night before the Creation Trial. I thought I'd be too antsy, too anxious to fall asleep. After meeting my grandmother and her Atoa last night, I thought I'd be too amped, too overwhelmed. But my body decided to throw in the towel. Days of revelations, curve balls and the damn near impossible had caught up with me. I looked in the mirror, examined the bags under my eyes. It occurred to me that it hadn't been days of crazy, it had been months. Weeks of loss, devastating truths, mortal danger and self-discovery, and here I was. I was still standing.

I tried to feel proud, but too many other emotions were vying for attention inside me. I settled for appreciation. Gratitude that despite the hurricane of circumstances around me, I was still here, and today I was here with a good night's sleep under my belt.

What do you wear to a Katuan Trial, I thought as I looked in my closet. None of my clothes seemed fitting. They were either too fancy for strenuous activity or too casual. Yoga pants and a sports bra felt disrespectful. I decided to shower. Maybe something would look better after I was clean. I toweled off and walked out to the kitchen for a second cup of coffee. There was a package on my dining room table. I looked around suspiciously. *Who had been in my apartment? While I was showering, no less?*

I poked at the package with my finger. When it didn't explode I decided I'd open it. I tore the first layer of wrapping. A sheet of paper slipped from the packaging. The cursive it was written in was delicate. It read:

To Ophelia

From A Secret Admirer

For the Occasion

"Well, that's not creepy or anything," I said aloud, but thought if someone was still in my apartment maybe I should keep my commentary to myself. My fingers found the seam I'd been ripping in the paper and followed it to where I could tear it completely open. The fabric inside felt soft and stiff at the same time, the way worn leather can feel. As I unfolded it, I realized it was a pair of pants and a cropped top.

"You've got to be kidding me," I said, exasperated. *I'm supposed to wear this in front of thousands of Conduits I don't know?* I grabbed the ensemble and sat with it on my lap, slumped on the couch. I placed the pants over my legs and held the tiny top over my breasts as I considered my options—work casual, yoga pants or Matrix Mama here. Matrix Mama was winning, mostly because I imagined if I didn't wear it, I would offend whichever creepy Conduit had snuck into my apartment to give it to me. I stomped into my room and pulled on the pants and top and examined my outfit in the mirror. Admittedly, it didn't look half bad. It fit perfectly, and despite the fact that I hated showing my midriff, it wasn't too risque.

"Matrix Mama it is," I agreed, nodding to the mirror. I pulled my hair up atop my head into a bun, refilled my coffee, and sat at the bar, trying not to think about what everyone else was going to think about this get-up. I watched the minutes pass by slowly, waiting for Elias to escort me down to the arena. He had insisted, and I was glad his face was the first I was going to see today.

I was waiting outside the door when he manifested in front of me. The look on his face said it all.

"Don't say a word. Someone left it for me and it felt rude not to wear it."

"I was going to say you look amazing." He muffled a smirk but I could still hear it in his voice.

I rolled my eyes. "Seriously? Am I going to be the laughing stock?"

"On the contrary, I believe you will fit right in." He took my hand in his. "Ready?"

"Am I ever really ready? Beam me up, Scotty."

ELIAS

*S*he really did looking amazing in her gifted attire, and she fit right in. It had me wondering who her secret admirer was. Whoever it was, I was grateful that Ophelia had one more ally among our people. Aside from Borte, Leviathan, Constance and Helia, the rest of the Pai Ona appeared to accept Ophelia and her unusual circumstances. I was grateful for the strokes, because that meant more Champions who would be sympathetic to her plight during the Trials, and Malarin willing, avoid hurting her.

Once more, I stared at the faces of those Conduits who would see Ophelia be harmed. After digging deeper, I was able to discover why the trio held animosity toward her, or rather me. There was nothing I could do about it at present, but I warned Ophelia on our way to the arena this morning. Between her allies and the armor Cline created, I prayed it was enough to keep her safe. I took my seat in the balcony I kept reserved for me and Ophelia when I thought we would be watching the Trials together.

"May I join you?" a soft voice inquired from behind the heavy curtain partition. "It is I, Jezebel."

I did not know Jezebel well, but Su loved her, and Ophelia admired her son and daughter-in-law. I also had her husband and grandson to thank, in many ways, for where we were today.

"Please."

Her pale curly hair came into view before her face did. There was a mass of it all about her head. Her skin was very fair, as well. Her eyes, however, were dark gray, like a thunder cloud.

"Thank you. The rest of my family were honored with Champion assignment. I am a proud matriarch." Her smile was half-hearted.

"It is an honor for most." I returned my own half-hearted smile.

"Almus speaks very highly of her. He is certain she will stay safe."

"It is good to know that she has many friends in the arena."

"And some foes?"

"You tell me." I knew Jezebel was a powerful Aura.

She looked down upon the arena where the Champions had lined up, waiting for the Masters of Ceremonies, Realto, to commence the event.

"I see many who desire goodwill, peace among all. I see others who are uncertain of their paths. And still there are those who would see your plans undone. But from this distance, it is hard to truly read their strokes." She looked at me. I felt like she was waiting for something, but then she continued. "You know that is all an aura is, the color of our strokes dancing around us in vibrant shades, perhaps our original shades. My Ruit, his aura was always vibrant blue. He had such reverence for life, for the power in it."

"I am sad I never met him." It was true. There was no point in lying to an Aura anyway. They were a lot like Rand; they would know. They may not know where your deception began and ended, but they would see enough.

"He would have liked you. He loved your father."

She got my attention and she knew it. "My father? He and Ruit were friends?"

"He never spoke of him?"

"No, I am sad to say he did not."

"Pity. They spent much time conversing. It was my Ruit who first devised the summit. Your father listened, but thought, as many of these people here do now, that we were safer in the shadows." She put her hands up in surrender. "Neither Ruit nor I blamed him. My family and I lived many peaceful years in the shadows, but Ruit and Cane discussed the summit in depth for many centuries. Part of me believes that your father was charged to action after Ruit's disappearance. Then, of course, you were born, and that was further fuel."

She smiled at me, this time with more sincerity.

"Why would my father never speak of Ruit?"

"Perhaps it was too painful. I will share their letters. Many of the broadcasts came from this place. Ruit helped your father install the two that he had so that they could communicate through the old channels."

I considered what she said, and it made sense. I just wondered why my father had never once mentioned Ruit. I wanted to inquire more but Realto's booming voice reverberated off the walls, interrupting our conversation and announcing the beginning of the Trials.

"If I may?" She looked at me for permission but I did not know what she was querying. "I have a few tricks up my sleeve."

Jezebel waved her hand in the air and it was as though we were placed in the middle of the arena floor. "The view is better here."

I looked up to see the thousands of onlookers, and to my left, completely unaware of my astral presence, was Ophelia.

OPHELIA

Sweat drenched my back from the anxiety swelling in my chest. Thousands of eyes were glued on us, seventy-eight individuals in a swarm of thousands. My outfit turned out to be the appropriate ensemble for the occasion after all. Everyone on the Opaly team was wearing black. Vosega wore black leather pants. Aruna had a modified black sari of sorts. Nara was in a majestic black outfit that looked more like armor than clothing. Sparkle, my dear Sparkle, was wearing a short glittery spandex skirt and what I would assess as a sports bra. But perhaps the most daring fashion award for the Opaly team belonged to Medusa. Her brown dreadlocks were pulled away from her face. She had a sportier pair of sunglasses on than yesterday, and she was covered from head to toe in a studded leather bodysuit. I always admired women who could wear bodysuits proudly. With the hundreds of sharp silver studs, her suit looked lethal. I'd need to say thank you to my fashionista fairy godmother.

"Deep breaths, Ophelia. We will be victorious." Vosega beat his chest proudly then flirtatiously crowed at Oya from across the arena, and she licked her lips in response.

Must be nice to not have to consider the fact that you could die, at any moment, in front of everyone.

Sparkle whispered in my other ear. "I won't let anyone harm you. Just do as we practiced. Your participation is integral."

I knew she meant that literally, since it was required that all Champions play their part during each Trial. If they didn't, the team was disqualified. We'd practiced all day yesterday, and my job was simple—don't get killed, and place the stone on the top of the construct. I felt the tiny opal in my pocket. The type of rock had no significance, but Vosega asked what kind of stone I thought would make the perfect finishing touch, and opal was the first thing to come out of my mouth—like Opaly, our team name. Everyone thought that was a hoot.

I patted the stone one more time, confirming it was still there. When Realto's voice erupted on the stage, I jumped. It was time. I had to pay attention to the rules. Every Trial was different. The instructions were crucial to ensure success, and I'd be damned if I was going to ruin our chance at victory because of a technicality.

"Welcome, Champions!" The arena erupted. "Welcome, spectators!" I admired Realto's costume for the day, a bright pink speedo with a fuzzy silver vest, knee-high black leather boots, and his hair was down.

"Today is a monumental day. Today we commence the first of three challenges in the Katuan Trials. The last Trials were over three thousand years ago." A cheer flew through the crowd and Realto paused appropriately. "Today we make history, as we have the first Unconsu to ever be chosen by the Stones in the arena!" Everyone stood, and the volume of the excitement grew so loud it was ringing in my ears. Then, without warning and as the crowd still stood applauding, it went silent. In a panic, I looked around before I realized it was Renata. Her soft voice was easily heard in the void of noise.

"Today is no different than any other. Just do your best," she assured me. Then, just as easily as it had disappeared, the noise came back with a thunderous clap. Cheers, stomping, and yells filled the arena, bouncing off every surface, creating a rumbling that shook the foundation, or at least seemed to. I looked up at the balcony from where I knew Elias watched on. I wished I was holding his hand, that I had his warm skin to comfort me and ease my nerves.

I looked back out at the feverish crowd and shook off the sentiment. I didn't have his hand, and I wouldn't during this Trial. I had my armor and my wits and Winston's oatmeal, whatever that was, and fortunately many friends by my side, which was even more appreciated when I glanced across the arena to see the sharp eyes of Leviathan and Helia watching me. I was sure Constance was around here somewhere, as well, but I wasn't going to go seeking out the third set of eyes that would rather see me fail, possibly even die during the Trials. They were the trio Kassandra warned me about.

Elias had let me in on their vendetta against our cause, and because I was his Atoa apparently that included me. I'd seen them the day I was chosen and overheard their snarky comments but I just thought it was because I was Unconsu. I was wrong. After asking around, Elias had discovered that Helia blamed the Kraus family for her and Leviathan's parents' murders. When Cane started asking the Pai Ona to stand up and fight back, I guess their parents took that literally. They waged their own war, totally out of the realm that Cane meant, and it resulted in Helia and Leviathan's parents' deaths, and that of Constance's Atoa. In their heartbreak and anguish, the trio blamed the Kraus family.

This wasn't the time to let a misunderstanding fill my head with fear, though, so I squared up my shoulders and let resolve consume my body. I fortified my shield and suppressed all the extraordinary gifts that desperately wanted to seep to the surface to assist in my survival, and I was ready.

ELIAS

$\mathcal{J}$t was surreal, being in the center of the arena unbeknownst to anyone around us. I could not take my eyes off Ophelia.

Jezebel leaned over to speak in my ear. It was much louder where we sat. "As I am sure you have concluded, it's an astral projection enchantment. Our bodies are safely up in the balcony."

I just nodded. I could not speak; my mouth was too dry from the anxiety.

Realto hushed the masses. "The Creation Trial is, just as it sounds, an endeavor of creation, a collaboration of all y'alls Katans and all of the factions represented among you. It's required that all members of each team contribute to the formation of the creation in some capacity." He looked directly at Ophelia before continuing. "Today our Champions will create a Haven large enough to house each of them and formidable enough to withstand the Destruction Trial yet to come. The Haven will be considered complete when all the Champions of a single team say *Adoday* in unison. Remember, with creation comes great responsibility. As creators, we must manipulate the strokes, bend the will of the world around us. Beauty can arise in the swells of creation, but so can horror. It's our duty to lean into the side of beauty and good." Realto moved about the podium fluidly, like he was born to be the Master of Ceremonies. "So today, during the first Katuan Trial of Creation, our Champions will create beauty with strength. But because every creation comes with its difficulties, the strokes often spare us no misfortune. Among your team, you must assign three who can defend your Haven, as well as interfere with the construction of all other Havens."

I knew it would not be as simple as "build a nice structure and we will all admire its beauty."

Realto continued. "You have but a moment to assign your Mekoninis."

Each team huddled together and, one by one, three Champions from each huddle stepped forward.

From Opaly, Shiva, Nara and the Sand Man stepped forward. I was interested to see how the Sand Man would serve as a Mekonini. I turned my attention to the opposite side of the ring to see exactly what I had hoped I would not. Leviathan and Helia were chosen from the Finesol team, and Constance was among the three Mekoninis of the Quitsee team.

"These three Mekonini must still contribute to the creation of the Haven, but they have the added task of defending and meddling to ensure the success of their own team. No other teammates can intentionally destroy or interfere with another Katan's creation besides the three Mekonini." Realto looked on at each team for a nod of affirmation that they understood the guidelines. After he was satisfied with their responses, he continued. "It is time to initiate the Trials. May they commence!"

The moment he said the words, the arena began to shift beneath our feet, widening and elongating, creating space between the Katans. In the center, where we had just sat, grew an enormous mountain, and from it a large tree. The ceiling of the arena dissolved away, letting the world in, so that the Conduits could call upon their powers to help them. Realto's projection shifted around us until it was a hundred various vantage points, each targeting a different Champion. I found the one that focused on Ophelia's face. Although we were in the thick of the action, it was like watching a live sporting event. Sometimes it was easier to see what was happening from the big screen. All of this happened in seconds.

The Trials had begun.

OPHELIA

*A*runa was the first to act. Nince descended from the open sky, followed by two other thunder birds, each carrying the trunk of a redwood tree in their talons. As soon as they dropped the trees at Aruna's feet, they were off once more collecting others. Vosega put his hands to the soil. Spews of lava erupted from the ground all around him. Then it got silent, and all we could hear was each other; Renata had drowned every other noise out.

Sparkle took my arm and pulled me to the side. "Isn't it magnificent?" Her smile was, as always, infectious.

I looked around at all the moving parts. It truly was beautiful chaos. "I must help with the heavy lifting and Covening. Stay low and out of sight until your time to shine comes." Then she skipped away to stand beside Tete, who was in his gargoyle form, collecting huge boulders that Vosega had manifested from the earth.

Vosega shouted to Nara, "A little wind, please." Nara never turned her attention away from our opposing teams. She simply directed her right hand behind her. A cold gust of wind spiraled up and around each spire of lava Vosega built, thirteen to be exact. When he was satisfied with their solidification, he waved onto Sparkle and Tete.

The Creation Trial was about creating a Haven. A Haven was two things, a physical structure and magical Covening. The Covening part would be the hardest, because done right, it would require a little energetic donation from each Consu on our team. Right now, we were just trying to build the physical construct.

Borte's shrill voice rang out. She was standing between Kassandra and Shiva so she could translate for the two of them. "Kassandra just saw an attack on your birds, Aruna."

Aruna's face got tense. The shadow of her thunder birds with another drop of lumber came into view above us. Her creased brow suggested she was sending them away. Shiva turned his gaze to the sky just as a lightning bolt shot into the air, aiming straight for Nince. Conduits may be able to survive that, but I doubted any other creature could. I held my breath. Aruna screamed, but Shiva didn't hesitate—he dispersed the electric dart with a single glance. The sky splintered with crackling electric shocks. At night, it would have been the most incredible fireworks show.

I searched the arena floor for Oya, sure she was responsible for it. When I found her face, she was looking at Vosega with a sheepish it-was-worth-a-shot look.

Nince and the other birds returned after a few moments unscathed but Aruna didn't call them back after that load, and I realized we were a few redwoods short of what we had discussed during our preparation drills.

"You keep your birds at a safe distance, dear Aruna. Let me assist," Olmsted's friendly voice encouraged. I noticed Medusa running back from the mountain that had emerged in the center of the ring. In her hands she held a large mound of dirt. She placed it at Olmsted's feet. He stood in the center of the lava spires. Once he had the soil he needed, he pulled several seeds from his pocket, picked through them and dropped four into the dirt. Instantly, shoots of green shot up and out. One began to grow directly up, while the other three were ropey and grew in opposite directions, crawling on the ground until they found the base of the spires, at which point they began climbing up the cylinders.

My attention was pulled away when I caught a figure out of the corner of my eye moving above me. Two Conduits I was unfamiliar with collided in midair. I ran to my left, trying to avoid the open space between teams and the shower of falling bodies from the combat above. But when I turned back around they were still there, and I realized they were both flying, fighting one another in flight. The ground shook below me. I crouched lower behind a boulder, not sure where the next threat was coming from, when suddenly the large boulder I was hidden behind moved, now being maneuvered by a gigantic polar bear. The bear took the boulder in its paws and stood on its back haunches. He had to be forty feet tall.

"Shiva! Help! Nanook!" Borte shouted.

Shiva turned in time to propel himself at the bear before he lobbed the boulder at our Haven and destroyed what progress we'd made. The two Ancients clashed. I was directly in their path. I felt two cool, solid hands wrap around my waist, hard as stone. Then I was in flight. Tete had scooped me up. As a gargoyle, he had large wings, and for a moment in the chaos I wondered how he could fly. He was pure marble. He put me down on the other side of our Haven, near Medusa.

She casually walked over. "Closer to me is safer, darling." She pointed to the ball of fur and blue skin that was now barreling toward the Panjoin structure just as they made a catastrophic collision, demolishing any progress by the Panjoin team. "You see, there is no time constraint, but faster is better. Once we finish, then our Mekoninis can simply stay and create problems for the other teams. It'll get more and more difficult for them to complete the Trial. Don't you think?"

I didn't respond. I didn't know what to say.

"Now I have to move some of these trees with the rest of the gang. Please stay close." I watched as Vosega single-handedly carried a redwood trunk to one of the walls of our Haven that had been constructed with boulders and vines, between the lava columns. Shiva came out of nowhere, dusting himself off, and grabbed the trunk. He laid one end on the wall and the other on the thick canopy of the dragon tree that Olmsted had grown in the center. It was like a pleasant game of link-and-logs for him. Medusa climbed up Shiva's leg, shimmied around his waist and onto his shoulders, from there she jumped onto the carefully placed tree. She removed her gloves and gently placed her hands on the bark. Instantly, the entire panel of the Haven between the lava columns turned to stone. It was eerie to see how quickly the living plants were replaced with cold, solid stone.

Yesterday, Medusa had shared the other part of her gift. She had a reputation to uphold, after all. Her stare rendered someone frozen, but they were still very much alive. Her touch, on the other hand— that turned any living thing to stone.

She jumped off gracefully. Our strategy seemed to be working perfectly. We only had to do the same thing eleven more times to complete the structure. Then the rest of the team would perform the Covening and I'd place the opal. Olmsted was busy growing more vines, Sparkle and Tete were gathering boulders, Vosega was preparing and then moving the trees, Aruna, Renata and Kassandra were running around assisting however they could, with the periodic foresight from Kassandra and the translation shouted to anyone who would listen by Borte, while I was staying out of the way and out of sight.

ELIAS

"You have to breathe, Elias." Jezebel's voice was barely audible over the clamor of the Trials. I heeded her advice, because fainting due to lack of oxygen at a time like this would serve no one. I consciously inhaled.

"They are doing it," I said it more to myself than to her.

"It would seem they are."

I had not torn my eyes away from the Opaly team, but with their first panel in place, the bones of their Haven taking shape, I took a moment to see how all the other teams were fairing. Quitsee and MisaKa were a little further advanced than Opaly. MisaKa was in the process of building a roof. They had Lucia on their team. She was a Master Mason, so it made sense that they would be forging ahead during the Creation Trial. No sooner did I make the observation than a fireball dropped from the sky and exploded onto the structure that had been primarily built from timber. I searched for Aremis' face among the Champions. When I found it, he was smiling from ear to ear, and not far from him was Winston's boyish grin. They were on different teams but they passed a smirk between them. Lucia, on the other hand, had her hands on her hips, and a look of pure outrage on her face. Until she saw the two men—then she, herself, tried to hide a smile.

As I took note of the other Champions, I noticed a similar disposition in most. They were taking the honor of being selected Champion very seriously. However, the competition of it all was only fuel, not a reason to hold malice. All but Helia, whose face depicted utter disdain for anyone who got in her way. I followed her line of sight and realized who was next on her list. Ophelia.

OPHELIA

The eighth panel had just been transformed to stone. Our team had found a rhythm, and although Shiva was now busy helping and not defending, it seemed we were in good hands with Nara and the Sand Man. Nara's beautiful figure danced in the air, directing the wind around her, deterring water, fire and the occasional giant flying object from colliding with our Haven.

To my dismay, I realized Quitsee was ahead of us in their construction. They were preparing their Covening, from what I could see from my vantage point, when a familiar face popped up near Martin Luther King Jr. It was the Sand Man. With a wave of his hand, I saw a terrified expression wash across Martin's face. I felt kind of guilty for being so delighted by Martin's fear, not because I wanted him to suffer but because I was happy for the distraction. It gave us more time. I didn't want Constance free to destroy our Haven—or me, for that matter.

Then everything seemed to slow down. Time warped into slow motion as it can when you realize something is coming. I heard Borte's voice in the distance. "Helia and Leviathan!" I turned around to see both of their anger-bent faces only feet from me, charging at me, with nothing to stop them. If they took me out, my team couldn't succeed. It was an easy solution.

The wind picked up around me. I watched in horror as Leviathan crouched and leapt onto Nara. His super-strength launched him into the air high enough to reach her. The gusts stopped and Helia descended upon me. I fastened my shield. She was going to have to give me all she had to penetrate my armor. I squared up my shoulders, braced for impact, but instead of contact with Helia, I saw a waft of black and then her limp form on the ground. A few feet behind her stood the Sand Man, returning his glove to his left hand.

"Shall we?" He gestured for me to head toward the Haven, which was nearly complete. Medusa was leaping off the last panel, and as I took in the sight of the Haven I saw that it was beautiful. Trees, boulders and vines all transformed into stone, creating a majestic mosaic. I looked over my shoulder to see that Nara was quick on my heels and Leviathan was trying to rouse Helia.

"Two birds with one stone," the Sand Man said behind me. He was right. By incapacitating Helia, he'd saved me and distracted Leviathan from continuing his assault on Nara. I also saw that the Quitsee were reassembled and performing their Covening. Urgency came over me.

My twelve other teammates took their positions in front of the still-visible columns and outstretched their hands on either side, although they were far from touching one another. They had devised a mantra yesterday, one that would summon and dispense small amounts of their gifts on and around the Haven, embedding their magic into the structure itself. During our practice sessions we'd decided the Haven would have resilient bonds that made each piece nearly magnetized to each other. It would be strong, ridiculously strong. Medusa was going to try and include an element that would freeze an attacker. Between her and Sand Man, they thought they could do it. There were many more elements to consider but from what I'd learned about Covening, you couldn't always ensure what pieces of your gift the Haven would pick up.

I stood a few feet back, trying to watch for my cue and also watch my back. The Covening was meant to fortify the Haven, making it more difficult to destroy during our next Trial. It was the first time I'd witnessed a Covening by a Paksyon. Although I couldn't see what was happening, meaning there was nothing to necessarily see, I could feel the change in atmosphere around me, around them. When they'd completed the final incantation, the Haven somehow looked different. It was my turn to contribute.

I heard the Quitsee team say in unison, "Adoday."

It was now or never. Constance would be gunning for me the moment she could. I ran to Shiva as fast as I could, pulled the opal from my pocket, kissed it for good luck. Shiva knelt down and pulled me up onto his knee then up onto the stone roof. The Haven seemed to soften under my feet. I dug my heels in and skidded to a stop at the center of the dragon tree. There was one spot left green. I plunged my hand in and looked up. Constance was running full-tilt in my direction.

I only had to say one word. "Odetistif." It was a simple incantation that turned the final leaves of the dragon tree to stone, and held my opal within it. I watched the leafy green transform into the hard, gray, cool surface, and nodded at Shiva, letting him know it was done.

"Adoday!" I shouted the words in unison with my team.

ELIAS

$\mathcal{T}$he Creation Trial ended when the first four teams completed their Havens. The ball room had been transformed into an enormous banquet hall. Champion tables lined the walls whilst the rest of us sat in the middle. Rows and rows of long tables filled the vast room. A Conduit named Henri-Paul insisted on cooking for the assemblage. At eight o'clock we were served, just as Henri-Paul said we would be. It was a four-course meal that consisted of lobster bisque, antipasto salad, filet mignon and an assortment of desserts, none of which disappointed.

Ophelia still had not mentioned her grandmother. I wondered when she would be ready to talk about her. In the meantime, I caught Lilith glancing at Ophelia every time she could get her in her line of sight.

I sat between Dracula and Nostradamus during dinner. They were fascinating to talk to, but I was eager to convene with Ophelia in private. When the first Trials ended, the remaining teams were swept away, a formality I was told was crucial during the Katuan Trials. The Champions must all be revealed during the Victors' Banquet. Two teams were eliminated. The first was the Panjoin. They were never able to recover their Haven after Shiva and Nanook rolled over it.

The second was Klison. Although they had an amazing team of warriors, none of their skill sets seemed best met during the Creation Trial. Once the other four teams completed their constructions, it was impossible for the Klison team to defend their Haven and build it.

Unfortunately that meant that Helia, Leviathan and Constance would be participating in the Destruction Trial. I had hoped at least one of their teams would be eliminated during this challenge. As the banquet came to a close, I got more and more excited about sequestering Ophelia for some alone time. But when Susuda entered the hall, I knew that would have to wait. I quickly made my way to him. Realto met me there at the same time.

Su looked at the flamboyant Realto skeptically.

"It is okay, Su. You were searching for his partner."

"I found them."

"Aurora too?" I asked. He had been searching since last night.

"No, Mikkel and Filbert."

Realto gasped.

"One of them needs a healer."

"Take us to them," I asserted. We promptly left, and on the way to their room Su explained how they were found outside Chernobyl. I thanked the strokes for the insight to send him there.

The room was quiet when we entered. A single bed lay in the center of an otherwise empty room. The light overhead was dim, but it clearly illuminated the two figures on the bed. Realto ran over.

"Filbert." He knelt beside the damaged form of Filbert.

The other man, who I had to assume was Mikkel, spoke. "He is in bad shape."

"I know this is a lot to ask, but can I request that you leave me and Su with him for a few moments to tend to his wounds?"

Both men reluctantly agreed. Once they were in the hall, I got to work.

"Su, get water and wash cloths. Let us clean him up." Su disappeared and I climbed onto the bed and sat beside the still unmoving body of Filbert.

"They poisoned me," he mumbled through gritted teeth. "It feels like my insides are disintegrating."

"Just stay strong a few moments longer," I did my best to console him. I began to work my fingers along his spine until I could feel where the poison had taken root. It was in his gut. Poison healing was different from other types of healing. It required syphoning. "Please be very still." I placed my palm in the middle of his back and just below his rib cage on his abdomen. I took a deep breath and began to pull the poison from its root out of his body. Once it was dislodged, I could push it out. In this case, he would need to vomit. After just a couple of minutes, Filbert began to purge the toxin from his body. Su stood by, handing me towels. After ten minutes the vomiting stopped. Filbert was exhausted and fell back into bed, motionless once more.

I got to my feet and went to the door to let the men back in.

"I will be back later to check on you."

Filbert half-waved.

Mikkel followed me out the door. Su and I waited for Mikkel to speak.

"Thank you, both. I don't know what would have happened without your help." He paused before continuing. "But I feel you must know. I left the entire Nebas compound in a time warp. Until someone returns to disrupt it, they will be easy prey."

I understood what he was implying we should do. This was exactly why I wanted to be the one to heal Filbert, to avoid creating a belligerent mob. The last thing we needed was to storm into the compound unprepared. Still I had to ask questions.

"I hear what you are saying. How can we be certain the time warp will still be in place should we decide to act?"

"There is no way of knowing without entering the premises, at which point you yourselves could disrupt the warp."

"Thank you for this information. I will consider our options carefully." We turned to leave while Mikkel returned to the room.

"What would you have me do, Mr. Elias?" Su asked.

"Nothing. We cannot act on that information alone. We do not know what the compound entails. Will there be traps, are there captives? Now is not the time to be rash, when we are so close to the bidding."

I hoped I was right. Now was the time I wished Aurora was here to help guide me. I would send Susuda out to look for her once more. *Where was she? What was keeping her?*

OPHELIA

*T*he banquet was over and I imagined it was what a wedding would feel like. Busy, too busy to eat or visit or drink, so I was going to grab a bottle of wine and bring it up to my room. As I made my way down to the wine cellar, I heard the hiss in my ear again. It was hushed this time, almost inaudible. I turned around to make sure I was in the passage alone. There was no one behind me.

"Is anyone there?" I stopped and waited for a response. As I expected, I was met with silence. I continued to talk to myself out loud. "This is ridiculous. There is nothing but caves beneath us. It has to be the whisper of the caves below us."

Then it dawned on me—I knew someone who could definitively tell me if I was hearing the voice of the caves. I placed my hand on the wall, kept Vosega in my mind's eye, and held my breath. The Cathedral planted me in front of Vosega and Oya's door. I knocked gently, hoping I wasn't disturbing anything intimate. After a moment Vosega answered, shirtless and sweaty. My cheeks blushed pink. I had clearly interrupted.

I turned my eyes away. "I'm sorry, I didn't mean to interrupt."

Vosega brushed his brow, wiping the sweat on his leather pants. "Ophelia, you are doing nothing of the sort. I know what this must look like, but I assure you I worked up this sweat preparing for the Destruction Trial." He stepped aside to show me that no one was in the room with him. "Please come in."

"Actually, I was hoping you could come with me. I want you to listen to something for me."

He cocked his head curiously at me, but didn't object. He shut the door and took my hand as he entered the hall. I put my other hand on the wall to my right. Immediately we were back in the passage that led to the galley, where I most often heard the noise.

I whispered, "Remember when you told me that you understood the language of the caves? Well, I've been hearing a noise... and The Cathedral sits atop several caves. Can you hear it?" I put my finger to my lips but the problem was, I didn't hear it anymore.

"I do. But I hear nothing."

"I just heard it again on my way to the wine cellar. Will you wait with me—listen for the noise?"

He nodded and leaned against the wall, waiting expectantly for the noise to meet our ears, but there was nothing. I let out an exasperated sigh, sad that I'd missed my opportunity to get clarity from Vosega.

"Be patient, dear girl. Caves have an eternity to speak. They do not feel the pressures of time," Vosega assured me.

I leaned up against the adjacent wall, frustrated. We stood there for several minutes. When I thought I'd just throw in the towel, I felt the air shift around us. On the wind was the gentle hiss followed by a deep humming in my ears.

Vosega's eyes got big. He could hear it.

"You hear it? Is it the caves below us, the caves deep under The Cathedral?"

He shook his head slowly. His face was stiff. I waited for him to elucidate on the noise. It got louder, and a small thrumming picked up.

"What is it?" I asked.

"Let us go back to my chamber." Vosega took my arm, and instantly we were back in his room. "How long have you been hearing that voice?"

"So it is a voice?" I smiled widely, happy that my assumption was correct. "What did it say?"

He repeated his question. "How long have you been hearing that voice?"

We were standing awkwardly in the center of his room. I realized I didn't recognize the surroundings; it must've been a different mountain chateau than the one I'd visited in Costa Rica.

"Ophelia, this is important. How long have you been hearing the voice?" I noted the impatience in his tone this time.

"I don't know, I guess since Elias and I arrived. Maybe not the day of, but pretty soon thereafter. What's wrong?"

"That is not the voice of a cave."

The look in his eyes sent chills up my spine. He was gravely serious.

"What do you think it is?"

"Something older than a cave, something in the depths of The Cathedral's caverns, something older than ancient."

"Is it dangerous?" I asked reluctantly.

Vosega ignored my question. "Can you understand it? Do you hear words or only noises?"

I lied, because I felt I couldn't tell him that I heard it say Sulu—that would expose too much. "I haven't heard any words yet. Should I be worried?" I looked at him, and it was as though he'd just noticed my concern for the first time.

His face eased in its expression. "No, of course not. There are legions of Conduits who would protect you within these walls. I would not listen to the sounds," he said matter-of-factly. "Perhaps avoid spending too much time alone in the lower levels."

"You're scaring me. Should I be scared? Should I tell Elias? Do you think someone infiltrated the summit?"

"No, dear. I believe whatever is calling you has been here for many, many years." He pulled me to a large chaise and ushered me to sit down beside him. "Forgive me for being overprotective. I want you to be safe. Let us take extra precautions while I investigate the origin of this voice. Can we agree to that?"

I hesitated, feeling like I should let Elias in on Vosega's concerns, but Elias had so much on his plate already. "Okay, I'll be careful. But if you have any more reason to be concerned, more than you are now, we need to let Elias in on this. Deal?" I put my hand out to shake on it.

"Deal." Vosega shook it. "I will get to the bottom of this before too long, I am certain of it."

I smiled at him and ignored the gnawing in my stomach.

ELIAS

I woke up and hurried down to Ophelia's room, but she had already left for the day. It was the second drill-day for those Champions who qualified for the next Trial. Tomorrow would be the Destruction Trial. The name on its own implied treacherousness. Of course, we would not know the true nature of the challenge until Realto outlined the parameters tomorrow during commencement. But by the description of this competition, I felt it was safe to assume tomorrow's Trial would be more dangerous than the first.

Thinking of Realto prompted me to check in on Filbert. I shifted gears and teleported up to the room where I had last seen the three men. The door looked different this morning. I knocked, and after only a moment Mikkel answered.

"Good morning. How is he?"

Mikkel looked behind him and then slipped into the hall. "He's good, much better. But I must warn you, he is up in arms, ready to return to the Nebas compound and render vengeance."

"Mikkel, who is it?" It was not Realto's voice I heard, so it must be Filbert's.

"It's Viraclay. He has come to check on you."

"Well, let him in. What are you waiting for? We need to speak at once."

Mikkel gave me another warning with his eyes before we both stepped into the room. It had changed significantly. I was now standing in a chateau. The brothers were French, so maybe this was the replica of a childhood home. It was beautiful. The wall opposite the door was all windows that led out to a veranda. Where the bed stood was now a fashionable overstuffed sofa beside two mid-century-design accent chairs. The fabrics in the room were bright and detailed, with a variety of patterns. Filbert sat at a small desk in the corner. He turned to face us as we entered. His color was back and he moved without effort.

"You seem to have healed up nicely," I said as I sat on the arm of the sofa.

"I've been told I clean up well." Filbert stood and promptly walked over and gave me a hug. "Viraclay, the miracle—my miracle. You amaze me, how is it you have your mother's gift, before your consummation no less?" He kissed me on both cheeks before taking a seat on the couch and beckoning me over.

"It is an anomaly I assure you, one that I wish to keep secret." Both men looked at me and then at eachother.

"We wouldn't dare say a word. I assure you Realto will honor your privacy as well." Mikkel promised, but I noticed he kept a safe distance, as though he was preparing for a battle. I did not like what it implied.

Filbert wasted no time. "Mikkel tells me that he informed you of the condition of Chernobyl when we left. Esther was vulnerable. Did you strike?"

I considered my words before I spoke, and chose them as carefully as I could. "I am afraid we did not."

"Then surely your intention is to attack today?"

"It is not, but I must explain why. According to your brother, we have no way of knowing if the effects of the time warp are still in place without entering the grounds. By entering the grounds, we could inadvertently disturb the warp if it was still in place, therefore destroying its effects and losing our advantage. I considered a blitz attack, but we do not know who may be being held within the compound as a captive, such as yourself. We would risk too many lives."

Filbert looked at me with disbelief. "The Nebas do not take captives. I am lucky that Esther thought I had something she wanted." Filbert got to his feet, pacing agitatedly. "Take him with you. If you disturb the time warp, he can reinstate it." Mikkel came to his brother's side.

"Sit, Filbert, calm yourself," Mikkel urged, but Filbert would not have it.

This was exactly what I was afraid of. Filbert had not made an outrageous argument. His strategies were not nonsense. But by storming the Nebas compound we risked more lives, we risked being ambushed or losing the advantage. Some very influential Conduits believed there were captives within the walls of the compound. If I blindly attacked without ensuring their safety, it would be disastrous. By acting rashly I could lose the support of many of the Pai Ona who currently sat on the fence. I could not ask for a bidding for a siege, only for war. We needed the numbers.

"I understand your reasoning, your desire for justice, and I promise you, you will have it. Just not today."

Filbert was in my face now. "You do not understand. You are too young. The time is now. The advantage is ours."

"I am young, but in my years on this planet I have learned one very important lesson, Filbert. If it seems too simple, too easy, it deserves further examination. The Nebas have hidden in plain sight ever since the last open war. Why would that be?" I hugged him and he did not reciprocate. "I am glad you are feeling better. I will be back to check on you soon."

Filbert's frustration saturated the room, but I did not have the time to argue with him. I understood his motives, I knew them well, but my father had taught me to be patient, and it had brought me here. I needed to trust that.

I stepped out of the room and into the hall.

What if I was wrong? The words kept playing over and over in my head. I needed to speak with Aurora.

It was time to reach out to her again, assuming she was still in hiding and not a captive or worse. Susuda had found no traces of her anywhere, so I had to believe she was still safe somewhere. Begging was not beneath me. I would beg her to attend the summit. I transported down to the passage that led to the broadcast room. One more attempt. I would plead with her with my own words. She would come, I knew she would come.

OPHELIA

*D*rills were less scary today, now that I knew my team and that they had my back. Plus, I had some semblance of what to expect tomorrow, although everyone assured me that it would probably be more dangerous than our first Trial. But I'd survived, and what was even better, I'd survived without exposing my abnormalities. I had to believe that made the first day of Trials pretty darn successful.

We had our plan for tomorrow and I was feeling good. That was until I saw Borte waiting for me outside my door.

"Did I miss something at practice today?" I asked, trying to stay positive.

"No, you seemed to follow everything as well as can be expected for an Unconsu."

"Was that a compliment, Borte? I'm growing on you, aren't I?" I teased, knowing she meant it more as an insult.

"You banter like he did." She scowled. "He never took anything seriously either. Now look where he is."

I knew exactly who she was referring to, and her words tore open raw wounds I tried to ignore. Pleasantries were over. Borte had already thrown her first few punches. "Did you know Lucas, really?"

"Did you?" she spat back.

I recoiled. Again, it was too close, too heartbreaking. "What the fuck do you want?" *How's that for Lucas banter, bitch?*

She smiled, and I had to fight the urge to swing at her. She may be older than me in mortal years, but she had thousands of Conduit years under her belt, which meant she was faster, stronger, and far more lethal than she let on. Borte's gifts seemed more knowledge based than anything else, but her husband was a conqueror, and they'd survived thousands of years of war—I'd be an idiot to underestimate her, and I was no idiot.

"You have something that requires my assistance. The object, whatever it may be, screams for translation. There is something urgent about its message. Until I translate it, it will continue to pull at me."

"How do you know I have it?" I sneered, still unsure of what she was referring to.

"It is all over you. I translate words of men. Words leave fingerprints, marks on those that have read or heard them, even if they don't know their meanings. The imprint is still there, and you are covered in unheard words."

I considered what she was saying. "I've been exposed to many things I don't understand over the last couple of months. I'm an Unconsu, remember?" I said sarcastically. "Now, if you will excuse me, Borte, I have to rest. Us Unconsu are weird like that." I pushed past her and into my apartment. She didn't fight her way in, she just looked after me.

When my door was shut I heard her on the other side. "I will figure it out, girl."

ELIAS

*J*ezebel joined me in the balcony. I still had the confrontation with Filbert yesterday heavily weighing my thoughts.

"May I ask you a very personal question?"

"I don't waste my time with inconsequential questions, dear Viraclay."

"You feel your husband is alive?"

"I know he is."

"How? How do you know that?"

"How do you know your parents are dead?"

"I saw their bodies."

"No, you felt their souls transform, leave the space you were used to them occupying. Tell me I'm wrong."

I thought about the day they'd died, about the moments leading up to their deaths and the moments just following. *Was there a defining moment? An instance I felt my world shift?*

"There was a sensation, something I have never shared with anyone. A void, a black spot that seemed to sear into my heart. I felt a subtle burning pain and then nothingness, which was scarier than the pain itself." It happened when I was climbing the stairs, but I ignored it. It was a memory I never wanted to revisit. Yet here I was.

"When you lose an Atoa, I imagine that pain is amplified by a thousand. Losing my grandson left a mark on me, too. But I have not felt the void from Ruit's loss. He is absent, yes, but I have never felt his soul tear away from this world."

We sat in silence for a while.

"So where is he? How come your Rune cannot reach him?"

"I do not know," she admitted.

"Do you believe he could be being held captive in the Nebas compound of Chernobyl?"

She thought about my question, and I respected that. "It is possible. Anything is possible. We are here now, watching the Katuan Trials, something people believed was no longer achievable. We sit in the grandeur of The Cathedral, a place people believed was mythical. Who am I to say what is reasonable in this world? Ruit is out there. His soul has not been cleansed by the River Tins. Is he likely imprisoned by the Nebas? Yes. Is it likely it could be at Chernobyl? Of course."

This conversation fortified my resolve to not blindly attack the compound. We did not know what we did not know. I could not risk that Jezebel was correct, that the Nebas had been collecting captives, and that they could be in Chernobyl.

OPHELIA

$\mathcal{I}$ looked up into the arena. It wasn't quite as intimidating today. I squinted to try and see the balcony where Elias sat. He'd met me this morning to bring me here, but something was off. It was hardly the time to gush about my grandmother or Borte's pestering, or even the hissing that Vosega seemed alarmed about—more so than I expected him to be. Instead, we held hands and walked in silence. I looked at my palm. It was as though I could still feel his warmth there, and it comforted me.

Strange how some people can comfort you with their mere presence. That was Elias. He had become my comfort, my friend, and perhaps someday he would become my companion, my Lasteea.

Sparkle interrupted my thoughts. "Are you ready?"

"Yeah, I'm ready." I smiled at her.

"Remember, stay close behind Shiva. He'll deflect most of the shrapnel, and maybe even ill intent." Sparkle snarled at the menacing stares I was receiving from Leviathan and Helia directly in front of us, and Constance to our right. "These three are senseless. They don't even know you."

"Most hate starts there—with ignorance," I conceded.

Tete's voice came from my left. He hadn't morphed into his

gargoyle form yet. "Don't you worry, Olly. Tete won't let a hair on your head be harmed." He tussled my hair with his huge hand playfully.

"Hey, watch the hair, buddy. I'm about to go on stage," I joked. "Don't worry about me. Watch your own ass, Tete." I nudged him with my elbow. He'd really grown on me.

"And what an ass it is!" Sparkle giggled. I nudged her with my other elbow.

"Sparkle Bantee, do you have a crush?"

"It's been a while, but maybe I do." She winked at me. I was sure Tete heard that whole exchange.

Before I could ask more questions—which felt oddly like girl time, something that I'd been missing for a while—Realto appeared on his podium.

"Champions!" Everyone stood in the arena, a standing ovation. "Spectators!" The audience grew louder. "Today we look on as the remaining Champions engage in the Destruction Trial. Victors from this Trial will carry on to our final challenge, the Transformation Trial."

I noticed Realto had a little more pep in his step today. He looked like he was glowing. I wondered why that was.

"Destruction follows creation. In our first Trial your Champions created a Haven. Our creations are our legacy. We construct them with the intention that they'll survive beyond us, thrive in the world, withstand difficulties and ruin. We build them to carry on in our own image. But too often they fall, deteriorate under the pressure, are demolished or disfigured. Today we see how well our Champions created their edifice. Will it withstand the onslaught of ruination? Will there be anything left to transform?"

More cheering from the arena erupted all around me. Simultaneously, everything became muffled. Something Realto said had struck me. Elias had told me the Katuan Trials were designed to shadow the fable of the three brothers. Except I was feeling this intense connection to the creation myth Aremis had once told me. First the painter created, then his creations were defiled or destroyed, but the true beauty came when they were transformed. When the Imposer and Receiver were able to become one again. But this new being wasn't the same as the original beings the painter had made. They were something new. For the first time, I understood the true purpose of these Trials, and why Elias knew they needed to take place. He knew that by participating in them, it would reground the Pai Ona, plant them back into their roots, transform them into something new.

"Ophelia," Nara interrupted. "Did you hear that?"

"What? What did I miss?"

"Every Champion must participate in the destruction of each Haven, save for their own."

"Okay, got it. I have to throw something around at each Haven." Because that's what we decided my destruction would look like during our drills. I needed to find a chunk of the opposing team's Haven and throw it or stomp on it, break it somehow. It was ridiculous, but we hoped it sufficed for my part in the wreckage.

I tuned back in to Realto so I didn't miss anything else.

"The first two Havens to be demolished beyond repair will be eliminated from the Transformation Trial." Realto paused. "And Champions, there is no defending your Havens. They are to be left to their own devices, based on the gifts you bequeathed them with during creation."

Just like that, the stage descended and the four Havens appeared on a spinning platform above the arena stage.

The Cathedral teleported each Katan to stand in front of their construct. I looked down, and between the spinning and the height I felt extremely woozy.

"We're going to break things from up here?" I asked Sparkle.

She shrugged. "Apparently."

Oh, I didn't like this one bit. I hated heights.

"Behold your Champions and their Havens," Realto's voiced boomed from somewhere and everywhere. "Katan Opaly!"

I couldn't take my eyes off the ground. This height thing added a whole new level of fear. I wouldn't survive a fall from this height. *Did this armor protect me from that?*

"Katan Finesol!"

I looked up to see Helia's wicked smile. All she would need to do was push me off.

"Katan Quitsee! And Katan MisaKa!"

The applause was louder up here. I searched the balconies, looking for Elias' assuring eyes. We were at balcony height, but the spinning was disorientating me. On the third pass I saw him, but his eyes were not assuring. They reflected my terror.

ELIAS

"*W*e won't be needing to astral-project today," Jezebel said plainly.

I thought I was going to be sick. The look on Ophelia's face was pure dread. She hated heights, and this was far beyond a third-floor balcony. This was towering elevations. One wrong move, one misstep —or worse, a shove—and no gift she had absorbed nor armor she wore could save her. The arena had morphed into a spinning death trap, a ring that was made of stone and perhaps a quarter of a mild wide. Each Haven stood an equal distance from its neighbors. I stood up, not certain what my next move would be.

"Sit. Sit, dear Viraclay. Enjoy the spectacle," Jezebel insisted.

"She could die if she fell from up there."

Su appeared beside me. "There is something maniacal afoot, Mr. Elias. Both The Cathedral and I sensed a shift in Helia and Leviathan's demeanor. It's subtle but perceptible."

My heart beat quickened again. *What did that mean?*

Jezebel heard Susuda's assessment. "She has my son watching over her. Trust that no harm will befall her."

I knew there were several Conduits atop the moving arena that would die to save Ophelia's life, *but what if they were too late? What if she stumbled?*

"Su, keep an especially close eye on Ophelia."

"Yes, Susuda, do keep a close eye on Ophelia. She is precious." Jezebel said it sincerely, then firmly ordered me, "Sit."

I sat down, not because she had insisted, but because I did not know what I would do. The Trials had begun. Ophelia had made her choice. To meddle with them would mean I was forfeiting everything. I gripped the arms of my seat. It was the only thing that felt secure in the moment.

"The Champions know the rules. Commence the Destruction Trial."

OPHELIA

Shiva stood in front of me. He turned around to let me know he was ready to move. Renata muted the arena, everyone but team Opaly, so that we could communicate. I heard the tearing of clothes behind me and assumed that was Tete transforming into a gargoyle. For every single step of Shiva's I had to take five. I was jogging while he was casually strolling. Borte appeared on my right. She would have to keep up with Kassandra and Shiva to play her role in this game.

Medusa was leaping in front of us. The way she moved reminded me of a jack rabbit. We decided we would split up and regroup at the MisaKa Haven, then divide again so that each half of our team participated in the destruction of each Haven. Of course, yesterday, when we devised our strategy, we didn't know the middle would be absent a bottom. The spinning circle we ran atop reminded me of a giant Frisbee with a hole in the middle. I couldn't see very far ahead of me with Shiva's giant blue body blocking my sight, and I dared not look to either side, afraid of the view.

I heard the battle cries before I saw the opposing team. Borte shouted "Duck!" and I instinctively listened. We collided with the MisaKa team between their Haven and ours. Shiva took two sudden steps back and I had to dart out of the way. Inkenga, the enormous African deity, was ramming him with his lengthy horns. Almus smiled as he jogged past me, and I turned back to see that sweet little Lucia was already at the base of our Haven, trying to dismantle it. But every time she moved a stone vine or boulder, it would wiggle back into its place. That was Sparkle's addition to the Covening. She created joy within the pieces themselves. She said it created a bond between them, and that appeared to be true.

Aruna swept past me on Nince. She was going to start tearing apart the roof of the MisaKa Haven with the help of Nince's talons. She dove down, and Nince successfully tore two large clawfuls of the thatched roof, but by the time they swooped back around to take another load, the grass had grown back.

This was going to be more complicated than it looked.

I started to sprint, wanting to catch up with Tete or Medusa. Shiva was still preoccupied with Inkenga. I realized as the MisaKa ran past us that no one intended to necessarily hurt anyone on the other Katans—that is, unless they were a threat to their Haven, which Shiva clearly was.

Although the point wasn't to hurt anyone in the arena, I had a feeling I was the exception, based on how Helia and her two thugs looked at me. So I needed to play my part as a Champion and watch my back, while also making sure I didn't plummet to my death.

I caught up to Tete, who'd just began to take flight. He was going to find a way around this chia-pet roof dilemma. Medusa shouted up at him.

"Pick me up, big boy!"

He swooped down and took her in his arms. She took off her gloves, because she didn't have to worry about turning him into stone. When they were over the roof, Tete took Medusa by the legs and she dangled, stretching her hands out and grazing the growing grass. Instantly, it turned to stone, and this time when Aruna and Nince took a chunk from the building, it didn't grow back. I turned around to see how the other half of our team was fairing.

Vosega was busy developing a massive lava bubble beneath the

Finesol Haven. Nara was creating a typhoon around him, giving him the time he needed to do his best work.

Suddenly, the barricade that Renata created around the noise dissolved and a flood of sound exploded in my head. I looked around, alarmed at what this meant for her wellbeing. She was climbing on top of Nanook, the polar bear, who'd just pushed her out of the way to get to the Finesol structure. She looked pissed. I was wondering what she was doing, when my ears began to ring. Renata had screamed at such a piercing pitch, and so fast, that every Champion stopped to cover their ears, myself included, although nothing could keep that noise out. The huge bear toppled onto the building and took half the structure with him. Renata's smile was huge as she dusted off her clothes from the fall.

I guess if you don't have the strength you find someone who does.

Borte shouted my name, but I couldn't make out anything else she was saying. It was too late, anyway. By the time I realized what she was warning me about, I was already flying through the air. A rogue root was barreling straight for me. One of the Bustanys in the arena was destroying the foundations of the Haven with large tree roots. Kassandra ran over to get me on my feet.

"Are you okay? I tried to warn you."

The sound disappeared around us again.

I was shouting when I replied. "I couldn't hear Borte!" Embarrassed, I repeated far more quietly, "I couldn't hear Borte. Thanks for trying."

"Come on. We're waiting on your destruction, then Shiva will do his thing." She smiled at me. I made my way to the base of the MisaKa Haven. Between Nince's handiwork and Tete's fists, the place wasn't looking too good. Borte was doing her own dismantling, shredding wood panels off the siding like they were paper.

"Careful," Medusa said from the roof. "I think there is some kind of enchantment on the wood."

Of course there was.

"Like what? Borte looks fine," Kassandra asked as she reached for a piece to tear off. The moment her hand touched the wood, she went into a frenzy, shredding away like Borte. Then her body went stiff, and she began speaking with her hands. After thirty seconds, she came to. "Definitely something," she agreed.

"Why would they make an enchantment that made you want to rip at the wood, and why were you able to snap out of it but she isn't?" I asked.

Medusa answered, "Look at her. It's an endless job. She would be here for centuries trying to tear the thing down like that."

"My vision pulled me out," Kassandra answered the second question.

I walked over to Borte and waved my hand in front of her face. There was nothing, just mindless shredding.

"Well, I'm not touching it. If it does that to her, what'll it do to me?"

"You have that fancy armor on—let's see what it can do. Take it out for a spin," Medusa goaded.

"It will be destroyed in a second anyway. Shiva is just biding his time so we can all do our parts." Moments after Kassandra said it I saw a gust of wind carry Vosega, Nara, Renata, Friedrick and Sand Man to the frail remains of the thatched roof. They landed safely and instantly each of them began their own demolition in their own way. When each were satisfied, they jumped off, one by one.

I turned to see Shiva looking on patiently.

It was time for me to do my part, "Alright, but if I become some mindless drone, shoot me and put me out of my misery."

"Deal," Medusa cheered.

Both women waited expectantly to see what happened. I took hold of a piece of the paneling with both hands, because that's what I'd need to do to bring about any damage. When I didn't instantly feel like a zombie, I stuck my foot up on the wall to try and get some leverage. I heard splintering and then a crack, and fell backwards on my butt. The ladies laughed, and I shrugged. "I guess the armor worked."

"I think it's cheating," Aruna teased from a few feet above us.

Nara appeared by her side. "I think it's time. I would give Shiva space."

I scrambled backwards on all fours as Shiva sauntered up confidently to the structure. Right before he placed his hand on what was left of the wall before him, Tete swooped down and detained Borte from her shredding fury.

With a single touch, Shiva turned the rest of the structure to dust. Nara quickly swept the particles into a funnel, and they rained down like confetti on the entire arena. Renata let in the applause of the crowd.

Sparkle came over and helped me to my feet, and I turned back to see what had become of our Haven. I'd wanted to name it, but everyone else said to only do that if we survive the Destruction Trial. MisaKa and Quitsee, with a couple of Finesol Champions, were doing a good job of disfiguring our structure, but they still had a long way to go, and now that MisaKa was out of the running, they were being removed from the arena.

Sparkle's charm must have been broken, because the stones were no longer reuniting. But Vosega's addition was holding strong. Lava oozed from the columns and as they cooled they continued to grow the structure. Nara was sweeping half of our team to the Quitsee Haven. She'd tried to carry me that way yesterday during practice, but I didn't like it one bit so we decided good old fashion foot work was going to have to work for me.

On the other side of the MisaKa ruins was the Finesol Haven—Helia and Leviathan's team. I didn't see either of them, but that didn't make me feel any better. The other half of our team was already hard at work on the Quitsee Haven, having previously done significant damage to the Finesol structure. Vosega was standing gloriously atop a massive blister cave he was forming in the center of the construct. I laughed out loud when I realized that was Stalt's team, and this was sweet justice for Vosega. The blister cave rocked the foundation of the Haven but didn't destroy it. Friedrick was currently growing a tree from just outside the walls, hoping to have the roots burst through the center and weaken it further.

Nara floated by on a gust of air. "Come on. What are you waiting for? We have to destroy a second Haven before they complete their demolition of ours."

I took off at a sprint. Shiva was still admiring his handiwork as I ran by. Our plan—of me staying behind him—seemed destined to fail out the gate. But I was doing pretty well avoiding danger so far. There were a lot of large roots around the base of the Finesol structure, and I had to slow down to climb over them. The look of them reminded me of Angkor Watt in Cambodia. When the third root took me too close to the edge for my liking, I decided to take my time and find a way closer to the center. The roots had grown so large that I couldn't see over them. I clawed at the mass of tree in front of me. My pride didn't want me to ask for help, but this could take all day. I was ready to get someone's attention when Shiva moved beside me and put his hand out. I sat down, not sure what else he had in mind. *Where was that hovering Borte when you needed her?*

He scooped me up and put me on his shoulder, then effortlessly traipsed over the roots. My cheeks got hot. I must have looked ridiculous. *Swallow your pride, Olly. Now is not the time,* I internally scolded.

Shiva set me down in front of the tall fortress that the Finesols had built. It looked more formidable than the MisaKa Haven even with the damage that had already been inflicted.

"Go get 'em, tiger," Medusa teased.

I rolled my eyes at her.

Already, several Quitsee were climbing the tall tower, looking for a weak link. *What was I going to do?* Aruna and Nince landed on the top.

"Here, Ophelia. Catch." Aruna removed the flag from its pole and let it loose. It gently fell to the ground, where I picked it up.

"Go on." Sparkle smiled. "Rip it."

I took the fabric in both hands and I tore it clean in half. My team cheered around me, and even Borte smiled.

"Now stand back and let us see what we can do here," Kassandra said as she put her hands on the structure. She went into one of her fits.

Borte translated for her. "They have an enchantment that will not allow Shiva's gift to work. If he tries his tricks, it will only grow taller."

Shiva looked down at his hands, and with a roar, he planted his fist onto the stone. The impact left a mark but the tower didn't fall.

"Shiva says he can use his strength, but it will take some time," Borte explained.

"What are we waiting for?" Medusa began to scale the wall. "Let's get to it, Opaly!"

ELIAS

*A*s we watched on, my nerves settled some. The Opaly Katan had already eliminated one opponent and they were about to remove a second from the running, thus completing the Destruction Trial. They had all been keeping a close eye on Ophelia. Even Borte appeared to have kept her safe.

Ophelia had played her part, and now it was up to the rest of her team to complete the havocking. I watched as Aruna and her thunderbird tore at the root system that surrounded the structure. Ophelia was a safe distance from the wreckage, but when Aruna ripped up a root I saw a flash of Helia's face. I stood to try and get a better look but things were moving so quickly I could not follow where Helia had moved to. Then her face appeared again. This time it was behind Ophelia, only a few yards away. My heart began to race wildly. No one was watching, no one could help her.

OPHELIA

I leaned up against a root and watched as half of the Opaly Champions chipped away at the Finesol structure. The Quitsees who weren't working on our Haven were finding it just as difficult to penetrate and dismantle the structure. It was impressive.

Kassandra began to have an episode at the top of the tower. When the convulsions stopped, she was too close to the edge. I screamed as I watched her body fall to the ground. I ran over as she came to. Blood streamed from the back of her head. I cradled it in my lap. She began flapping around wildly. Borte wasn't watching. She didn't see or perhaps was ignoring the communication. Either way, Kassandra's eyes said it all when they shot open and got as wide as saucers.

"Ophelia, look out…" she choked out.

Then I went numb, all emotion, all sensation—gone. Like a static frequency, I felt unclear waves of something moving through my body… no, maybe it was my mind. Words, muffled sounds flashing in and out like a strobe light. Then it was gone too and I was weightless.

ELIAS

*I*t all happened so fast. Kassandra fell. Ophelia ran to her aid. From across the arena, there was a thunderous crash. I turned to see Leviathan with all of his supreme strength kick an enormous boulder that was dislodged from the Opaly Haven. The boulder did not shatter, as would be expected from his strength. Instead, he lobbed it into the air directly toward Ophelia and Kassandra.

Helia appeared from behind Ophelia. She flung Kassandra in one direction and shoved Ophelia in the other. Helia's power rendered Ophelia numb to all sensation and all thought. You could see it on her face as her body was thrown from the arena platform. I watched on in horror as she flew through the air then began to plunge to her certain death.

The screams that clawed their way out of my throat were violent and full of disbelief. When she was only feet from the floor, Aruna caught her with the talons of her thunderbird.

What came after that was pure pandemonium. The Cathedral transported me to the arena floor, where Ophelia lay. Her body was limp in my arms, but she looked unscathed.

"Ophelia?"

"What happened? Did we win?"

I heard the ruin above us, the uproar.

Su appeared at my side. "We should move." He quickly returned us to the balcony.

Jezebel was gone. Ophelia stayed in my arms, groggily coming to from the disorientation of being compelled numb. I watched on as the Opaly Champions wreaked pure unadulterated barbarity on the Finesol Haven. By the time Ophelia was completely lucid, there was nothing left.

"I missed it," she moaned.

OPHELIA

The other Opaly Champions and I waited outside to hear the Directorate's ruling. Helia and Leviathan claimed the incident in the arena was an accident, and that without Helia's help I'd be dead.

"This is so fucked-up," Tete said for the fifteenth time. "We all know it wasn't an accident."

"The Directorate will make the right decision," Sparkle insisted.

I looked at each of my teammates with a new tenderness, even Borte. After Helia threw me off the arena stage, after Aruna saved me, they went berserk. Absolutely insane, as Elias tells it. Each of them found the strength to pummel the Finesol Haven to dust. It took four Ancients stepping in to stop them from dismembering Helia and Leviathan next. Su also had to explain that the Katuan Stones would virtually self-destruct if they went so far as to kill my would-be assassins. Now here we were, waiting to hear if the Directorate would be expelling the two from The Cathedral or if they would believe their story that it was all a big fat accident.

Elias had been with me for the last three hours, but finally agreed to go mingle and tend to his diplomatic duties as a host when I promised him I was fine.

The door to the conference room opened. "Ophelia Banner, can we see you for a moment?" a red-haired man named Zenos asked.

I looked at my Champions, as I was starting to think of them. "I'll be right back."

No one said a word, but as the door closed I heard Tete say again, "This is so fucked-up."

"Please take a seat." I looked at the twenty-six members that made up the Directorate assigned by the Stones. Two Ancients, Ganesha and Ixchel, and several other faces I didn't recognize. Elias said these were the wisest and fairest of all the Conduits—that was why the Stones had chosen them.

A round Asian man spoke next. "Ophelia, my name is Confucius. We have not met before. I find your courage admirable." Several heads nodded at this statement. "Today your life was in danger. These two Conduits either acted maliciously or recklessly, putting not only your life but all of our lives in jeopardy by breaking the code of conduct as a Katuan Champion."

Helia objected, "We told you, we didn't realize a death in the Trials would result in the Katuan Stones self-destructing, and it was an accident."

I internally rolled my eyes.

The familiar German accent of Berty addressed the room. "It's our job as the Directorate to determine if these two individuals should be punished, banished, or given the benefit of the doubt. What would you have us do, considering that you were the one they attempted to harm?"

Helia was going to object again, but Berty put his hand up to silence her. I considered my options carefully. I didn't need any more enemies. I knew Elias wanted to build loyalties and trust with the summit. *What better way to do that than to extend an olive branch?* On the other hand, these two clearly weren't trustworthy. But by repri-manding them we risked losing allegiances from anyone who aligned with them. I didn't know who that was, or what kind of impact that would make on our mission. I had plenty of people I could trust—my team had proved that today. I felt I could spare these two and see if mercy won us more allies.

"I think it was a terrible accident." I tried my best to sound convincing. From some of the looks I got, my performance may not have been very good. "I believe in second chances. People make mistakes, but they deserve forgiveness."

Helia's jaw might've hit the floor. Leviathan looked just as shocked.

"If you're asking my opinion, I think they deserve to finish out the summit."

It was quiet until a female voice called for a vote. "We have heard the arguments, we have what evidence we could accumulate. It is time to decide. Those in favor of banishment say *Aye*."

Several *Ayes* echoed through the room. "Those in favor of mercy, as Miss Banner would have it, say *Aye*."

It was a close vote, but the mercy verdict won.

"Very well, but hear me now. If anything should happen to Miss Banner during the remainder of the summit, it will be assumed that you two are to blame, and without her here to advocate for you, mercy will not be administered a second time."

Helia gave me one more confused look before leaving the room. The rest of the Directorate gave me solemn nods, all except Berty, who gave me a jovial smile. I shuffled out last to an expectant group of Opaly.

"So? Are we torturing the assholes?" Tete asked.

"No, we're not. They get to watch the rest of the Trials like everyone else, in the stands and as losers."

That warranted a cheer or two from Sparkle and Kassandra, but everyone else looked slightly dejected. "I think it's its own form of torture to be stuck in a room full of Conduits that know you're a deceptive coward who bullies others. Don't you?" I meant what I said —this would be torture for them in its own way.

"I guess, but now we have to go see them at the lame banquet tonight," Medusa added.

"Do we?" Vosega smiled. "We are the Champions. Can we not decide how to celebrate?" He winked at me.

"Yeah! Who needs a stuffy banquet? Let's boycott," Tete joined in. "The spectators can hang out with the Quitsee team."

"Nay, they can hang out with Stalt," Vosega sneered.

I laughed. "I'm up for a little hooky."

Everyone else nodded or gave a cheer of agreement, everyone except Borte.

I walked over to her. She was standing a few feet away from the rest of us. "What about you, Borte?"

"It seems wrong to celebrate with my husband missing." Something flashed across her face. I couldn't tell what it was—sadness maybe, but paired with something else. "Where will you be meeting?"

I looked back at everyone else. "My apartment?" There was a unanimous agreement. "Yep, my apartment."

"Let me freshen' up. I will see how I feel then."

Under the gruff exterior was a woman who was missing her partner. I could empathize with that.

I nodded and she put her hand to the wall and disappeared.

"It looks like we're going to need a lot of wine. Vosega, Tete, come with me. The rest of you are welcome to meet us up there." I had a moment of wishing I'd cleaned up the apartment better, but then thought, screw it, these were my friends.

Vosega, Tete and I manifested into the wine cellar. I pointed to a box I knew had been acquired for me. "Tete, you can grab that one." Vosega was rummaging around.

"What are you looking for?"

"I know it's here. I had it delivered."

"What? What's here?"

His eyes lit up when he spotted what he was looking for. "My finest batch of mead." Vosega took hold of a large barrel. "Are you ready?"

I picked up a second case of wine and realized this night would be one to remember. "Am I ever!"

ELIAS

"*D*o you think she's alright?" Aremis asked me while I sat at the island in the galley. "She missed the banquet."

"I think it is likely she is hung over." I smiled at my dear friend. "Based on the amount of alcohol they consumed last night. You know our Ophelia, always sure she can do what anyone else can. She probably challenged Shiva to a drinking contest."

We both laughed at that.

"I am sorry that your team did not carry on after the first trial."

"No matter. I have never been one for competition, although I would have liked to have been up there yesterday when our girl was ambushed."

"As always, I know she would have been in good hands if you were there, watching over her," I assured him. "On one hand, I wish the Opaly team would have lost yesterday, so that she was no longer in danger. But on the other, the world loves an underdog, and everyone is excited to see Ophelia and her team succeed." It was true. She was already, without knowing, uniting the Pai Ona.

"That, they do," Aremis agreed. "What is on your agenda for the day?"

"Well, I think I will start by bringing Ophelia coffee and breakfast in bed."

A voice with a thick German accent spoke up. "I don't mean to interrupt, gentlemen, but may I speak to you in private, Viraclay? My name is Albert, but most people call me Berty."

Aremis looked at me then excused himself.

"Berty, how can I assist you?"

"It's about Miss Banner."

Well, now he had my full attention. "Please sit." I gestured to the stool beside me.

"I've been watching her closely over the last few days, week rather. You know my gifts?"

"I am familiar. You see energy, or rather the way the strokes move."

"I do, and there is a curious thing about the way Miss Banner's presence manipulates the strokes around her."

This was my fear, that someone would see her abnormalities. I clenched my jaw. "In what way?" I asked, playing ignorant.

"She is a vortex. I have no better way to put it. But that isn't the most curious part."

"What is the most curious part?" I leaned in unconsciously.

"Whatever she is absorbing in this vortex is preparing to funnel somewhere else."

"What do you mean?"

"I wish I knew more, but I'm afraid that's the depth that my abilities will allow me to see." He got to his feet. "I thought you should know. She is special, but you already knew that. Now, what shade of special... that remains to be seen."

OPHELIA

*A*lmus' voice about split my head in two. "We missed you last night at the banquet."

"Holy shit!" I shouted and grabbed my head.

"What is it? Are you okay?" Worried images flashed across the back of my eyelids that I had yet to open.

"I'm fine," I responded internally. "You just scared me, and I have a massive headache." I recalled last night. It was one for the history books, at least my history books. We drank and laughed until—I cracked my eye open and saw the clock—just a few hours ago. Even Borte had decided to join us. She kept her distance but she drank and occasionally laughed. When her face lit up, I saw that she was a very attractive woman.

Almus seemed to finally catch my drift, not by anything I was intentionally trying to convey in my words, but I must've been leeching some of the pain from my headache into our connection.

"I will leave you to it, then. I just wanted to convey to you that Inca and I missed you."

"I missed you too," I mumbled before signing off.

I let my body relax again, ready for sleep to heal me of my nasty hangover, when I felt the air shift around me. I instinctively sat up in bed.

"It is just me." Elias stood with a plate of food and a warm cup of coffee beside my bed. "I thought you might need this." He set the tray down on my nightstand. "And these." He wiggled his fingers.

I'd completely forgotten about my ability to heal, although healing myself would've required me lowering my shield, which was strictly forbidden until after the summit. So I was grateful to have Elias' digits at my disposal.

I nodded, and he crawled into bed beside me. His fingertips found my temples, and he began to trace gentle circles. Instantly, the pain subsided.

"Did you have fun?"

"A ton of it. It was totally worth it, even if you couldn't make me feel better." I opened my eyes, now feeling right as rain, to look at him.

"I thought I was going to lose you yesterday." His voice was serious.

"I know. I'm sorry."

"You needn't apologize, but it put things into perspective." He pulled his hand from my head and took my free hand in his. My other hand was still stuffed under my pillow. "I think we should reconsider our approach to consummation... not immediately, of course, but a few days after the summit, perhaps we can revisit the subject." He gently kissed my hand, lingering on my middle finger for a second soft and sultry kiss.

I knew what his words implied. I no longer had a headache but I was still clearing out the fog from lack of sleep and alcohol. Elias still had my hand pressed to his lips when I suddenly became self-conscious of my breath, hair and general disarray.

I gently pulled my hand away. "I'm all for revisiting, but—and I don't mean to be a pain—but it tastes like a small animal shat in my mouth last night, and I know I smell like a tavern. Can we pick this up at a later date?" I asked, afraid I offended him.

But Elias just laughed. "Anytime you want." He pulled himself out of bed, pointed at the breakfast tray. "My mother used to make me one of these sandwiches after a late night with my father. I hope it helps you the way it helped me." With a wink, he strolled out of the room.

I was still uneasy having him in the space that I'd shared with Lucas. Lucas' presence tainted any intimacy I had with Elias. When I looked around, all I saw was my past.

I dragged myself out of bed. We'd have drills today to prepare for the Transformation Trial tomorrow. I should get ready. The food Elias had brought smelled amazing. I lifted the lid. An egg sandwich on a croissant—just what the doctor ordered. I sat at the edge of my bed and took a bite. It was delicious. I took a sip of my coffee. It was just the way I liked it.

While I chewed on my breakfast I let my thoughts wander. Elias was ready to start a life with me. *Was I ready to do the same with him?* I considered what Talia had told me during our brief friendship: "Follow your heart." If I was being honest with myself, following my heart would always lead me to Elias.

I wanted to hear more wisdom from the familiar words of my friend Talia so I reached for her journal where I'd stashed it, between my mattress and box spring. It wasn't there. I took the last bite of my sandwich and stuck both my hands under the bed, my fingers looking feverishly for the familiar leather binding. I threw the mattress off the bed entirely. It was gone.

ESTHER

*T*ears streamed down my face. *How long had I been standing here? How much longer would I have to endure the scent of my lover, of my Yanni, fused with the certain smell of burnt flesh and ash?* The combination was haunting, ripping the shreds of my sanity apart.

My body was frozen in a slow, unending movement. The way Mikkel warped time slowed it down so that every passing second felt like an eternity. The muscles in my arms ached from disuse and yet contracted all at once.

It could have been years since they had escaped, for all I knew. Time would tell the story when the warp was finally disturbed by someone new entering into it at a normal speed.

When Lucifer's face flashed in front of my eyes, my body collapsed to the ground.

I lay there in a heap, trying to will strength back into my exhausted extremities.

"Mistress?" He knelt beside me. "What happened?"

"How long have you been gone?"

"Five days."

"Where are the rest of my men? Bring me Akiva at once," I demanded.

"Yes, Mistress."

I still had not lifted my head. "And Lucifer, get a message by way of the pixies. I want all Nebas called to arms, even those in secret alliance."

"Yes, Mistress."

OPHELIA

I stormed out of my apartment. *That bitch had tricked me.* She never wanted to hang out with any of us. It was all just a ruse to get into my apartment. To go through my things. I wondered how I'd been so stupid. Plus, I'd never put two and two together. The translation she saw—it was always the journal. It wasn't the part I valued, so I never paid much attention to it. Talia's words were what mattered to me, not the odd language that preceded her pages.

The Cathedral presented me in front of Borte's door. I was still in my pajamas. I hadn't even bothered with brushing my teeth or pulling back my hair.

My fist hit the wooden door hard and didn't stop thumping until she opened it.

"Ophelia." Borte grinned at me, shamelessly holding Talia's journal in her hand. "I've been expecting you. Come in."

I pushed past her and reached for the journal at the same time.

"Ah-ah-ah. Not yet. I am almost finished. Take a seat." She gestured to a bench against the wall. It wasn't very inviting.

"Give it back, Borte!" I demanded.

"Please sit. There is something I want to discuss with you." She was trying to manage her tone, keep it pleasant and light, but you could tell it strained her to do so. I refused to sit. "This is an interesting read. I must say I am not surprised to find out about Lucas' betrayal. He was always rotten."

I lunged at her. "Give it to me now!" I felt my skin start to burn, like I was boiling my own blood, and struggled against the powers that were only too eager to manifest. I needed to keep my temper under control—I knew from my interaction with Di that I could expose too much if I didn't—so I took deep breaths. "I'm going to ask you one more time, and then there will be no more asking."

"Idle threats, little Unconsu." She had no idea. "Talia's journal, Nandi, whatever you would like to call her, is no real care of mine. But these markings, do you know what you have here?"

She knew I didn't. "Stop stalling."

"This language is Kata, the language of the Stones."

Familiar figures flashed across my mind's eye. I was connecting the dots. I knew the engravings on the stones had looked familiar.

"The interesting thing about Kata is that it is not a language I can freely translate, because my gift is limited to translations of humans and Conduits. I can't understand animals, or in this case, rock." She was tapping the journal she held in her left hand with her right. "Surely someone very old wrote the markings to begin with, but the language evades me entirely, or at least it had until this text." She held it up.

"So then you got what you wanted. You got to read the text you were hounding me about. You're welcome."

"Not exactly. I could only translate very little of the markings. I believe you need to be in proximity for me to complete the conversion. You are funneling something to or through the markings. I am certain of it."

"That's impossible."

"I agree. Yet it is true."

"Why do you care?"

"The few words I deciphered indicate there is something below this Cathedral, and if Elias is to be believed, that is where my husband is."

"What? What is below The Cathedral?"

"I do not know."

I'd had enough of this. I wanted my journal back. "I don't care about your husband. If The Cathedral sequestered him, he must be a bad man," I growled through gritted teeth. "Give me the journal or I will—"

Su manifested out of the air behind Borte. "No need to threaten Mrs. Khan, Miss Olly. She will hand over your property now."

Borte turned to face Susuda. He was ordinarily a mild-mannered man, on this side of the gate, but the fire in his eyes at present suggested he could turn at any moment. Borte complied with Su's request without question.

"Come, Miss Olly. You need to freshen up."

I took Su's hand and we were gone before Borte could say another word.

ESTHER

I looked at the small mass we had congregated since only this morning. They were too few. I had many more allies, but something was making them jumpy, skittish.

I turned to Akiva. "Where are the rest of them?" I demanded.

"Mistress, I summoned everyone, and this is the lot that responded." Akiva's eyes moved back and forth as he spoke. He was aware that I was not happy and he wanted to avoid my wrath.

"Summon them again," I said through bared teeth.

"Of course." Akiva bowed and began backing out of the room, afraid to turn his back on me. He was such a good servant. Obedient, submissive, aware of the consequences when he displeased me. A thought occurred to me. "Wait." I put my hand up just before Akiva would have disappeared into the shadows of the corridor. "I think I should personalize the summons. Help the others see the urgency in these matters."

"As you wish, Mistress." Akiva stood erect and walked to my side. The compound had a central space where hundreds if not thousands could congregate. I avoided the masses and took my rightful place above them. The second story had a balcony that overlooked the larger open space on the first floor. I stood at the railing as I evaluated the group below. Akiva came to my side and he too took inventory of our guests.

"How many are down there?"

"A little over a hundred."

I had to hold back a scoff—what a pitiful turnout. "Collect Visius and Jillian."

Akiva raised his eyebrows but said nothing.

"Oh, and, Akiva… be discreet."

OPHELIA

"Thank you, Su," I said as he delivered me to my door.

"Miss Olly, please do not enter into those sorts of situations without me. That woman is not nice. She cannot be trusted."

I smiled at him and put my hand on his shoulder. "You're right, and I won't do that again. It was silly of me."

Su was satisfied with my answer and quickly dissolved away. I really did love that man. I shut the door and decided to jump into the shower. A glance at the clock said drills would be starting soon.

The water felt good on my scalp. I considered what Borte had said. *What did it mean that I was funneling something into the Kata symbols? And was there something lurking below The Cathedral?*

I needed to speak with Vosega before the drills.

I finished up in the shower, threw on some clothes and arrived at Oya and Vosega's room ten minutes later. I knocked and Oya answered the door, looking as sexy as ever. I had a new-found respect for the Conduit who'd saved my mother's life.

"Oya, is Vosega here?"

She shook her head. "No. I thought he was with you. He was returning his mead barrel to the wine cellar and then heading to the drill room to get some extra practice in. He is eager to defeat Stalt." She smiled coyly.

Of course he was. "Oh, okay. I'll catch him down there." I waved goodbye as she shut the door.

I landed in our practice hall a few moments later. Medusa and Tete were there, but no Vosega. I met them where they trained, at the end of the room.

"You're up early. I thought you would be down for the count today. You fucking rock!" Tete winked at me.

"Our girl Ophelia is a pro." Medusa smiled.

"Hahaha," I poked back. "Have either of you seen Vosega?"

"Not yet," Tete replied between blows. Medusa was practicing contact maneuvers, and since Tete was already made of stone, there was nothing for them to worry about. "But everyone should be here soon."

"Yeah," I said and walked a distance away to wait for the others to arrive. Something wasn't right. My gut was screaming at me.

ESTHER

*A*kiva threw Jillian's frail frame in front of me. She looked broken, disfigured. While Visius, who sat in a chair behind me, looked valiant, strong and vital. I knelt down to better see Jillian's face. She retreated into the fetal position, trying to squirm away from my touch.

"Tsk, tsk, tsk. You needn't be afraid of me, Jillian. You have confessed your sins. You are hereby absolved of any treason." I spoke softly, sweetly. I looked up to see Astrid and Claudia enter the balcony. There was much to be seen from this vantage point. Alliances being made, whispers bouncing off the walls. The Nebas were a curious group. United by vengeance or the lust for power. It made allegiances weak, but one thing kept those loyalties strong, one element united them all under my command—fear.

I nodded to Akiva, Claudia and Astrid, so they immediately took their places at my side, overseeing the congregation of Conduits below. I looked down at Lucifer, who in turn nodded. He was ready.

I spread my arms into a warm welcome. "Good evening, friends." I smiled the smile Yanni said endeared others to me. "I am so pleased with your arrival to the compound. It has been many years since we have congregated as friends, perhaps not since the last open battle."

There were some nods and whispers of agreement. "It has come to my attention that the Pai Ona are mobilizing."

That created more of a stir. I put my hand up to silence them. "I know, this is disturbing. And although most of you maintain your allegiance to the Nebas in secret, I know they have orchestrated a way to divine who is with them and who is with us! Your secrets are useless to you now!"

The room erupted this time. Once again, I put my hand up. The statement wasn't an entire truth, but I had reasons to conclude this must have happened.

"There is nothing to fear, my friends. For we are many, and they are few." Then I paused and looked around, feigning surprise. "Wait, are we many? For years we have been fighting in the shadows. Those in secret allegiance to the Nebas have killed many for our cause— domination over the humans, reclaiming the power we lost..." I looked around again. "But so few are in attendance today." I hopped up on the banister of the terrace and began to pace. "Which makes me wonder, where are the rest of our comrades? Why do they forsake my summons, my call to action, in our time of need?"

I deepened my voice, allowing the menace and conviction I often controlled to leach into it. "It has occurred to me that perhaps many of you here and far have thought me weak upon Yanni's passing. Many of you think my position has diminished, that losing Yanni's gift somehow makes my agenda compromised. Perhaps you may even think I cannot find you anymore, that my reach is less penetrating." I took a deep breath, feeling the rage boil up to the surface, and growled, "Let me assure you, I am not weak."

I put a hand out to either side. Akiva instinctively drew their bodies to me. On my right was the crumpled form of Jillian, and on my left was the pragmatic Visius.

"I believe you are all familiar with Jillian." I put my index finger under her chin to raise her swollen face. "This poor misguided fool also thought I was weak. She thought she could discharge herself from my company, from our cause, from this war! But you see her now—she is a pawn, broken and malleable. Are you familiar with her abilities?" I looked on at the crowd. Those who knew shuddered, others looked around anxiously for the answer. I turned my gaze to Visius. "Visius here is a crusader. Like you, he has come to the call, showed up when summoned." I caressed his cheek gently, seizing control of his body. "Do you know what these two have in common that those who have declined my invitation do not?" I met the stare of every Conduit who dared make eye contact with me. "Fear." I almost whispered the word. "They know to fear me and the consequences of displeasing me."

I commanded Visius' hand to take hold of Jillian's. Both of their bodies stiffened. Jillian was a Conveyor. She could articulate any message, feeling or sensation to anyone within a certain radius. Visius was a Decimate. He could make anything explode with a single touch, including parts of the body. What a brilliant combination.

"I want to make it clear—to you, to all of you—that you are not out of my reach. That if you try to abandon the Nebas, I will hunt you down and I will kill you myself."

I whispered a simple order in Jillian's ear and at the same time commanded Visius to decimate his own heart. His body fell to the ground, my control broken by his temporary unconsciousness. Jillian's eyes rolled back into her head, the only indication that she was sending a message. Then everybody in the room stiffened and crumpled to the ground, their hearts having exploded in their chests.

I looked down at the mob of bodies. They would come to soon enough, and when they did, each of them would have a newly charged fear of me. The only real way to rule over anyone is with fear.

ELIAS

"There's something wrong," she asserted as she paced in my room. "He wasn't at drills, and he didn't attend the play tonight."

I walked over and put my hand on her cheek. "He didn't attend the banquet last night."

"None of us did. That's different."

"Is Oya concerned?"

"No. She said he does this. That he's probably meditating or some bullshit." Ophelia pulled away from my touch and threw her hands in the air. "Don't you trust me?"

"Indeed, I do." I sighed, wanting to comfort her, but not wanting to raise any alarms for a Conduit who was known to appreciate his privacy. "Let us compromise. If Vosega does not appear for the Trial tomorrow, we will sound the alarm."

"What if it's too late?"

"What if he is off collecting his thoughts, preparing for a stand-off with his greatest opponent?"

She reluctantly succumbed to the fact that that was a possibility. "I told you about the hiss when I first heard it. I wish I would've told you Vosega's reaction sooner. Borte said something was down there. I worry that these two incidents are connected. Vosega knew about it too."

"All that matters is that you told me. We will get to the bottom of it."

"I should get to bed. Big day tomorrow." Frustration laced her every word.

"Do try and sleep, Ophelia."

"Yeah," was all she said before leaving my room and disappearing into the hall.

Once she was out of sight, I tried to assuage my own fears by telling myself that it was just one missing, perhaps not even missing, Conduit. But it was not just one missing Conduit. It was possibly a fourth missing Conduit, and still no sign of Aurora.

OPHELIA

The third day of Trials. I woke up early and went straight to Vosega's room. Oya said he still wasn't there and she still seemed unconcerned. My gut on the other hand was screaming at me. I knew something had happened to him. He was my friend and I would not forsake him. I'd not rest until I saw him again.

So now here I was. We all stood there on the stage, waiting for Vosega's arrival. Realto waited patiently to begin the Trial.

He came over to us after several more minutes had passed. We huddled together. "I'm afraid we can't wait any longer, y'all. The Stones have spoken, and they've instructed me to forfeit your place as Champions and convene the Directorate for further direction. You cannot compete with an incomplete team; therefore you are disqualified."

Tete began cussing, and Medusa's mouth was no better. I couldn't wait any longer. Something was wrong, and I knew where to begin my search for Vosega.

I jumped off the platform and walked toward the closest threshold to transport to my room and collect my things. Behind me, Realto's voice boomed over the stirring audience.

"It is the day of Transformation! True beauty is found through resilience and renovation." Then I touched the wall and was back in my room, in the quiet.

I was going to find Vosega.

PART IV

ELIAS

I saw Ophelia jump down from the stage before the rest of her team were removed by The Cathedral. She must be seeking out Vosega. At this point I had to assume her fears were warranted. I could not imagine him disappointing his team or missing an opportunity to challenge Stalt.

Su appeared at my side just before I stood to teleport to Ophelia's room.

OPHELIA

I knew what I had to do. Borte had translated enough of the journal for me to suspect that Vosega's disappearance had something to do with the mysterious noise I kept hearing. Vosega had promised to get to the bottom of the sound. Maybe he had, and now he was in danger. I wasn't going to lose him. He was my friend, Lucas' father—a good man. Any one of those reasons was enough to venture into the unknown to find him. I thought about reaching out to Oya while I packed a small bag in my room. She would help, but I couldn't bring myself to put anyone else in danger.

I'd leave a note for Elias in the galley. I wanted to grab some food and water in case this expedition took me longer than I expected. I looked in the bag one more time to make sure I had everything I thought I needed: a long sleeve shirt and some extra socks—it could be cold down there—Talia's journal, and a blank sheet of paper and a pen. I slung my backpack over one shoulder, tied another sweater around my waist, and looked around the familiar apartment one last time before stepping into the hall and placing my hand on the wall just outside my door. The Cathedral planted me right where I wanted to be, in the galley. I had to move fast, before Elias came after me—

and I knew he would. I tore the blank sheet of paper in half and scribbled a brief note to Elias and Su.

I think I know where Vosega is. I'll be back soon!
Don't worry about me,
Olly

Short and sweet, and if I was lucky this adventure would be just like that, as well. I swiped three bladders of water from the pantry, along with duck jerky, saltine crackers and four apples. I stared into the bag and wavered. *Was it enough? Was I being too cautious? You can never be too cautious, right?* With that thought, I swiped another bag of jerky.

I needed to get moving. I wanted to be back by nightfall, for the arguments and the Victors' Ball. If I was quick, then maybe no one would notice my absence. I pulled the backpack onto my back and started down the hall. If I'd been a little more aware, maybe even a little less distracted, I might have noticed I wasn't alone in the galley.

ELIAS

"Someone is here." The way Su said it I was sure we were going to be facing the Nebas outside The Cathedral gates.

"Who is here, Susuda?"

"She would not give me a name, but she requested she see you." He looked at me skeptically. "I am not sure it is safe."

It had to be Aurora. "Take me to her."

"Are you sure, Mr. Elias? She has an unsavory attendant. I don't know what it is, but I don't like it."

"I understand." I tried to be calm. I had to greet whoever was here and then hunt down Ophelia. My stomach was twisted in knots. "What did the woman look like?"

"She is cloaked."

"I see. Take me to her, Su."

Su argued no further. Moments later we were atop the Bengharh Fort roof. In front of us stood a tall woman with a short escort, both wearing hooded cloaks.

"How can I help you?"

There was a long pause. No one moved. *Had I made a grave mistake?*

OPHELIA

J walked down the dark passage with my flashlight, hoping to hear the hiss, but all I heard was silence. In the silence, I was left with my thoughts.

I hoped Elias found my note, and that it wouldn't distract him from his preparations for the arguments. I grappled with my decision to leave him hanging when he was so busy. But in the end, finding Vosega seemed more important, and Elias couldn't come with me and take care of six thousand Conduits at the same time. He'd understand.

The interesting thing about the lower depths of The Cathedral was that the teleportation magic stopped working below the third basement floor. I wondered why that was. Su had explained to Elias that anything deeper than the level I was on now was governed by a different kind of magic. Not even he could teleport beyond this point without getting permission from The Cathedral. I'd have to venture on foot, and I kind of liked the normalcy. It occurred to me that perhaps the lack of teleportation was to keep others out. *What did that mean for me or for Vosega?* I guessed I'd find out.

The back of my ear began to tickle. It was Almus, or Inca.

Almus' voice manifested in my head. "Ophelia, where have you run off to?"

I quickly joined the conversation by rubbing my Rune. "I need to see to a quick errand before I can make my way back to the arena. Will I see you and Inca at the Victors' Ball?"

"Ophelia?" Almus asked peculiarly. "Are you there? Ophelia?" His voice was full of alarm. I saw a flash of Inca's face. She had worry lines across her forehead.

"I'm here, Almus. I'm okay." But there was nothing. Our connection was gone. I stood there in silence and felt eerily alone. *I didn't have a signal down here?* Almus had never mentioned poor Rune reception before. I had a sudden urge to head back, to explain where I was going, so at least Almus wasn't concerned.

But no sooner did the thought cross my mind than I heard the shuffle of feet behind me in the dark. "Hello? Who's there?"

I turned the flashlight on my stalker to find the all too unpleasant figure of Borte.

"What on earth are you doing here?" I asked.

"I need to find my Khan."

"So you're following me?"

"I knew you wouldn't let me come with you willingly. That journal you carry is the key. What choice did I have?" she spat and pointed at my bag.

"You could wait for The Cathedral to return him," I suggested.

A scoff escaped her lips before she responded. "My husband has done nothing but keep his family safe, only to be imprisoned by a Haven. I think not."

I didn't know what The Cathedral would do with her prisoners or why she took them to begin with. *If I were Borte and Elias was Khan, could I sit back and see what became of him?* It only took me a moment to know the answer. No, I couldn't. I wouldn't. "Very well, but be quiet… and try and not be such a bitch," I added.

We heard a chuckle in the dark behind Borte. A flicker of flame illuminated two of my favorite faces. Aremis and Sparkle were traipsing down the hall.

"That will be very difficult for Borte." Sparkle's face lit up even in the dim light of the flame.

334

"What are you guys doing here?" I moaned halfheartedly. On one hand, I was appreciative to have friends with me when just a moment ago I was feeling desperately alone, but on the other hand, *was I leading more of my friends into danger?* I couldn't do that to them; I loved Sparkle and Aremis too much to risk their safety. "Did Elias send you to follow me?"

Aremis was the one to answer. "No, Miss Ophelia. On the contrary, we were looking for you in the galley when we saw Borte slink by. When we realized she was following you, we decided to trail her." Aremis' youthful smile warmed my heart.

"I expect you want to join me on my exploration, as well."

"If you insist." Sparkle laughed again and pushed past Borte, making her way by my side, where she squeezed my arm in a friendly hello. "It sounds like an adventure."

"It's more of a rescue mission," I admitted. "I need to find Vosega, and my gut tells me he's down here."

I turned off the flashlight. Aremis realized that this was my invitation for him to lead the way. His friendly dancing sparks forged ahead in the dark.

"You three are ludicrous," Borte whined, but she didn't protest any further. Instead, she walked at the back of our line as the corridor narrowed.

The floor began to decline at a subtle angle and curve to the left. I didn't remember any other corridors like this. I'd thought this tunnel would dead-end a lot sooner. We walked for another fifteen minutes in relative silence before the inevitable question came up.

"Why do you believe Vosega is down here?" Sparkle prodded.

"A hunch." I paused. It was time to be honest. "More than a hunch. I heard something down here, and Vosega seemed interested to discover what the noise was. I think he decided to explore the lower levels of The Cathedral and got lost."

Borte snorted. "More like got abducted."

I turned on her. "Why would you say that? The Cathedral has been nothing if not hospitable to you."

"If that is what you call sequestering my husband."

My head was swarming with a dozen snarky responses but before I could retaliate, Aremis interrupted me.

"It seems we have reached a dead end, ladies." It was the wall I'd run into the two other times I'd been down here.

I traced the crevices, looking for a sign of a door or secret passage, like Hafiza had.

The humming erupted in my ears, louder than it had ever been. "Do you guys hear that?"

Aremis and Sparkle shook their heads while Borte ignored the question.

"Are you going insane?" she asked excitedly.

Then there was silence, heavy silence. My eyes met Aremis' just as the floor beneath our feet disappeared and we dropped into a black abyss.

ELIAS

"*A*urora." I sighed in relief. "You are here. I was so worried you would not attend."

"I am sorry for my absence thus far, Viraclay. I had to take extra precautions to avoid detection. Esther knows the Pai Ona have congregated. I have seen it." She saw the alarm on my face and put her hand on my shoulder. It was awkward, because Aurora avoided intimacy. "Worry not, my boy. I left no trace of my whereabouts."

I turned to her attendant, who had yet to remove their hood. "Come, let us get you to your room. You must be exhausted from your travels." Su opened the gate and we entered The Cathedral. There was a roar from the crowd in the arena. "The Transformation Trials have only just begun."

"How many are in attendance?" Aurora looked alarmed. It had been centuries since she had seen more than one Conduit at a time, I was certain of it.

"Over six thousand," I said proudly.

"That may lead to many arguments."

"I do not believe you will preside over as many as you would expect. Being that there are no Nebas here, most of the Pai Ona are carrying on very peaceably."

"Surely there are aged disputes?"

"Perhaps, but I have to say that between the two weeks of arrivals and the banquets, most of our people have reasoned their differences with each other. Fellowship can be a good thing." I hoped she understood what I meant. "I have one concern, though."

"What would that be?"

"The Cathedral—she has taken her own prisoners. Three, possibly four." I was including Vosega now in that number.

"Her own prisoners?"

"I was hoping you could tell me something about it."

"Who has she taken?"

"Genghis, George Thracian and Cadmus." I hesitated on the last name. "Possibly Vosega."

"But you are certain of the first three? Why are you unsure about Vosega? "

"He only went missing yesterday. The other three were sequestered upon their arrival. I have promised the families we will return them, but I haven't the faintest idea what she intends to do with them. I have held out hope that she wants to present them to you for evaluation. But now that Vosega is gone, I do not know what to think," I admitted.

We continued to walk as we talked. I was not certain where we were going. Susuda appeared to be buying me time with The Oracle.

"Where do you think she is keeping them?"

"Below us, in the caves. You have not seen any of this?"

She shook her head.

"The gatekeeper does not even venture down there."

"That is because something dark resides in the depths of this Haven. I can feel it now, rumbling beneath us, hissing, thirsting for blood."

"Hissing?" Ophelia had heard hissing.

"Hissing," Aurora repeated.

The bottom of my stomach dropped through the soles of my feet and a waterfall of ice cascaded down my spine. "Susuda, see Aurora to her room." I reached for the closest wall, hoping against hope that I was not too late. I had to find Ophelia.

OPHELIA

"How can you be sure this is the right way?" I asked Borte. She'd taken the lead after we fell for what felt like forever into this maze of tunnels. They weaved in and out of each other in what seemed like nonsensical ways.

"I do not know which is the right way. I just know we won't get out or find my Khan without moving."

"Then perhaps we should take a moment to get our wits about us?" Aremis suggested patiently. "Instead of ambling aimlessly through these halls."

"I'm with Aremis," Sparkle chirped. "I think we should make a plan, so we don't get lost down here."

I stopped but Borte kept walking. "Borte, stop," I said.

The slight woman with her long black hair turned to face the three of us. "I am looking for my husband. I am not on your whimsical quest to find the Vulcan." She turned back around and huffed off. "Leave me be."

Aremis grabbed my arm when I started after her.

"Are we really just going to let her take off like that?"

"I don't think we have a choice, Olly." Sparkle met my stare. Her eyes looked just as worried as mine. "Borte seems determined."

"That, she does. We needn't concern ourselves with her errand. Tell us why Vosega came down here."

Aremis squeezed my shoulder gently. I looked into his face with the distinction of wisdom in his eyes then glanced after Borte one more time. She'd do anything to find out where The Cathedral was keeping her prisoners. The ancient Mongolian woman had seen her share of violence, so I had to assume she could take care of herself, at least until I figured out how to find Vosega and get us out of here. I resigned myself to moving forward with the reason why we'd come down here and not worrying about our AWOL companion.

So I explained everything to Aremis and Sparkle, from the first time I'd heard the hissing, and although I trusted both of them, I left out the time I thought I heard it say Sulu.

"Vosega said it wasn't the caves that were whispering to me, or hissing at me—whatever. It was something else, and it concerned him."

"Do you hear the whispers now?" Sparkle asked.

"No. I haven't heard anything since we fell through the floor," I said, discouraged. "But Borte translated the journal and said there was something down here." I rubbed my brow. "I don't know what to do."

"Well, we are here now. All we can do is move forward," Aremis asserted.

"Yeah, so which way does your gut tell you to go?" Sparkle asked.

I looked after Borte one more time before digging into my gut and deciding that my instincts said to continue straight and not leave this tunnel until we saw where it ended.

ELIAS

J stared at the note. Almus appeared in the doorway of the galley. "Is Ophelia with you?" he asked.

I handed him the piece of paper.

"I cannot contact her with my Rune. I have tried multiple times. Where would she have gone to look for him?"

"Below us. She believes Vosega is in the caves beneath The Cathedral." I sat down, dejected, on a stool.

"Where is she?" Su's voice commanded. "I can't sense her anywhere on the grounds, and that wicked Mongolian woman is missing as well."

"Borte is missing?" I looked at him in disbelief. "Ophelia would not be going anywhere with Borte." I thought back to Borte's threat to harm her. I was a fool. I should have banished her on the spot. Instead, I empathized. Without thinking, I lashed out at the first thing I could reach, a clay bowl on the counter beside me. My arm made contact, flinging it against the wall and shattering it to pieces.

"We will find her." Almus stepped forward to assure me.

"I cannot see any further than this level. I am afraid I am of better use here than venturing down into the caves," Su noted. "The Cathedral has only ever permitted me down there a handful of times in our long years together."

"Why would she allow Ophelia down there, then? Unless Borte forced it, or worse—hurt her." My mind was spinning with terrible scenarios. "Is anyone else missing?" I was grasping at straws.

Susuda took a moment to take roll. "Two more, Sparkle and Aremis."

Almus and I made eye contact. "It is highly likely she is in their company," Almus deduced, and I agreed.

There were so many moving parts. I did not wish to spook anyone, especially not Aurora, into leaving. The Cathedral had been a gracious host. For the most part, I had no reason to think we were in danger.

"Susuda, I need you to keep a close eye on the comings and goings within your reach. If any of the missing Conduits surfaces let me know immediately." Su nodded. "And Su, no one can know about this. It would create a panic. Double your wards on the gate. Aurora indicated Esther may know something is happening." Then Su vanished.

"Where are you going?" Almus asked.

"I am going to at least try to find her."

"May I attend?" Almus took another step toward me.

I just nodded, afraid to speak, knowing my words would come out shaky at best. We began toward the passage located just off the galley that Ophelia had described to me. I took off at a clip and Almus kept up behind me. In minutes we found a dead end. My hands traced the wall. There was nothing out of place. I slumped down, defeated, lost.

"Her trail ends here," Almus confirmed what I already knew.

She was gone.

ESTHER

$\mathcal{M}$y message must have worked because I was pleased to see our numbers had risen from a hundred or so to over a thousand in only a few hours. More continued to pour in.

"Beautiful," I purred as I looked over the balcony into the now-buzzing courtyard. "This is more as I expected."

I turned around to face my most trusted soldiers—not because they loved me or truly believed in what I was creating, but because they feared me.

"How many more can we expect to arrive within the hour?"

"At least five hundred more. Perts the pixie just reported his current numbers," Lucifer promptly responded.

Perts was my most recent conquest. I'd broken him just like I broke the others, and so far I appreciated his enthusiasm.

"Excellent. Tell him to double his efforts. I know we have far more comrades to call upon and I want them within these walls before sunset. Now excuse me, I am going to take a bath." I was almost out the door. "If they refuse Perts' order, tell him to kill them."

344

OPHELIA

e'd been walking for hours. My eyes hurt from seeing nothing but Aremis' flame ahead of us. I held onto Sparkle's hand. The flame disappeared in front of us, and I was afraid we lost our light. The other two would be able to see fine, but I would be blind. It turned out the flame had just flew ahead then turned a corner, and when it did, the tunnel opened up, exposing a large cavern. No, not a cavern—a tomb.

We stood in a huge cavernous hall that expanded as far as the eyes could see, at least three stories high. Skulls of all shapes and sizes filled every crevice. There was no wall to be seen, only bones.

"Catacombs," Aremis almost whispered.

Clearly many of the skulls were human, but many of the bones in front of me I wasn't familiar with. I thought I recognized the remains of a troll. A massive circular head with two huge ocular cavities, no nostrils, and a wide jaw with needle-sharp teeth. Other skulls were elongated, square, thicker, or animal altogether.

Aremis had sent his flames far and wide in every direction so that we could see the greatness of the hall.

"What on earth?" I asked no one in particular.

We just kept walking.

"How far do you think Vosega went into the depths?" Aremis asked. I heard the skepticism in his voice. I felt the same. I started to wonder if someone would continue this journey after the fall we'd experienced and then finding this chamber. It was starting to seem more likely that he was being held captive by The Cathedral at this point.

"Let's just follow the hall. There must be an end. Maybe Vosega is waiting there." I said the words but didn't even believe them myself.

We walked slowly past the remains of countless creatures. I began to wonder what had happened to them. *How did they end up here, as they were, in a precisely constructed display?*

I latched onto Aremis' arm, seeking his reassurance and finding surprisingly less than I thought he'd be able to give me. His unease amplified my own fears. This was new territory for him. The unknown was especially scary to Conduits who'd experienced so much in their lifetimes.

"Why would The Cathedral have catacombs?" I asked the question more to myself than anyone else.

Sparkle decided to answer me. "Maybe they were sacrifices," she suggested. "We don't know much about The Cathedral, do we? But the name suggests it was a place of worship, sacred. I think they were sacrifices to her."

"To the Haven itself?" I decided to follow Sparkle's train of thought, because it was better than the anxiety I was feeling in the pit of my stomach.

"Perhaps, or perhaps to those who lived in it."

"We really don't know anything about how The Cathedral was made?"

"It was thought to be a legend, a myth, just like all the other fables and stories we heard as children," Aremis interjected. "Leave it to Viraclay to reveal The Cathedral's true existence."

"Well, what did the legend say?" I squeezed Aremis' arm, hoping he'd share the story. He was still looking around at the catacombs in an uneasy way, sending his flames yards ahead, and when he couldn't see anything, then returning them to our sides.

He cleared his throat. "I'm afraid I don't know that one well, Miss Ophelia."

"I do," Sparkle chirped. "May I tell the story, Olly?" I nodded and Sparkle hooked an arm into my free right one.

"It is a legend that is as old as the brothers and their games. Created before the Rittles. So it goes that after the first strokes, the painter saw an odd shape on the horizon. It was not of his creation. He moved his paint brush over the anomaly, but the strokes within did not pay heed to his direction. The painter grew frustrated. He tried again and again to manage the discrepancy with his brush but still it would not obey his will. He began adding paint to the odd spiral smudge, trying to paint over it, but his strokes, the paint, and anything else he used to try and cover the spot simply absorbed into the spiraling smudge on his masterpiece." Sparkle squeezed my arm. "I have to be honest, here is where things can change depending on the person telling the story. I was always told the smudge is why the brothers were created in the first place—to undertake the task of governing this unruly spiral of color. But I've heard other renditions where the brothers are suspected of producing the enigma in the first place. Do you care which fable I tell?"

I shook my head. "Tell me the one you like best."

"Very well. As it was said to me as a child, the painter grew tired of supervising the renegade smudge. He had tried all he knew to rectify the problem, yet it persisted. It was then that he decided to create his first sons, Fih, Tindle and Priloc. Each had his own gift. Fih preferred breaking lines and building his own. Tindle built connections and created beauty. Priloc loved everything in creation. He wanted nothing more than to heal and mend all broken things. Once established, the painter charged his sons with the important task of fixing the disorderly spiral of color upon the horizon. The brothers were eager to make their father happy, so they set to work straight away. As they worked, the painter decided to sleep, confident that his sons would rectify his problem and restore his painting to perfection. As he slept, the brothers worked tirelessly. Fih attempted to break the pattern of the spiral, interrupt the colors and stop the continuous blending of strokes. Tindle tried to mold the spiral into something else of beauty with his hands. Priloc admired the wild strokes, spoke to them, encouraged them to please their creator. Each brother tried and each brother failed.

The painter began to stir from his slumber. The brothers were worried about what he would say upon waking and seeing their failure. Fih declared the worst. 'He will rise and smite us from his creation when he realizes our failure!'

Priloc protested. 'He will do no such thing. He loves us. The painter will realize we tried our best.'

But it was Tindle who came up with a solution. 'We cannot change or violate the smudge. Let us create and reconstruct the strokes around it. Create beauty to mask the unsightly.'

Priloc and Fih agreed, and they began hastily erecting pillars and spires. Fih created lines to box in the smudge. Tindle created beauty by adding details with ribbons of color and connecting spires to pillars. Priloc secured the couplings with love and his will. When they finished, they stood back to admire their work. It was a thing of grandeur, something never created before. Vast, formidable, and precious to those who'd devised it.

Just then the painter rose from his nap. He saw what his children had made from the smudge he detested. The painter applauded them, because it was surely a thing of magnificence.

Two things happened that day that were not clear at the time. The Cathedral was made to contain a wild energy created by the painter himself. The Cathedral only quelled the spiral of strokes, the medley of color—it did not change what it was. The latter thing would affect us all. By creating The Cathedral, Fih created his first lines, his first box. The sensation of destruction, separation and creation would haunt him until he would later determine the fate of us all by melding the colors to gray and eventually separating the whole. When the day would come that the painter divided his children, blended all the colors into blacks and whites, lines and segregations, he did not know of the swarming of color within The Cathedral. Therefore, the painter knew not to open The Cathedral's doors, so it is here, in these walls, where the original strokes still reside, and with that, all of the creatures that once were or could ever be. The Cathedral holds the last of the source magic."

I didn't say anything. No one did for a long while. *What if the fable held some truth?* It would explain why this place in all its glory was unbelievable, even among legends and monsters. I looked at the catacombs again, this time through a different lens, and wondered if the creatures whose bones we could see had been trapped when the brothers had built The Cathedral.

ELIAS

*T*he Transformation Trial ended nearly an hour ago. The Directorate had concluded upon the Opaly team's ineligibility that the MisaKa team would participate in the Transformation Trial. They performed an informal vote on the two teams that had been disqualified in the Destruction Trial. Due to Helia and Leviathan's conduct, the Directorate found it easy to make a decision. The MisaKa Katan took the place of the Opaly Katan in the final Trial. They were at a disadvantage since they were not the creators of the Opaly Haven but they confounded everyone by finishing victoriously.

I had missed much of the challenge, busy trying to find a way to locate Ophelia and the others. We were unsuccessful and I was feeling dismal but everyone else seemed unanimously thrilled for the victors. Spirits were high. Next, we would proceed with the arguments. Of thousands of Conduits, only three came forward, and one was against Helia. No surprise there—she obviously made a habit out of behaving poorly. The arena was metamorphosing into a courtroom of sorts.

Aurora met me at her door, her eyes staring blankly back at me. She invited me in while she unpacked the rest of her belongings. I took it as an opportunity to discuss how the arguments would go.

"We have three Conduits awaiting arguments." She did not

acknowledge anything as I spoke. "You will be presiding over the arguments upon a podium. After you hear the accused's story, you may ask anything of them to determine the validity or the severity of the crime."

"Anything?" She turned to face me.

"Some books depict the overseeing Ramalan taking the accused's blood. Other texts suggest the residing prophet smells the aura of the accused. I suppose it would depend on how the Ramalan's gifts work."

"I see. Fortunately for the onlookers, I needn't draw blood or taste auras. As long as they are free of charms, I should be able to see their innocence very clearly."

"Yes, that is fortunate."

"You are distracted. Worried about Ophelia?" Aurora looked at me through squinted eyes.

"I am."

"She isn't going to break, my boy. She is harder than you think. Stronger than I could have imagined."

"I know that. Deep down, I do. I am afraid she will get too hard for even me to penetrate. I am afraid she will lose her way. The prophecy does not say how she may turn—become bad, if you will, to be used against us. I have feared that it would be my fault, that I would push her from her righteous path."

"That is a huge weight to bear. We all have a destiny, a destination that cannot change. But we all have choice, too. The painter made us this way. The destination may be unchangeable, but the path we take to get there is our own. No one decides that for us. To try and control her path would be like trying to control the heart—it is as wild and as unique as the chest it beats in." Aurora put her hand on my shoulder. "Let it go."

Another rare intimate moment with the usually icy woman, and it felt odd. So I was grateful when Di interrupted us. She knocked on the open door and bowed slightly as she entered.

"Oracle, Viraclay. I have come to tell you that the hour is near and the Pai Ona are ready for the arguments to begin."

I looked at my watch. It had been three hours since I had found

Ophelia's note. She had wanted to see the arguments, and now she would miss them. I hoped she was okay, wherever she was.

"You are right. Let us begin," I agreed. "Aurora, are you ready?"

"I am. Let loose the tide. May the Conduits in attendance see this broken woman I have become."

Although the words were sad, the tone in which she said them was in reverence. She wore her scars like a flag, a sigil to her plight. Her captivity was as much a tragedy as it was a badge of honor. This was why it was so important she be present here, at the summit. I needed the Pai Ona to remember the horrors the Nebas had inflicted. And to show them that we could all break free, as Aurora did, if we banded together and fought. Her courage, her choice to be here, to leave the shadows, would inspire everyone to step out, into the light. It had to. They would concede to the bidding.

OPHELIA

*O*nce the hall of bones ended we were directed into a long, deep, dark passage with wide cold bricks. If I'd thought the catacombs had felt endless, the monotony of this tunnel was suffocating.

"You should eat, Olly," Sparkle advised. "We've been down here for at least twenty-four hours, and I haven't seen you eat once."

My stomach agreed with her. But time felt so distorted, being in nothing but darkness. "You really think it's been that long?" I considered how terrified Elias must be by now. I hadn't meant to worry him. *This was so ridiculous of me.*

"It has most definitely been twenty-four hours, Miss Ophelia. Please let us sit while you eat," Aremis insisted.

We looked around for somewhere comfortable to sit, but the hall was just an endless brick wall.

"I guess here is as good as any spot." I pulled off my backpack and let my back slide down the wall behind me until I was sitting on the floor. I rummaged around until I felt one of the familiar bags of jerky I'd swiped from the galley. "Want any?" I held the bag out. But as expected, both of them declined.

"I'm going to run ahead. See if I see anything," Sparkle said.

"Okay," I agreed through a mouth full of jerky.

When she was out of sight, I took a moment to say what had been on my mind for the last two hours as we walked aimlessly in the dark.

"I'm sorry, Aremis. I'm sorry you guys followed me down here on this ridiculous errand." I swallowed what was in my mouth and took a sip of water. "But I'm also thankful. I'd be lost without you, stumbling around in the dark. Just like when we first met in Hafiza, you're my light, my protector." I smiled at him.

"I am not sorry, and I know I can speak for Sparkle when I say that she is not sorry either. We followed you because we love you and we trust you. If you say Vosega is down here, then we must find him."

I appreciated Aremis reminding me of the reason why we were down here in the first place. To rescue a friend, to make sure he was safe. "I wish I had as much faith in me as you do." I laughed slightly and took another bite. "I don't know where we're going. I wonder if Borte has had better luck than us."

"Never mind her. I have the mind to believe that voice you hear will be what truly guides us."

"But I haven't heard it since we got down here," I said exasperatedly. "Not a whisper." I bit down hard on the jerky in my hand.

"Things come to us when they are meant to," Aremis assured me.

"Hey, guys!" Sparkle's voice echoed down the hall. "The passage forks up here."

I quickly threw the water bladder and the jerky back in my bag and maneuvered it back onto my back. "C'mon, let's check it out."

Aremis followed behind me. Sparkle's petite figure emerged from the shadows feet ahead, and sure enough, it was a clear fork in the road.

"One appears to go downward, while the other ascends. Which way do we go?" She looked at me with the real question in her eyes.

Do we continue on this expedition or do we throw in the towel and hope Vosega and now Borte make it out of here alive?

ESTHER

*C*laudia sat across from me, while Akiva paced restlessly on the other side of the room.

"Akiva, come sit down."

"I cannot, Mistress. My nerves are on end."

"I understand, but pacing will not speed up the impending battle."

He stopped and looked at me. I knew that look well. He was evaluating whether he could say what he wanted to say.

I stood up and walked over to him. "Come, come, Akiva, share what ails you."

It was too late for him to hold his tongue now. "Mistress, I wonder why we wait. The Nebas are ready, eager to serve you."

I brushed back a lock of his thick black hair. "I know they are."

He continued. "More arrived after your message was received. We have the numbers. We will be triumphant. We need to move while they are still enthusiastic."

"You are so eager. I appreciate that, Akiva." I laid my hand on his cheek and seized control of his body. I clenched his fist and heard the bones break in his right foot. "We are waiting on a signal."

Lucifer, Claudia and Astrid were all standing now, not certain what I would do next. I continued to make my point. "Carefully laid

355

plans are only effective when executed with accuracy, not whimsical emotion." I flipped my hand in the air and Akiva's body crashed against the stone wall violently. "I would love nothing more than to harness the enthusiasm the Nebas have in this moment and take it with us to battle. But we don't know where the Pai Ona are congregated at present, so no amount of enthusiasm can trump information or waiting for the right moment to strike." My teeth were grinding together as I spoke. Akiva still lay on the floor where is body had landed. I crouched down and took his face in my hand, released the control I had over his body, and he immediately straightened himself up. "Do you understand?"

"Yes, Mistress," Akiva mumbled, still looking down at his broken foot, refusing to make eye contact with me.

"Excellent. Now sit down. Relax. We will leave when the moment is right."

I sashayed to the table. As I sat, so did the other two women. Lucifer stood patiently by the door. The room was electrified with uncertainty. I loved the effect I had on my subjects.

OPHELIA

"We're going down. We have friends to find," I said confidently, and I meant it. "We aren't leaving this place until we find Vosega."

"Here, here!" Aremis agreed, while Sparkle just beamed.

So we started our descent. It got steep quickly and my feet began to slip and slide. I wasn't graceful. The descent plateaued about thirty minutes into the walk.

"Can we take a second? My legs are shaking like all get-out."

"Of course, whatever you need," Aremis quickly answered.

I leaned against the wall and put my hands on my knees.

"Are you okay?" Sparkle leaned in to see my face.

"Yeah, yeah, just out of shape." I thought that was enough fuss. We didn't have time for me to recover entirely. I put my hand against the wall to push off and it dissolved behind me. The next thing I knew I was flying down a shaft and landing on a dusty floor face down and alone.

ELIAS

The first arguments were against a Conduit named Prudence. The Gifland family claimed she had seduced their son, which eventually led to his assassination by the Nebas.

I wanted to be present, but I was too distracted to really listen. Almus stared at me from across the courtroom, eagerly waiting to signal me if Ophelia reappeared back in his Rune range.

Susuda was hovering behind me. He too was ready to let me know Ophelia's whereabouts the minute she was detectable. In the meantime, I acted as though I was interested in this family's tribulations. Having to feign concern felt callous and wrong but it was as Aurora had said—to feel any different would be like trying to tame my heart. It was not possible.

"Prudence, come here, child," the Oracle asked after she had heard the father of Don Gifland describe the events leading up to his son's death. Aurora sat atop an enormous imposing podium. Unlike the arena, the courtroom was flat. All seats faced toward the center platform. There were three seats directly below the podium, one for a witness, the accuser and the accused.

Prudence stood in front of her assigned seat and crept toward Aurora.

"What say you to these accusations?"

"I loved Don. We happened upon the wrong place at the wrong time."

"Harlot, murderess!" Don's father shot up and shouted.

"Ruth Gifland, you will keep your mouth shut during these proceedings," Aurora reprimanded, and the man quickly sat down, shame all over his face from his outburst.

"Give me your hand, Prudence." Aurora reached down and Prudence raised her shaking hand to meet the Oracle's palm.

A moment passed and the spectators held their breath, waiting for the sentencing.

"Return to your seat, dear." Aurora stood on the podium, more as a symbol of authority than for anything else. "Gifland family, I am deeply sorry for your loss. You have suffered at the hands of the Nebas, like so many of us here in this room. But I have looked into this child's past, examined her intent and her heart, and she is innocent of any wrongdoing concerning your son and his demise. I am sorry."

Whispers moved through the seats of the audience and I half expected another outburst from Don's father but the realization of the fact that he had no one to blame within reach broke him. He and the rest of the family began to sob. But the shocking moment was when they invited Prudence into their arms to cry with them.

Many Pai Ona broke down as well at the show of solidarity in grief.

OPHELIA

"Aremis! Sparkle!" My hands traced the wall in front of me. It was smooth, like marble, and cold to the touch.

"Ophelia! Where are you?" Aremis asked. I could hear the anxiety in his voice.

"I don't know where I am. I can't see anything." It occurred to me that I had that flashlight.

"Are you okay?" Aremis called down the shaft after me.

"I think so." I took an internal inventory while I looked for my flashlight in the dark. I didn't feel any wounds or broken bones. It didn't mean there weren't any, but if I was scratched up or bruised, they weren't catastrophic. "I'm fine," I said more confidently. I found the flashlight and clicked it on.

The room I'd fallen into illuminated to show three barren stone walls and an arsenal on the wall behind me. "I think I landed in an arsenal. There are all sorts of weapons down here." I looked up to see a small flame appear in the opening of the channel I'd slid down. After a moment, when no one flew down the tunnel after me, I walked over to look closer at the objects behind me. They were strange weapons. They looked archaic. As my eyes categorized each one, I realized the higher shelf held random objects, not weapons. "Wait. Maybe it's a

360

storage unit. Not everything is a weapon." I went to reach for an object that looked like a crystal ball. My fingers were so close I could feel a buzz of energy coming from it.

"Don't touch anything!" Sparkle's voice had a command to it I'd never heard before, so I listened and stepped away. As I did, I realized there was a crack in the wall to my left. It was oddly shaped. It appeared to be man-made, not a natural crack. My index finger traced the line until I felt a lever of sorts. I lifted it and heard a click in the wall, the sound of a lock unfastening.

"You guys! There's a door." I stepped outside of it and looked up, shining my flashlight with my gaze. My light caught movement, and I saw Sparkle and Aremis leaning over a banister two stories above me. They both gingerly jumped from the balcony and landed in front of me as soft as two feathers. "You've got to see this."

They looked at me and then back at each other before warily entering the secret chamber. Aremis stayed at the door while Sparkle and I examined the objects placed on the shelves.

"You didn't touch any of them, did you?" Sparkle held her breath, waiting for my answer.

"No. I learned my lesson after being thrown into the Trials for touching the Stones. What are they?"

Sparkle looked over my shoulder at Aremis. "They are the stolen Rittles."

ELIAS

*A*urora commanded a room like no other. I watched how the Pai Ona revered her, her wisdom, her strength and resilience in the face of what she had endured centuries before.

"Viraclay, are there any more arguments to be heard?" She looked down at me from her perch.

I in turn looked to the crowd. "Does anyone else have an argument to be heard by the Oracle?"

A familiar voice called out. "I do." *When had he entered The Cathedral? And why had he asked me to keep his whereabouts secret if he now showed himself in front of all the assembled Pai Ona, and not only that, he put himself the spotlight?*

"I would like to present the case against the murderer of Alistair Tallus." Rand said it casually as he approached the podium. He waved at me then addressed Aurora. "May I sit, great Oracle?"

She nodded at him and he abruptly sat.

"Who are you arguing against?" Aurora asked.

"Myself."

My heart froze in my chest. Almus, Inca and Jezebel jumped to their feet. "What is this?" Almus demanded. "What game do you play, Rand Garrith?"

Rand turned in his seat to face the Tallus family. His face was sincere and empathetic. "I play no game, Almus. I am here to confess."

"This is unconventional, Rand."

"I understand, Oracle, but I feel compelled to explain my actions."

By now the room was on fire with murmurs and questions.

"I will hear it."

"And I will confess it."

OPHELIA

"**W**hat are they doing here?" I asked.

Aremis was scrutinizing every article meticulously. There were assorted weapons, and I counted six random objects. Aremis stopped when he arrived in front of a large book. I came to his side to see what had caught his attention.

"What is it?" Sparkle appeared on his other side.

She answered for him. "It's the lost Pierses." Her voice was barely a whisper.

Aremis reached for the huge book. "Wait," I said, putting my hand on his. "Aren't we supposed to avoid touching them?"

"This is not a Rittle. There is no magic to harm me when I touch upon its pages." He lifted the book from its resting place and traced the binding with his finger before moving his palm over the crest on the front. "This could change everything."

"How?" I was trying to remember what Elias had said about the Pierses. I replayed our conversation in my head. He'd said they were books full of Covening spells, sister volumes that were linked. We knew the whereabouts of one, but couldn't use anything in it because it was assumed the other was in the hands of our enemies, the Nebas. But it wasn't. It had been here all along. I also considered the stacks of

Pierses paper we used to send the broadcast to the Pai Ona. Elias had said that was a rare find, as well.

"The magic, the words on these pages…" Aremis seemed to be at a loss for what he was trying to say. "It is the equivalent to having an atomic bomb while our opposition only has a cannon."

The analogy made me shiver. I understood he meant this would give us an advantage over the Nebas, but did that include destruction, I wondered. *What was the cost of using the magic within these pages?*

Sparkle just stared at the book.

"Who has the sister?" It seemed like the next obvious question.

"The Oracle. It was decided after she was freed from her chains that she be given the Pierses. It was supposed to signify some sort of recompense for her suffering. In my opinion, it was a pathetic attempt at a peace offering. But she took it nonetheless and has kept it safe," Aremis concluded.

"What is this stuff doing here?" I looked at both of my stunned companions.

"I haven't the slightest idea," Sparkle answered. My question seemed to pull her out of her daze.

"Do we leave them down here?" That question brought Aremis to complete awareness too.

"I believe we have to," Sparkle answered.

"But we don't even know how we got down here. If we leave them, we'll never find them again. What about the Pierses? We should definitely bring that, right?" I was rambling now. "What if someone not so savory stowed them here in the first place? Shouldn't we take them for safekeeping?"

Sparkle put her hand on my shoulder. "We should leave them. They've been here for many, many years, perhaps centuries."

I turned to see what Aremis thought. "We should consider our options very carefully," was all he said. Sparkle gave him a hard look but didn't object. "Why don't we sit on it, think about the consequences of moving these sacred and powerful objects first? Because although they could help us defend ourselves, once they are revealed they become a new target, and if they are seized by our enemies, we would never be able to stop them. Sometimes the best thing to do is nothing."

Sparkle seemed more satisfied with that response.

I watched as Aremis put the book back where it had lain. I knew what he said had truth, but all of that assumed that we'd let our enemies know we were wielding this type of power. I wanted to argue but decided that, whether I disagreed or not, we'd have to come to an agreement or at least a majority, and clearly that meant taking time to think about it.

"Let us sit—outside the room. It is musty in here. You must be ready to rest again. I don't know when you last slept," Aremis said to me.

He was right, I was running on limited to no sleep. We'd been down here for at least a day and I'd hardly shut my eyes. I didn't want to be the one to slow us down, but maybe I could think more clearly if I rested.

"I could use a nap."

The three of us moved into the hall. Sparkle plopped down cross-legged and tapped her legs, gesturing for me to rest my head there. Now that the prospect of sleeping was so close, I found my eyes getting heavy and bleary. I cuddled up next to her and put my head in her lap. My eyes closed and sleep washed over me instantly.

I DON'T KNOW HOW LONG I SLEPT, BUT SPARKLE AND AREMIS' HUSHED conversation coming from the secret chamber full of the Rittles and the Pierses couldn't have been what woke me; they were too faint. I strained to hear what they were saying, all the while making sure not to move a muscle.

Sparkle's sweet voice was a little easier to hear. "I don't think it's a good idea, Aremis. We don't even have a way to transport them. They shouldn't be handled."

"And the book?" Aremis asked. "What say you to delivering the sister Pierses to Elias?"

"I'm concerned that revealing the second book will create more discord among the Pai Ona. Some will want to use its magic while others will strongly oppose messing with the ancient spells. It's been said that not even the Ancients remember how to use many of the incantations," Sparkle reasoned.

"But maybe, just maybe, having the book will bring others to our aid, even dissuade the Nebas from continuing this rampage of death, fearful of what we may do to strike them down."

I was about ready to engage in the discussion when I heard the familiar hissing pick up in the hall. I hadn't heard it once since we got down here, and now here it was, as plain as day, buzzing in my ears. But something was different this time. The noise was accompanied by a deeper drumming within the hiss. I strained to hear past the conversation I'd been eavesdropping on. I attempted to distinguish between the two noises coming from below. The drumming got a little louder, and I realized it wasn't drumming at all. It was a deep baritone voice, and it was clear. "Leave them be. Leave them be. Leave them be."

I sat up abruptly. "We cannot move anything in this room," I blurted out.

Aremis and Sparkle quickly moved to kneel down beside me.

"You're awake. Did you have a bad dream?" Sparkle asked, looking concerned.

My heart was pounding. I had sweat on my brow.

"No, I heard the hissing again. But this time there was a voice." Aremis and Sparkle's eyes met then returned to me. "It told me to leave them be."

ELIAS

*R*and stood, circling the podium, or rather working the stage, and I wondered what my father's dear friend was up to. I did not understand any of this. He had asked me who had killed Alistair when I saw him a few weeks ago. He wanted me to discover who it was, to consider who had motive besides the Nebas. I did not have time to discuss it with him because he ran off so quickly, and now here he was, confessing. *But why? Why would he kill Alistair?* Even more disturbing was the fact that Almus had already shared with me that he believed whoever killed his son betrayed him and was a defector.

"Come, Almus, Inca and Jezebel, join us," Aurora invited them. Once they were situated in the three chairs on the platform, she prompted Rand to continue.

"I had been monitoring Alistair for three years before I took his life. He was residing in Ontario and then moved to Chicago where Viraclay would seek him out. When I saw that Viraclay had arrived in Chicago I knew his intent. I knew because his father, Cane, had charged me with keeping Alistair safe until he could map the where-abouts of a safe location for the summit, which he did the very night before he died. This was how I came to find Alistair in Ontario." Rand kept darting his eyes back to me, looking for something, a reaction, perhaps recognition. "When I saw that Viraclay had made contact with Alistair I knew it was time to act. I could not sit back and hope to stumble upon the answers I had hoped to find through surveillance alone."

Inca interrupted, her rage boiling over. "What answers were worth my son's life?"

Rand answered simply, "Who had he acted with when he took Sorcey and Cane Kraus' lives."

OPHELIA

"**W**here is the voice coming from, Olly?" Sparkle asked.

"I think it's coming from below us, deeper into the caves."

"Then deeper we must go," Aremis concluded. "Come, we must move while you can still hear it."

Aremis pulled me to my feet. The baritone voice had disappeared but the hissing persisted.

I started to pick up my pace, eager to find Vosega and get to the bottom of the mysterious voice. My fast walk turned into a jog.

"Be careful not to fall," Aremis said as he trailed right behind me.

"Just keep things lit so I can see where I'm going. I'll watch my feet."

We kept at that pace for forty minutes or more, every step moving us deeper into the belly of the cave channels. Without warning, the tunnel we were following stopped, ending at a wooden spiral staircase.

"Too late to turn back now, right?" I turned around to see the troubled faces of my friends, but they agreed—we needed to forge ahead, or in this case downward.

We moved slowly down the spiraling staircase. I was afraid of losing my footing, and everyone else kept with my pace. Aremis' familiar flame danced in front of me. My legs started to ache and shake.

"How long do you think we've been descending these stairs?" I paused for a moment to give my legs a rest.

"Many hours," Aremis replied. I looked behind me and up at him.

"I'm sorry to hold us up but my legs are starting to get weak."

"Want me to hold you?" Sparkle asked from behind Aremis.

"No, thank you, Sparkle." It was a sweet gesture but it would be humiliating to have Sparkle's little frame traipsing down the stairs with me in her arms. I shook off the silly visual and looked over the side of the railing.

I couldn't see the bottom of the cave, even after hours of descending the stairs. The hissing had stopped then started again several times. I didn't know anymore if we were going in the right direction. There was no reason to believe Vosega had come this way either. I didn't want the others to see the panic I was starting to feel welling up in my chest. Questions began circling my thoughts. *Would we be able to find our way out of here? What if Vosega went missing for another reason? What if he was dead? Where was Borte? Had she found Genghis?*

"Ophelia, look." Sparkle's sweet voice drew me back to the present and brought my attention to the approaching floor. Relief inflated my chest. I picked up my pace, taking two steps at a time. I didn't know what waited for us down here, but it had to be better than an endless spirally abyss. As soon as my feet hit the ground, Aremis' flame extinguished in front of me. I took two steps forward to make sure Sparkle or Aremis didn't run into me in the dark. Pitch-black, smothering darkness filled the space.

"Aremis, where is your light?" I asked gently, trying not to let the anxiety I felt slip into my tone.

"I do not know, Miss Ophelia. I cannot resurrect it, and there is no other to command within my reach."

"It's okay, Ophelia, we are here," Sparkle assured me.

"But where is here and how will we ever get out of here? Can either of you see anything?" I asked.

"No. For the first time since I was mortal, I feel blind," Aremis conceded.

"I can't see anything either," Sparkle agreed.

I was feeling the weight of my decision to investigate these caverns. *Had I led my friends into a trap?* The anxiety was pressing on my chest, heavy and hard. I gave myself an internal pep talk. *It's going to be alright.* Sparkle didn't know about my abnormalities, but in the face of the unknown, it seemed like I had to at least try to do something, even if it meant exposing myself. I reached for my shield, to pull it down and see what I was capable of doing down here. But it wasn't there. It was gone.

The hissing returned in my ear. Loud and vibrating. "Do you guys hear that?" I asked, hoping this time it was loud enough for their perception.

"No, I still hear nothing," Aremis said.

"Nothing," Sparkle agreed.

The hissing transitioned into a buzz, and it grew louder and louder until it felt like a cacophony in my head. I put my hands on either side of my ears, trying to dull the chorus of noise. It did nothing. I thought my head may explode, but then the noise suddenly stopped and the cavern floor lit up beneath our feet. Millions of minute glowing golden flecks littered the ground.

Sparkle and Aremis looked just as alarmed as I did. I felt for my shield again but still there was nothing.

"There is no magic in here that I cannot control," a thunderous voice announced. "This is my sanctuary."

I looked to see if Aremis or Sparkle had heard it—they must have heard it—but their expressions said they hadn't.

"Something is down here with us. We've stumbled into their space," I translated.

"How do you know that?" Sparkle leaned into me.

"It spoke to me, and I can hear it. The same way I can hear the hissing and the buzzing and you two can't."

They both just nodded their heads in understanding.

"Why do you think you can hear me when most cannot?" the voice rumbled.

"I don't know," I admitted.

Aremis and Sparkle looked at me severely but said nothing.

The voice laughed boisterously. "I have been beckoning Viraclay, but you come in his stead."

"I don't think he could hear you. He doesn't hear the caves."

"Oh, my dear girl, you are so misguided. I am no cave. I am Cataphet." For the first time, I noted the feminine nature of the voice. Before then, the volume had made it difficult to distinguish.

"Cataphet the cave, from the Three Brothers fable. You were friends with Tindle, the brother who created things," I asserted, feeling proud of myself for remembering the story as well as I did. Aremis and Sparkle still stood astounded and quiet.

Again, the voice laughed. "You are right about one thing, girl. Tindle and I were dear friends. But I am no cave." Just then, something moved deep in the dark, beyond the scope of the light below us and deeper than the shadows.

My voice was shaky when I responded. *What on earth could stifle a Conduit's gift, be as old as the beginning of time, and live in the dark?* "What are you, then?"

Alarm replaced astonishment on Aremis and Sparkle's faces. The dark moved once more. This time it grew and swelled and filled the space in front of us. When everything stopped moving, the gravity of the situation became clear. I was talking to a dragon.

ELIAS

*N*ow I was advancing on the platform. "What are you talking about, Rand?"

He turn to face me. "I tried to tell you, my boy, but while we sat in the cafe in Bairat I heard Inca's familiar voice. Afraid they knew what I had done and would serve retribution, I escaped."

"How could they have known that you killed Alistair?"

"There were two assailants the night your parents died. They gained entry to one of the most secure Havens in the world. How do you suppose they did that?"

"The Loktpi," I whispered.

"Exactly."

Almus interjected, "Huan had already been murdered. They could have confiscated his."

The room was buzzing with curiosity. We were giving so much away.

"That is certainly a possibility. But I saw one of the intruders' faces when I tore him off Viraclay. It was your son. I didn't know it at the time; I had never met Alistair. When I saw him in Ontario I didn't yet understand what had happened. Why would he betray Cane after he agreed to help him? He had to be working with the second assailant, or for the Nebas. I needed to flush out the other assassin, so I sat in wait. Until the night Elias tracked him to Chicago. I couldn't sit by any longer, I couldn't let Elias befall his parents' fate." Rand's eyes were pleading for my understanding. "I confronted him. He denied it, but I laid it out, all of it. At the time I did not know of the Loktpi. Only after Viraclay uncovered The Cathedral did I put that piece together. Alistair had the means to enter the Kraus compound in South Africa... but what was his motive?"

"Yes! What was my grandson's motive? Give me that!" Jezebel demanded.

"Love. It was love. Almus has been saying for years that Ruit was still alive, captive somewhere. Huan died for the very cause, trying to infiltrate the Nebas and discover his father's whereabouts. Someone playing both sides manipulated your son, your grandson, into believing he could save his grandfather by betraying the Kraus family. But instead everyone lost."

The look on Jezebel and Inca's faces said they believed what Rand was saying held merit. Almus was not as ready to concede.

"Did my son confess to treachery?"

"No, he did not, but the night I dispatched him he obsessively traced this symbol that marked his hand." Rand held up a sketch of the Rune I too had seen Alistair rubbing the night I met with him. "What is this?" Rand asked the question knowing the answer.

"A Rune, an incantation that my father created allowing his family to communicate silently with one another." Almus looked defeated. Mentioning the Rune confirmed something he already knew in his heart.

"Can they be shared?"

"Yes, with only one other." Almus was rubbing his forehead.

"The night I interrogated your son he was sharing our exchange with someone on the other side of this Rune. I know it wasn't you or any other of your attending family because you would've recognized who I was when I arranged a run-in just before you three entered The

375

Cathedral. I tasted your emotions. None of you knew who I was. Nandi would be the only other living Tallus during the time of the Kraus murders, but given that she virtually arranged the discovery of The Cathedral, I find it hard to believe she was acting as a traitor. So that means if we find the Conduit who bears this mark, we find the second assassin and the defector in our midst."

OPHELIA

"Can you hear it?" I asked Sparkle and Aremis once more.

"No, but I sure see it," Sparkle replied.

"You are in no danger. You are not who I expected, but I have a message that you can pass along to the Sulu," Cataphet explained. Now I was happy they couldn't hear her since she'd just inadvertently outed what I was. That explained why I could hear her—because I was the Sulu. She mistakenly thought it was Elias. For two reasons, I saw no point it correcting her. One, she was a dragon and I wasn't sure how dragons felt about being corrected, and two, I would have to say what I was in earshot of Sparkle. So I just agreed.

"I can relay a message."

"Perfect," she hissed as she moved closer to the light. I watched her move. It was like nothing I'd ever seen before—serpent-like, but also as ferocious as a lion. Her scales were black, but underneath each scale was a fleck of gold. I couldn't tell if they reflected the light from the ground or had their own luminescence. Until I understood the flecks on the ground were one and the same. We were standing on a bed of illuminated dragon scales.

Cataphet's head came down close to where we stood. It was five times taller than I was and as wide as a truck. Her mouth was huge, but I didn't see fangs, not even this close up. Green, gold eyes stared at me. Where white would be surrounding the irises, it was black. If I wasn't so scared, I could've stared at her for hours and would probably still have missed some incredible detail. "Tell Elias that the battle will occur where the world ends. Only then will the rebirth succeed."

"Will he understand this message?"

"He will, someday." She smiled and chills ran down my spine. "Now I will send you away. It is nearly time for you to return to the summit."

"No." Cataphet's eyes got wide. She was obviously not accustomed to being told no. "We came down here to collect our friends. Do you have them? Or does The Cathedral have them? Do you know where she's keeping them?"

A roar of laughter echoed off the walls. "Silly girl, The Cathedral and I are one, formed from the same strokes, birthed at the same time. There would be no Cathedral without Cataphet and no Cataphet without The Cathedral."

"So you have our friends?" Aremis and Sparkle stepped forward, realizing I was getting answers even if they couldn't hear them.

"I do. They must pay for their crimes." The dragon tail flicked and Vosega, Borte, Genghis, George and Cadmus appeared in front of us. I fought the urge to run to Vosega and squeeze him. They were comatose, in some kind of trance. None of them were moving. They were expressionless.

"What have you done to them?"

"They are fine, girl, just sleeping, awaiting my judgements."

"For what crimes?"

"These two are guilty of stupidity and meddling in affairs they know nothing about." She flicked her tail at Vosega and Borte. "But these three are dragon slayers. They killed my sisters and they must pay the price."

"What is that?"

"Death by fire."

"What is she saying?" Sparkle whispered.

"She is saying that Genghis, George and Cadmus have to die by dragon fire and she called Vosega and Borte nosey."

"You cannot kill them," Aremis demanded. "They came to the summit believing they were safe, that they were supporting Elias and the war against the Nebas."

"They were misinformed," she hissed.

Think, Ophelia, think. I pressed, "What if they paid their debt?"

"A life for a life is the repayment."

"Are you the last dragon?"

"No, certainly not. We are all in hiding, forced to live in separate corners of the world. Only one Haven, The Cathedral, is large enough for more than one dragon to survive in, and I occupy it alone."

"What if they helped bring the other dragons here? Conduits have gifts. We could hide them or something. Would that help?"

Cataphet closed her eyes as she considered my suggestion.

"How can I trust that these three will not betray me and kill more of my kind?"

"We can enter into a bidding. That's a super-serious contract, right?" I knew from Elias that it was the most serious contract a Conduit could make, and by the look on Sparkle and Aremis' faces it was a very serious suggestion.

"A contract resulting in their death if they do not succeed? I would expect all of you to make it, all eight of you, today. You would have four full moons to fulfill it."

"That seems reasonable." Honestly I had no idea what was reasonable for transporting dragons, but I knew I wasn't leaving here without them.

"Very well. We have come to an accord." She grinned wildly and I had the sneaky suspicion that I'd just bargained for way more than I knew. Cataphet flicked her tail again and the other five came to. I ran to Vosega and threw myself into his arms.

"Thank God you're alright." I squeezed him as tight as I could.

"Ophelia, there is a dragon behind you," Vosega muttered in my ear.

ELIAS

Those in attendance turned to the Oracle for confirmation that what Rand said was true. There was shouting.

"Everyone must be screened!"

"Find the traitor!"

"What does the Oracle see?"

Aurora stood up and ushered the assembly to sit down. "I see that what Rand says is truth."

That prompted more yelling from the audience. But when Inca stood they went silent.

"Will there be justice for my son? Traitor or not, we do not allow murder to go unpunished."

Rand had killed him to avenge my parents, to save me. Now he would be punished for his allegiance to my family. I had to at least attempt to sway them. "When will the killing stop?" I said as I took to the platform. "I understand Inca's distress and desire for justice, but Rand was seeking justice for my parents' death and he gave Alistair an opportunity to confess. Rand came here today to expose the truth at his own detriment. Does that not earn him leniency?" I looked to Aurora, hoping she would give her support.

Everyone waited in silence for her judgement. "This is no easy decision to make. On one hand, Rand murdered another Conduit, and on the other, he may have saved us all from further betrayal. Is it my responsibility to deal the hand of death to another for justice? I do—" Aurora's eyes got big. She looked as though she may faint. "They are here."

Susuda manifested at my side, disheveled and weak, barely able to stand. "Mr. Elias, they had the Loktpi. I couldn't stop them... there were too many."

OPHELIA

"That's Cataphet. She has agreed to set you all free." I looked behind Vosega at the other prisoners I didn't know. "On one condition. You all killed her sisters, so in exchange for your freedom we're going to help bring the dragons that still exist back here to The Cathedral. The alternative is death by dragon fire." I added that last part hoping they'd understand the severity of the agreement I'd just made.

Vosega whispered in my ear, "What kind of agreement?"

"The bidding kind."

"I was afraid of that." He looked over my shoulder again. "We are so grateful for your mercy. Aren't we?" He directed the last question to the others.

They caught on, but weren't very convincing.

"We dragons abide by a blood bidding. Words are not enough. Especially of this dishonorable lot," Cataphet thundered. "I need their blood."

"What is she saying? All I hear is a very low hiss," Vosega asked.

"You hear a hiss?"

"What is she saying, Olly?" Vosega insisted.

"We need to give her our blood for the bidding."

"I'm not doing that," a slight man with long stringy hair said as he tried to back away.

"Yes, you are, Thracian. We all are. Ophelia helped us greatly by bargaining our freedom." Vosega grabbed Thracian by the arm, pulled out a knife from his pant leg and sliced the tip of Thracian's index finger. Cataphet raised a single claw, at which point Vosega smeared Thracian's blood on it. "Who's next?"

I stepped forward. One by one, we all donated our blood to the dragon.

"Excellent," she hissed. "It is time to return you. Susuda will need your help soon. He is my dear friend and only companion. Take good care of him."

"Will anyone still be in The Cathedral? We've been down here for a couple of days."

"Your absence has only been a few hours long on the surface. Time moves differently here in the caves."

"I see." I looked to the others. "It's time to go back to The Cathedral. Cataphet, one more thing." She cocked her head curiously. "You have the Rittles and the missing Pierses."

"I do."

"You seem to want Elias to succeed in his endeavors. Is that why you're sending him a message?"

"I do. His victory would be best for this world."

"Can we have them, then? The Rittles and the Pierses?"

"I will consider it. Oh, and girl, tell the one born in fire that the answers he seeks will reveal themselves in the gates of hell." Then she flicked her tail and the world seemed to flip upside down and inside out.

My head was spinning when we landed in the banquet hall. My ears throbbed with pressure, my scalp tingled, and my eyes were clouded with stars and rainbow orbs. I sat down to steady myself.

"Aremis, Sparkle? Are you here? Are you as dazed as I am?" There was no response. It was silent.

I felt around on the floor. My hand landed on a foot. My vision was starting to come into focus. The foot moved under my grasp and a hand reached out to take mine and pull me to my feet. When I stood, it was like a clarity light bulb coming back on, and all of my refined senses returned. Sparkle held my hand. Behind her stood the others—Aremis, Vosega, Borte, Genghis, along with George and Cadmus.

No sooner did my senses return than I heard the heart-wrenching sound of battle cries and the unmistakable echo of Conduit flesh being torn.

Susuda appeared in front of me. "Miss Olly, we must go." He took my arm. I pulled back.

"Su, what is going on? I'm not just leaving everyone. Where is Elias?" I asked desperately. "Is Elias okay?"

ELIAS

*I*t took several minutes for my mind to catch up with what my eyes were seeing. Hooded Nebas were flooding into the courtroom from every entrance. I glanced up to see an indiscernible look on Aurora's face. I could not say what it meant, but it left me with a sense of foreboding like I had never experienced before.

My thoughts shifted to Ophelia. I had to find Ophelia. I propelled myself from the center platform. Rand was behind me and Susuda was gone.

"Where is she, Elias? We must get to her." Rand's words rang in my ears so loudly—where was she?—that I nearly missed Esther croon my name over the crowd.

"Viraclay! I am coming for you and your pet! Vengeance will be mine!" Then she cackled at a bone-chilling pitch. I had no idea where she was in the room. Her laugh bounced off every wall.

Rand took a leap in front of me, stopping me in my place. "We cannot simply flee." He grabbed my shoulders. "I know you are worried about her. I am worried about her too. But you prepared for this, did you not? Your father—you—chose this place for a reason, for its ability to give you a tactical advantage. Do not let your fear of losing her distract you!"

His words brought me to the present. Reminded me that the best thing for Ophelia was making a stand. It was what I had been working for, what *we* had been working for. Rand tasted my resolve.

"That's good. That is good, my boy," he assured me. "What do we do? Where does our stand begin?"

I pointed to the center of the massive room where chaos had broken out. Thousands of Conduits were fighting the figures in black cloaks. We had the numbers but they had the surprise. I pointed to the Stone in the center of the podium. "Our defense is in the Stones. When The Cathedral and the Katuan Stones collaborated, Su slipped in a suggestion. When the first Conduit is killed, the Stones will begin to dismantle the entire space they built. Anyone left will perish, fire need not apply. The Stones will dismantle them. Susuda was supposed to send a broadcast warning the Pai Ona, but he has disappeared." I pointed to the four large decorative pillars around the room. "There is an entire arsenal hidden inside those columns. We just need to unleash it."

Rand looked up. "Very clever—hidden in plain sight. How do we arm our friends?"

"Susuda, the gatekeeper—he is the key to our defense." I looked around, desperately trying to find his face among the carnage. It did not reveal itself. "I do not know where he is. I begged him to keep watch on Ophelia. Perhaps he found her and is taking her to safety." I let hope touch my heart.

"Well, that does not serve us at present. We must improvise, buy some time." Rand pointed to Nara. "She is wondrous at creating a distraction."

We both took off in her direction as fast as our legs could carry us. Rand made it to her before I could. She was fighting a Nebas who appeared to have the upper hand. Rand swept through and landed a ferocious blow to her combatant's head, knocking it clean off. Rand quickly explained what we needed just as I arrived. Nara looked at me intently.

"How will this help, Viraclay?" she asked.

"We need time. Su will return."

She nodded. "I can create a distraction." She began to spin. Her body rose up with the gusts around her. She was creating a tornado.

"We'd better get out of her way." Rand took my arm and pulled me toward one of the cooridors.

I spotted Esther, she stood in the balcony I had watched the Trials from. She pointed her sharp finger at me. "Kill him!" she screamed.

I heard a growl from behind. Akiva leapt several feet and landed only inches from me. Astrid was behind him. She flew at Rand like an electrified missile. She struck her target and he howled in pain. I looked to see where he landed but did not see him. "Rand!"

"My mistress wants you dead," Akiva drew my attention back to him. "Therefore you shall die." He flipped his wrist and I flew into the cyclone of the tornado. The winds dragged me high up into the air.

Nara saw Akiva on the ground, not more than twenty feet from where she elevated in the air. She abandoned her twister and dove toward him, drunk with revenge for her Valerian.

My body began to fall, without the wind tossing me about like a rag doll. I reached for the only thing I could—the wrought iron chandelier that hung from the ceiling.

I swung my legs, to get momentum so I could kick them up onto the large circular base of the chandelier to stabilize myself. Just as I hooked my leg up onto the rail, a huge stone shot past only inches from my head, colliding with the ceiling. I looked down to see Akiva smiling up at me. But it was not for long, because Nara was aiming for him. He saw her fury. Despite his abilities, it was enough to frighten him into forgetting to attack immediately. She pinned him against the floor with an intense onslaught of wind.

The chain that held the chandelier had been struck. It swayed wildly in the air. The ceiling was crumbling where the stone had made contact, and the chain was slacking as it moved. The impact was going to make the chandelier plummet to the ground.

I swallowed any fear that was bubbling to the surface. As I rocked in the air atop the massive iron fixture, I watched as the Nebas appeared to gain the upper hand. *This fight could not end that way, I would not allow it!*

My weight threw off the chandelier, and the chain link that secured the iron piece to the ceiling began to tear apart. I was going to die. My stomach lurched as I began to fall.

Then the world went still. My eyes fixed to the ceiling as my body felt weightless. The only sensation still intact was my hearing. I heard a scream, a terrifying scream. I knew that scream. It shook my soul. It was Ophelia. She would be here to see my death.

She did not deserve that.

OPHELIA

"$\mathcal{H}$e told me to find you the moment you reappeared. This was before the Nebas infiltrated our walls, but it matters not to me. I need to get you somewhere safe," Su explained.

I turned to my companions, exasperated.

Vosega spoke first. "You should go. The gatekeeper will know how to get you out of here safely. You do not need to fight, Olly."

Sparkle's sweet voice chimed in second. "He is right. We cannot lose you; you are too important." She reached out and took my hand. Just then the walls shook violently.

My head was moving through scenarios in rapid succession. My heart panged with worry for Elias—for everyone, but most of all for him.

Su leaned in again. I could feel him over my shoulder. "She is here, Miss Olly. Esther is here. We need to go."

I swiveled around to see my dear friend—my keeper—shaking. I hadn't noticed it before, but I saw it clear as day. The look of terror in his eyes. "I will not go," I practically whispered.

My own anxiety, fear, resolve hardened instantly.

I stepped back, so that I could see all of their faces—so that they could all see mine. Borte held onto Genghis, Aremis looked like he already knew what I would say. Only Vosega and Sparkle held out hope that I would run. George and Cadmus didn't know me, so they weren't sure what to think.

"I will not run! This is my fight just as much as it is yours or hers or his." I pointed to each of them. "I have lost in this war. The people I love have lost in this war. I will not stand by, not when I can help." I had a second of hesitation before deciding it was time to let them see what I was truly capable of.

My shield disappeared. I rubbed my fingertips together until sparks flew from my right hand. I wanted to see what I had absorbed from Vosega. I was determined to use everything I had at my disposal. I lay my hand on the tile floor beneath our feet and moved the earth until the ground shook beneath them all. As I rose back to my feet I called on the closest weapon I could sense. A spear from a far-off room catapulted through a window, shattering the pane of glass before landing in my hand in perfect fighting position.

"I'm a Sulu, and I will not let our people endure any more loss." My voice was forceful, unwavering, and I meant every word. I expanded my shield to envelop my friends, to guard them, but to also feel how they felt about me. The true me, the Ophelia that was growing more powerful every day and was just as much a mystery to me and she was to them. All I felt was admiration, love, excitement and awe coming from my closest friends. Only Borte and Genghis held reservations, but there was no animosity.

I let my hands fall to my sides, still holding the spear.

"Are you ready to carry out the plan that you and Elias devised?" I looked at Su, he realized I wasn't backing down. "It's time."

ESTHER

I watched in giddy anticipation as the esteemed Viraclay was seconds away from his death. The chain of the chandelier creaked with the disproportionate weight and wild sway. With every squeal of creaking metal, my heart soared. Yanni's death, my partner, my beloved would be avenged.

I smiled and laughed wildly. The room seemed to slow. I looked around. It had to be Mikkel. *Where was that spineless asshole?* Temporarily distracted from watching Viraclay fall, I scanned the crowd.

The columns that stood erect around the large room dismantled, exposing a large arsenal. Daggers, swords, spears, and hammers flew through the air, and within a blink of an eye every Pai Ona was armed with a lethal weapon. The grin on Ying's face told me he was responsible for the swift equipment. This was not Mikkel's doing. This was something more. I took a step in Ying's direction but ground to a halt when a scream like nothing I had ever heard before tore through the room, sharper than any blade.

My attention returned to Viraclay, who was now floating in midair. I looked for the origin of the scream. My eyes followed everyone else's stunned gazes to where the Unconsu stood on the podium, her hands outstretched, anguish on her face.

I smiled as I thought about how terrible this would be for her, watching the miracle boy die in front of her eyes—her destiny dying with him. I looked back up at Elias to see his body had still not moved. I paused for too long, my attention divided. My focus returned when a huge fireball landed at my feet. The dress I wore went up in flames. Between the smoke and flame I saw a flicker of Conduits appear beside Ophelia on the podium. Among them was... *Aremis?* It could not be. My skin began to sizzle just as a wave of water washed over me. At the same time Viraclay safely landed into the arms of his Ophelia. It took a moment for my thoughts to catch up with what was happening, to become fully aware of what she was.

I ground my teeth as realization after realization flooded my mind. She was Sulu.

OPHELIA

took him into my arms. "I almost lost you." I pulled back
and caught his face in my hands. For the first time, without
restraint or any reservation, and without a shield, I kissed him. I
kissed Elias like I never had before. I let our connection penetrate us
both. When I needed to breathe, only then did I pull away. I pulled
him close again. "I can't lose you."

Elias pulled me in tighter. "I love you."

"I love you," I whispered in his ear. Then I was brought back to the
present by Aremis' hand on my shoulder.

"We should arm ourselves." Aremis pointed to a pile of weapons
just beyond the podium. Without a second thought, I commanded the
metal and armed anyone else around me who did not have a weapon.

Elias took hold of Su. "You have to send the broadcast." Su nodded.
"And Su, find the Oracle."

Susuda disappeared. Seconds later, the terrifying cries of one of
our people going up in flames echoed through the room.

A mass exodus of the Pai Ona commenced immediately.

"Do not let the Nebas leave this room!" Elias shouted, and all those
who needed to hear understood the message perfectly.

ELIAS

*T*he room began to shake. The Stones were playing their part —they would destroy the arena. All we needed to do was keep them from spilling into the other parts of The Cathedral. Ophelia held my hand as we backed up the stairs to the nearest exit. We were almost there when the wind moved around us. It was Aruna atop of Nince, with a second thunderbird in tow.

"Climb on top of Jelso. She will carry you to safety," Aruna instructed. Jelso the thunderbird knelt low enough for me and Ophelia to climb onto her back. "Hold on." The bird took off, flapping her enormous wings. As soon as we were in the air I saw why Aruna had come for us—the Ancients were taking a stand. Each of their huge frames filled the arches through which they had first revealed themselves during the Trials' Open Ceremony. Simultaneously, they began to push back the resisting Nebas, forcing them into the crumbling center of the room. Stones began to fall from the ceiling and all around. Jelso successfully dodged and wove through the falling debris.

One skirmish caught my eye. It was Nara and Akiva. She was still pinning him to the ground under a current of wind.

"Nara! We must leave this place. It will bury us."

She ignored me. She never took her eyes off Akiva. Instead, she walked over to his battered form, unsheathed a knife from her thigh and struck him in the heart, over and over and over. He was no longer moving but her rage fueled her. Blood spattered everywhere around her, carried by her wind. When she finally looked up at us circling above her, the rage was replaced with sorrow, pure sadness.

Then the floor began to fall beneath her. I pushed Jelso forward. We dove down as fast as we could but the Stones beneath her feet disintegrated and she was pulled down into the depths of an unending crevice.

ESTHER

I looked around at my soldiers, the Nebas all around me. We were losing. The Pai Ona were sequestering us into this dilapidating structure. Akiva's lifeless body lay a few feet away. I needed to get out of here. I looked up to see the smug Viraclay and his pet Ophelia flying around on the back of one of Aruna's thunderbirds.

The earth shook beneath me and I lost my footing. I saw a crossbow on the ground in front of me. I reached for it and fell to the floor. An arrow lay in the shaft. I cranked the trigger. I would take them with me.

Once the bird was in my line of sight, I fired. The arrow speared the bird's left wing and hit my mark. Ophelia reached for her side, where the arrow had struck.

Then the vision of my revenge was gone. I was on Lucifer's back as he raced through the debris and falling ceiling with his intense speed, seeking safety.

OPHELIA

I couldn't breathe, and now we were falling. Elias was trying to steer our wounded thunderbird to safety but his voice was panicked as he tried to asses me.

"Ophelia, talk to me. Are you okay?"

I tried to speak but the impact had been so hard I couldn't make it happen.

We landed on the ground outside the arena. Poor Jelso was squawking in pain. I looked at my hands, expecting there to be blood, but there was nothing. Cline's armor had saved me. Elias searched my body for wounds. When I finally caught my breath, I spoke.

"Help Jelso with her wing." He hesitated. "I'm fine. Cline's armor worked. He'll be so proud."

Elias tended to Jelso while I recovered. Chaos ensued around us.

I searched for familiar faces in and throughout the battles that were taking place in the hall. I wanted to help. My eyes fell on Renata's face. She was far in the distance. There were flames on either side of her, where she fought a hooded Nebas. A wicked scream echoed through the hall. It sounded like a banshee. It made my ears bleed. Even with that blow, Renata was struggling. I got to my feet and began to sprint toward her. The closer I got the thicker the smoke was. I found it harder to breathe. It slowed me down. I was almost there when her attacker jumped on top of her and the sound of Conduit flesh ripping replaced the deafening pitches she was using to distract them. I watched as the monster flung her body into the flames —first her head, then her arms and lastly her torso.

Shock rippled through me, shock mixed with anger. I commanded the closest weapon I could conjure and sent it flying toward the figure. It struck the asshole in the shoulder. I'd missed—I was aiming for the heart.

He ripped off his robe and plucked the blade from his shoulder. When he looked up, I had no doubt who this monster was. It was Nestor, my father.

"Well, hello." He smiled a crazed smile.

The sight of him shook me. He advanced. I stepped back and stumbled over a body.

"Aren't you a pretty one!" he leered, drawing closer. Then a ball of fire flew through the air, hitting him in the chest. Nestor ran, to try and put out the flames, and by the time I got to my feet he was gone.

ELIAS

"Thank you, Aremis," I said as I took hold of Ophelia's arm. "We need to find Esther. If we cut off the head of the snake, the others are likely to surrender."

Susuda appeared at my side as we ran. Jelso was spooked and took to the air as we passed. I had healed her, but the ordeal had frightened her.

"Have you found Aurora? Did you get her to safety?"

"No, but I will keep searching." Then Su was off again.

"Aremis, where would Esther go? She has not left."

"I don't believe she has left either."

"Why wouldn't she leave?" Ophelia asked.

"Because she wants Aurora, and because if she had, the Nebas would have begun to disperse. They do not fight for a cause, they fight for fear of the consequence of not doing Esther's will."

"Those who didn't get buried alive by the destruction of the Katuan Stones have been cornered into the ballroom," Aremis explained.

OPHELIA

e ran toward the ballroom. There was so much
destruction all around us. I started to worry about my
friends. "Aremis, where is Sparkle?"

"I do not know, Miss Ophelia." His face reflected my concern.

Just then I heard a loud thunderous noise behind us and a scream.
I turned to see Sparkle being tossed around like a rag doll by an enormous man. "Sparkle!" I shrieked. "We have to save her!"

Before I could say any more, I felt the air move above our heads.
Tete's gargoyle form was in flight, aiming straight for the back of the
big guys head. The sound the collision made was deafening. It was
enough of a distraction that the Nebas threw Sparkle aside. I ran to
her. She was bleeding, badly.

"Sparkle, Sparkle, talk to me," I pleaded. Elias was already next to
me, working his magic on her wounds, and I tried to do the same.
Another loud noise and I turned to see Tete was losing. The huge man
had him in a vice and was just about to break his stone head clean off.
I don't know what came over me. I just screamed.

But it wasn't just any scream, it was Renata's scream. Tears ran
down my cheeks as I replayed her broken body in my head, empow-
ering the borrowed gift. My ears began to bleed and it was only when

I saw the blood streaming from Elias' ears that I was able to contain my emotions.

The Nebas had fallen to his knees with my scream, but it was too late. Tete's crumpled body was separated from his head.

"Aremis, get his head!" I demanded. Sparkle was coming to. "Elias, heal him. Get them both out of here." I slowly walked toward the large hooded Nebas. My anger was boiling, overflowing.

"Ophelia, we need to go," Elias said, reaching for me, but I shoved his arm off.

"Get them to safety. Heal them," I repeated through gritted teeth. I met his eyes and he saw my determination. Aremis was dragging Tete's body and had his head in his other hand while running in the opposite direction.

"You fucking coward!" I growled. The large Nebas was still disorientated by my scream. He didn't see me approaching. "You pick on little women. Pick on me, asshole."

He looked up and I immediately started my onslaught. I threw a variety of weapons and other metal objects at him. With every penetration I felt my anger escalate. He was getting to his feet, trying to avoid my metal shrapnel, but there was nowhere for him to go.

When he was standing I stopped the assault, just so he could see my face. "That was my friend you've just hurt. These people are my friends. These people are your people. What the fuck is wrong with you?" I didn't even know what I was saying. I was just so angry.

ESTHER

*L*ucifer set me down outside the collapsing arena.

"We need to find the Oracle!" I ordered. "Now!"

I could feel the impending failure, the loss of this battle weighing on me. *Maybe I was lost without Yanni?*

Lucifer said nothing as he sped away again in search of Aurora. Once he was out of my sight I fell to my knees. No one could see my weakness or doubt. I put my head in my hands and it was then that a familiar voice rang in my ears. Filbert's voice. Rage replaced the fear of failure. He had tortured me for days. I would kill him, now.

I got to my feet. My dress was in tatters, barely holding on after being lit on fire. I must have looked like the demon I was. I searched the corridor for Filbert. He was nowhere in sight.

I closed my eyes and realized the voices were coming from a nearby room. Realto's southern drawl found my ears.

Perfect. They were together. I would kill Realto first. I slinked down the hall and peered around the corner, into the room I suspected they occupied.

There they were, burning the bodies of my men.

"Hurry, throw his torso in there before he starts to piece himself back together." Filbert's French accent sounded odd directing such violent actions. I searched the wrecked room for Mikkel. He wasn't in there.

"Gentlemen." I stepped into view. I had them cornered in here.

They both jumped when they saw me. I saw it in their faces—anger, fear and resolve, all in a moment. They knew they were no match for me, but they would try.

"We will kill you, snake," Filbert spat through gritted teeth.

I laughed as I stepped into the room slowly, deliberately. "Is that so? Two prancing princes against a queen. I think the odds are in my favor."

Realto stepped in front of Filbert, to shield him. This battle would not be waged with gifts, it would be a victory determined by skill. Filbert scurried to grab a sword he had behind him. Realto still stood tall in front of me. I didn't need a weapon to kill these two. My bare hands would suffice.

Filbert charged forward, the sword aimed to spear me. I leapt high in the air and kicked against the west wall, spinning my body so I was now at Realto's back. I took his neck in my hands from behind. He didn't even know I was there. With a swift twist, his head snapped clean off and into the fire they so graciously provided for me.

Filbert turned to see the horrific expression on his Atoa's face as his fleshed burned.

"Thank you for preparing your own pyre." I wafted my hand in the air. "Smell that, that's the smell of your lover's burning flesh."

Wailing, Filbert flung himself at me. I had hoped to torture him longer but I was feeling better after killing Realto and decided to just end this waste of time. I disarmed him, ripped off his arms at the same time, then jumped on top of him to quickly dismember the rest. It happened too fast. He probably died before he had any idea it was over.

I wiped the blood on the pieces of my dress, took a deep breath and let this minor victory rejuvenate my spirit.

ELIAS

Sparkle was on her feet now. "We have to stop her," she yelled.

But I realized as I watched her defend her friends that there was no stopping her, no holding her back. She was a force, a Conduit like no other, and she could take care of herself. I put my hand up as Sparkle moved forward to intervene. "Leave her be, Sparkle."

The look on my face must have been enough for her to agree to my request. I looked down at Tete to see that he too was still healing. He would recover, but this Nebas would not be so lucky.

Ophelia continued to fill the gap between her and the giant assassin. He pulled off his hood to reveal a face I was unfamiliar with.

"You stupid cunt!" he yelled at her in a brutish voice. "Now I, Dohin, will kill you!"

"Dohin? What kind of name is that?" Ophelia spat back. "I don't care what your name is, you're sentenced to die for killing your own people, asshole!" Then she outstretched her hands and before Dohin could advance he was dust, or perhaps mere particles. She had obliterated him, just as Shiva could.

Sparkle and Aremis ran to her side immediately. I was right behind them when I heard a voice I had hoped to never hear again.

"Viraclay, you have unfinished business with Salzar!" Before I could turn around to see where he was, his vine-like fingers were around my throat. "You do not have your tiny prick on you today." He laughed.

I twisted under the grip he had around my neck to face him. As soon as I could see his face, I kicked as hard as I could. It was enough to jar him and stop him from tightening the noose around my neck. I ducked down and scrambled a few feet away.

"We do have unfinished business, Salzar."

He jetted his fingers out toward me again. I maneuvered left. Suddenly a long axe appeared in my hand. It must have been from Ophelia. I did not have time to look, I just swung as hard as I could. It did not hit his body, but it sliced through his ropey fingers so they fell to the floor like squirming spaghetti. He howled in pain.

Without a second thought I swung again, this time decapitating him. A ball of fire instantly descended on his body and Ophelia was at my back now.

"I'm so sorry, I don't know how to use these gifts very well. I didn't want to poof you too."

I turned to face her and took her in my arms. "Is that what you call it? Poofing?" I smiled and then I put my mouth on hers and kissed her hard.

OPHELIA

"*L*et us keep moving," Aremis' gentle voice interrupted our intimate moment.

We both reluctantly pulled away. Now that my shield was down every touch felt like lightning penetrating every part of my being.

Sparkle giggled as she helped Tete up, who was almost fully recovered with Elias' help.

"Thanks, guys, I really needed my head," Tete teased. "But Aremis is right, we should keep moving." Then Tete transformed back into his gargoyle form. Sparkle jumped atop his back.

I looked around to see several skirmishes happening all around us. The Pai Ona seemed to be winning. We were successfully rounding up or killing anyone who wouldn't surrender.

"We should get to the ballroom." Elias took my hand and we continued down the corridor.

ELIAS

*W*e turned the corner. The ballroom was in sight. I paused for only a moment when I saw who was working together to man the entrance. Vosega and Stalt were at either end of the three entry arches through which one could enter the room. When a Nebas would approach or attempt to escape the room, the two rivals would work together to stop them.

"Stalt, to your left!" Vosega shouted.

Stalt responded with a geyser of lava from the ground. It jetted nearly twenty feet in the air in front of the fleeing Nebas. Vosega then lobbed two huge lava rocks at the hooded figure. The second made impact. Stalt calmly walked over and dragged the Nebas back into the room.

Ophelia and I shared a glance before she waved at Vosega and we entered the ballroom.

OPHELIA

 e had them cornered. We had the numbers. This would end. No one else would need to die.

No sooner did I think the thought than I heard Esther's wretched voice bound off the walls.

"Oh my poor, poor broken friends." Her voice rang from the middle of the herded Nebas. Slowly they moved, trying to give her space to speak. But I still couldn't see her in the crowd "You think you have won a victory here? You have won nothing. You have proven nothing." She pointed to me and Elias, and I tightened my shield onto the cowering group of Nebas. "This was always the plan—a diversion while we took what we wanted. Thank you for dragging her out of hiding for me."

A gasp moved through the Pai Ona as we all realized at once who they had come for—the Oracle. Su had not returned with her. Elias had known, he did his best to find her. We just hadn't been fast enough to cut them off.

When the crowd finally gave way to expose Esther in the middle I saw Aurora's limp body hung over one of the Nebas' shoulders like a rag doll. Su was gagged and bound with strange chains beside her. My heart broke, seeing the fear in his eyes. I wanted to shoot over there and rescue my friend. Without thinking I raised my hand toward them, not sure what gift I would use, but ready nonetheless.

Esther wagged a finger at me. "Don't even think about it, pet. If any one of you tries to stop our departure, we will kill her. The great Ramalan, the Oracle, and the reason for this war to begin with. All the lives you've lost will be for naught. Worthless."

I felt the rage consuming the room, the fear and anxiety.

Then Nestor appeared beside Esther, half-burned and gripping Lilith by the throat. He whispered something in Esther's ear and she laughed.

Elias took hold of my arm. I was shaking. That monster had my grandmother again.

Zavier came out of nowhere, wielding an ax and flying toward Nestor. I saw Esther's hand move slightly. She had hold of someone's body. With a flick of her wrist, Zavier imploded.

"Anyone else feeling brave?"

I couldn't stay silent. "You may leave here today, Esther. But I will hunt you down, I will find you, and I will incinerate you just like we did Yanni."

She growled, hissed and bared her teeth at me. She was ready to lunge, I could see it, to start the carnage again, to sacrifice it all to avenge her Atoa. I took hold of Elias' hand, showing her that I still had my other half. I still had my partner. Anger, pain and fierce hatred burned in her eyes. She raised a hand toward me, sure she could ruin me. I was ready. I was confident Cline's armor would deflect it. I was going to finish this now, today. But instead Esther reached for Su, and the entire mob of defeated Nebas disappeared. With control of Susuda's body, she had access to the gifts of the gatekeeper. They were gone.

ELIAS

*W*e healed the wounded and gathered what remains we could find of the dead. There were no surviving Nebas to dispose of, but we looked anyway. After what felt like hours of picking up the pieces, we were back where the carnage had started. I did not know what would happen next. *Would the others rally behind Ophelia's promise or would this battle divide us all once and for all?*

When those who could attend returned to the ruins of the arena, we stood there upon the podium, the last place we saw Aurora. And when silence took the room, only then did I speak.

"Brethren, today we lost a lot but we also gained insight into our enemy. We fought back and we won on many fronts."

The crowd mumbled indiscernibly to that. I continued.

"They have made their stand clear—there will be no surrender. We saw today that we have the numbers, we have the abilities to defeat them in open battle."

More murmurs, louder and clearly disgruntled. A voice trailed up from the crowd. A tall, thin male Conduit got to his feet.

"What more do we need to lose before we realize the enemy is too great even with those advantages? They took the Oracle again!"

More people stood and agreed with the man's insight.

"I understand. I know that we have all lost so much. But we will only lose more if we stay in the shadows. Simply because we have not witnessed the death in this magnitude does not mean that they are not mercilessly slaying our Atoas, our friends, and our family. They have been picking us off one by one. We cannot ignore the casualties any longer."

A dark-skinned female Conduit stood on the opposite end of the arena. "Viraclay is right. We've let this go on for far too long, and now they've taken the Oracle again. If we let this stand, then it has all been for nothing."

Aphrodite stood a few people down from the last woman. "I will not let them ruin her. She has already been through so much."

"Haven't we all? Today we mourn more brothers and sisters, more wives, husbands, sons and daughters. We will do best to hide, like the Ancients have."

Horace stood, his huge animal body towering over everyone around him. Borte stood by his side, ready to translate. "I speak for all Ancients when I say that we have been wrong to ignore the war. We have sat in the dark for centuries, passively ignoring the strife in our world. That will no longer be. We stand beside Viraclay and his cause."

Murmurs erupted through the arena. Another voice rang out from across the crowd. "It is not enough. We had the numbers and the advantage today, and still, we were defeated!"

Cheers of agreement rose up among the surviving Conduits.

"I will not lose another comrade for a war we cannot win. We are not ruthless enough to defeat Esther and her mercenaries. We haven't the cunning to think like the abominable witch."

Another chorus of agreement.

Di spoke up again. "Who will follow Viraclay, save the Oracle and end this war? Stand if you are with us!"

I watched in horror as only a quarter of the survivors stood up. It would not be enough to win the war. We needed everyone.

I looked to Ophelia. I leaned in and whispered in her ear. "I do not think I can persuade them."

OPHELIA

I watched on, more deflated with every opposition. I thought of what we'd lost so far. Of how close we'd come to ending this. I thought about Su and Aurora and my grandmother, about how afraid they must be.

Watching only a quarter of the Conduits rise to our cause in the arena and seeing the defeat in Elias' face when he admitted he didn't think he could persuade them made something in me snap.

"Give me a moment." I jumped down from the podium. Friedrick was standing just behind us.

"Can you plant me a small tree, here? And make the roots shallow, please. I need to touch one." I pointed to where we stood. He looked at me strangely but complied.

I heard a voice I didn't recognize shout over the crowd, "See, even the Sulu abandons him." I wanted to march back up there and scream at the naysayer, but instead I had a better idea. I squatted down, holding the Hillio in one hand as Friedrick stepped back from the small bonsai tree he'd grown.

I reached out to Fetzle, sent the message through my fingertips, repeated our phrase while simultaneously begging The Cathedral to get my message to the she-troll through the tiny roots. I had no way of knowing if the message went anywhere, but I kissed the coin and put it back in my pocket.

Then I replaced my hands to the floor, this time asking The Cathedral to reach into her depths to give Cataphet a message from me. After I said all I could think to say, I prayed to Malarin for some lucky strokes.

I returned to my place beside Elias and put my hand on his arm. I didn't say anything but he understood what I was asking—I wanted a chance to speak to them.

So he stepped back and I stepped forward. The shouting between individual Conduits had begun to fill the arena. I cleared my throat and watched as some Conduits began to leave.

I reached up, forming a huge fireball in the center of the wreckage, where the iron chandelier once was. The crowd hushed. I put my hand down but let the fire ball hover above us all.

"I'm Ophelia Banner. I have yet to meet many of you, and you have no reason to trust me. Better yet, maybe this power," I pointed to the ball while at the same time raising every piece of metal in the arena several feet from the ground, "frightens you. Perhaps you want nothing to do with me and whatever I am. I wouldn't blame you. But you trusted Viraclay enough to come here, to hear what he had to say. To hear what his father wanted him to say. And for a few days we felt what it was like to be free, to connect and expand and grow—to not cower in the shadows. For a few days we knew freedom from fear! Viraclay gave you that, and he wants to build a world where that is how we live together, all of the time. And if anyone could do it, it would be him. I trust him with my life, with the lives of those I love. We all lost today, but we will continue to lose if nothing changes. And it will only change if we decide to come together to transform our world. You may not be sure of what my power means, but I'll promise you this, it will make me a powerful ally—I'll fight for our freedom, for our true transformation!"

The room buzzed again, then became eerily silent. I saw the shadow fall over my shoulder before I realized what had left such an impression. I turned to see Fetzle and four other giant she-trolls standing behind me.

"Fetzle, queens of the trolls, rightsful heir to the portals of Listy says Ophelias Banner will not be fighting alone. The trolls fight with their friends the Conduits." I looked up at Fetzle and smiled bigger than I ever had before. She tapped me on the head with her giant finger and leaned in to whisper. "Fetzle's took magics to speak just likes you."

"Thanks, Fetzle."

I turned back to the crowd that was still silenced. A moment later I felt the ground shake beneath my feet. Not sure what was coming next, fear lurched into my chest. We all began to look around, poised for the next attack, until I realized what was happening. I pulled Elias back to my side and took his hand. He looked worried. "Trust me," I whispered.

Not a second later, the Rittles manifested in the center of the arena before us.

"We have the stolen Rittles and the lost Pierses. We have the Ancients, and the trolls, we have each other, and we have something to fight for!"

I waited for the spectacle in front of them to sink in before I spoke again. "We are stronger together, and we are not alone. So let me ask again, stand if you will join us in ending this war once and for all. Stand if you will do the bidding!"

Without jeers, shouts or a word, every survivor stood in unison. Even Helia got to her feet, her face was stained with blood and tears, she nodded at me as she rose. My hand trembled in Elias' grip as I realized... We had united the Pai Ona.

ELIAS

*a*fter Ophelia had successfully united the Pai Ona, each of them took part in the bidding ritual. It was simple enough, a blood bond that swore them to our cause. When it was time to act, they would be called upon.

When the rubble was cleared it became more evident whom we had lost. Those who could not be accounted for were assumed dead. Realto and Filbert were gone, Nara, Renata, two of the Ancients, Anansi and Tezcatlipoca. Berty and Korbin, and so many more. But despite our losses our numbers were still strong, and if the number of Nebas that had sieged The Cathedral was any indication of their true figures, then we now had them outnumbered three to one or perhaps more.

Olly acquiring the Pierses and the Rittles, along with aligning with the trolls, put our odds in great favor. The question was what to do now.

Many Conduits had already returned to their homes, or wherever they felt safe at present. Thirty of us still remained in The Cathedral, and we were ready to decide what our next course of action would be.

Borte translated for Shiva, "We must wait to act. Now is not the time to be rash. Let our wounded heal, let the other Ancients be called upon." There were several nods.

Stalt stood up. "But they are weak, weaker than we are. Now is the time to strike!"

Vosega sat beside his new-found friend. "I agree. Now is the time." More murmurs circulated around the room.

Then Ophelia stood and everyone was silent. She had won their allegiance. They respected what she said. "We can't go in blindly. I want to get our captives back. I want revenge just as much as each of you, trust me, I do. But look at what happened to the Nebas when they struck in our territory. They thought they had the upper hand, but they were wrong. We won't make that same mistake. I'm no war strategist, I assure you. But I learn quickly." She made eye contact with everyone she could. "We need to approach this on our terms, where we decide, not at the Nebas compound. We'll travel the world determining the best place to hold the *last* open battle." That created a stir and a few hushed whispers. "But there is something else. The Rittles were not given freely, they were gifted by the dragon Cataphet, and some of us here are bound to honor a promise to the dragon. We must fulfill this promise in order to maintain control of the Rittles and the advantage they give us. Will those who are bound to this task please rise?"

One by one, Vosega, Borte, Khan, Thracian, Sparkle and Aremis stood. Cadmus had died in battle. I stood as well, knowing I would follow Ophelia wherever I needed to. She took my hand. Ophelia opened her mouth to speak, but before she could, Medusa and Tete stood.

"We go with you," Tete said. "We've already decided."

Oya stood and took Vosega's hand in silence.

"As do I." Helia stood, it was distressing to see her alone. Both Leviathan and Constance had fallen during battle. "I owe you both a great debt, for my behavior. Let me make it right."

Ophelia just nodded. I was astounded by her ability to forgive. "So who will take on our second mission and find the optimum location for the last open battle?"

416

Lucia and Winston, Ying, Aruna and Di all stood. Friedrick, Almus, Jezebel and Inca also got to their feet. One by one, the rest of the room stood.

"Excellent. Before we leave The Cathedral tomorrow night, we will decide how we'll all communicate without running the risk of tipping off the Nebas. I want to thank each of you for your courage. We'll win this war once and for all!" That final statement resulted in cheers and hugs around the room. Ophelia and I silently excused ourselves.

"Did I do okay?" she asked when we were in my room.

"You were brilliant."

She let out a huge sigh and collapsed on the sofa. I took a seat by her side. She leaned into me and I took my mouth to hers. The heat between us was electrifying and all-consuming. It was difficult to concentrate on anything else when I was around her now that she was unshielded. I was starting to believe it was in everyone's best interest if we consummated and ended this distraction.

I pulled her body closer and she moved rhythmically with me. Erotic noises between breaths were making me hard.

Then she pulled away suddenly. I opened my eyes to see utter shock on her face.

"What? Is everything alright?" I cupped her face with my hand. She was shaking under my touch. The color in her cheeks was gone. "You are scaring me, Olly."

"It's Lucas. I feel him. He's alive."

GLOSSARY

Adfector~ A faction of Conduit that manipulates emotions.

Alalli~ The Asagi word for mother.

Amplifier~ A Conduit that can enhance any other Conduits abilities around them.

Ancients~ A faction of Conduit that is very old and has a variety of gifts.

Animo~ A faction of Conduit that manipulates consciousness.

Armorist~ A Conduit that creates shields.

Aromatic~ A Conduit that can manipulate smell.

Asagi~ Conduit Language.

Atoa~ A Conduit's other half or partner.

Aura~ A Conduit that can see the color of the strokes around another Conduit, because of this they can sense intents and truths.

Brilfalti~ The secret word that incited the Katuan Stones to rebuild the arena and manage the Trials.

Body Snatcher~ A Conduit who can manipulate others physical forms.

Bustany~ A faction of Conduit that manipulates plants or vegetation.

Circuitu~ A faction of Conduit that manipulates objects or elements around them.

Chitchakor, Malarin, Dalininkas~ The master painter and creator of all life in the world.

Conduit~ A semi-immortal being that expresses extraordinary powers when consummated with their other half, or pair. Upon consummation Conduits no longer age. Conduits are always coupled as a receiver and an imposer.

Consu~ A consummated Conduit

Conveyor~ A Conduit that can articulate any message, feeling or sensation to anyone within a certain radius.

Corpori~ A faction of Conduit that manipulates the body.

Covening~ The act of Conduits gathering to perform the ancient magic.

**Dalininkas, Chitchakor, Malarin, **~ The master painter and creator of all life in the world.

Decimate~ A Conduit that can make anything explode with a single touch, including parts of the body.

Directorate~ The committee of Conduits assigned by the Katuan Stones to oversee the trials.

Elemental~ A faction of Conduit that can manifest or create the earth, wind, water or fire.

Epochus~ A Conduit that can distort time.

Eyok~ An ancient morning ritual that includes a guest and a host sharing stories. It is customary for the host to start the ritual with a story of their own choosing. The host can then ask their guest to share a story of the host's choosing. It is customary for the ritual to last the entire length of the guest's visit. The purpose is to share Conduit history and build each Conduit's legacy

Giant~ A Conduit that can grow in size.

Gilly Mead~ A breakfast mead produced by Vosega. It has less alcohol and is fermented differently than other meads. It is served hot.

Haven~ A place of ancient magic, often a safe house created by Covening.

Healers~ A Conduit that can heal.

Hillio~ The medallion used to communicate with Fetzle the troll

Illusionist~ A Conduit that can create things that are not there.

Incubus~ A Conduit that impregnates women.

Imposer~ A Conduit that can impose their will or energy onto another being or object.

Incantor~ A faction of Conduit that creates or manipulates magical elements/

Kata~ The language of the Katuan Stones.

Katan~ A team in the Katuan Trials.

Katuanak Arena~ The arena built with the Katuan Stones.

Katuan Trials~ The trials that take place in the Katuanak Arena. There are three, The Creation Trial, The Destruction Trial and the Transformation Trial.

Lasteea~ A connection and feeling deeper than love.

Lantern~ A Conduit who can absorb and reflect light.

Loktpi~ A magical key that can dissolve any wards and unlock any door, revealing the location and passage into any Conduit Haven.

Malarin, Dalininkas, Chitchakor ~ The master painter and creator of all life in the world.

Mapper~ A Conduit who can create maps to various locations or create paths to otherwise obscure locations.

Master Mason~ A Conduit that can build anything with anything.

Mekoninis~ The three Conduits who can defend and make mischief for the other teams during the Creation Trial.

Minerals~ An earth elemental that can command control of metals, stones, salts, anything that is found in the earth in its most basic form.

Nebas~ Evil or 'bad' Conduits who most likely align with Esther and Yanni, either in secret or openly.

Pai Ona~ The 'good' Conduits, those fighting to unite and end the war.

Paksyon~ A small congregation of Conduits, who are usually participating in covening..

Pealatunic- The Asagi word for magic.

The Pierses~ Sister books that contain ancient magic spells.

Phoenix~ What Aremis believes he has become when he returns to life after being killed by his own flame. There is still much to discover about this type of gift.

Plitos, Milti, Damilton~ The phrase needed to transfer a Rune, it means 'mine is yours, ours is theirs.'

Poginuli~ A broken Conduit pair, an individual Conduit whose partner has been slain.

Projector~ A Conduit who can replay memories or project a scene into a larger capacity or screen.

Ramalan~ A faction of Conduit that can see the future.

Receiver~ A Conduit that receives or absorbs another object or being's energy.

The Rittles~ Weapons forged with magical poisons that inflict severe injury.

The River Tins~ The magical river where your colors can be cleaned, according to the creation myth of the Conduits.

Shape Shifter~ A Conduit who can take a different form.

Shield~ A Conduit who can camouflage or energetically guard against gifts or detection.

Soahcoit~ A consummated Conduit pair.

Sulu~ A beacon of energy, often in the form of a group of Conduits. In rare occasions it is an individual Conduit that creates an energy vortex.

Swali~ A human that has some Conduit heritage, or a demi-god.

Tahwil~ A faction of Conduit that can manipulate their own form.

Taqa~ A faction of Conduit that manipulates energy.

Timbress~ A Conduit who can manipulate sound.

Truth Sayer~ A Conduit who can detect the truth or compel you to tell the truth.

Tulaswaga~ The Asagi word for gift.

Quakers~ An earth elemental that can shake the earth, move the plates within the earth's surface.

Unconsu~ A Conduit that is still mortal and has not been consummated.

Varon~ A faction of Conduit that influences animals.

Vulcan~ An earth elemental Conduit that has the power to control and manifest or create volcanic activity.

FACTION DIAGRAM

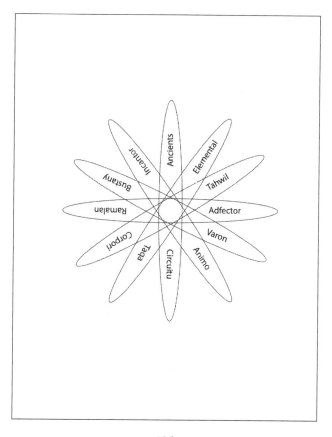

EPILOGUE

OPHELIA

I sat in my grandmother's room in silence, trying to determine what I should do next. They hadn't brought much that needed to be packed. But I found myself sifting through it all meticulously. I wanted to know her better. I didn't know if I'd ever see her again.

I moved to a small bookshelf with only three books in it. One by one, I picked them up and looked at the titles. Did Lilith read these, or Zavier, I wondered. Then something fell from the third book, *The Catcher in the Rye.*

I sat on the couch, staring at the envelope with my name on it. I took a deep breath and ripped open the seal.

Dear Ophelia,

I don't know how to say this or where to start. I will tell you that many things start from forgiveness, so I will ask that you forgive me. I wish I would have asked more questions, demanded more answers and fought harder to be a better person. But sadly, I did not. So now here I sit, writing you this letter, hoping without reason that you will forgive me and allow me to become a part of your life.

Lilith never told me until today that Eleanor was my daughter. She had always said she was pregnant before me consummated and I never once ques-

tioned her. I know now and knew then that everything she did was to protect her child. She thought she was doing what was best by letting Eleanor live a normal life. She knew that if I had known she was mine I never would have allowed us to part with her.

The last few days, here at the summit, seeing you, hearing your mother's story, has been eating Lilith alive. I have watched her tormented and broken over what has happened to her family because of her decisions so long ago. She told me the truth knowing that she risked losing me or at least a piece of what we share when I learned of her deception, all to save you the torment of believing your father was also your grandfather. You are no abomination, child. You are my blood and my bone, and I will live the rest of my life making certain you know you are dearly loved.

I hope you will forgive us both and give us an opportunity to share in your life.

Love,

Your blessed grandfather,

Zavier

The letter fell from my hands, and with it, the tears.

ACKNOWLEDGMENTS

As always, I want to thank my family and friends for their outpouring of love and encouragement. Specifically I'd like to thank my writing buddy Rachelle for keeping me on track, and Alicia for letting me bounce things off you.

My VIP team got to get their hands on Fallen first. You guys are super fans, I appreciate the enthusiasm and reading gusto!

To my editor Ella Medler, you take my rough drafts and shreds of imagination and make them masterpieces—thank you.

I need to thank Cherie Fox for her artistic prowess and using it to make my cover vision into a reality.

And I can't forget my readers—thank you for navigating through the Conduit world with me!

A NOTE FROM THE AUTHOR

I want to say thank you so much for taking the time to read *FALLEN*. *The Conduit Chronicles* has been a dream of mine for many years. I am so excited to take you on this journey and introduce you the Conduit world.

If you would like to get the latest publication news for the next book in the series, FATED, please visit my website and make sure you join the READERS CLUB to get a FREE Bonus Content. Learn what Rand saw happen at the Kraus compound the night that Sorcey and Cane died.

https://ashleyhohenstein.com

If you enjoyed the book, please take the time to review it on Amazon.com or Goodreads. I am so grateful that you took the time to read *FALLEN*. I would love to hear what you liked about the book.

ABOUT THE AUTHOR

Ashley Hohenstein lives in Northern California.
Ashley has been a massage therapist and health educator for
seventeen years. She has owned several businesses and has found
entrepreneurship to be dynamic and fulfilling.
She was an avid reader at a young age and enjoyed getting lost in
other worlds. Her dream has always been to become a published
author. *The Conduit Chronicles* came to her on a backpacking trip
through Europe. It took seven years to get the first book written and
published.
If you want to learn more about the author visit her website:

https://ashleyhohenstein.com

ALSO BY ASHLEY HOHENSTEIN

You can find Ashley Hohenstein's latest publications on her website, at
Amazon.com and is available in the Kindle Unlimited library.

Made in the USA
Middletown, DE
23 May 2022

66086569R00262